About the Author

Tony Bury, born in 1972 in Northampton, England, has had a passion for writing songs, poems and short stories since an early age. He has taken it more seriously since having children, writing in several genres including horror, crime, children's books and screen plays

PREDATOR ISLAND

Also, by Tony Bury

The Alex Keaton Crime/Thriller Series:

Intervention Forgiven
Intervention Needed
The Intervention
Darkness Falls

The Edmund Carson Horror Trilogy:

Inside Edmund Carson
Edmund Carson - The ONE. The Only.
Edmund Carson Is the Alphabet Killer

Ane the Last Witch

Tony Bury

PREDATOR ISLAND

Vanguard Press

*Vanguard Press is an imprint of
Pegasus Elliot MacKenzie Publishers Ltd.*
www.pegasuspublishers.com

First Published in 2019

**Vanguard Press
Sheraton House Castle Park
Cambridge England**

Printed & Bound in Great Britain

Dedication

For Ana… there will always be a locked door
waiting for you… x

Chapter 1

Father Matthew watched apprehensively as Chris James, the head guard at the prison, unlocked Jacob's cell for the very last time. As Father Matthew entered, Jacob was sitting on his bed with his hands and feet tied together by a single chain which was securely attached to the bed, and to a hook cemented firmly into the ground.

Jacob was facing down towards the floor, the remainder of his last meal was on the bed next to him. Chris James entered the cell, leaned over, picked up the tray, and left the cell without saying a word to either of them. He handed the tray to another guard who swiftly disappeared and then he stood just outside the cell door facing away from Father Matthew and Jacob. Having worked at the prison since the day it opened, Chris had no interest in hearing another inmate's last confession.

"I am sorry I am later than we discussed. How are you today, Jacob?"

Jacob didn't answer. He sat staring at the ground, deep in thought of what lay ahead of him. Father Matthew had seen this all too often, he wasn't going to push him into a conversation. A few minutes of silence and reflective prayer were a good thing at this time in the process. Father Matthew patiently sat, looking at Jacob as he stared at the floor. After a few minutes, Jacob's head came up. For a moment both men sat just looking directly at each other, both knowing something needed to be said.

"Sorry, Father, I am well, and you?"

"I am good too, Jacob." There was a faint smile from Jacob. Father Matthew was glad that he had started the conversation. Despite everything that he knew, deep down Father Matthew believed that Jacob had tried to be a good man.

"I am here, Jacob, to ask one more time if you would like to say anything to me or to your God. As we have been discussing the last few weeks, this is clearly your choice. I can stay or I can go." There was another moment of silence. They had shared a lot of silence over those last few weeks during Father Matthews visits. Jacob throughout his life had been a man of very few words.

"Stay, Father, a little company would be nice."

Compared to Father Matthew, Jacob was a giant of a man. He was six foot six and built like a barn door: solid and strong. Jacob had worked on his father's farm his whole life. The manual labour had ensured that there wasn't an ounce of fat on Jacob. His size had actually increased over the last five years he had spent in prison. During that time, he had little else to do other than hit the gym on a daily basis. That and prayer were the only two things that had filled Jacobs day.

"Some people take this opportunity to confess their sins, Jacob. As a religious man it may bring you some comfort. Is this something that you would wish to do?"

Jacob didn't answer. His head raised for a second, and then it dropped again towards the ground. Father Matthew waited patiently again, a short while later, without looking up, Jacob answered.

"I don't think I would know where to start, Father."

"I understand that, Jacob, but once you start talking you will find how easy it is to share. Why don't you start with why you asked for breakfast to be your last meal? It is quite unusual that an inmate requests a morning breakfast as his last meal." Those words stuck in Father Matthew's throat a little. Even though it had been a couple of years he still hadn't become used to spending time with an inmate just after they had eaten for the very last time.

"They tend to ask for a late supper, just to give them a little more time. What I mean to say is that you could have had the day to yourself."

Jacob's head came back up and he looked Father Matthew in the eye as he spoke.

"I like breakfast, Father. On the farm, my mother would always make sure we ate a big breakfast: bacon, sausage, egg, black pudding, white pudding, tomatoes, beans, if there were leftover potatoes from the night-before dinner, she would fry them up with a bit of pepper too. Best meal of the day my father used to say."

Father Matthew noticed the smallest light in the corner of Jacob's eye. For a moment, there was a memory. Jacob had finally shared a happy memory. This had not happened in all the time they had been together.

"He always said, 'Get up and get on with it, Jacob'. That's what we do on the farm. No point in putting things off, Father. Get up and get on with it."

"That sounds like a nice memory, Jacob. It sounds like a real family farm life. Tell me, what else do you remember about the farm?"

Father Matthew knew it was a leading question. He was a little worried he had made it too blunt as soon as the words came out of his mouth. Jacob went silent again and his head was back to pointing down at the ground. Eye contact wasn't something forthcoming from Jacob with Father Matthew, not if he was going to have to confess his sins. Jacob was fully aware of what he had done.

Jacob and his family had a healthy respect of the church. In his community, back home, the church had played a big part in everyone's day to day social life. The church had been the place where he was first introduced to his wife Michelle.

Jacob had been dreading this part of the day with Father Matthew as much as what was going to come after.

"They weren't always good times on the farm, Father. No, not good times."

Father Matthew never wanted to push a confession out of anyone. This was their time, and he had come to notice that even here, confession troubled some people more than others. But in the end, everyone wanted to say something. Father Matthew could see Jacob's confession was troubling him. His real concern was that he also believed that confession coupled with the last rites would give Jacob at least a chance to get into heaven. Father Matthew wanted that for everyone.

Father Matthew was a devoted Father to his community, in all sense of the word. He always wanted to do what was right for his congregation. Now that he had the prison as part of his community, he wanted to do what was right for them also. Although in times of reflection, over the last couple of years of visiting the inmates, some of the confessions he had heard started to question his faith in mankind.

"It must have been very hard, Jacob" Father Matthew knew exactly what he had said. He was hoping it would open the door for Jacob to, in turn, open up to him.

"It was, Father. We had some bad days, Father. Some very bad days... I wasn't going to let them happen again."

There was a pause. Jacob was clearly remembering those days. This is what Father Matthew had hoped for. He knew this was his opening if he was going to be able to help Jacob.

"What happened on the farm, Jacob? If I hear your confession, it will help God to forgive you. That is what you want, isn't it? Do you seek forgiveness, Jacob? Absolution for everything that has happened?" Jacob's head stayed still, pointing directly at the ground.

"I want to help you, Jacob, as much as I can."

Jacob didn't raise his head to speak.

"Father, when I met Michelle, my wife, it was the happiest time of my life. She was so pretty. So, so pretty. You should have seen her, Father: long, dark hair, and a tiny little thing. Some days, I swear, I felt like I could pick her up and put her in my pocket. I would have liked to have done that, Father. Keep her in my pocket. Safe in my pocket." There was a slight pause and a sigh. Father Matthew picked up on it, he knew this was going to be very hard for Jacob.

"She liked me too, she really did. First girl that ever did, Father. I asked her to marry me after about three months of courting. I wanted to after the first week, but mother said no. She said girls don't like that. So, I had to wait the whole three months. She agreed, there and then. Just like that. She told me that she would have said yes after the first week. I never told mother that. She even came to live on the farm after we were married. My father and mother were so happy about that. They were getting older, and she helped out so much. Michelle practically ran the house, she did. That was until Jacob Jnr was born. My son, Father, you should have seen him. So strong, not like me. He will be a big one, I tell you. So much stronger than me. And smarter father. And smarter."

"I would have loved to have met him, Jacob." As soon as those words left his lips, Father Matthew regretted them. Jacob's head pulled up a little at that and glanced a smile at the Father, but quickly returned back down before making eye contact.

"You see, as my boy got bigger, he would help out more and more around the farm. Like I did when I was his age. Feeding the cows, the pigs, and the chickens. He was a good boy, Father, he was. But sometimes forgetful, that is all. He was still smart. Just forgetful." Jacob paused again at that thought. All these memories were flooding back to him. He had tried to block them out for the last five years, but now the flood gates were opening.

"It wasn't his fault the foxes got into the chicken shed. That door was always a little sticky. I meant to fix it, Father. I really did, so many times. There is just so much to do on a farm, Father, so much. There is never enough time. That is why we had to get up and get on with it." Father Matthew was nodding at Jacob although he couldn't see it. It was almost in encouragement to keep the confession going.

"He was still only a young boy, Jacob. Mistakes do happen."

"He was young and a little forgetful, Father. That is all. Just a little forgetful."

There was a longer silence. Father Matthew knew what was coming, he knew Jacobs story and he was prepared to listen to all of it. He was always prepared to listen to all of their stories.

A change in the law had been passed six years ago. The whole trial had to be reread in court before the public, exactly five years after the initial death sentence conviction. Father Matthew always attended these as they were now happening in the court room on his island. He had attended Jacob's rereading six weeks ago to the day. Father Matthew told himself that he listened to the case in order to understand the man he would be spending the next six weeks visiting and talking to.

During the six-week period between the reread and the last meal, the inmate or representative could request an appeal to the sentence. To this day there had never been an appeal to what was now known as the second sentencing, and today it had been six weeks since Jacob's case was reread in court. Jacob knew nobody was coming to defend him.

"My father didn't like sloppiness, he just didn't. When he came out that morning and found the chickens, they were nearly all dead father, he was mad so mad. There were still a couple which were just injured father, but Michelle said he broke their necks himself in his temper. She knew as she was watching him from the kitchen father. He was so angry. I was in the barn sorting out the cows... The first thing I knew I could hear Michelle screaming. It was so loud. So loud. I ran into the house and my father had his belt out... To my boy, Father. He was my boy, Father, not his. He had no right to do that to my boy, Father."

Jacob fell silent again. Father Matthew had heard the whole case as it was reread six weeks ago. Jacob had been beaten as a child and as a teenager and even as a man by his father. His back was covered in whip marks, some of which, judging by the photographs taken for the court case, must have been almost to the bone. His mother had been a trainee nurse before meeting his father, so it was a rare occasion that Jacob was taken to a hospital. The only time he was, was when the beatings were so severe, she worried that she couldn't stop the bleeding herself. Even then she would blame it on an accident on the farm. Most of the time she would dress his wounds, stitch him up and then they would just carry on like nothing had happened. The beatings became part of their family life.

"My mother was holding onto my Michelle, saying the beating was for his own good. She had always said that to me, Father. She always said that I brought it onto myself, for being stupid or useless. I tried not to be, Father. I tried so hard. Sometimes I just couldn't get it right. It was never good enough for him." Jacob paused again. Father Matthew knew that those thoughts were hurting him. The reflection part of confession was difficult for almost everyone he met, and those that truly want to confess felt it the most.

"I tell you, Father, she had brought my father's temper onto herself a few good times too over the years."

Jacob's father's attention had changed to be more dedicated to Jacob as he got older. He needed his wife to cook and clean for them and ensure that the farm ran smoothly. She had kept all the finances as well as the house. Jacob's father wasn't an intelligent man. Although, he had been intelligent enough to ensure his wife never left him. Jacob was getting stronger, and his father knew he could take a beating and he wouldn't fight back. That was until the day that Jacob's father took the belt to his grandson. Until that day Jacob had never stood up to his father. That was the day that everything changed.

"He is my son, Father. Nobody gets to whip my son with a belt, nobody!"

Father Matthew could tell from Jacob's voice that he meant that. There was a passion and determination to protect his son coming through loud and clear. Father Matthew looked back at the chain attached to the floor. He wasn't convinced that if Jacob got really angry it would be able to restrain him.

"I understand, Jacob. What happened after you entered the house?"

"I ran at my father. I grabbed the belt out of his hands and threw it to the ground. I then turned to my father. Before I knew it, my hands were round his throat and I was shouting at him! What do you think you are doing? Who do you think you are? That is my boy you are hitting."

Jacob was reliving the situation directly in front of Father Matthew. Jacob's voice was raised higher than ever before. Chris James had turned from outside of the cell to ensure that everything was safe. Father Matthew had caught his eye to ensure that he didn't come in. Jacob needed to tell his story.

"I can hear the words now, Father. I remember the look on his face, Father; he really wasn't expecting it. All those feelings as a child were coming back to me. I always wanted to know. Why did he hit me? Why doesn't he love me? Why am I so stupid? Why did he always call me useless? I never want my son to have those feelings, Father, never. I had never laid my hands on him." The silence that followed lasted five minutes. Father Matthew didn't move. He didn't even want to breathe hard at that point. Jacob eventually looked up and directly at Father Matthew.

"All those feelings were in me, I knew they were. I just never thought they would come out, and for the first time I wanted to know why he did what he did. I don't know if I was asking for me or for my son. I guess I was asking why he felt he could do that to another person."

Father Matthew wanted to say something to comfort him, but he knew that keeping the flow was key to getting all of the confession. That would help Jacob more.

"Suddenly I could hear the screaming, Father; I think I had blocked it out with my thoughts. Michelle had broken free from my mother and was now trying to stop her. My mother had picked up the belt and was whipping me with it; she was doing it to get me off my father. Over the years, I had become immune to the pain, Father; I hadn't even noticed. My mother was now as bad as him. She had never hit me before, Father, never. But she was now whipping me like a dog. Like he used to do. With one hand still around my father's throat, I pulled my other hand backwards and grabbed the belt as it hit my back, pulling the belt towards me. My mother stumbled closer to me, and I struck her round the head with my fist. Not full fist, Father, I promise. It was more of the back of my hand. Just to stop her, Father. To stop her whipping me. She fell backwards and hit her head on the corner of the table. Instantly I could see the amount of blood pouring out of her head." Jacob paused again. The image was clearly running through his mind.

"Michelle was screaming. I turned back towards my father. I knew what I had done. I let go of Father and ran to her, trying to pick her up off the kitchen floor. Michelle was still screaming, and Jacob, my son, he was crying so hard. He was now hiding in the corner of the kitchen curled up in a ball, hiding his eyes. Like I used to. I could see him. I wanted to go and comfort him, Father, to say it was all going to be OK. I wouldn't let anything happen to him. But I had to help my mother first, Father. I had to patch her up. I had to do something to try and save her, Father. That's what she used to do to me; she could always make it better, she could always stop the blood... But it was too late. I was apologising to her, but she couldn't hear me... I was apologising to my father too as I knew what was coming. I was waiting for the belt to hit me again as I was holding my mother on the floor. I deserved it, Father. I deserved the beating that was going to come. I had killed my mother. I didn't mean to; it was an accident. It really was an accident. I just wanted her to stop hitting me. That was all, Father, just too please stop hitting me."

Jacob wasn't crying. There were tears in his eyes and they were streaming down his face, but he didn't make a sound. He just took a deep breath, and then another.

"The belt didn't come. After a while of holding my mother, I realised that the belt didn't come. I turned and saw my father lifeless on the floor." Jacob took a bigger deep breath as if he had finished his confession. He had finally admitted to himself what had happened to his parents that day on the farm.

"The policeman in the court had said I had snapped his neck at the first grab. I hadn't noticed. I was just so mad at what he had done to my son. I was so mad, Father, so mad. I couldn't let him do what he done to me, Father. I couldn't let him whip my boy. Not my boy, Father. He didn't deserve that." Jacob was shaking his head as he spoke as if to back up his point.

"It was understandable given everything that you had been through to have these emotions, Jacob. You had yourself suffered through years of abuse and torture at the hands of your father."

Jacob fell silent again. He didn't like the words abuse and torture. He didn't see it that way; he had seen it as discipline from his father. Those words weren't used where he came from. They were the fancy words that the lawyer had spoken in the courtroom in aid of his defence. Father Matthew knew there was some remorse in what had happened that day. Jacob had not intended any of it. That was the day Jacob's whole life had changed.

"I have to ask you, Jacob, do you regret killing your mother and father? Do you know it was wrong? Do you ask for forgiveness for this act, Jacob? Because if you do, you need to tell me. I need to hear the words from you, Jacob, not just a retelling of your story. That is the meaning of a confession. Do you seek absolution for your actions, Jacob?"

Jacob sat still, head down looking at the floor. The silence seemed to last a good ten minutes to Father Matthew. In truth, it had probably been closer to three. It was the anticipation of the response that had made it seem longer.

"OK, Jacob, if you don't want to confess, I can't begin to ask for forgiveness for you." There was still no response from Jacob. Father Matthew was concerned he shouldn't push him anymore. He also knew that they were both religious men. They both believed in the power of forgiveness, and if he was going to help Jacob, he needed to hear the words. All the words.

"Jacob, do you want to talk about what happened next? Maybe we should try to talk about that now?"

Jacob's head came up, and he looked directly at Father Matthew. There were no tears in his eyes now; there was just rage. Pure rage. Father Matthew could feel his whole body jump back five inches.

"No! I don't want to talk about that, Father!" His voice reflected the anger in his eyes. He seriously didn't want to talk about it. Father Matthew sat back upright, and looked towards the corridor. Relieved he saw Chris standing not ten feet from him. He had heard the change in Jacob's tone and was now in the doorway ready for anything that could happen. That was comforting. Father Matthew spoke in a soft voice to try to calm Jacob down.

"Jacob, I understand it is difficult for you to talk about. You will not be forgiven if you don't confess the whole story. You need to absolve yourself of the sins you have committed. That way you will be cleansed of them, and you can enter the Kingdom of heaven."

Father Matthew held his bible tight, as if it were a shield against anything that might come next.

"We are done, Father! Guard! I am done with Father Matthew!"

Jacob stood up. Whilst he couldn't move any further, he towered over Father Matthew. His three years working in this prison had taught him something. That something, was that if an inmate looked at you the way that Jacob was looking at him, it was time to get out of there as soon as possible. Whilst there was clear evidence that Jacob was restrained, he didn't want to take the chance of those chains breaking. Jacob was a strong and powerful guy; Father Matthew had no doubt that the bed and the hook on the floor were not going to be enough to stop him if he chose to attack.

"OK, Jacob, I understand that we are done. I will still walk with you when it is time if that is OK with you?"

Jacob didn't respond, he just sat there looking at the floor. Chris had entered the cell as soon as Jacob stood up, and Father Matthew had to step around him to get out into the corridor. He stood outside of the cell for a further fifteen minutes until he could see the rest of the guards heading towards him. He had pushed Jacob as far as he could go during the confession, he was not going to get any more from him. Not now, now Jacob was being prepared to take his last journey.

The act of killing his father and mother had sent Jacob into a downward spiral. He buried them both on the farm and didn't tell a soul what he had done.

His wife, Michelle, had seen another side to him that day and it terrified her. She was now scared of her husband, and so was Jacob Jnr.

Until that point Jacob had been a gentle giant of a man, the most attentive and loving person Michelle had ever met. That day had changed him. Jacob started to drink heavily like his father had done before him. Within less than a month he had hit Michelle for the first time. She, like her mother-in-law, had taken a beating and acted as if it had never happened.

Within two months he was hitting his son with a belt. Jacob had turned into his worst nightmare, his father. Three months after killing his parents, the police started to ask questions about their disappearance.

Jacob's father was a prominent farmer in the community, and as such he would always be trading cattle or wheat. In all the years he had been farming he had never trusted Jacob to do this alone. Other people had also started to ask questions. Holidays were never taken in the farming industry, and Jacob's family had never left the farm before. Jacob returned one afternoon from a cattle market to see a police car just leaving his premises. He had been drinking the night before, and Michelle had taken the best of his temper. She hadn't said anything to anyone about what had happened. She told the police officer she had been kicked by one of the cows when trying to get something out of its hoof. Jacob hit the front door like a missile. Before she knew it, he had his hands around her throat screaming at her as loud as he could. Jacob Jnr was in the corner of the room. He hadn't seen him when he had burst through the door. Jacob Jnr didn't wait thirty-seven years to stand up to his father. Even at the age of nine he knew wrong from right. He took a knife off the kitchen table and jumped on his father's back, plunging the knife into his father's shoulder. As he did, the pain Jacob felt made him tightened his grip around Michelle's throat. He snapped her neck in the same way that he had killed his father three months previously. Jacob swung around as Michelle's lifeless body fell to the ground.

Jacob shook his son off of him, and grabbed him by the throat also lifting him off the ground. The rage made Jacob squeeze the life out of his only remaining family member.

Unbeknown to Jacob the policemen had returned. The explanation of why Michelle's face looked like she had been pounded on by a two-tonne gorilla had left one of them feeling uneasy. They were just moments too late.

Jacob was on the floor with his wife and son in his arms when they came through the front door. The knife was still firmly in his shoulder. Jacob was handcuffed and taken to the police station. He confessed the whole story about his mother and father, gave them the location of their bodies, and described the events of that day. He knew what he had become; he had been battling with it every day, he had just been too scared to face it. Now he had no choice.

A decade ago the mindset in the United Kingdom had begun to change. The government had been placed under considerable financial pressure to bring back the death penalty. The whole country had given its support, and fully swung behind a campaign.

The incarceration of a murderer was costing the tax payer in excess of thirty-five thousand pounds per year. At an average age of twenty-eight when they were convicted, studies showed that these inmates would spend an average of thirty-five years in prison in their life time, mainly due to re offending. The country now knew this was in excess of one million pounds of tax payer's money per head to keep murderers alive and well. Unfortunately for the UK, crime was on the rise.

The Campaign for Death Sentences had used those figures all over the country. Posters, billboards and TV adverts airing five times a day starring Jonathan Ledger, a notoriously nasty serial killer who had killed and raped seven teenage girls over a seven-year period. The reward for his crimes, according to the TV, was a cell with his own fifty-inch, flat-screen HD TV, three square meals a day, and an hour down at the gym every day. The prison he had been placed in also had its own pool which they could use three times a week.

Jonathan Ledger had a place in what the press were now dubbing 'millionaires' row'.

This campaign had been the last straw. The government listened to the people, and the law changed. Jacob had been given a PDS verdict: Potential Death Sentence. Five years after the case was concluded the prisoner would be moved to the PDS Prison. His full case notes would be read out in court again which was open to the public to attend. There would then be a six-week appeal process. If there was still questionable or new evidence about what had happened, then a trial would be restarted. If not, the sentence would be carried out.

Nobody had appealed for Jacob. There was nobody left in his family to do so. Jacob wouldn't have asked anyone to step in on his behalf either. He knew he needed to pay for his sins.

The guards had unchained Jacob from the bed and led him out of the cell; four guards escorted him as he walked through the cell block, with cells either side of him. There was the sound of banging on the walls from the other inmates as he passed by, but there were very few words spoken. Father Matthew followed closely behind Jacob as he walked. When they approached the final locked room that Jacob was going to be placed into, he stopped in his tracks and turned to Father Matthew.

"Father, I am sorry for what I have done. You have to believe me, I didn't mean to do it."

"Yes, Jacob, I believe that you are."

There was nothing else to be said on the matter. Chris James and the other three guards escorted Jacob into the room. Father Matthew took the door to the right which was for visitors.

In the room were Michelle's parents and Dr Steve Mitchell. There were three rows of six seats. Michelle's parents were sitting in the middle row in the centre seats, and Dr Steve Mitchell was sitting in the front row by the door on the opposite side of the room.

Michelle's parents had made the journey over on the boat the night before, and had stayed in the only hotel on Callington Island. Dr Mitchell was there, as always, to ensure the procedure was followed correctly.

Father Matthew walked over and sat behind Michelle's parents. He didn't say a word, he just wanted for them to know that he was there should they have need of him.

The screen covering the big glass window lifted in front of them. As it did, Dr Mitchell disappeared out of the door.

Jacob was strapped to the reclining table in the centre of the room. In the room with him was Chris James, the head guard from the prison. The prison director, Albert Finlay, and Father Matthew's soon-to-be son-in-law, Michael Peterson.

Michael was understudying with Dr Mitchell at the prison. He was also the only licenced mortician on the island after he had taken over from his grandfather who had passed away two years ago. Michael was seriously thinking about going off to medical school after the wedding and felt that understudying with Dr. Mitchell would be the best use of his time on a very quiet island. Previously the only people dying on the island were of old age. The prison had made the job a little more interesting but, as a mortician, it was still more of a part-time job for Michael. He also performed other duties in the prison, one of them was being the third person placed in the room to release the fatal injection.

To make it easier on the executioner's three injections were set up and connected to the drip. Two of them were saline solutions, and one was the fatal dose.

Three switches had to be pulled in order for each of the vials to empty. It wasn't much of a comfort in what they were doing, but it did give them a sense of doubt in whether they had killed the person in front of them. Dr Mitchell was the only person who knew which vial contained the fatal dose.

Albert walked across to Jacob and whispered in his ear. He shook his head. Chris James then moved the recliner so that it was sitting slightly upwards to look out at the people in the opposite room. Michelle's mother buried her head into her husband's chest as she cried. Her father stared directly at Jacob. Jacob didn't return the stare. He continued to look down at floor.

At ten thirty a.m. the first switch was thrown, and at ten forty-five, after Dr Mitchell had entered the room,

Jacob was pronounced dead. Michael wheeled him out of the room and down the corridor to the morgue that was now on site in the prison.

Father Matthew paid his condolences to Michelle's parents. He knew nothing he could say was going to help them. They just needed time to say goodbye to their daughter and grandson and put this all behind them, again. This was always a difficult day for anyone entering and leaving that room. He sat with them for a further five minutes in silence whilst they consoled each other then he left the room.

Within a few minutes he had left the prison. Saturday morning executions were quite rare; in fact, it had been a first in his time at the prison. This meant Father Matthew was finished with the prison for the day, but he still had a full day ahead of him.

Chapter 2

Father Matthew always took a moment to himself when he walked out of the prison. It was his own sense of freedom kicking in; he knew few people had this privilege inside those walls. The island air always smelled that little bit better just after he left. This feeling had not disappeared in the three years of visiting the inmates.

When the government had passed the law to bring back the death sentence the whole country had gone out to celebrate. Worryingly though, whilst ninety-seven percent of the country voted in favour, none had wanted the prison to be built in their county.

Father Matthew had seen an opportunity to do some good for his congregation. There was a derelict navy base on the west side of their island which had been empty for twenty years. Cutbacks and efficiencies in the defence budget had meant that it was no longer needed for naval manoeuvres.

Callington Island was located about six miles off the UK coast, just to the south of Dover. It wasn't a big island; before the prison, it had housed less than a thousand people. Fifty percent of them had gone to the island to retire.

Father Matthew had approached the government to strike a deal. He had preached his intentions to do this at church and at the local community meetings for months beforehand. Receiving the full backing of the island, his idea was expected to bring significant investment which was also expected to increase security and trade. The community had been seriously struggling, surviving on holiday makers and the local fishermen for revenue. Father Matthew had been acting as the mayor of the island as well as their priest for almost a decade now, and the residents of the island trusted him.

The deal had been struck. It was perfect for the government as it kept the whole business away from the media as much as it possibly could. In return of the acceptance of a Death Row Sentence prison on the island, Father Matthew had secured a number of deals for Callington Island. A new old-age pensioner's home next to his church for at least one hundred people was his greatest achievement. Extra facilities for a small nunnery, and a small orphanage close by too. These were all to the east of the island where Father Matthew lived which was a twenty-five-minute drive across from the prison based in the west. He felt that was a suitable distance from the prison.

In the centre of the island was the main living accommodation area. Father Matthew had secured investment for a new hotel for tourist as well as to help house visitors of the prisoners. Also, the few shops and restaurants that were already there would receive some upgrade grants to extend their premises. Housing for around four hundred and fifty people was already situated in the middle of the island. These houses had stood for hundreds of years and gave the whole centre an old rustic village feeling. There had been over forty new houses built to the northwest of the island closer to the prison. These were purposely built for the guards and other prison workers so they could reside on the island. The locals hadn't wanted the new buildings to affect the feel of the traditional main town.

To the south of the island was the only port. It was the only way on and off of the island and where the main fishing trade came from. There were a few fishing boats of various sizes. Generations of tradesmen all loyal to the island. A new ferry, with a private compartment for moving the prisoners, and big enough to carry supplies to and from the island, had also been included in the deal.

The locals had one request for Father Matthew. They requested that they didn't see the criminals when they were travelling to and from the island. Father Matthew had delivered on that request too. There was a locked area on the bottom floor at the back of the ferry where the prisoners would have to wait until everyone else had left. As soon as the passengers had departed, most of the doors and windows in the port area would close, and the streets would become empty. The locals in conjunction with Chris James had worked out a flag system to show when they had a new visitor to help with the process. A few of the younger residents though took a fancy to watching the people led off the boat. No matter how much their parents had been against it.

The fishing port boasted accommodation for another three hundred people. The remainder of the thousand residents originally based on the island were scattered in various points around the coast with views of the sea. Mainly secluded retirement homes. The port also boasted the only public house on the island. Apart from the hotel in the centre and through sales in the only supermarket, this was the only place to get an alcoholic drink on the island. This attracted locals and prison workers to socialise together.

Father Matthew made the twenty-five-minute journey across the island. He had promised his wife Mary that he would help with making the lunches at the old people's home. This was something he liked to do if he had the time on a Saturday. This morning his wife had asked for his assistance.

Overnight, and out of the blue, one of the nuns, Sister Sarah, had disappeared back to the mainland without telling anyone. Apparently, she had packed her bags in the morning and had taken the early ferry out of the port. She had been living in the nunnery with the other sisters for two years and none of them had expected this. It wasn't until after morning-prayer that the sisters started to notice she was gone.

There were only two ferries a day: one departing at six a.m. and the other departing at six thirty p.m.; these were scheduled for anyone that wanted to work on the mainland. You had to book a ticket in advance for both directions; it was part of the protocol given by the prison. The government wanted to know and keep a record of who was leaving or coming to the island. This was how Mary had discovered Sister Sarah had returned to the mainland. She had checked the schedule after they couldn't find her in the nunnery or at the old people's home.

On arrival to the home, Father Matthew found his wife Mary in full cooking mode with Sandra Hills, the resident cook for the home. Mary was a slender, five foot four inches, long dark-haired woman. Father Matthew had imagined, less than two hours ago, that she had been very similar to Jacob's wife, Michelle. In their twenty years of marriage they had never had as much as a cross word. Sandra on the other hand had the build of the lunch lady from school. Exactly what you expected a cook who loved her food, and loved her life too much, to look like. Father Matthew always seemed to catch Sandra with a rolling pin in her hand, which was a clear sign that she was making a pie. Sandra's cooking was a thing of legend on the island, her apple pie had become everyone's favourite dessert.

"Morning, ladies, I am here now. How may I be of help?"

Mary turned and smiled at him, blowing him a little kiss as she did.

"Thank you, Father Matthew. I think that Mary has already done most of the work, as always. We will be ready to plate up soon, so if you wouldn't mind, can you start laying the plates on the side?" Sandra nodded over to the stack of trays in the trolleys.

Sandra ran the kitchen with military precision every day. She was the boss and nobody saw fit to challenge that.

"No problem, Sandra, my wife is a great little helper. How many trays would you like me to set out?"

Sandra looked at the list above her head.

"We are expecting circa forty-five, but let's lay out fifty, just in case. You never know who might be hungry today."

One of the biggest challenges Father Matthew found with opening and running an old people's home on the island was at meal time. You were never sure who was going to show up. Due to the financial situation of the home, they needed to make every penny count. They relied on the government and donations from the mainland plus a few private patients that paid for their place at the home, but it was always tight which meant he needed to keep a close eye on expenses at all time. As the residents became older, they tended to eat less and less. Some would sometimes not come for lunch, and others who still had friends or family on the island, would be taken out. This was especially the case on a Saturday or Sunday. At full seating, they had eighty-two people in the old people's home, but very rarely they fed that many at a sitting.

Father Matthew started to create the trays that he was going to pass to Mary to fill. Just a plate, bowl, knife, fork spoon and a napkin. Suddenly the swing door to the kitchen area burst open again.

"As if by magic she appears. We are saved, our other little helper is here, ladies." Mary looked up from preparing the vegetables and smiled.

"You are just in time. Come on, Alana, you can help me with the plating up."

Alana, as always, did as she was told. She went over to the tray area and got stuck straight in to help Father Matthew. Alana had arrived at the orphanage when it opened. She had been their first youthful resident; they took her in at the age of fourteen. Alana's parents had been driving home one night from a party at a friend's house when, at no fault of their own, they were hit by an oil tanker. The driver of the oil tanker had been an intercontinental driver who had been driving over his legal driving hours. When the case finally went to court, the haulage company responsible stood by the story that they believed the driver had had an assistant and they had been double-shifting his truck, but that wasn't the case. He had been working eighteen hours straight and claiming double the salary. The CCTV footage showed that the driver had fallen asleep at the wheel for less than ten seconds, and the truck swerved to the other side of the road and hit Alana's parents head-on. Alana had been told they would have been killed instantly, before the car had disappeared in a ball of flames, but this was little comfort.

With no grandparents, aunts or uncles, her mother and father had been her only family, Alana had been orphaned in a brief moment whilst she was asleep safely at home. Father Matthew had been so touched by the story that he had read in the paper that he had made the crossing to bring her back to the island.

Alana was always dressed in black; it had started out as mourning for her parents, but after a few years it has just become part of who she was. Almost gothic-like, but she didn't go into the dark, black make-up. She was the only almost gothic-like person they had on the island, so everyone knew who she was. Although her appearance stood out, and despite the clothes, she was a very attractive girl. Alana didn't think so and would usually made herself disappear into most backgrounds, especially in the home. She did as she was told and was never any trouble to anyone. She was never rude as she very rarely spoke. Father Matthew would make time to speak to her every day in order to try and coax some more words out of her. The days that this happened were few and far between. He was becoming increasingly concerned that, although she seemed happy there, as soon as she was of legal age, eighteen she was going to leave them. He knew he had a couple of months to get her to start opening up more and enjoying herself more in their company.

"So, let's make a conveyor belt. Alana with the tray and plate, passes to me for the rest of the equipment, Sandra main, Mary dessert, and then lid on and done. I think I could have probably worked as a manager on a production line. I always knew my real talents were wasted here."

Father Matthew looked for the smile from Alana; it didn't come, but Mary threw him one. Alana stood next to Father Matthew. They made a conveyor belt as he had suggested and within fifteen minutes fifty meals were set on the trolleys and ready to be served.

The dining room was visibly half empty today. The lunch was always scheduled for midday, so the people that had arrived were all they were getting. Father Matthew passed out the trays to the residents, speaking to each of them as he did. He knew everyone one of them personally. Whether they were original islanders, or not. If they had been mainlanders, he would have been responsible for interviewing them and then bringing them across on the ferry. Having people from the mainland helped with the government grants, and Father Matthew tried to ensure the home was at capacity as much as he could to help with the financials.

Alana disappeared into the hallway with a trolley to deliver lunch to the bedridden patients. Father Matthew finished handing out the last lunch and then, as he sat down to start his own, there was a familiar voice from behind him.

"Hellllooo, F-Father Ma-atthew." Father Matthew immediately stood and turned around.

"Hello, Alex, how very nice to see you. Are you going to be joining us for lunch...? You will be more than welcome."

"Y-es pl-pl-ease."

Father Matthew pulled out a chair for Alex; with Alex's disability he struggled with the use of both his hands, although he always tried his best. Alex sat down, and Father Matthew pushed his chair in to make sure he was comfortable.

Alex was brought to the home by Judge Reynolds two years previously. The judge had moved to the island himself when the prison opened a year previous to that. The judge had been given the task of reading the case notes out loud to the public in the new court room next to the prison on the fifth-year anniversary of the sentencing. The second sentencing had been attracting too much attention when read in the original court house. Moving it to the island had been the government's plan to quieten everything down. It had worked. Over the last few years, people had stopped caring about the second sentencing.

The judge had spent his whole life in law, and was now turning sixty-seven years old. This was seen as a quiet, but deserved end to an interesting and colourful career.

Having lost his wife a few years ago and with no children, the island seemed like a retirement home calling to him.

Apparently, Alex was the son of a long-time family friend of the judge. Alex too had suffered a great loss; his father had been murdered and his mother, who had been a friend of the judge, was no longer able to care for him. The judge had explained the whole thing to Father

Matthew before bringing him to the island, including the fact that he was suffering from motor neuron disease, but it wasn't as progressive as other strains. Alex's hands and feet were affected quite badly, his hands were almost claw-like, he had no real grip to speak of and one foot was forced to the side which made it difficult to walk or to carry anything. He could just about make it to feed and dress himself on a daily basis, so he wasn't that much of a burden to them. The judge had explained how the stutter had always been there, but now his speech was a lot more slurred due to the reduce control of the mouth and tongue. It made understanding him hard at times, but everyone was patient with him and treated him like one of the family since the first day that he arrived.

"So, Alex, how has your day been?" Father Matthew, like everyone else at the home, had a soft spot for Alex. They all ensured to keep him included in everyone's conversation no matter how long it took him to reply.

"G-gggood. Been Goooo-o-d."

"I am glad to hear it. I hope you haven't been teasing the ladies? I know how you like to do that."

Alex started to blush and turned his head. In the home he had become an outrageous flirt with the staff and nuns alike. Religion hadn't stopped his advances. He was harmless enough, bringing the ladies flowers and sweets, even attempting to write them little cards to say thank you and how much he appreciated them.

If it hadn't been for the disease all the women, including the nuns, in the facility believed Alex could have been quite the ladies' man. He was tall, dark, and a very handsome man, which made it even harder to see what the condition had done to him.

"N-n-nn-oo… Nn-ever."

Father Matthew knew that was a little white lie. Alex and Father Matthew went back to their lunches. When Alana returned from dropping off the trays to the bedridden patients, she started to clear the trays from the tables. She wasn't one too often sit down and eat with them. Father Matthew finished his lunch, got up, and helped her. Within ten minutes the dining room had cleared, and Father Matthew and Alana were loading the dishwashers.

"So Alana, what do you have planned for the rest of the day?" Alana just shrugged her shoulders.

"You do know you don't have to keep helping out around here? You are a resident too. You should be out enjoying yourself. I am sure there is lots you could be doing on the island." It was Father Matthew's turn to tell a little white lie. He knew there was little for teenagers to do on the island. He had tried running a youth club for a couple of months, but with only a few participants it slowly fizzled out.

Alana shrugged her shoulders again.

"I was thinking, we should plan something nice for your birthday. I know it is still a couple of months away, but that should give us plenty of time to make it special. I will speak with Catherine later, and maybe she can help us plan something? That would be nice, wouldn't it?"

Alana shrugged her shoulders again for the third time.

Catherine was Father Matthew and Mary's daughter. She was a little older than Alana at twenty, but Matthew had hoped that when Alana came to the island, they would have been close. He had imagined them coming together in a sisterly way. That was something that never really materialised. Catherine's distraction had been Michael. They had been dating since the age of twelve. They were also best friends and inseparable from that first date. Like her father, Catherine always tried to make time to speak to Alana when she could, but Michael had been her main focus. Michael proposed to her at her twentieth birthday party a few months ago. He had done everything by the book, even asking Father Matthew first for her hand in marriage. He gave his permission straight away. The whole community was becoming increasingly excited about the wedding of the century.

Catherine was classically beautiful; she would have passed as a professional model anywhere in the world. On Callington Island she stood head and shoulders above all others. Michael had been lucky enough to catch her, before she met the world, or the world met her. Living on the island meant that you didn't meet very many people.

There were very little choices of relationships. All of that aside, it was the real thing. They truly loved each other. Whilst they had been together since the age of twelve, they were still waiting to have a physical adult relationship. Catherine believed in saving herself for her wedding night. Whilst her father and mother hadn't strongly placed this idea in her head, it had been something that she herself had a moral compass on. She had made this decision herself as part of the religious upbringing that her father had given her.

As a father and a Father, Father Matthew had been thankful and proud on the night that Mary told him of her beliefs and her decision.

Michael was also happy to wait. In truth, there was nobody on the island that was going to turn his head as much as Catherine. He knew he had struck the Callington Island lottery by forming a relationship with the most beautiful girl on the island.

"OK, I am going to take that as an agreement. I will see her this evening and ask her to help us plan something special."

Alana didn't even bother to shrug her shoulders that time. She just finished loading the dishwasher and turned it on. She turned and left the room at the same time Mary walked in.

"Let me guess, three words? You do try, my love. She is just not a talkative girl. Woman, sorry, I guess she is fast becoming a woman."

"You will be surprised one day. One day you will walk into the room and think, will she ever shut up. I guarantee it."

Mary walked over and hugged Father Matthew. They were never shy about their emotions or feelings anywhere. In front of an audience or not. Mary had been in love with him from the first day that he arrived on the island. The feeling had been mutual. They too were childhood sweethearts of the island from the age of twelve which made them even happier for Catherine and Michael.

"That is something I cannot wait to hear, my dear. All your effort will pay off; I am sure of it. So, what's next on your, I am sure, incredibly busy agenda?"

"Well, I am about to drive into town as I promised I would go to see Miss March. Then I will be heading back home to write tomorrow's sermon." Father Matthew kissed his wife on the forehead, walked over to the sink, dried his hands on the tea towel and then placed it on the side.

"We have made lasagne for dinner tonight, so it's all done and in trays in the oven. Sandra and Alana, with the sisters' help, can cope with that. So, I will meet you at home when you are done." Mary paused. Father Matthew knew what was coming next. He had heard the same thing from Mary a hundred times over the past few years.

"And I know you don't like to hear it, but be careful with Miss March. I do worry about people like that. There is something unstable about them. Something that probably requires professional help." Father Matthew smiled at his wife.

"She is just a little confused, dear. I said I would sit with her and hear her view on the case. Let's see if we can get her to go home." They were both gently nodding at each other.

"She is not the first visitor we have had with these intentions, and I am sure she will not be the last."

"OK, you are too thoughtful sometimes, Matthew. For me though, be careful. I will see you at home." It was Mary's turn to kiss him, and then she left the room heading home to prepare their dinner for this evening.

Father Matthew waited a couple of minutes to make sure she had left. Quietly he walked over, pushed the door open, and looked inside the dining room to ensure that nobody was still remaining. There wasn't anyone, it was completely empty. He then turned, grabbed one of the remaining lunch trays off the trolley, and headed out of the kitchen.

An hour later, Father Matthew took the drive to town.

It was less than fifteen minutes to the centre of town, and a pleasant afternoon drive. Arriving at the hotel, he was greeted by a Hayley Keating, wife of Kevin Keating, the hotel manager. If truth be told they both ran the hotel. If anyone was really in charge, it was Hayley.

"Hi, Father Matthew." There was always a jolliness to Hayley, in fact, to the both of them, Hayley and Kevin. They were what Father Matthew called the salt of the earth. Do anything for anyone. Always seemed to have a spring in their step, even though neither of them was light on their feet. Hayley and Sandra were the top two chefs on the island and as such both ran kitchens. Both had sampled far too much of their own cooking. In turn, both of their husbands had also been well fed.

"Hello, Hayley, and how are you on this lovely Saturday afternoon? And how is Kevin?"

"We are both really well, Father. Thank you for asking. Although, I think Kevin is off somewhere, hiding, having a second lunch. Have you eaten, Father?"

"I have, Hayley, I am fine." Father Matthew was waiting for that question. Hayley was always trying to feed him. It was in her nature.

"Well, if you are sure. I presume you are here for the young Miss March?" Father Matthew just smiled at Hayley.

"Takes all sorts to run the world, Father, that's what I say. And we do get all sorts since the prison, don't we, Father?" Hayley was almost laughing at that point. The prison was always the talk of the island. Father Matthew hadn't expected that it would be so popular. He had envisaged that, due to its location, it would have been separate from the day-to-day life of the island. Nevertheless, it had become part of the day-to-day conversations in their lives very quickly.

"That we do, Hayley. That we do."

"She is in the study, Father, on her own. We are very quiet this afternoon. I think everyone is down by the port watching the sea, with a beer in hand. I can't blame them for that. Now, are you sure I couldn't tempt you with a sandwich? I could bring it straight in to you?"

"I am fine, I assure you, Hayley."

Father Matthew walked into the hotel, and through to the study. Sitting in the chair was Miss March. She was a professional-looking lady: smart suit, long blonde hair, and very attractive. She could have passed for a lawyer as she sat there. Miss March had come to see Father Matthew at the church over a week ago when she first came to the island. She wanted to appeal the death sentence of one of the inmates, and as an appeal had never been logged, she had asked around for some help in doing this. Hayley and Kevin had directed her to Father Matthew as the main man on the island. The man with the most influence. Whilst she dressed the part, and certainly looked the part of a lawyer, it wasn't who she really was.

"Hello, Father, so happy to see you again." A smile came across her face as father Matthew walked in. Not many people had spoken to her on the island. She wasn't the first woman of her type to arrive, others had come, but never to log an appeal. They came to say their goodbyes or be close to a loved one at the time of their departure from this world. Most of the islanders gave them a wide berth for this reason.

"Hello, Miss March, sorry I am a little late."

"Father, you can call me Kacie, and that is fine; it is just ten minutes. I am sure you are a very busy man." Kacie gestured for the Father to sit down, and he took the chair opposite to hers.

"Thank you, and how are you today, Kacie?"

"I am fine, Father. It is a beautiful day outside. I spent the morning walking the town. It is a very beautiful place."

"That it is. That it is." There was a moment's silence. These were always hard conversations to start up, even for Father Matthew.

"Kacie, have you thought about what we talked about the other day? The reason you are here?"

"I have, Father, and whilst I understand that all of the evidence points towards my Damien, I know he has been set up. I know it in my heart, Father. He is a good man. A really good man."

Matthew stopped and paused for a moment. Kacie was smiling at him. She looked so happy. His first thought was, you haven't listened to a word of what has been said. But then he thought of Hayley, and her comment just now as he was walking in. It takes all sorts in this world, Father.

"I am sure you think he is, Kacie. May I ask you again to run through your reasons behind this? Given everything we discussed and everything we know." Father Matthew leaned in to ensure that Kacie knew he was listening. She was smiling back at him. She had no trouble with explaining it all over again. She loved to speak about her Damien to anyone that would listen.

"Because I know him, Father. We have been writing to each other for over four years now. I know the man he is. He could have never done what they say he did. He is just not that type. My Damien is kind and gentle. He is a loving, Christian man, Father. Does that sound like a murderer to you, Father?"

Kacie had been writing to Damien Winter for four years. She started a year after he had been convicted of the murder of four women. He was given the PDS verdict in a court case that lasted less than a week, and now he had been moved to the island.

Damien had been a predator. He would stalk his pray for weeks before killing them. He would send them little gifts and flowers to their work, almost courting them in his own mind. The victims only ever got one actual date, and they were never expecting it when it happened. Three of the women in question were married, and one was single. All professionals, and all long blonde hair.

After reading all the reports in the newspapers, it was Miss March that had started the correspondence. His picture had struck something within her. His eyes had told her that he was not a killer. She wasn't a natural blonde; she had made herself into the perfect victim for Damien before sending him some photos, and trying to engage him in conversation.

"Besides, we are to be married, Father. Does that not count for anything? Married people just don't do that sort of thing. He would never do that sort of thing."

Kacie pushed out her hand to Father Matthew; there was indeed an engagement ring on her finger: a large solitaire diamond ring. She bought it for herself about a year ago after her correspondence had started to become daily with Damien. She was convinced of his commitment in their relationship then. Telling the few friends that she had that it must be love due to the effort he was now putting in to communicate with her daily. For Damien, there was little else to do in his cell all day but write to his fans. Surprisingly there were a few of them. Even after all the day-to-day communication, Kacie and Damien still hadn't met. Damien had made a promise in all his letters that this had been a mistake, and he would be released soon. Each one of his fans believed this, but only one had believed it so much that they made the trip to the island with the intention of helping him.

After making an application it took ten days to receive a visiting order from the prison. Kacie had now been on the island for seven. She had visited the outside of the prison every day so that she could write to Damien and tell him she was close. The prison had allowed her to drop off and pick up the mail directly from them instead `of using the postal system due to the nature of the island. They had continued to be corresponding daily.

"That's very pretty, Kacie. When did he give it to you?" Father Matthew was hoping for some kind of reality check from that question, but he didn't get one.

"He proposed to me in one of his letters. He even picked the type of ring I should have. He knew my taste in jewellery, Father. That is how connected we are. When he comes out in a couple of weeks, he will pay me for it; he has money tucked away. He was just waiting for the right person to come along. We will be starting our life together very soon, Father. We are both still young, and both want a big family."

Father Matthew knew Damien was never getting out of prison. He had been at the hearing, and that was where he first met Miss March.

It had been a highly publicised investigation. Damien had waited until the victims were alone at home before breaking in. He would gag them and tie them to the bed, undressing them with a Bowie knife, slice by slice through the clothes. Taking his time to torture his victims. Then he would force them to have sex. When he was finished, he held his hands around their throats and strangled them until there was no life left in them.

Damien would then cover up their private parts with anything he could find: a pillow case, a cover, a T-shirt, and then leave. Damien wasn't an intelligent killer; there were traces of his DNA everywhere. There was also security footage of him entering and exiting the buildings. He didn't even disguise himself. More importantly, he had confessed to everything, and his reasons for doing it. Something Father Matthew had mentioned to Kacie on several occasions since she arrived on the Island.

Damien Winter had been rejected by the woman he considered to be the love of his life. In reality, this woman, a lawyer by the name of Rebecca Castor, hadn't really known Damien. He ended up speaking to her in a bar one night. She flirted with him and gave him a kiss on the cheek, and a fake number. It had enraged Damien, and he snapped. First, he tried to hunt her down. Rebecca Castor was married, and lived out of town. He never found her, and she never knew how she had affected him. Even when it was all over the news, she didn't know it was because of her.

"Miss March, you have to understand that there is a chance that he will not be coming out of prison. You do understand that, don't you?" Father Matthew reached out and grabbed her by the hands.

"Father call me Kacie. I know the evidence is strong. They created it that way on purpose. But our love, well, that is stronger, and I am going to see him in a couple of days. We will be able to sort it all out then, and I will help him build his appeal, Father. The judge will see the caring and considerate side of my Damien. He will see how he is around me and realise they have made a huge mistake."

Father Matthew knew she was not going to stop. She did look the part, and although he was confident that a supermarket assistant shelf-stacker did not have the knowhow to overturn a murder charge, Father Matthew had some sympathy for her.

It wasn't uncommon for PDS inmates to strike up relationships with lonely women on the outside. It was almost becoming a common occurrence for them to end up on the island. More common than Father Matthew had expected anyway. All that he could do was council them while they were there, and send them on their way as soon as the sentence had been carried out.

"OK, Kacie. Why don't we talk again after you have met with Damien? But for now, let's have some tea and some of the delicious cake that I presume Hayley is standing by the door with in order for us to try." Father Matthew had clocked Hayley's arrival a couple of seconds before. It was, as Father Matthew had presumed, so that she could get him to taste her cake. He also knew that Hayley didn't like the thought of him leaving without having something to eat.

"That sounds like a good idea, thank you, Father. You are so kind."

Hayley entered the room with cake, and Kevin wasn't far behind with a pot of tea. Father Matthew stayed another thirty-five minutes talking to Kacie about her family, her dreams, where she wanted to be in five years' time. She didn't want anything different than most women her age. A couple of kids and a house with a big back garden in a little village. Just to love and be loved in return. The trouble was that, in her head, it was all with a guy they had nicknamed the Sheffield Strangler.

Father Matthew eventually made his excuses and headed home to write his sermon for the following day's congregation. On the fifteen-minute journey he decided that, given the last twenty-four hours, it should all be about facing up to reality. Something quite a few people he had spoken to lately didn't seem to be able to grasp.

When he arrived back to the vicarage, Catherine and Mary were cooking in the kitchen, and Michael was sitting at the dining room table talking to them.

"Isn't this a pleasant sight to come home to, all cosy in the kitchen, just like a real family." Catherine came over and kissed him on the cheek.

"Dad, we are a real family, and we are making dinner. Michael is helping. Don't worry though, you have a couple of hours for your sermon writing before we sit down to eat."

"Good, thank you, dear, and, Michael, how are you today?"

"I am fine, Father Matthew." There was a look shared between them. Neither of them ready to speak about what they had seen today. Neither wanting to discuss Jacob and his last day on this earth. They both kept that part of their lives from their partners; it certainly wasn't something they wanted to discuss over the dinner table. They never even discussed it on the odd time that they were alone.

"Well, I will be in my study then. Call me if you need me for anything or when that lovely smelling dinner is ready." Father Matthew went to his study. He sat down at his desk and pulled the bible from the right-hand drawer. Holding it open, he thought about where he would find guidance on the sermon of reality. This took him the whole two hours to write, longer than he had first expected.

Just as he finished, he was called for dinner. Michael was joining them, and the four sat discussing the old people's home whilst they ate and enjoyed a glass of wine before retiring to the living room. The after-dinner conversation turned to the wedding they were planning. It was a few months away, but excitement had taken over most evenings for Catherine and Mary.

"Dad, we do have someone to marry us now, don't we?"

Father Matthew had been trying to sort this out for weeks. Whilst he knew a lot of Fathers, it wasn't very often they got together. Well, this was mainly due to where he was based and the huge workload that he had undertaken. A Father on Callington Island was quite a solo profession.

"Yes, of course we do; I forgot to tell you. He is an old friend of mine. Travelling up from Cornwall none the less. Father Andrew will be proceeding over your service. He is a good man. As for me, Catherine, I can't wait to give you away."

Father Matthew smiled at Catherine and Michael. They knew exactly what he meant. Even if it was done with a wry smile.

"Thanks, Dad. I am so excited, we have the dresses for the bridesmaids and flowers, and we are going to the mainland for another fitting for my dress in a week. I know it is months away, but it has to be perfect."

"It will be. I am sure your mother has it all in hand." Nobody had any doubt that with the amount of planning that had gone into it, it was going to be the perfect day.

"Michael, I do notice that you never seem to say a lot on the matter. That is not a good start for married life. You have to speak up a little more." Father Matthew was almost laughing as he spoke.

"I never get a chance, sir." Michael smiled back at Father Matthew.

"That is what I thought. I would get used to that if I was you." Mary quickly reached out and playfully punched her husband in the arm.

"Anyway, it's late and I have to leave. It is a shame that I will not be able to look through the flowers again, Catherine. Maybe your father would like to do that with you?" Michael gave another smile at the Father. It was his parting playful gift.

"I will see you all at church in the morning." Michael stood and started to leave the room, so did Catherine.

"Yes, Michael, see you in the morning." Mary got up and kissed him on the cheek, and Father Matthew just smiled in his direction. Michael and Catherine disappeared into the hallway.

"She is so excited, dear. It will be a wonderful service. I am really looking forward to it." Mary started to clear the books away.

"Yes, it will. It only seems like yesterday she was in the corner playing with her dolls. And look at her now, planning a real wedding and not the make-believe ones we all used to have to partake in." Father Matthew shared a smile of remembrance with his wife.

"I know, dear, but don't worry, I think our little girl is still in there somewhere. It is getting late, should we all retire? You know how Sundays drain you out, what with three services to give now."

Father Matthew did know this. Since the prison had arrived on the island, he had included two more services on a Sunday. He started his Sunday with an early session at the prison, then he had his normal service, and he had added another one at evening song for any of the officers that were working in the day. All giving roughly the same speech with the hope that people weren't attending twice in one day.

"You go to bed, dear. I think I am going to take a walk just to clear my head."

Mary didn't question him; it wasn't abnormal for him to still be thinking about his sermon late on a Saturday night. Especially after a day at the prison. Those days always took their toll on her husband. Mary knew that today had been an execution day. The island was always updated on execution days. The local newspaper would publish the dates just to prepare the island for any visitors. Mary got up to leave, walking over to kiss her husband before heading to bed. As she opened the door to the hallway, she could see Catherine heading up the stairs.

"Good night, Catherine."

"Oh, good night. I was just getting changed into my PJs. Are you retiring?"

"Yes, I think so, dear. Your father is taking a walk, but I am tired; it has been a long day."

"OK, night, Mum, night, Dad." Catherine turned and headed back up the stairs to her bedroom.

"Night, sweetheart, sweet dreams," Father Matthew shouted to his daughter from the living room. Five minutes later Catherine and Mary were upstairs getting ready for bed. Father Matthew could still hear them talking about weddings as they did. He went into the kitchen and pulled open one of the drawers. He took out a large torch, and checked it on and off. He then wandered over to the cupboard and pulled out a rucksack. He placed it on the table, unzipped it, and checked the contents. It was all there; he had prepared it earlier today before heading into town to see Miss March.

As quietly as he could, he opened and closed the back door and headed out of the garden. The night was cold, but Father Matthew knew it wasn't that far to go; he could leave his jacket at home.

Chapter 3

Sundays were a long day for Father Matthew. He was up at six, went to the church and said his own prayers then headed home, ate some toast, and drank a cup of coffee. By seven twenty-five he was in the car heading to the prison. If prisoners wanted to pray on a Sunday, they would have to be in the church for eight a.m. It was common for the chapel in the prison to be full. Father Matthew figured that either there was little else to do in prison on a Sunday morning or the closer to death you become, the more you wanted to hear about the afterlife. He had certainly noticed this in the old people's home as nearly all his residents had started to attend both his services on a Sunday.

Today was no different. As he walked into the prison chapel, he could see rows of inmates all sitting down awaiting his arrival. There were only five women in the prison, so Father Matthew had changed their service to Thursdays. There was all manner of vicious people in the prison, and even he knew it was not a good idea to have men and women in the same room at any time.

All the prisoners were still handcuffed in church. This was to stop any fighting, but they weren't shackled at the ankles any more as it made it hard to bend down and pray. It was very rare that there was any trouble. By the time they reached the island, most of the fight was out of the inmates. Father Matthew stood behind the podium, made the sign of the cross, and then started his sermon.

"Good morning, gentlemen. I wanted to take some time today to discuss reality. Reality in its purest form. The reality of what we are, and what we have done." Some cheering happened at this point which Father Matthew didn't acknowledge. When writing his sermon, he knew some of the words were going to get a reaction out of his audience. He could hear comments like: "you know what I have done", and, "I know what he has done." There was a type of hierarchy amongst the prisoners on Callington Island. In the prisons where they would have spent the last five years, this would have meant something. It would have delivered them benefits to be top dog. But here, it was more to do with fame than power. There was very little to be gained from power as they were all there for such a short time. Fame, on the other hand, which depended on what you had been convicted of, distinguished one inmate from another. There was one particular inmate whose fame would surpass the walls of the prison, and even those of the UK, he would go down in history. Father Matthew had scouted the room on his way in to see if he was there today, he never missed an opportunity to be closed to him, except today. He wasn't there. There was a little sigh of relief for that although it did worry him where he was? Father Matthew recognised all the other faces but ignored them all to continue with his sermon.

"As I sat in my study at home, I started to reflect about my own reality. Just because I perceive there to be a god, it doesn't mean that he is real. Certainly, I am sure he is not real for a lot of people. Some may believe in my god or other gods or no gods at all." Father Matthew paused for a second. He knew the story of every man sitting in front of him. Some he had heard as they had arrived on the island, but most of them he knew from before their arrival. They all had a belief; they all believed there was a reason for their actions. Some thought it came from a higher power, and others from something within themselves. He was hoping this would make them all think.

"For me, I concluded that my reality is in fact my faith which is a contradiction in itself. My reality is what I believe it to be. The people in this room have their own reality of life. What they perceived to be the truth is in fact their reality. So how and why does reality differ?"

The noise had quietened down. It was working, the inmates were listening to what he had to say.

"Is reality faith or physical? Do we need to believe it? Or experience it for it to be true? I myself believe I have a calling, a calling to do someone else's work. God's work. I have listened to many cases over the years, and there were a lot of your fellow inmates who have said something similar: 'Mine is God's work', and in many cases your past inmates were perceived to be doing the work of... Well, let's just say someone else." There were a few laughs again from the inmates.

"Some other voice; a voice that had been speaking to them. That was their reality. That was what they were supposed to do. Now I would question that against my reality, so which one is real? In life maybe we each have to have a set of rules to work by? When you really think about it, is that what reality comes down to? Faith in a set of rules in which we must operate? Rules that we need to follow and always have present. If my god were to tell me to commit a crime, I have the rules that he has laid down for me so I can question his request. If you follow the rules, then the true reality will materialise whether you like or agree with it. Maybe that is the answer?"

Father Matthew knew he was preaching to people who couldn't follow the rules, at least not the rules he lived by. They were now all living their own reality. As he glanced over the faces, he singled out Damien, and fixed his gaze on him while he spoke. He carried on his sermon with very little response from his audience until the end when he had them all praying for a reality of life.

When they had all finished praying, he asked one of the guards to ensure that Damien stayed behind. Once the chapel had emptied Father Matthew guided Damian to the pews close to the guard who was standing in the corner keeping a careful eye on the Sheffield Strangler.

"Thank you for staying behind. I just wanted to let you know that I met with your fiancée yesterday, Damien. Kacie is a lovely, remarkable woman."

Damien's glance didn't change. He looked directly at Father Matthew as if he hadn't heard a word he had said. Damien wasn't a god-fearing man. He wasn't actually an anyonefearing man. The time that he had spent in prison over the last five years had really shaped him. His crimes on the outside world had been against women, and there were a lot of inmates that didn't like that. As such Damien had spent the last five years fighting his way through his sentence. Damien's last few weeks on the island was the most peaceful time he had had in prison.

"She informs me she is coming to see you in a couple of days, isn't she?"

"Yes, she is, Father." Damien kept looking directly at Father Matthew. He knew what he had been doing to her, but writing to anyone who wrote to him had been his only escape inside prison.

"Can I ask you to do something for me, Damien?" Father Matthew knew the best way to help Miss March was to let her move on.

"Yes, of course, Father."

"Let her go, Damien. This is no life for a young woman who has her life ahead of her. This isn't something that she needs to be a part of." Father Matthew gestured to the prison around him. Damien turned his head, but then looked back directly at him.

"I didn't start this, Father. She wrote to me, nearly every day for a year before I answered. I didn't start this." It had been four months before he had replied to Kacie's letters. It had only been when she sent her first photo that he picked up the pen. She had been a brunette her whole life until the point that she had wanted to get the Sheffield Strangler's attention.

"I know you didn't start this, but why did you answer her, Damien? What was going to be the benefit in that?"

"Because she was so persistent, she told me she loved me. She knew from the first time that she saw my picture on the TV. She told me that she was lonely and just needed some company. There is no harm in that." It was Damien's turn to pause. He had picked up the pen because, since his conviction, he had spent his whole time alone in his cell. He had family, but after his arrest they had disowned him. The only time he had company was when he was being beaten in his cell by other inmates or the guards.

"I guess I felt the same, Father." Father Matthew could see the change in his face. It was no longer that cold stare. His face had softened.

"Prison is a lonely place, and although I know it will not materialise to anything, I was glad of the company. It was nice to think that someone was thinking of me." The way Damien had just spoken almost had Father Matthew feeling remorse for him.

"I do understand, Damien. I am sure it is a very lonely place, but what about today? Knowing where you will be going in a few weeks' time? Is it not time to let her get on with her life? If, as you say in your letters, you care for her, don't put her through all of this anymore." Father Matthew was trying to appeal to his sense of morals. Hoping that he still had some in him even if he was the Sheffield Strangler. It was in his nature to try to find a little piece of decency in everyone.

"I am still lonely, Father. That hasn't changed, and is there any harm in some company for the last few weeks of your life?" Father Matthew did understand that too. The thought of facing death alone would not be pleasant for anyone, no matter what role they had taken in their life. Part of him understood the need for company. But another part of him, not the man-of-God part, also thought about saying that he didn't deserve company at the end after what he had done.

"Time will come for your sentence to be carried out Damien for the crimes that you have committed, and if you were able to let someone have their life back before you pass over, that will hold you in great stead for the afterlife, my son."

Father Matthew didn't like using the 'my son' quote and avoided it as much as possible. Damien didn't seem to want to change his view, but he may be the type to respond to a little emotional, religious blackmail. Father Matthew knew it would be healthier for Miss March to leave the island before the day his crimes would come to justice. He never wanted anyone in that room with him when that happened. It was not healthy for victims or family. Damien paused as if to reflect on what Father Matthew had said.

"OK, Father, I will not promise anything, but I will see what I can do." Father Matthew released a sigh of relief inside. It wasn't a victory yet, but at least he had Damien thinking about it. Damien knew he would have to sit with him again for his confession, and he would want that to go well. He would not want to feel guilty for failing to do something he had promised a Father.

"That is all I can ask from you, Damien." Father Matthew placed a hand on his shoulder. There was a faint smile from Damien as he did. Father Matthew knew that was another good sign.

"Father, can I ask something of you in return?"

"If I can help I will, Damien." Damien was now looking directly at him. Whatever he wanted meant something to him. There was now a purpose in his eyes.

"In your reality, can you see the difference?" Father Matthew paused as if trying to understand the question.

"Difference?"

"Yes, Father, can you see right from wrong? You talk about the urge to follow the rules. The rules set out by your god. Is there any time that you don't follow the rules, Father? Is there any time that it is permitted to break them?" Damien paused as if remembering something important.

"Because the lines are blurred for me. There are times in my life that I wished they weren't. I wondered if they are blurred for everyone. Are they blurred for you at times, Father?"

Father Matthew was quiet now. He could almost feel his head drop to the ground. Even writing the speech, there had been some guilt tying him up inside. He knew what he was preaching, and why he had chosen the subject, but some of its content had been weighing on his mind for quite a while.

"Damien, all I can say is that we each have a path to follow; we need to stick to the rules as closely as we can. I can see right from wrong, and, as most people, I always have the best intentions in my actions."

"I think it must be just as hard to be good all the time, as it is to be evil, Father." Father Matthew held his breath at that statement.

Father Matthew had been contemplating that thought for years, ever since the prison had arrived. So much evil locked up a short ride away from his home. But he didn't want to think about it anymore today, he had had enough. Father Matthew made his excuses to Damien saying he had to leave due to having other services he had to give. He made the sign of the cross in front of him, and headed out of the prison.

Father Matthew breathed a large breath of fresh air as soon as the prison doors closed behind him. That last conversation had his head thinking over and over again. It was hard to follow the path that had been chosen for him. Father Matthew headed over to the church. It was always a tight turnaround but he made it with minutes to spare. The church was full again and ready to hear his speech.

"I wanted to start today to discuss reality."

His speech was virtually identical to the first, other than a little less play on the guilty aspect of what reality was. His first audience had been made up of fifty inmates who were responsible for over two hundred and twenty-seven deaths between them. There had been a particular inmate missing from the morning sermon which was still playing on his mind. Father Matthew had thought about that on the drive all the way back to the church. In the short time that he had been on the Island he had never missed a service or a chance to see Father Matthew. Always asking for a little extra time at the end to talk to him. Father Matthew was thankful of the break. It was frightening to think that if he had been there, his audience's death toll would have been double.

In front of him now were who he considered to be the normal folk of the island. Over one hundred people in the church, which was about average for a Sunday morning. Father Matthew was glad about that. When the service was done, many of his congregation stopped for a quick chat as they left the church, which always took about as much time as the service itself. This also gave Mary and Catherine time to clean up behind them as they left, and the church was made ready for the evening song.

"Well, I think that went well, Mary?"

"It did, my dear. Very profound. I can't believe it went down as well at the prison this morning. Reality must be something they don't see very often."

"It was a little rowdy in parts, but it went better than I expected. I think we had a few people thinking on their

actions. That is all I can do for them at this time."
Catherine had finished with the last stack of bibles and
joined them in the porch way to the church.

"Good sermon, Dad. I really enjoyed it."

"Thank you, Catherine. I am glad." Catherine
cuddled up to her father giving him a tight squeeze.

"So, ladies, shall we go and make ourselves
available for Sunday dinner service at the home?"

They both nodded. This was part of the Sunday
tradition. They would help the staff and Sisters with the
dinner, and then eat with them every Sunday. They took
the short four-minute walk over to the home and entered
the kitchen. Sandra was in full cooking mode, and Alana
was working on dessert. They all pitched in. They had
all been doing this for nearly three years so there was
little to be said. The sisters were fetching the elderly
from their rooms and bringing them to the dining room.
Sister Bethany, Sister Katie and Sister Grace were all
floating around the dining room as this was the dinner
nobody wanted to miss.

Father Matthew wheeled out the first trolley-load
out of the kitchen to a slight applause. He started to lay
the trays on the table and the sisters were up and
helping. Alana and Catherine soon followed with
another trolley-load. This continued until all the people
in the room had their dinners laid out in front of them.
It was a big crowd even for a Sunday. Sandra had taken
the trolley to the bedridden patients, giving them all
time to eat their dinners. During dinner the Father
received praise for a great sermon, and everyone
commented on how good Mrs Hills' Sunday dinners
were. Both were normal conversations at the dinner
table on a Sunday, and as always, they all agreed

Sandra's cooking had been the better of the two, including Father Matthew.

Mr Hills had been the local builder on Callington Island and received huge amounts of work when the Father made the deal with the government. Sandra didn't need to work at the home; she did out of a sense of pride for her Island. Her husband, David, had made enough money for them to retire, although he also still did odd jobs around the church, old people's home and its grounds for free. Mostly he did it to be able to get fed whilst his wife was busy in the kitchen.

"Sister Grace. How is it that you are so tiny, yet you seem to eat more than the rest of us?" Father Matthew smiled in her direction.

"I don't know, Father. I guess I am blessed with a fast metabolism." There was a smile as Sister Grace took another roast potato from the extra bowl that Catherine had brought them from the kitchen.

"And what of Sister Trinity? Where is she today? Is she joining us for dinner?" There was a silence with blank expressions coming back from them all. For a moment the table froze. Nobody knew the answer to Mary's question.

"You know, Mary, until you mentioned it I didn't notice that she wasn't here? She is so quiet at times. Has anyone seen her?" Sister Bethany looked at the others. There were shakes of the head all around the table. Sister Bethany was the senior sister of the nunnery, so by all accounts she should have noticed one of her sisters missing.

"Was she at prayer this morning?" Both Sister Katie and Sister Grace looked back at her, shaking their heads once more.

"It is not unusual for her to rise pretty early some days, so we don't always see her." Sister Grace was nodding in agreement with Sister Katie.

"But she was at church today, wasn't she? She doesn't normally miss the Father's speech." Sister Bethany was now looking directly at Father Matthew. His glance then went around the table.

"You know, I am unsure, Sister Bethany. Mary, did you see her?"

The blank looks continued from everyone.

"No, I don't think I did." Whilst nobody wanted to be the first to mention it, they all suddenly had the same thought in their heads. It was Mary who finally said the words.

"You don't think she is another one who has just disappeared to the mainland overnight, do you? Why would she do that?" Each of the guests at the table felt a little worried at that thought. Sister Sarah's disappearance had come as a great shock to all of them. Father Matthew knew he needed to be the one to reassure everyone at lunch. The look on each of their faces was changing from worry to fear. Fear that they had lost another Sister without truly understanding why.

"I am sure she is fine, ladies. Let's not worry unnecessarily. She is just probably taking some silent time for prayer. Or the morning off. We all need a morning off every now and again. Do not get yourselves worried. After we finish this amazing lunch, we will go and see her to check that she is fine."

Whilst they all returned to their dinner, there was a clear doubt in the air about Sister Trinity. There was no more talk at the dinner table. Sister Sarah's sudden and unexpected departure to the mainland meant there was a genuine concern for Sister Trinity now. It had been so out of character for Sister Sarah to leave without saying anything; the whole home asked themselves for days why she had done it. Now they all feared another Sister had left them.

Suddenly there was bloodcurdling scream echoing through the dining room. Father Matthew recognised it immediately; it was Sandra Hills. He was the first to react, closely followed by the sisters and Mary. They all jumped from the dining room table and ran out the door from which Sandra had left to deliver the meals. As they turned down the corridor, the screaming seemed to have them running towards Sister Trinity's room. Father Matthew was the first to arrive. Sandra Hills was still standing in the doorway, and in front of her, on the floor, lay the body of Sister Trinity.

She had been de-gowned and laid naked apart from a pillow case that had been taken off of her bed, covering her private parts. Her habit which had been removed was folded neatly on the chair next to her, and her long blonde hair had been exposed for the world to see.

There were now screams from the sisters and Mary. Father Matthew quickly became aware that everyone could see her. Alana arrived shortly followed by Alex. They had been eating together in Alex's room just three doors down, they had heard all the commotion, but Alex couldn't move as fast as the others.

"W-w-w-w-what i-i-s it?" Alex pushed his way past Alana and Mary and got into the room.

"N-N-N-N-OO, N-N-N-O, Sister Tri-in-init-it-y." Alex fell to the ground in front of the sister. He was trying to hold her, but with his crippled hands he was barely able to get his arms around her. He stopped trying to pick her up and just laid over her, crying and trying to call her name. Father Matthew had a quick reality check of his own; the residents were now watching along with the sisters, and his wife and daughter. He needed to get them all out of there. This wasn't a sight for any of them.

"OK, everyone out of the room. Mary, grab Alex, Catherine and Alana, take everyone back to the dining room. Sisters, go and get her some clothes or a blanket or something." Father Matthew spoke with authority. Mary was the first to move, practically tearing Alex away from Sister Trinity. He didn't go quietly, insisting on kissing her on the forehead before he did. Alex was playing out everything that they had all wanted to do as soon as they saw her lying there. The room had been to in shock to move, but Alex played his heart on his sleeve. The others then one by one all disappeared to do as they were told.

Once Father Matthew was left alone with the body, he closed the door, and sat on the bed. He didn't move for three minutes staring at Sister Trinity. He was completely fixated with what was in front of him. Then, all of a sudden, he knelt on the floor next to her and held her hand. Father Matthew then proceeded to give Sister Trinity the last rites. Although it was too late, he knew he would feel better if she had received it. All the time holding and stroking her hand and her forehead as if to soothe her. Just as he was finishing, there was a knock on the door. Sister Bethany had brought a spare robe.

"Thank you, help me dress her, Sister Bethany." Sister Bethany handed over the robe to Father Matthew.

"Shouldn't we be leaving her for the police? Maybe there are clues or DNA that can help with what has happened, Father?" Sister Bethany had stepped back from the body and was still standing by the door as Father Matthew was starting to stand up. He was shaking his head.

"Do you wish Sister Trinity to be seen naked by the police and the doctor as well as all our guests, Sister?" She shook her head in return.

"No, I suppose not, Father." Father Matthew started to lift Sister Trinity's body off the floor; together they pulled the gown over her head. They removed the pillow case and left it on the bed. There was another knock on the door. It was slightly open now from when Sister Bethany had entered. Mary walked in.

"Are you sure you should be doing that, Matthew?" Father Matthew just nodded his head. Sister Bethany and Mary looked at each other worriedly, it was clear they both thought differently.

"I have called the police. I know as much as they are. I have also rung for the doctor. Matthew shouldn't we be waiting for them to arrive before moving anything? It just doesn't seem right?"

"I fear it is a little late for a doctor, Mary. Tragically Sister Trinity has left us already."

"I know, but I am sure they will be able to help with the body or something. Let us know what happened. Fingerprints and that type of thing? They, I mean he, will find out who has done this to her." Mary started to cry softly. Sister Bethany stood next to her, and put her arm around her.

Although they had thought it, nobody mentioned the likelihood of foul play up until that point. Father

Matthew could see bruises around her neck, and some dried blood sitting on her bottom lip. The most worrying thing was that she had been covered with a pillow case on her private parts. That fact had sent all their minds racing to someone on the island. Whilst only a few people would attend the second sentencing, everyone on the island had become an expert on the cases of the inmates. It was something that Father Matthew was not happy about.

"The Father thought it was better to cover up her body; she was a sister of the church after all, Mary." Sister Bethany wanted to ensure that Mary knew it was not her idea to move or touch the body. She agreed with what Mary was saying.

None of them were used to this type of thing. For an island full of murderers there had never been an actual murder on Callington Island, until now.

Father Matthew recognised the crime scene as soon as he walked in. Blonde young woman, naked apart from the covering up of her private bits. He was convinced that this was the same M.O. as the Sheffield Strangler. What was going through Father Matthew's mind was that he had spoken with him this morning, so he knew Damien was safely locked away in prison. There was no way that he could have done this.

"It is for the best, Mary. I wouldn't want anyone seeing her like that. I am sure the doctor and the police will have all the details they need. I suggest we just carry on with the daily routine with the residents. We don't want them all getting upset, so let's get them to finish dinner, and we can put a movie or something on in the lounge. That will help try to keep their minds off other things. I will sit with Sister Trinity until the doctor and Nigel arrives."

"Nigel." Mary repeated the name as if she had never heard it before. At the same time remembering that is who she had just spoken to. Her heart had sunk when she put the phone down; that is why she made the call directly to the doctor. If anyone was going to help in this situation, it was going to be him. Nigel, was just Nigel. Father Matthew detected the tone in Mary's voice.

"Like it or not, Mary, he is the closest thing to a police officer we have on the island. He is going to need all our support in order to get through this."

"I know, I never really thought about it like that until I made the call. I just called the station. You do, you just call for the police at times like this. Forgetting who was there. It is Nigel." Mary stood just shaking her head. Nigel was the only police officer on the island. Even when Father Matthew made his deal with the government, there was no need for another. The prison would maintain itself, totally, that was the deal. It wasn't going to take resource or time out of the community.

The only exception to this had been Doctor Mitchell and that was only because he applied for the role at the prison. He had been spending his time maintaining one thousand generally fit human beings. Either that or visiting the people in the OAP home where he did the rounds once a week to deal with a common cold or an aching back! Being the only doctor on the island didn't keep him very busy. Before the arrival of the prison, he could spend days without seeing a patient.

Nigel's role had been pretty similar. Crime wasn't something that happened in such a small community.

The most interesting thing that had happened in the last three months was one of the young fishermen's boys was caught shoplifting from the local sweet shop. It was actually his father who called Nigel and asked to lock him up for the night. Which Nigel did. Although he was a policeman, he generally did as he was told by the locals. The cell hadn't seen anyone else for the previous six months, and then the only visitor was a drunk from a night out at The Fleece Public House.

This was going to be a real test of Nigel's skill set. Although nobody on the Island believed he actually had a skill set. Three years after graduating out of the police academy, he finally had a case.

Out of the two of them Nigel arrived first. After putting the phone down, he had been in shock, but it had not lasted long. All the way over to the old people's home he had been excited about the thought of a case. For the first time he even got to use his flashing lights across the island. This caused a stir with the locals as he passed as they had never been seen before. There were now people jumping in their cars to follow him to find out what all the commotion was about.

Nigel was a small man around five foot seven and eight stone if he was wet through. At twenty-three years old he still looked like he had just come out of school. Father Matthew intimidated him; if truth be told, everyone intimidated Nigel, but Father Matthew the most. When Nigel arrived at the home, he was shown to the room where Father Matthew was waiting. He almost fell backwards when he saw the body on the floor. Even though Mary had explained quite clearly on the phone that she thought someone had been murdered, Nigel still didn't believe it until this point. This was the first dead body he had ever seen.

"Nigel, come in and close the door. I would prefer it that the residents and staff don't see this."

Nigel did as he was told. He closed the door and stood with his back almost touching it.

"Good lad, I hope you didn't broadcast this all the way from the police station. I don't want the other people arriving to see her like this, Nigel." Nigel just shook his head side to side to indicate no to the Father.

He knew he had broadcast it to the whole island. Father Matthew was going to be cross with him at some point. But there was no point in owning up to it now. Not with what he had laying on the floor in front of him.

"What happened to her?" The words stumbled out of Nigel's mouth.

"We don't know, Nigel. Sandra was taking the food trolley around and found her like this about thirty minutes ago." Nigel was just now able to look directly at her. He was trying to remember his police training, but for a moment everything he had learnt had fallen out of his head.

"Who is it, Father?"

"Who is it, Nigel? It's Sister Trinity!" Father Matthew looked up at Nigel to see a blank look just staring back at him.

"Oh OK, I just didn't recognise her. You know, with the hair, and everything. I didn't even know she was blonde."

Nigel was never going to be the best detective. As soon as the words came out of his mouth, he almost felt embarrassed by what he had said. He took a minute and tried to compose himself. Taking three deep breaths; he started to focus. His training started to come back to him. Now was the time to switch into work mode. It had been one of the first things that he was taught. This is not personal. This is just about the cold facts.

"So, the body was found exactly like this, Father?" Nigel's voice had deepened, and he tried to sound more like a police officer.

"No, we dressed her, Nigel. She is a sister of the church." Father Matthew spoke with a higher command.

"But I think, we are…"

"Nigel, did you want the world to see a naked sister laid out on the floor." Nigel's head was just moving side to side.

"She was naked?" Father Matthew gave Nigel a look. It almost embarrassed him. Father Matthew was sure that Nigel had never seen a dead body or a naked woman before he entered this room. He was right.

"No, I guess not, I need to go and get my camera from the car to take pictures of the crime scene." He looked at the Father as if to ask permission to leave. Father Matthew nodded at him.

"OK, you go do that." As Nigel left the room, Dr Mitchell arrived.

"Father." Dr Mitchell wasn't really a religious person. He believed in his job and he believed in medicine. Praying was never going to cure you of anything. For him it was a waste of a Sunday morning. Although he did have time for Father Matthew. This was mainly because of everything he was always trying to do for the island and its residents. Father Matthew, in his book, was one of the last good men.

"Dr Mitchell, thank you for coming."

"This is Sister Trinity I presume? Your wife told me her name on the phone. I never did actually meet the woman."

"Yes, we found her like this about thirty minutes ago, but with a few less clothes."

The doctor just looked directly at the Father and bent down over the body. He checked her pulse with his watch and his right hand at her throat. He then started to move her head from one side to another. The bruises were very clear to see.

"Did you mean she was naked, Father?" Dr Mitchell looked up from Sister Trinity.

"Yes, well, almost, other than a pillow case that had been placed over her private parts."

At that the doctor froze, and looked directly at Father Matthew again. He knew the case as well. Whilst he wasn't attending many of the second sentencings, he did read the local newspaper every day, and they would always lead with the more famous of the inmates' cases.

"Damien Winter, the Sheffield Strangler? I must say she certainly fits the description, doesn't she?"

"I believe so, Doctor. Given the hair and the build, she certainly would have been his type."

The doctor returned to his patient and inched up Sister Trinity's gown, examining the area that had been covered by the pillow case.

"I need to do more tests, but I would say Sister Trinity definitely had unwilling sexual intercourse. The cause of death also seems to be strangulation which would fit his MO. He almost crushed her windpipe." There was a pause. Neither of them had seen anything like this before, and the thought of someone with their hands around a sister's neck was firmly in both of their minds.

"Damien is still in the prison, Doctor. I saw and spoke with him myself this morning. So, what worries me more is that it could not have been him. Could it?" Thoughts ran through the doctor's head of the possibility of escape from prison. The same thoughts had been running through Father Matthews mind for the past thirty minutes. Father Matthew had also thought about Damien's fiancée back at the hotel. Everyone on the island knew that she was there. This would be the perfect distraction on the case for her. She had only just told him that her Damien was being framed. Now there was a case to be answered. Doctor Mitchell tried to dismiss the theory of an escape from his mind. He had been at the prison daily over the last few years, and there was no way anyone was getting in and out of there undetected.

"No, there was no way he could have escaped. Nobody could." Doctor Mitchell said what they had both been thinking. Although Father Matthew now thought that if anyone was capable of escaping it was the one inmate who had been missing from church that morning. That thought had started to make him feel sick in his stomach. The thought of it was so bad he didn't even want to say the words out loud. The doctor brought Father Matthew out of his own head.

"My first indication would be that she died last night, Father, somewhere in the last twelve to sixteen hours. Do we know what time she was last seen?" Father Matthew was back in the room and shook his head.

"If that is the case unless he escaped, and then decided to break back into the prison to go to your service this morning; I agree with you father he cannot be our guy."

Nigel knocked to announce himself before he entered back into his crime scene.

"Doctor Mitchell. I am glad you are here. I would have called you as soon as I had understood the crime scene. We need you to give a time of death and to do a thorough examination of the body." Nigel had googled what to do as soon as he had left the room. The answer had been from a TV show, but he figured they will have done their research also.

"I am sure, Nigel. I see you have your camera. That is good thinking."

"Yes." Nigel just stood there with a grin on his face. In turn they both looked back at him. Waiting for him to move.

"Shouldn't you be taking pictures then?" This was the hint that prompted Nigel to move.

"Yes. Pictures, right. Take pictures, let the doctor do what he needs to do, and then search the room for clues of who committed the crime." Nigel went behind the lens. Doctor Mitchell got up and stood by the door to give him access to the whole room.

"OK, Nigel, you do what you need to do. I am going to see if I can get one of Sandra's Sunday dinners. As soon as you are finished, you need to come and get me, and I will take the body to the morgue at the prison. I can do the autopsy there." Doctor Mitchell nodded in the direction of Father Matthew and then disappeared out of the door.

"OK, OK, Doctor. Yes, let's do that." Doctor Mitchell didn't hear any of those words. He was practically in the kitchen by the time Nigel had stumbled his way through them. Nigel started to take pictures. Later, when he got back to the station, he realised the first three had been of a desk, a bed and a flowerpot. One of them did include half of Father Matthew's shoulder but that was actually as close to the victim as he had got in the first ten pictures.

Father Matthew watched as he helplessly tried to take photos of the scene. After a few minutes he had to join in, and guide Nigel through the process. Once they were confident they had enough photos they started to go through Sister Trinity's possessions. She didn't have many. Sisters didn't really want for anything, other than a roof over their head and somewhere to worship. They all led a pretty simple life.

"Are you OK, Nigel?" Nigel's hands had been shaking through most of the ordeal. He had been trying to hide it, but Father Matthew had been watching him intensely since he arrived.

"Yes, I am fine, Father. I am just a little nervous, I think. It is my first real case." Nigel paused.

"Father, do you know anyone who would want to hurt Sister Trinity? She is a nun, right. They don't have enemies, do they? They are always so kind to people."

"No, Nigel, I don't. I agree I do not believe they have many enemies. You should start thinking about who would have something to gain from a copycat murder. That is where I would start." Father Matthew didn't want to put words into his mouth or give him suspects, but he was helping Nigel to think like a policeman.

"A copycat, Father?"

"Yes, Nigel, a copycat. Sister Trinity was a blonde girl, she was found practically naked, raped and, according to Doctor Mitchell, strangled to death. Someone had covered private bits with a pillow case. Doesn't it sound familiar to you?" Nigel just stared blankly at Father Matthew. It was as if he was speaking a foreign language.

"She was raped? She had a pillow case over her, her lady bits? And she was strangled? Father, I didn't know any of that? You didn't mention any of that to me before?" It was Father Matthew's turn to look confused. He played the last forty-five minutes back in his head. All of those facts had actually been discussed, but it was with the doctor. Nigel wasn't in the room.

"Yes, Nigel. I thought you were here when we discussed this?" Nigel just shook his head again. Father Matthew glossed over it, although he did realise now that he hadn't told Nigel.

"Then you need to keep up. All those facts that you have just heard, Nigel. Where do they lead to?" Nigel was deep in thought but not speaking.

"Nothing? Nigel, where were you last Friday? Not the Friday just gone, the one before?" Nigel stood thinking, about two minutes later it was as if a light bulb was switched on in his brain.

"The Sheffield Strangler, Damien Winter. This was how he killed his women, wasn't it, even with the pillow case? Or just something to cover up, you know, the ladies' bits." Nigel stood waiting for his reward for answering the question.

"Well done, Nigel, yes, but before you get excited, he is in prison. I know because I met with him myself this morning. So, he has not escaped. That is unless he broke back into prison this morning. If you remember the doctor said it happened late last night. Maybe sixteen hours ago." Nigel almost looked disappointed in this. This could have been a closed case by tea time if he had escaped.

"But his fiancée, Miss March, she is still on the island. Isn't she, Father? She could have had something to do with this?"

"Now you are thinking, Nigel. I think that is where I would start my questioning, if I was working for the police, that is."

They continued to search the room. Nigel almost had a spring in his step now. He knew he needed to get this done so that he could interview a potential suspect. He had never interviewed a potential suspect before. Nigel picked up Sister Trinity's bible, and as he did, a small black envelope dropped out, the size of a small mobile phone. Holding it up to the light, he saw that it had black bold lettering on it; there was just a single M on the front of the packet. He ran his finger over the raised M, it was quality lettering.

"Father?"

Father Matthew turned to see Nigel opening the envelope. He tipped the contents out onto the night stand. It was a white, almost grey, powdered substance and it covered everywhere. Nigel stuck his finger into the powder and put his finger to his mouth.

"Nigel. Is that wise? You don't even know what it is." Nigel thought twice about what he was doing and brushed it off his finger.

"You are right, Father. I will put some of it back into the envelope and give it to the doctor." His spring was a little dented again as he looked sheepishly at the floor. In his mind he was doing so well up until the point he nearly tasted the unknown substance.

"That's a better idea, Nigel." Father Matthew smiled over at him.

"I wonder what it could be. Do you think it could be drugs, Father?" There was a pause as both men thought about that from two completely different stand points. Father Matthew brought them both out of their thoughts.

"Nigel, what would drugs be doing in an old people's home? Besides, Sister Trinity would never get herself involved with things of that nature. She is a sister of the church."

Father Matthew and Nigel knew drugs had no place on the island. With only one way on and off the island, and the fact that the ferry was checked every trip, it would be almost impossible to get them on there.

"Yes, you are right, Father. I would know if drugs had gotten onto my island." Nigel felt confident in his statement. Drugs had never been an issue on the Island. He returned to searching the room, but there was nothing else to find. Once he was finished, he turned back to Father Matthew.

"I am sorry about Trinity, sorry, Sister Trinity, Father. She was a lovely woman. I always liked her."

"Me too, Nigel. It's a great loss to us all. I just hope the people in the home can deal with this and move on quickly. It's going to be hard on all of them. Be mindful of that, Nigel." There was a tone to that last sentence. Nigel had picked up on it. He knew Father Matthew meant for him to be gentle around them all.

"Yes, of course Father."

"You have to play your part though, Nigel, and keep this under wraps for the whole community. The last thing we need is people thinking there is a murderer on the loose on our island."

"Yes, Father. I understand."

Nigel stood looking at the Father as he took the sheet off the bed and covered Sister Trinity.

"Father, just so I know though. There is a murderer loose on the island?"

"Yes, there is, Nigel, but it is to be kept quiet, Nigel. Secret, Nigel. We don't want panic, panic will just confuse everything. We need to deal with this under the radar."

Nigel was nodding his head. Father Matthew knew it was going to be of little consequence. He would tell the whole island he is investigating the murder of Sister Trinity by teatime.

Chapter 4

Father Matthew and Nigel finished with Sister Trinity's room. Doctor Mitchell then arrived and took Sister Trinity to the morgue at the prison to do the autopsy. Nigel, with some advice from Father Matthew, set up the dining room as a temporary interview room so that he could interview everyone that had been there when they found the body of Sister Trinity. The news of the murder had now spread across the island. Everyone knew. Half of the fishing community were even taking bets on how long it was going to take Nigel to solve the case. Within three hours of the discovery, this had ranged from one year to not in his lifetime. The doctor had given Nigel an approximate time of death, and this is what he used to lead the questioning.

Where were you at the time of the murder? This was his number one question. Well, it was, until he sat down, the only real question he had come up with. Sandra Hills, the cook, had been home with friends and her husband having a dinner party. It was a rock-solid alibi. She had told Nigel that herself.

Catherine had been home with her parents and Michael although Michael had left around ten p.m. According to him he went straight home. Nigel had written this point down three times. This was something he needed to check out. Whilst his leaving time was conveniently close to the time of death, the main reason for his disbelief was his dislike for Michael. Since their days together at school, Nigel had envied Michael. Michael was everything that Nigel wasn't: charming, popular, and above all had loads of friends. When Michael started dating Catherine, his envy turned slowly into dislike.

Nigel interviewed some of the residents, but they had neither seen nor heard anything, the same as the sisters. After evening prayer, they had all retired to their rooms. There was only Mary and Father Matthew left to interview.

"Please sit down, Mary." Mary took the seat on the opposite side of the table to Nigel.

"Hurry up though, Nigel, I need to get back to Alex. He was very close to Sister Trinity. He is in pieces, and I don't want to leave him long." Mary intimidated Nigel just as much as Father Matthew.

"Yes, ma'am." Nigel cleared his throat.

"So, where were you last night between the hours of…"

"I was at home with Catherine, Michael and Matthew, Nigel. You already know this so don't look at your pad. Catherine already told you."

"OK, and that was…"

"Yes, all night, Nigel, all night."

Nigel was scribbling down in his note pad every word that everyone was saying. He had been wishing all afternoon that he hadn't forgotten the tape recorder on the side at the station. That would have made him look so much more professional. As he looked up, Mary gave him the look. He could tell that she wasn't happy to be there.

"Michael left you though, didn't he?" Nigel flicked back through his book.

"At ten I believe." Nigel didn't need to flick, but he had seen it on a crime show where it spooked the person that was being interviewed. He had tried it with everyone. Mary wasn't going to be intimidated though, especially not by him.

"Yes, Nigel. He left to go home. He went straight home." Mary was keen to point out that this was an avenue that Nigel didn't need to go down. Michael wouldn't have done this.

Nigel kept his head down.

"And then, when Michael left, you all went straight to bed?"

"Yes, that's right, Nigel, err, no, not right actually; Catherine and I went to bed. Father Matthew stayed up a while."

Nigel's head came up just for a quick glance, and then went straight back down again. He didn't really want to have eye contact with Mary. It was going to put him off his questioning.

"Father Matthew stayed up? To do what exactly?"

"To work on his sermon, I believe. Now, that is enough, Nigel. You know none of us have anything to do with this. I have things to do. People to care for. This is not the time for questions." Nigel remained still, looking at his pad. Remembering his training. Remembering this was exactly the time for questions. That is what police do. That is what he wanted to say to Mary.

"Thank you, Mary. You may go." Mary was already out of the chair and heading out the door. As she walked out, Father Matthew walked in.

"Father, please sit down."

"Thank you, Nigel." Father Matthew smiled at him. He sat in the same chair that Mary had been sitting in. It was encouraging to see him acting like a real policeman.

"So, Father, where were you last night?"

"I was at home with my family, and when they all went to bed around ten, I took some night air for about an hour, going into the church, saying some prayers, and then I returned home to bed, Nigel. That is all." Father Matthew was keen to get this over and done with as soon as possible. The longer that Nigel played detective in the dining room, the longer the residents would continue to think about the tragic circumstances of the afternoon.

"Alone?" Nigel's head came up briefly. As with Mary, he didn't want to catch the Father's eye.

"No, Nigel, with my wife."

"No, I meant the walk, Father. Did you go on the walk alone?"

"I just said that I did, Nigel. I was alone, with my thoughts, and my God of course."

Nigel had a moment of clarity. For a moment he felt like a real policeman, almost saying the words: 'but your god, he can't vouch for you?' Almost saying those words because, as soon as he looked up again to Father Matthew, his nerves got the better of him. The thought had made it seem like he had paused for quite some time. He wasn't sure if that made him look like a real detective or not at that point. Nigel was struggling in his head on what to ask Father Matthew now.

"How are you, Nigel? How are you coping with everything?"

A sense of relief came over Nigel's face as Father Matthew started the conversation again.

"I am good, Father. I am nearly done with the crime scene questioning. I think?"

"Good, because it looks like we have a murderer to catch, doesn't it? I don't want to tell you how to do your job, Nigel, because you are far more qualified than I am in these things, but, if Sister Trinity was killed last night that means there has already been one ferry leaving the island... So, our killer may have gotten away. The second boat leaves in a couple of hours, so you should probably be checking that also. Check all the records for the last forty-eight hours of coming and going; we may find someone new has come to the island. I think you should also interview the one person linked to the Sheffield Strangler as she is staying in the hotel in town, and you never know when she may leave. She has the most to gain if the Sheffield Strangler has been falsely accused. Check with the doctor on the facts and what DNA or fingerprints have been left on Sister Trinity. It may also be worth contacting the mainland with regards to the mysterious powder in the black envelope with an M on it. It was very well designed, something that couldn't be done on this island, it seems like a brand to me, Nigel. It may be something they have seen before?"

Nigel was writing as fast as he could into his note pad as the Father spoke. He knew he was the one supposed to be asking the questions, but this sounded like exactly what he should be doing.

"Nigel, not to frighten you, but murderers that are not caught in the first seventy-two hours tend to kill again, or so I have heard somewhere. You don't really have a lot of time to get this underway. As I said, I don't want to tell you how to do your job, and you probably want to get on and do that now. Don't you?" Nigel looked down at his pad.

"I understand what you are saying, Father, and I was just about to say that we are done here. I have a lot to do."

"Good, Nigel, I knew you would have it all in hand." Father Matthew stood up as an indication to Nigel that they were definitely done now.

"I think the first thing I am going to do is go down to the docks to get the manifest for the ferry, and I am going to stop people leaving the island." Nigel looked at Father Matthew for his approval. He gave Nigel a slight nod.

"Good, Nigel, I am so glad we have you here to help us solve this horrible situation."

Nigel puffed his chest out a little more as he headed out the door. Father Matthew waited for him to leave the room and then walked over into the kitchen. A few minutes later he emerged with one of Sandra's famous roast dinners and headed towards the back door.

Evening mass was full; the news of the murder had brought everyone over to the east side of the island. Father Matthew had to change his service, both this morning's services were based on reality and the new reality was, someone had murdered Sister Trinity in their home.

He spoke about family, togetherness, and all the things that you wanted to hear about when you had lost someone close to you. As the service ended, Mary informed her husband that she had received a call from Dr Mitchell, and he had requested that he come to the prison morgue. After he said his goodbyes to his congregation, he took the twenty-five-minute drive across the island to the prison, as he walked into the morgue. Doctor Mitchell was standing at his desk. The body was still out on the table in the middle of the room but Doctor Mitchell had kept it covered up.

"Hi, Father, thanks for coming. I hear from Mary you had quite the church full."

"Yes, bad news travels fast I am afraid. Anything I can do to help people get through though, I am glad to. I just hope we can clear this all up, quickly."

"My sentiments exactly, Father. I am glad you said that." Doctor Mitchell paused and pointed at Sister Trinity's body. They both walked over to the table.

"Are you going to be OK if I uncover the body again?"

"Yes, that is fine." Dr Mitchell pulled down the sheet that was covering Sister Trinity's body. The sight did take Father Matthew back a bit, but he hid it well.

"I think we both know, Father, Nigel is going to need some help with this. I have invited him over here also, but before he gets here, I just wanted to go over it with you."

This wasn't a surprise to Father Matthew. He was everyone's council on the island. As acting mayor and Father, he was included and ran almost every decision the islanders made.

"As we suspected, she was strangled and that was the cause of death. Previously to this, however, she had been raped. I have taken a swab of the seamen, and we can check all the males on the island against their DNA. I don't have the kit here, but I think if we have a suspect or suspects, I can take the sample to the mainland."

Neither the morgue, nor the doctor's surgery held any equipment of significance. They were only really built to monitor and maintain the wellbeing of the islands residents. Anything serious would always be sent to the mainland or if really urgent Doctor Mitchell would take the trip himself.

"Father, I did want to point out something to the both of you when Nigel arrives. Whomever this was, he, and I mean he, was a strong person. Look at the bruises around her wrists and her throat. Sister Trinity tried to fight this guy off her, and she put up one hell of a fight. There is skin underneath her nails from the murderer also. So wherever he is, he will have some deep scratches and is missing a couple of layers of skin." Father Matthew was deep in thought about Sister Trinity's last moments. Her last moments in an old people's home that he had built. A home he had invited her too. This wasn't how this was all supposed to end for her.

"So, we can discount the residents then?"

"I think we can. There is no way a ninety-year-old man is going to be able to do this, Father. Sister Trinity wasn't a big girl, but she is plenty big enough to fend an old man off. Whomever this was, they were fit as a butcher's dog as my dear old mum used to say. The strength you would need to crush someone's windpipe with one hand, Father, well, that is no mean feat either."

"What about the Sheffield Strangler? There is no way he has left the prison, is there?" Father Matthew didn't really think there was, but it was a plausible question and one that needed to be answered. The islanders were already whispering that there must have been an escape from the prison. Father Matthew knew that type of conversation would only lead them all somewhere that he had feared. They would be blaming him for the only ever murder on the island, for it was him that brought the murderers there.

"No, none whatsoever, I did check as well. You can see him go into his cell on lockdown last night and then emerge this morning to go to church. The only person he has been in contact with from the outside world would be you, Father; I believe you have spoken to him twice in the last seven days?"

Father Matthew felt a little uncomfortable in the way that Dr Mitchell had said this. He had spoken to him twice. He liked to visit the inmates after a couple of days of readjusting to their arrival in the prison and then on Sunday.

"I did. I asked him to let Miss March leave the island. To drop this nonsense about an engagement. He has struck up a friendship with her, and she believes him to be innocent of his crimes. She is a very troubled young lady who needs to get on with her life, her life away from here." Father Matthew was confident in his speech to ensure the doctor that he wasn't afraid of any questions he may have.

"I would say she would be our number one suspect in that case, Father. Although she couldn't have done this, not without a male accomplice, if you know what I mean." Father Matthew was about to ask if any other inmate could have escaped until he heard the sound of approaching footsteps.

Father Matthew turned to see Nigel entering the room carrying a stack of paper printouts from the ferry company.

"Doctor Mitchell, Father Matthew."

"Nigel, perfect timing, we were just discussing Sister Trinity."

"This is police business, Doctor; I am not sure the Father…"

"Shhh, Nigel, we are all here to help you." Nigel bowed his head slightly. The police work had been giving him more confidence all afternoon, but he knew he was no match for this conversation. He was however now ready to be part of it. Nigel puffed out his chest and stood tall again walking towards Sister Trinity's body.

"Right one more time the victim was raped, Nigel, before being strangled. The murderer and Sister Trinity fought; she has bruises round her wrists and ribs and the force would indicate a strong male. I would say early twenties to forty, fifty years old at most." Nigel was nodding in agreement.

"Let me get this right then, if you discount the old people's home, that leave's pretty much any man on the island that could have done this?"

They both just looked at Nigel. They knew that was true. Nigel put the papers down, took out his notebook, and started writing down everything Dr Mitchell had said.

"Time of death, as we concluded, somewhere between ten p.m. and one a.m. last night. The M.O. fits the same as the serial killer, the Sheffield Strangler, Damien Winter. I have checked this out for you, Nigel; he was here all last night and again this morning. Verified by CCTV. He then met with the Father this morning after his sermon. Not that I believe this prison is escapable."

"What was the meeting about, Father?" Nigel spoke without lifting his head.

"It was a polite conversation around Miss March, and her delusions of love. I asked Damien to let her go. She is a troubled young lady, and I wanted to convince him that what he was doing with her wasn't healthy for either of them. She needed to go home and start a new life with someone else."

"And what did he say to you, Father?"

"He didn't commit to me either way, Nigel. All he said was that he would try his best, so I left it with him to mull over. I am convinced he will do the right thing in the end." Nigel carried on writing down in his pad.

"Did he say anything else to you, Father?" Nigel didn't get a response. He raised his head long enough to know that he shouldn't have pushed that question. Both the doctor and Father Matthew were staring directly at him. His head went back down.

"No that is all he said Nigel." Nigel continued to write in his notebook. There was silence as he did; they both waited for him in anticipation to finish.

"What have you discovered, Nigel, on your trip to the port?"

Nigel picked up his stack of papers.

"I have been through the logs and there are no strangers or abnormal activity on and off the island. In fact, other than usual suppliers, none of the locals have been on or off the island this weekend."

"Which suppliers?"

"The supermarket, hotel, pub, that sort of thing. The same people delivering as always, and they are regular deliveries so nothing out of the ordinary."

"So, we have a suspect list of about a thousand then, Nigel?" Father Matthew caught his eye.

"Nigel, she went back out on the boat that Sam Purnell came in on." Father Matthew was confident in his understanding of what happened. Nigel wasn't budging though. His new-found purpose had given him the confidence to question Father Matthews view.

"No, that is what I am saying, Father, she didn't." Nigel paused as if he was gaining his confidence even more.

"I didn't know that, that was what everyone thought. Not until I interviewed the sisters earlier. The boat as always has the sniffer dog search as soon as it docked. They then transferred the prisoner into the van. Then the boat stood still. I know as I personally went on because I like to pet the dogs after they have finished their work. I have always wanted one for myself. A dog. The boat sailed with nobody on it. I know, Father. I am positive of it." Father Matthew didn't respond.

"So, do we think we have a potential missing person or a second murder on the island, Nigel?"

"I don't know, Doctor, but I am concerned. Sister Sarah can't be missing for forty-eight to seventy-two hours without someone seeing her. The island isn't that big. Plus, why would she have packed a bag? Murderers don't pack bags for victims. The sisters confirmed she took all her clothes." Nigel's afternoon had him creating a lot more questions since his first interviews around the dining room table.

"Doctor Mitchell, Nigel, we need to keep a lid on this until we know for sure. The island is already worried about the first murder; we don't want to tell everyone that there is a further... problem." Father Matthew was now trying to control the rumour mill. That had always been part of his role on the island. He was concerned that Nigel's loose tongue would start a panic.

"What further problem?" Albert Finlay, the director of the prison, entered the room. Albert was a long-term prison director forty years in the service. It seemed that the island attracted people who were about to or wanted to retire. Albert was certainly the latter to that.

"We have a missing sister, Mr Finlay, and a murdered one." Nigel couldn't help himself. He was proud he had a case. Especially one that was becoming more in-depth by the hour. Father Matthew and Doctor Mitchell were looking directly at Nigel. He was careful to not make eye contact with either.

"We do, Albert." The doctor and Albert had been friends before Albert came to the island. Albert's wife had died, so he took the position on Doctor Mitchell's recommendation. It was an easy job. All his inmates knew when they arrived, they were only there for a short visit. So, they were no trouble. Their friendship had bloomed again since their time on the island together. They could often be found together down The Fleece pub propping up the bar.

"There is no way anyone is escaping from this facility, is there, Mr Finlay?" Albert Finlay was almost appalled at the question from what he considered to be a less than average, at times not even average, village bobby.

"No, Nigel, sorry, Constable. There is no way anyone is getting out of the prison other than in an urn. So, are we saying we have a serial killer on the loose on Callington Island?"

"No, nobody is saying serial killer, Mr Finlay. So far, we have one murder victim, but it is one who has the same MO as the Shef—, sorry, Damien Winter's." Nigel's confidence had clearly been growing all afternoon, now everyone could see it. There was a time when he wouldn't have spoken out loud to anyone. Now he was starting to command a conversation.

"Really? An interesting choice for a copycat especially given who else we have in the prison this week." There was a slight nod from Father Matthew and Doctor Mitchell at that point.

"I have just approved a visitor order for Damien tomorrow from a Miss Kacie March."

"Yes, the Father has spoken to Kacie, Miss March, and she is another groupie, if that is the right word for them? Someone who believes they are in a relationship with an inmate from the prison." Nigel suddenly realised that Father Matthew had spoken with Miss March and Damien all within twenty-four hours of the murder. He grabbed his pad and wrote that down, being careful that Father Matthew didn't see what he wrote.

"In my forty years in the prison service, Nigel, I have seen many things, but one thing is for sure, never trust someone who falls in love with a lifer. They are deluded and capable of anything. If I were you, I would be paying that young lady a visit." Nigel was nodding approval at Albert's statement.

"Thank you for your advice and support, Mr Finlay. I will be doing exactly that as she is in my notebook." Nigel held up the notebook as if to show all of them that he had control of the case right there.

"Well, I don't think we are going to find out any more here tonight." Albert was keen to get going. He was only still there waiting for Doctor Mitchell to finish.

They were heading for a drink straight after he had met with Nigel and Father Matthew.

"No, gentlemen, I don't think we are. I am going to interview Miss March on my way home. And so that you know, I have notified the boat master to contact me first should anyone be looking to leave the island."

Nigel picked up his papers, and then dropped a couple of pages on the floor. He bent down, picked them up quickly and headed out the door closely followed by Mr Finlay.

"He is a good lad, Father; his heart is in the right place."

"His heart is, and he almost had me convinced for a moment there, but I sense we are going to need his brain to catch up and quick. I will be speaking to him tomorrow after the Purnell hearing."

"That would be good." Doctor Mitchell turned back to his folder on the bench behind him, and Father Matthew headed out of the door.

"Crap, I forgot, oh, sorry for swearing, Father." Doctor Mitchell turned around to face Father Matthew and pulled out the black envelope.

"The black envelope, the substance inside. You are not going to believe this, Father, but Nigel was right. It is cocaine." There was a genuinely shocked look on the doctor's face as he said it.

"It is what?" It was the Father's turn to demonstrate a look of shock now. Which he did very well.

"It is cocaine, Father, cocaine and, as much as I can ascertain, some kind of wood ash. That is what is giving it the grey colour."

"How did cocaine get into my old people's home?"

"How did cocaine get onto the island, Father? Every boat to and from the island is searched with dogs. It is one of the rules you made, isn't it, Father, as the islanders were worried about drugs in the prison. You know those two things go hand in hand in most prisons."

Father Matthew stood and looked at Doctor Mitchell for a moment. He returned the gaze, looking into each other's eyes waiting for someone to come up with an answer. It was true. There was no way to get cocaine onto the island, yet here it was. There were no chemists on the island, and the only medicine man was there, standing in front of him. For drugs to be on the island meant something was broken. Father Matthew started to strongly suspect the two issues were heavily linked, and this would have something to do with the murder of Sister Trinity. He took his time, but he finally broke the silence.

"Something just isn't right here. This doesn't happen on Callington. What, a murder and now drugs? We are a small community. We would know, we should know everything that goes on around here. We have always prided ourselves in the fact that we have kept the island under control." Father Matthew paused. Lots of things that didn't happen on the island had started to. He also knew that standing in the room were the two men who should have known everything that was going on. The doctor was as much a part of the structure of the Island as he was.

"It is what, nearly nine? I will ring Nigel later, once he has finished with Miss March, and give him the news, Father. He did ask me to send it to the mainland, but I thought I would check it first. It would seem we have a dead sister and a missing one. Couple that with a drug problem all into one day. This island has never seen so much activity. Outside of the prison walls, that is."

"I agree; drugs have no place on our island doctor. We need to find the person or persons responsible for these things as soon as possible." They both paused at that statement. They both knew that would normally be a job for the police. They also both knew Nigel was the police.

"Any idea about the M on the front of the packet; is that something normally associated with cocaine?"

"I don't know, Father, not really my thing. It looks like it may be some kind of logo of the manufacturer. I do remember reading something about a new drug on the market last week in The Times newspaper. I am sure that Nigel will discover this pretty soon. There are all kind of designer drugs nowadays. Gone are the days where it used to be smiley faces or pictures of cartoon characters on sheets of acid. I would suggest kids want cooler, hipper drugs."

"The world, our world, is certainly changing, Doctor."

Father Matthew said his goodbye and left the prison. He still took his moment of clarity when he exited, although he hadn't been to see an inmate. Standing just outside, breathing the fresh air, he contemplated his next move. Drugs, murder, and a missing person. All of that in one day, and Nigel was leading the case. Father Matthew knew he needed to head home to bed. It had been a long day and he already knew that tomorrow was going to be just as bad.

Chapter 5

Father Matthew was up early. There was a nine a.m. hearing, of the Sam Purnell's case. He had been to say his own prayers and was now sitting drinking coffee in the kitchen of the vicarage. As he stared out the window, he could hear someone coming down the stairs and entering the kitchen.

"Good morning, darling."

"Good morning." Mary walked over and kissed him on the back of the head.

"You were late last night. I went to bed at eleven, and didn't hear you come in."

"Yes, I was trying to be quiet. I didn't want to wake you. It had been a long day for everyone. How were the residents after I left? How was Catherine and the sisters? I hope they weren't too much of a burden, given the afternoon we had."

Mary pulled out a chair and sat down next to her husband.

"Everyone was a little shaken, but with God's blessing we will get through this. Catherine and the sisters were great with everybody. Even Alex had started to come around by the end of the evening. What took you so long?" Mary put her hands on her husband's and gripped them tightly.

"I was at the prison. Dr Mitchell gave Nigel, Albert and I an update on the body... I mean, Sister Trinity.

Then we spent some time discussing how we can help Nigel in order to get this to a swift resolution." Mary was nodding.

"He is a good person, Matthew, but I am not sure that he is the right person to help us here. There are a lot of worried people out there, and they need some reassurance. Especially that this isn't going to happen again. At times like this, you need to look to a leader." Father Matthew knew what Mary was saying. He got up and walked over to the sink to rinse his cup.

"I know, Mary, and I believe it will be our job to help him, to give that confidence to our community. Nigel will come good. I have faith in him. He was really sounding the part last night. Already enforced controls at the docks and he has already started to create a shortlist."

"I fear it will take more than sounding the part. You are too kind with him, my dear. This is really serious. Matthew, we don't know what is going on. We don't even know if it will happen again?"

Father Matthew was silent. Mary was right; what if this was the start of something.

That had been the conversation for most of the evening in the home. Father Matthew had told his wife about the packet of suspected drugs found in Sister Trinity's bible. He didn't want it to come from Nigel. All she could think was that it was all linked together. A conclusion that a lot of people were starting to come to as Nigel repeated the story to everyone he met about the white powder.

Father Matthew knew it was cocaine. This wasn't information he wanted to be shared, so he kept this to himself. He hadn't even told his wife, and he was hoping the doctor hadn't told Nigel yet. He didn't want to add fuel to the fire. Rumours started to have a life of their own on Callington Island.

"No, I am afraid, my dear, we don't. I am going to go to the hearing of Sam Purnell. And then, then I think I will have a conversation with Nigel about him getting some help here from the mainland. If you can spend some time reassuring the residents today that would be a great weight off my mind, Mary. They will all be feeling the loss even more today, after sleeping on it." Mary got up, walked over to the sink and hugged her husband as tightly as she could. She knew he had the weight of the world on his shoulders. At least, the weight of their island. His island.

"Of course, I will. I promised Alex I would go and sit with him again today anyway. I told him I would keep him up to date with the events. He was so shaken up. He has the closest occupied room to Sister Trinity and heard nothing. I think he blames himself, not that he could have done anything. I think that is what is bothering him the most. That he couldn't have saved her either way." They were both nodding at that point. They knew Alex to have a heart of gold since the first day that he arrived.

"It must be awful to lose your functionality like that, and in the prime of your life."

"He is a good kid, Mary. But please, let's try to keep the police business out of conversations. The less it is discussed, the closer we can keep a lid on it. Let's see if we can get Alex back to just being Alex. He will then help bring a little happiness back into the place once he gets his head right."

Father Matthew grabbed his coat and headed out of the house for court.

The court chambers were part of the prison and they had been built purposely in order to hear the second sentencing. On the drive over, Father Matthew began to feel as if he was living on the road across the island as this was his fourth journey in seventy-two hours.

On his arrival he saw Nigel was already there sitting in the stalls; he always attended these hearings with Father Matthew. In addition, there were a couple of the twenty-something males that Father Matthew recognised from the fishing port. There was no one else. This was becoming more common. In the early days they had lots of visitors and the worlds press on the final read-through. Not anymore. Now Father Matthew and Nigel were normally the only attendees. Well, that was in all previous readings except the one about six weeks ago. That had captured the interest of the world again. The island had seen nothing like that since the prison opened. There was press camped out for days to ensure they secured a place in the court chambers. Previous to that though, the most they had seen in the last year was one, maybe two, visitors from the mainland. Once a PDS sentence had been given, it was almost closure for the families. They were confident justice was going to be done. It always was, the prison had a 100% completion on time record.

Judge Reynolds entered the courtroom and sat in his chair. There was no formal announcement like a crown court case, but everyone still stood up and sat when he did. The judge nodded at the Father, and at Nigel. He gave a discerning look at the teenagers who were just there for kicks. This had become free entertainment to some of the locals. Especially if there had been a lock in at the fleece. The cases had become topic of conversation down the Fleece of a night time. As such they would often get half sober attendees in the morning.

Part of the change in the law had been around a rereading of the case five years after the PDS sentence was given. A shorter version in the presence of the murderer and any members of the public that wanted to attend. Most of the time it was as short or as long as the judge deemed necessary. That generally depended on his mood, and the Judge wasn't generally a morning person. He was as grumpy as you expected a judge in his retirement to be after dealing for forty years with the criminal world. The Judge also looked like you would expect a high court Judge to look. He was a heavy-set man who Nigel had always imagined could crush a man with his bare hands. He often thought that was the reason nobody ever made an appeal to him. They were too frightened to do so.

The prisoner was brought into a glass room in the corner by Chris James, the head guard at the prison. As he stepped in Chris gestured to the judge and Father Matthew with a nod of the head as if to welcome them to another hearing.

"I shall begin. Firstly, are you Sam Purnell of thirty-four High Street, Islington?

Sam Purnell nodded at the judge.

"I will take that as a yes. Sam Purnell, you were charged in two thousand and fourteen with three counts of murder. You pleaded guilty to this in a court of law with no remorse or defence against the crimes that you committed. Is that correct?"

Sam Purnell nodded again.

"The murder of your wife, Nicole Purnell, took place on the night of November the twenty-fourth. You stabbed her seven times in the stomach, and left her for dead in the address previously mentioned. Leaving the residence, you walked approximately one mile to the Red Lion public house where you took a further two lives: Mr Terry Jones and Mr Mark Smith. Is that correct?"

"Yes." There was finally an answer and there was some strength behind the word yes. Sam almost sounded proud of that action.

"As per your own words you believed that the aforementioned gentlemen were both engaged in a sexual relationship with your wife."

Sam Purnell was back to nodding.

"I could go on, but to me it seems as if you rejected legal advice at every point in the trial, and confessed to the whole event. Is there anything that you would like to say before I pass final judgement, Mr Purnell?"

Sam Purnell stood up.

"I know what I have done, and I am not sorry about it. They all got what they fucking deserved... Sir. I am sure I will now get what I deserve."

"OK, Mr Purnell. It is my duty to inform you by Her Majesty's service that your conviction of a potential death sentence is now changed to the Death Sentence. In exactly six weeks from today, pending no more evidence or appeals, your sentence will be carried out by lethal injection. Are there any appeals that would like to be lodged at this time?"

The court room was silent, and the judge nodded at Chris; he took Sam Purnell back into the prison. The judge took a final glance at the Father and disappeared out of sight. The two teenagers soon disappeared too leaving just Nigel and Father Matthew in the court room.

"Well, that was short. These things generally last at least half an hour." Father Matthew nodded in agreement.

"The judge sounded a little off to me. Did he sound a little off to you, Father?"

"Yes, Nigel. It certainly was the shortest hearing to date. The Judge wasn't mixing his words this morning, was he?"

"Do you think he is OK? I think I will need to speak to him. They say that you should watch for people acting out of the normal? It is one of the first things you should look for in a murder case. And he certainly wasn't acting normal."

"I don't know, Nigel. Maybe it is worth a conversation. The judge is an old man though, I don't think he is going to be one of our suspects." Nigel sat in thought looking directly at the wall next to Father Matthew. He knew he should be taking advice from Father Matthew, but it is was his case. He needed to make the decisions on who he should be speaking too. The Judge was old, but he could still crush a windpipe with one hand and he was male. He fitted the description of the killer. He needed to speak to him. That is what policemen do, no matter who it is.

"Talking of conversations, how did you get on with Miss March last night?"

"She was… well Father, she has an alibi for the night, and I don't believe she is working with someone. She is going to appeal to the judge today. Given the evidence, I don't think I blame her. We did have a long conversation about how Damien may be innocent of all these crimes given the events of yesterday." Father Matthew feared that was how the conversation was going to go. She was very convincing, even for him. She was bound to make Nigel think twice.

"You don't believe that he is innocent, do you, Nigel?"

"Of course not, Father. I believe she really does though. She seems so normal. I don't think I have spoken to one, one of those types of women, for that long before. There is a calmness about her that makes it all seem real." Father Matthew was nodding at him. He had had his fair share of conversations with inmates' girlfriends. More than he ever thought he would.

"They always do, Nigel. They always do."

Father Matthew was still worried that Nigel was going to tell the whole island everything. The more he worked alone, the more worried the Father became.

"Do you think you may need some help, Nigel? Have you considered calling in anyone from the mainland?" Father Matthew tried to say it as nicely as possible.

"No, Father, I have this under control. I have logged it on the mainland as that is what I have to do. They have offered advice and support if I need it, but I don't, I have been trained for this."

There was a moment's silence whilst they both thought about that last sentence. Nigel had been trained, that was true. Nobody on the island thought he would pass the induction, but he did. But, although Nigel seemed confident in his training, Father Matthew was more confident he was going to need help with the case, and most of all, with the Islanders.

"I can solve it, Father. I was up till late last night working on my lists of suspects. Look."

Nigel retrieved a list of names out of his pocket, and handed it to the Father.

"You see, I was at the disco Saturday night, so I can personally vouch for all the people who were at the Fleece. Most of them were there till two a.m., and in no fit state to drive across the island, let alone fight with someone. When I was at the hotel last night, I got a list from Hayley of everyone that was there all night and checked the CCTV." Father Matthew looked over the list.

"But there must be fifty names on this list, Nigel."

"Yes, Father. If you remember there were one thousand last night, so I consider that to be huge progress. In less than a day I have taken out ninety-five percent of the possible Unsubs. Sorry, possible murderers, Father. Unsubs is what they say on TV." Father Matthew couldn't argue with the logic. He had made more progress than anyone on the island would be giving him credit for.

"So, all of them just need to be checked out, Father. That will bring us closer to the killer." Father Matthew continued to work through the list.

"Nigel, I have noticed that Doctor Mitchell and I are on the list also?"

"Yes, sorry, Father. I am just doing my job." Nigel hung his head. He spoke in a softer voice now almost guilty of the fact that he had included them.

"But you don't have an alibi, Father, and neither does the doctor. You went for a walk, and he left the bar earlier than most and went straight home. Alone. I have to be thorough with everyone, Father." Father Matthew knew he was only doing his job. It did show that Nigel was taking it seriously. A few days ago, Father Matthew would have doubted Nigel had the courage to have that conversation with him. His confidence was continually growing by the hour in his new role as a detective. Father Matthew felt a sense of pride in the person he was becoming.

"I agree, Nigel, and that is exactly how it should be."

Nigel was relieved to hear that. He looked back up at Father Matthew.

"I thought I would just go through the list one by one and cross them off; whoever is left then, that is potentially the killer. That makes sense, doesn't it?"

Father Matthew looked down the list; he knew almost all of them by name. Some had been on the island their whole life. He couldn't see any of them as potential murderers.

"It does, Nigel. It really does. Did Dr Mitchell call you last night to discuss the black envelope?"

"Yes, he did. He rang me at home late last night. I was nearly in bed." That was a relief for Father Matthew. It meant that Nigel couldn't have confirmed the story too anyone else.

"That is good, Nigel. I don't think we need anyone else to know about that yet. So let's just keep that between us." Nigel nodded in agreement.

"I agree, Father, but I am stumped. It doesn't make sense; how would it get on the island, let alone why would Sister Trinity have some in her possession? Do you think she was on drugs, Father?" Father Matthew was shaking his head.

"Do you think there is more on the island or in the home, Father? I have never even seen it before other than on the TV. The doctor seemed to think he had read about it. So, I will look into it when I get time, Father."

"I hope there is no more at the home, Nigel, but I assure you I will conduct a thorough search myself and let you know." Father Matthew handed the list back to Nigel who placed it back in his pocket.

"Thank you, Father, I am going to be doing the same. I know a lot of people don't have faith in me, Father, but I will solve this. This is what all my training has been leading up to. I dreamed of cases like this. Not that I wanted anyone hurt, Father; I didn't mean it that way. I just wanted a case to get my teeth into. To prove to you all. I am a good policeman, Father. I really am." Nigel was speaking with passion and vigour. It was refreshing for Father Matthew to hear.

"It's OK, Nigel, I know what you mean. I am sure the doctor and I will also give you all the support you need. We will get through this." Father Matthew put his hand on Nigel's shoulder. They both felt a lot more comfortable as they spoke about what was going to come next.

"Thank you, Father, I know you will. You both will."

Nigel's phone started to ring in his pocket, but he just sat there looking at the Father as if he didn't hear it. It continued to ring until Father Matthew spoke up.

"That is you, Nigel. That's your phone ringing."

"Oh, yes. Sorry, Father, it never used to ring and now it has not stopped in the last twenty-four hours. I still don't get used to it." There was almost a smile on his face as he said that. Nigel didn't get many calls; in fact, the call from Mary yesterday had almost shocked him. He had been cleaning the bars in the little cell they had at the station just to pass the time. It had been the first need for a police officer in months. The second was now ringing in his pocket.

"Hello…What…? Where…? I will be right there. Don't touch anything. I mean it; don't touch anything. It is a crime scene."

Nigel hung up the phone. The colour drained from his face as he looked directly at Father Matthew. Father Matthew could tell that something was wrong immediately and whatever it was it was serious.

"There is another body, Father, out the back of the hotel. I am so sorry, Father. So sorry. It is Alana, Father, it's Alana." It was Nigel's turn to put a friendly hand on a shoulder. Father Matthew froze as he heard the words that Nigel was saying. They kept running through his head over and over again. The name Alana was stuck on his tongue. It felt like he was dreaming. He finally shook it off, he needed to focus.

"How, Nigel? Are you sure?" Father Matthew could barely get those words out.

"That was Hayley, Father. She knows it is Alana. She is gone, Father. I am so sorry." Tears started to roll down Father Matthew's face. He didn't cry. Nigel had never seen this happen before, but he knew how much Alana had meant to Father Matthew.

"We have to go, Father." Father Matthew nodded and got shakily to his feet. He followed Nigel out of the court room.

"Are you going to be OK to drive, Father?" Father Matthew just nodded at Nigel. He knew he needed some time alone to absorb the tragic news. The first thought running through his head was how was he going to tell Mary? And Catherine? They were going to be heartbroken. They each took their own cars and drove to the hotel.

On arrival, a large crowd had gathered inside the hotel, and in the garden out the back, Hayley and Kevin had placed a bed sheet over Alana's body.

"Nigel, Father Matthew. I am so sorry, Father. We just found her like this."

"Hayley, can you lock the back door and close the curtains so that people can't see out here. Also, can you call Doctor Mitchell and ask him to join us here."

"OK, Nigel." Hayley was surprised at the sound of his voice. Nigel sounded authoritative; this was the first time she had heard him like this. Hayley still shot a look at the Father for approval; he nodded, and she did as she was told. Nigel bent down and pulled back the sheet; he was expecting to see her as Father Matthew had described Sister Trinity. Another copycat murder of Damien Winter. She wasn't; she was fully dressed. All in black as she usually was. There were rips in her black shirt around her stomach area. They could both see the blood seeping through. Nigel reached into his pocket and took out a pen. He used it to lift up the shirt. He had seen it done on TV. When he did, he could see several stab wounds to her abdomen. He stood up and placed the sheet back over her.

"Father, can I have a word, please. In private."

Kevin had still been standing next to the body, so Nigel needed to pull Father Matthew over to one side.

"I am really sorry, Father, but by the looks of it, she was stabbed in the stomach more than once. I think I counted at least three times."

"I could see, Nigel." Father Matthew couldn't say any more. The sight of Sister Trinity on the trolley in the morgue and now Alana in the space of a few hours was too much to bear for him.

"Sam Purnell, Father, that's what he did. He said that not an hour ago in the court room. He stabbed his victims in the stomach, repeatedly. It is the same."

Father Matthew stood back a bit from Nigel. He really was thinking like a detective as this hadn't even occurred to him. The Sam Purnell case, as with many others, had been over the news recently. As a PDS sentence was due to be carried out, the press liked to relive it a week before they were scheduled to go to the island. Especially when there was no other news to report. Nigel had started to think about this last night, what if this had something to do with the press? Or maybe someone was mimicking the prison and the activities associated with it?

"Nigel, do you think we have another copycat murderer here?"

"I don't know, Father, but it can't be a coincidence, can it? We have had two murders in twenty-four hours, both with different MOs, both imitating serial killers that have been all over the press lately. Surely that is what is going on here?" The thought was running through Father Matthew's head, but then, there were so many murderers on the island now, that any murder could be considered a copycat to at least one of the inmates.

"No, it can't be, not here. I mean, it can't be a coincidence, Nigel. Although I am sure the people inside the prison have killed in every way possible. It would be quite easy to link anything to them." Father Matthew was playing that over in his head again. Two murders in twenty-four hours. They hadn't even experienced one on the island before. What was happening to his island? Somewhere deep down, Father Matthew knew this was all his fault. He was responsible for everything that was going on, on the Island.

Father Matthew also knew that Nigel was talking sense. He just didn't want to believe it could happen. Dr Mitchell was standing behind them before they knew it. He hadn't waited for the official call. Kevin had already rung him when they discovered the body, and he had set off straight away.

"Gents, is it true? That it is Alana under there, Father?" Father Matthew turned and nodded his head.

"Yes, I am afraid it would seem so, Doctor."

"Then I am so sorry for your loss, Father. I know what she meant to you and Mary." Father Matthew's thoughts went directly back to Mary and everyone else at the home. This was going to devastate them all over again. So close after the loss of Sister Trinity. Especially Mary and Alex who loved Alana.

"She was stabbed, Doctor Mitchell, in the stomach. More than once."

"Uh… Umm." Kevin had wandered over to the three of them. Trying to introduce himself into the conversation.

"I have a marquee, Nigel." Kevin tried to say it as softly as possible.

"Sorry, Kevin?"

"I have a marquee, over there by the back door. It's one of those pop-up ones I use in the garden if it's raining and people want to smoke. I just thought that if you wanted, we could put it over the body and zip it up like, so you can examine the body where it is. Like they do on the TV programmes." Nigel looked at Father

Matthew and Dr Mitchell; Dr Mitchell nodded at him. Nigel had come to realise the only experience anyone from the island really had in murders had come from the TV. This gave him a little more confidence. Nobody knew more than him about detective shows. That was all he watched on TV.

"Thank you, Kevin, that's a great idea."

Father Matthew, Kevin and Nigel went over and picked up the marquee. They carried it over to the centre of the garden and placed it over Alana's body. They then zipped themselves into the inside of the tent.

Kevin went back into the hotel where half of the town were now standing in the bar drinking. Most of the conversation had been around Nigel. There was still no confidence in his ability to solve this. If there was a murderer loose on Callington Island, then there was a good chance that they would all be dead before Nigel captured them.

"Let's have a look then." Dr Mitchell pulled back the sheet, and Alana's body laid on the floor in front of them. Dr Mitchell put on a pair of latex gloves from his bag and then lifted her top to reveal what looked like three stab wounds to the abdomen. He then checked her pulse and her eyes.

"I would guess she has been here since late last night. That being the case, I am surprised that it took so long to find her lying here on the grass. The body was hardly hidden, was it? And there are no signs that she was dragged here. It looks to me that this is where the crime took place." Doctor Mitchell was looking directly at Nigel when he said that.

"It will be because of Mondays. Mondays are a late breakfast in the hotel, Doctor. Hayley always runs it later as some of the OAPs, sorry, old age pensioners from the home come and have a walk through the town on a Monday. She doesn't start cooking till eight thirty, and they found the body at nine thirty." Nigel really did know all the activities on his island. Something Father Matthew hadn't noticed before. This, and the way he had conducted himself in the last twenty-four hours, had his admiration.

"Well, that being the case, I would say she has been lying here for at least twelve hours. I would say the murder took place around ten p.m., maybe a little later."

"Roughly the same time as Sister Trinity, Doctor?" Nigel was very quick to answer. All three of them looked at each other. All with the same thought, it couldn't be another coincidence.

"That may be, Nigel, but my early indications would tell you that we are not dealing with the same killer."

"What! Are you sure?" Nigel was sure he had a copycat murderer on his hands, and now there was a chance that he had two. Father Matthew remained silent and focused on the body on the floor. His thoughts were of her birthday party, the fact that they had only discussed it a few days ago. Now, because of him, she wouldn't be reaching eighteen. Because of what he had done.

"I am never sure until we have all the facts, Nigel, but as you can see, this person was stabbed in the right-hand side at the front. If I were to do that to you, Nigel." The doctor stood up and moved over to Nigel, twisting his shoulders so they were facing each other and made the gesture of stabbing him in the same place.

"If I were to do that. What would I have to be, Nigel?"

Nigel thought for a moment before he answered. He knew this was a teachable moment, and the last thing he wanted was to get the question wrong.

"You would need to be left-handed?"

"Exactly, Nigel, and from the bruising on Sister Trinity's body, my diagnosis would favour a right-handed attacker; that is certainly where the bruises were more prominent."

There was a silence again at the doctor's findings. The thought of one murderer on the island was unthinkable. Nobody had a word for the thought of two murderers.

"So, we have two murders and two murderers?" Nigel decided to state the obvious.

"I hate to say it, but yes, I would think so, Nigel."

"What else do you notice though?" The Father had remained quiet through the demonstration until this point. The sight of Alana lying on the ground was as much as he could take. She had been almost a daughter to him. As he kept looking at her, he was the one that noticed something that he wished he hadn't. Both the doctor and Nigel looked down at the body.

"Her shirt, gents. Isn't it on inside out? See, the label is still showing."

"It is inside out." Nigel knelt down by the body to check.

"I know Alana, and they were the same clothes that she had been wearing yesterday at lunch. It certainly wasn't on backwards then as she was helping us in the kitchen. She always helps out way too much for a guest. I always tell her she doesn't have to, but it doesn't stop her. That is just the type of person she is." Nigel and the doctor could see that Father Matthew was lost in his own thoughts for a moment. They gave him the moment of reflection.

"When was the last time you saw Alana, Father?" Nigel was back up with his notepad in hand.

"It was at evening mass. She was properly dressed then. I remember as I wanted to spend some time with her afterwards. One, just to make sure she was OK after the events of yesterday afternoon, and two, we were going to give her a party for her birthday. I wanted to get her excited about it. But Mary had received the call from yourself, Doctor, so I told her we would do it today. She didn't mind. She just shrugged her shoulders like she always did. Not saying a word." They could both tell from Father Matthew's voice that he was getting upset at the thought of Alana's body being laid cold on the ground in front of him.

"So, were you the last person to see her then, Father?" Nobody answered that question. As the words left Nigel's mouth, he knew it probably wasn't the right time to ask it. Silence continued until the doctor spoke.

"So, at some point between then and ten p.m. last night she had undressed and redressed?" Nigel wrote that down.

"Nigel, Father, I am no detective but a seventeen-year-old girl in the grounds of a hotel with her shirt on backwards would lead me to come to one conclusion: she had been seeing someone at the hotel. Does she have a boyfriend staying in the hotel?"

"Or in the town; we all used to cut across the grounds to get to the high street. Saves about five to ten minutes and Hayley never minded. Even after they did this place up, she still left a space in the hedge to get through for all of us." Nigel looked inquizatively at the Father.

Father Matthew had tears in his eyes. He wiped them away. The thought of Alana having a boyfriend had started to turn his sadness to a little anger. He didn't see her like that. She was more of a daughter and she was still too young. The Alana they were speaking about wasn't his Alana.

"Gents, she doesn't have a boyfriend. She barely spoke to anyone and spent all her time in the home. I know her." Nigel and the doctor could see that this line of questioning was going to be upsetting for the Father. Nigel wrote that down in his pad. He was trained to watch for something out of the normal, and Father Matthew fazed and upset, that was out of the normal.

"Doctor, can you see if she has a room key in her pockets or any clues to where she had been?"

The doctor leant back down and went into her left-hand pocket: nothing, and then the right. As he placed his hand in, he could feel something. He looked up at both of them. He then pulled out seven little black envelopes with the M sign on the front. He threw them on the floor; one emptied as he did on the ground next to him. It was the same powder substance that was found in Sister Trinity's Bible. There was a moment of shock. Nigel shared a look with both of them. None of them knew what to say next. It took Doctor Mitchell to break the silence.

"Maybe she wasn't the shy retiring girl you believed her to be, Father?" Father Matthew didn't move. He just stared at the ground. That was two ties to drugs and his home. Let alone the two murders. Maybe Doctor

Mitchell was right. He hadn't known her as well as he had thought.

"I don't believe it. More drugs. Where from? There is a lot as well; do you think she was a dealer? Father, I never remember her leaving the island. How could she be? Do you think she was making it here? How do you even make it? Can you make it?" They were all silent. Nobody had answers to Nigel's questions, and Nigel had a lot of questions. He had certainly developed in the last twenty-four hours from the time he sat at the dining room table with one question in his head.

"Nigel, it would seem I didn't know her. I didn't know her at all." There was a clear sadness in Father Matthew's voice.

Nigel looked at the both of them and then took his phone out of his pocket and started scrolling for numbers.

"Who are you calling, Nigel?"

"We need some help, Father. Help from the mainland, I can't solve this on my own. Two murders, two murderers and a drug ring or cartel, whatever they call it. On a totally secure island. I am going to need some support in closing this down as quickly as possible." Nigel left the marquee. The doctor and Father Matthew shared a moment of silence, both looking at the body and the drugs.

"I think we both know this is a little out of his capabilities. He will need some support and fast because whatever is happening here, Father, it seems to be escalating."

There was a pause as the doctor checked her back pockets and shirt pocket, but there was nothing else to be found. Father Matthew was thankful for that at least.

"There is nothing else, maybe she was just cutting across the lawn when she met someone that she shouldn't." That was a little more comforting to Father Matthew. The drugs were one thing, but the thought of Alana in a hotel room with a man was another.

"I meant to ask you, how is Michael, Father?" The question brought Father Matthew away from his thoughts.

"Michael?"

"Yes, Peterson, he didn't show for work at the prison this morning. I presumed he was ill or helping at the home given what happened yesterday." Father Matthew was trying to think. He hadn't spoken to anyone about Michael.

"It's not that we had anything to do, just that he often comes in and floats around. He is an early bird like me Father and you know how keen he is. I thought he would have at least wanted to go through the autopsy with me this morning." Thinking about it Doctor Mitchell was probably right with his initial thoughts, Michael would probably be helping Mary and Catherine. He wouldn't have wanted to leave Catherine on her own, not after the events of yesterday.

"Oh, maybe he is at the home then. Mary did say they were short-staffed what with Sister Sarah and Sister Trinity now gone. And now, thinking about it, I guess Alana would have been missing from work too today." Father Matthew paused at that. He hadn't even thought about the fact that his resource at the home was disappearing fast. They were now three people down in a week.

"I left really early, Catherine wasn't even up. I would expect they called him to help." The doctor

124

watched Father Matthew as he ran all those thoughts again for a moment. He snapped out of it.

"I think I had better go and help Nigel control the masses, I can hear the noise level rising from in there. The last thing we want is a posse with pitch forks roaming the town. Are you going to be OK here, Doctor?"

"Yes, I will take some pictures with my phone for Nigel and send them over to him. Then I will take Alana down to the morgue to sit with Sister Trinity. I am presuming we just want to keep the bodies until support arrives. I don't really have a chilled facility as generally after the sentence is carried out, we put them straight into the furnace." The doctor was looking at Father Matthew for the answer. This brought Father Matthew back to normal. This was what people did often on the island. This is what he was good at, giving the people guidance.

"I would think so. If Nigel is calling for backup, let's let them decide what to do with the bodies when they arrive. I am sure they will be here on the next ferry once they hear the latest development."

Father Matthew left the marquee and headed into the hotel. Half of the town was there, and they were all surrounding Nigel. There were comments being thrown at him from everyone. He was stuck in the middle of them and fighting to get out or a word in.

"Stop... I said stop." They turned to see Father Matthew standing by the door of the reception area. They all knew his voice. The noise level disappeared immediately.

"Nigel, come over here." Nigel did as he was told. Father Matthew sounded like he meant business. He was not in the mood for nonsense from anyone.

"If you let Nigel speak, he will give you a full update on the last twenty-four hours' events. Please do not interrupt him. This is a difficult time for all of us, and something that is unprecedented here on our island."

The crowd turned their attention to Nigel and Father Matthew. Generally, when Father Matthew spoke the island listened. This was one of those times.

"OK, OK. Thank you, Father. I know you all have questions? But the first thing I would like to tell you is that I have called for backup from the mainland, and they will be here on the six o'clock ferry." There was continued silence. A lot of people were nodding with agreement at Nigel's statement.

"As for what has happened over the past twenty-four hours, Sister Trinity, who we all knew, and loved was found dead in her room yesterday. We believe this to be of foul play. Alana..." Suddenly Nigel realised that he didn't even know her second name. He looked towards Father Matthew, but his attention was fixated with the crowd which kept them under control.

"Alana who worked and lived at the home, some of you may know her, has also been found this morning dead in the grounds of the hotel. We also believe this to have been of foul play. I am with immediate effect putting a nine p.m. curfew on the island. You are not to leave your homes or the hotel after that time. The detectives that arrive will be set up with me in the police station. I will stress though; early indications are that these two murders were not committed by the same person. We do not have a serial killer loose on the island. I repeat, we do not have a serial killer loose on the island."

Father Matthew knew as soon as the words came out of Nigel's mouth that he had said too much. He had been doing so well until he had decided to tell the island that there were two killers on the loose, and they were not to think that it was the work of a seriail killer. That last statement was met with raised voices from the bar: "not connected", "two killers", "of course there is a serial killer on the loose". There were chants from the crowd that prisoners must be escaping, and asking Nigel what he was going to do about it.

"Listen, listen. We can confirm nobody has escaped from the prison. I have the full records of everyone on and off of the island, and we will be processing these. We will also be interviewing everyone who cannot be accounted for between the hours of ten p.m. and two a.m. last night and the night before, hence the curfew. You need to bear with me. All of this noise isn't helping."

The noise started to disappear. Nigel was starting to make them listen on his own.

"We are tracing the sequence of events, and that will lead us to the murder suspects. We have already eliminated ninety percent of the island from our investigation."

Nigel was slowly winning over the crowd. Although he wasn't that confident in himself, the way he spoke actually sounded like he knew what he was doing. Father Matthew continued to stand close enough to give him as much confidence as possible.

"If you are not a resident, or an owner or worker in this hotel, can you all please go back to your homes? You are in a potential crime scene and anything you disturb could cause harm to potential evidence."

The crowd were listening, and they started to drift off almost immediately. Nigel looked at Father Matthew to check how well he had done and got a nod in the right direction. Everyone cleared out apart from Miss March, Kevin and Hayley Keating and David Hills, Sandra Hills' husband who had been doing some work on the hotel that morning.

"OK, that's a little better, and a lot less noisy." Father Matthew was settling down the smaller crowd. Despite his own feelings of sadness and loss, he was putting on a brave face; his community had to come first despite the circumstances.

"Hayley, how many guests do you have currently at the hotel?"

"We already discussed this Nigel. Miss March here is the only one. It's been a quiet couple of weeks, and as the kids don't break up from school for a couple more it's going to be like this until then."

"So, was Miss March the only other person in the hotel last night?"

"The only resident, yes, we had a few walk-ins for a drink at the bar. David and Sandra were both here. Sandra was so shaken up she needed a drink after the events at the home yesterday. William and Julie Peterson, Michael's parents, were here also." As Hayley said this, she nodded at Father Matthew. She had wanted to offer her condolences about Alana, but she felt that this wasn't the right time.

"The judge, and then, yes, Miss March. That was about it, I think, Kevin?"

"Yes, that was it. We were all in the lounge bar, mostly talking about Sister Trinity and how there had never been a real crime on the island, let alone a murder. And now we have two? And one of them was in our garden? Imagine that."

Nigel didn't comment on Kevin's rhetorical questions. He had to stay focused on the task ahead to ensure he had all the right information before his colleagues arrived. The call had started to concern him. It was the right thing to do, it was what his training had taught him, but he was worried that once they arrived, he wouldn't be the lead in the investigation. He had started to think that making the call to the mainland may have been a mistake.

"And what time were they here until?" Nigel was quickly getting the hang of asking the right questions.

"I was in the bar from around nine p.m. and didn't leave until I went to bed around eleven, sorry eleven thirty." Miss March was keen to say that she wasn't outside at ten o'clock. She already felt the eyes of the island on her after the murder of Sister Trinity.

"I went straight to my room, and it does not pass the door to the garden. I know this hotel has cameras, so you can check my story if you like." Miss March paused but still held Nigel's stare.

"Can I go now? I have to be at the prison for two p.m., and don't want to be late, I have been waiting so long for this visit with my fiancée." Nigel looked back at Father Matthew for some reassurance. Father Matthew nodded at him.

"Yes, that is fine Miss March, but don't try to leave the island, and make sure you are back by nine in time for the curfew." Kacie left the hotel and headed over to the prison to visit her fiancée, Damien Winter. Despite his conversation with Father Matthew it seemed Damien was ready to spend some time with her, and he had no intention of letting her leave the island any time soon.

"That is what happened, Nigel." Hayley said "Miss March went to bed at eleven thirty, the Petersons left shortly after and Sandra and David stayed for a late one."

"Yeah, we did, we were out of here for one a.m. Are you saying Alana was lying dead in the garden whilst we were all in here?"

"I am afraid so, David… What about the judge? Where was he in all this?"

Father Matthew was surprised that Nigel had twigged that no one had mentioned him. He figured that Nigel must have still been thinking about his attitude in the court room that morning. David and Kevin both passed a look over at Hayley.

"He passed out around ten p.m. He does that quite often, and we have an agreement that if he drinks too much, he shouldn't drive. It is not safe."

"So, one of you took him home?" There was a shaking of heads at this question.

"No, it was Sunday night; we were all in shock, so we all had a drink. I put him in one of the rooms. I checked on him this morning, but he had already gone. He said he had an early reading this morning." Although it was only Nigel, there was still a sense in the air that they had just told the police that there was a suspect.

Nigel looked directly at the Father. They had both been questioning the judge's attitude. They knew something was wrong with him. In Nigel's mind the judge had just become the number one suspect.

"So, we will be able to check the CCTV for any activity of him roaming the halls after ten p.m. like we did the night before with Miss March?"

"Yes, I suppose we could." There was a silence across the room until Kevin spoke up.

"But… we put him in room one which opens up to the garden, doesn't it? He could get out of there without being seen by the camera." Kevin knew what he was saying. It was what they were all thinking.

"Wait, he must be seventy years old, and a judge. We are not saying we think he has anything to do with this, are we?" Hayley was the first one to protect the judge.

"Nobody is saying anything, Hayley. What we need to do is just follow the facts and the evidence. The judge would have been close enough to hear the goings-on of the garden though, so that does make him a person of interest."

Again, there was silence. Kevin had started to feel guilty for almost accusing the judge. He had been a loyal friend to the hotel. Nigel had controlled the situation with great ease despite his own thoughts on the matter.

"I doubt he would have. He was pretty wasted. He passed out on the bed as soon as we put him on it. He wouldn't have moved all night. He never does. Plus, we could still hear him snoring in here." It was Kevin's turn to defend the judge one more time. There was then silence again. Each person was now thinking before they opened their mouths. Although they all had doubts about Nigel, he was starting to sound like a real policeman. Nigel could tell they didn't want to say anything more.

"I think we are done for now. I am going to follow the doctor to the morgue to see if he has found anything else out, then I will give the judge a visit." Both Kevin and Hayley were convinced it was their conversations that were pointing the direction for Nigel.

"Father Matthew, I would welcome your company until the other officers arrive." There was a sigh of relief from the audience. They all knew that Father Matthew would ensure the job was done properly. Nigel also knew that he needed a witness if he was going to speak to a suspect, and Father Matthew was the most honest person he knew.

"It is not a problem, Nigel. Happy to help where I can."

Father Matthew and Nigel left the hotel. There were still a few people outside the premises watching the coming and goings. Neither the Father nor Nigel acknowledged them as they left. Taking Nigel's car, they headed over to the prison morgue. Not a word was said during the journey. Father Matthew was reflecting on the morning activities, and Nigel had still been going through the list of suspects in his head. He had narrowed it down to almost fifty in Sister Trinity's case. On the other hand, in Alana's case, everyone was a suspect from what the doctor had said, but at the moment the judge was his number one person of interest. Dr Mitchell was examining Alana's body when they arrived into the morgue.

"Dr Mitchell." The doctor stopped and looked up from Alana's body.

"Nigel, Father, just in time. I have just taken Alana's clothes off and bagged them over there for evidence. I was about to go over the evidence one more time."

The doctor walked up and down the body looking closely at everything one more time before he spoke again.

"Nigel, if you look at her hands, she did try to protect herself, to a certain degree. There are slices on both her hands as if she had tried to stop the blade before it went in, then she tried to push it away, but it seems that as she did, it was thrust in again." The doctor was making the motions to demonstrate what had happened to Alana.

"I would say from this she certainly wasn't expecting this. Whilst the first stab was a quick one, the next stabs were slow as if whilst they were purposeful, they were also somehow thoughtful... Thoughtful is probably the wrong word. Just purposeful. Look how the first stab mark has ripped open a little; the others were slow and a straightforward in and out...Maybe the attacker was thinking about the attack rather than the action he or she was taking, if that makes sense. Stab wounds are normally more erratic. Full of passion. These seem to be purposeful and intent... If you both wouldn't mind looking away for a minute." Father Matthew and Nigel turned their back on Alana and the doctor.

"Thank you... I am just testing to see if there is any semen in her body. It was the last thing I had to do. I have had a quick look and there is no bleeding so if she were to have had sex, I would come to the conclusion that it would have been consensual. What I mean to say is there are no bruises or blood in that area."

"Alana was a good girl, Doctor, and as I said, she didn't have a boyfriend. I don't believe she will have ever had…" Father Matthew was back to protecting his adopted daughter.

"I know, Father, so you said. OK, you can both turn around now. Now just to mix this and if it changes colour then, yes, she has had sex in the last twenty-four hours."

The doctor went over to his desk and mixed the swab. They all waited and looked at the glass; it changed colour. Father Matthew had been saying a little prayer in his head hoping that it wouldn't change, but there was definitely a blue substance in the tube now.

"As I said before, Father, I don't believe we knew who she really was. I would also say from the examination that this was not her first time. There was no discharge which you would find the first-time round." Father Matthew was now struggling to look at Alana's body. She had been a sweet complex girl from the home which he and his family had taken in as one of their own. This wasn't supposed to be how this ended for her. He had brought her to the island to give her a better life. He didn't even know the life she was living.

"So, our second victim has also had sex in the last twenty-four hours, but this time by choice? Is there a way of checking the semen to see if it is from the same person?" Father Matthew and the doctor were stunned by the question. Given the doctor had pointed out that there were two different murderers, it was clear to them now Nigel was thinking of every angle.

"Err, yes, Nigel, I think I can do that. It will take a while, but we can definitely do that."

"OK, Doctor, thank you. If you could call me on the mobile with your findings, that would be good. Father Matthew and I will leave you to it and go to see the judge."

"The judge?"

"Yes, Doctor, he was at the hotel last night and stayed over; we need to see if he heard anything. When we were with him this morning, he seemed a little off from his normal self. Wouldn't you say, Father? That makes him a person of interest in my book." Doctor Mitchell looked at Father Matthew for approval, but for the first time ever didn't get it. Father Matthew was still wrapped up in his thoughts about Alana. Nigel placed a hand on the father's shoulder to bring him back into the room, and they both left. The doctor finished writing up his report, and then headed out of the prison not long after they did.

The judge lived just north of the town; he was one of the few residents that didn't live in a cluster of houses. It was a small modest farmhouse-style building which had been empty when he arrived on the island. After about six months of living in the hotel, the workman had upgraded the house to his design. He had built a strong friendship with Hayley and Kevin over that time; hence the reason he could crash out in the hotel whenever he needed to free of charge. It was also why Kevin had felt so guilty at the point of almost accusing him of Alana's murder. The car journey was going to take them less than fifteen minutes.

"You are very quiet, Father. It must be hard to see both of them like that in the last twenty-four hours. Both a part of your close family." Nigel wasn't a great detective, but he knew that both of the victims had very strong ties to Father Matthew. He had thought about that statement for five minutes before blurting it out.

"I am sorry. I guess I was lost in my thoughts. It is extremely hard, Nigel. Such terrible goings-on, these things they tend to knock you off balance."

"It is understandable, Father, but we can't let it get to us; we have a murder, sorry, murders to solve. I really do appreciate your help with this. It means a lot to me that you are here."

There was silence again.

"But not you, Nigel, I have been very impressed with you. You would have made your father and mother proud today with the way you have handled yourself and the situation." Nigel was almost blushing at this. If there was anyone's approval he sought for what he was doing, it would be Father Matthew's.

Nigel's father and mother had passed away when he was very young. It had been heart breaking given the lengths they had gone to, to have a child. Nigel had been there only one. His mother had died of cancer, and it was felt that that had led to his father giving up on life. He died a few short years later, leaving Nigel to be brought up on the island by his Aunt Marg who he still lived with.

"Thank you, Father. I am trying to do what is expected of me. After such a long time I just never thought it would all come at once."

"You are standing up to it, Nigel, and your aunt, she must be so proud too, is she well?"

"Very well, Father. She was shocked at the goings-on of last night. I can't imagine what she is going to think of today when I get home."

"The less she knows the better, Nigel; some of this is very distressing. Especially for a woman of her age." There was a tone in his voice that Nigel knew only too well. One that was telling him to keep a lid on things. A mixture of excitement and adrenaline had Nigel spilling the whole case to whomever he spoke to. Father Matthew knew he needed to help him keep the case confidential, if not for the case itself for the detectives that would be arriving shortly.

When they arrived at the judge's house, he was sitting in the garden with a book drinking a jug of Long Island Iced Tea.

"I presume you are here to talk to me about last night, gentlemen?" There was shock from both of them as they approached the garden table.

"Yes, your Honour. How did you know?" After forty-plus years in service, the judge knew they would get there sooner or later. Even if it was Nigel investigating. Besides, Kevin had rung the judge as soon as Nigel and the Father left. He had told him everything that had gone on, and mentioned that they were heading to him after the prison. The Judge was just keen to put them off guard as soon as they arrived for his own amusement.

"This is a small island. Well, sit, sit then. I can save you some time though, I didn't hear or see anything. It was Sunday, my day off, and I can assure you I was completely out of it."

"Nothing at all, your Honour? A young girl was murdered outside your room, and you didn't hear anything?"

"As I said, Nigel, not a thing. I don't even remember Hayley and Kevin carrying me to bed. Force of drinking too much over the last fifty years I am afraid. As soon as I am out, I am out. My wife used to say they could drop a bomb next to me and I wouldn't move." There was a moment of silence as they both stood looking directly at the Judge.

"Sit down, chaps, come on. This doesn't need to be so formal." The judge gestured at them both to sit at the table. It was a big table with eight chairs which, in all the years the Judge had been on the Island, had never been used. Only Kevin and Hayley had ever been invited to visit, and that had only been for a brief dinner inside. The judge was a very private person. Father Matthew and Nigel sat directly opposite to him.

"And what time was that, Your Honour? What time did you pass out?"

"No idea, Nigel. I am sure Hayley will remember; she is good like that. I started early that day. It was Sunday, the day of rest and all that, Father you know all about that." There was a wry smile from the Judge in the Fathers direction. He knew all too well that the Father didn't have a day of rest in him.

"Judge Reynolds, do you remember seeing Alana at any time yesterday evening?" As the words left his mouth Nigel looked in the direction of Father Matthew. That had been the one question he hadn't asked anyone at the hotel, the simplest of questions, and he had missed it. He knew he should have asked everyone that question.

"No, sorry. I was here in the garden most of the day with a few drinks, and went down to the hotel from about five o'clock I would say. Didn't see many people, just the usual suspects. That blonde girl was there, I think she came in around nine, but nobody else. None of us left for more than a couple of minutes to go to the bathroom, and that faces the main street outside." The judge was strong in his answers and direct. As far as Nigel was concerned, he was the law on the island. He certainly knew more about it than anyone else. So if he said he didn't see anything, then he didn't see anything. This avenue was already starting to feel like a waste of time.

"OK, Judge, sorry to have wasted..." Nigel moved to stand up.

"Drink some Long Island Tea, lad, and rest a moment. You still have a while before the boat comes in. Tell me what you have so far, and I will see what I can do to help; I have been doing these going on forty-five years you know. I have learnt a bit in that time about murderers and their actions..."

Nigel sat back down and proceeded to tell the judge everything they knew so far. There was the odd look in Father Matthew's direction as he did, but they both knew that the Judge had more experience in murder cases and law than anyone on the island. He was the man you could tell everything too.

"And you say the nun, what's her name, Sister Sarah is missing as well?"

"Yes, your Honour, we presumed she caught the ferry across as she booked a ticket, but she didn't embark. I know, your Honour; I was there." The judge was silent for a second.

"Are there any obvious links, Nigel, between the three of them? The nuns and the young girl? Apart from the drugs linking at least two of your victims." The Judge was looking directly at Nigel as he spoke. Making eye contact with the judge didn't feel natural to Nigel. In fact, it made him more than just a little nervous.

"Sister Sarah isn't a victim." Father Matthew was keen to express that point. He felt the need to chip in as Nigel was telling his story to ensure that the Judge knew she was just a missing person.

"Not yet, Father, but in my opinion missing nuns very rarely turn up. Well, not alive anyway. Nigel, what is the obvious link?" Nigel looked between the judge and Father Matthew.

"Like what, Judge?"

"Nigel don't ignore the obvious because he is sitting in front of you. I was just testing to see if you would say it in front of him. Father Matthew here must be suspect number one at the moment. He is the likely candidate shall we say, with access to all three victims or potential victims. The drugs are surrounding his premises, and he, above all others, travel on and off the island on a weekly basis. I can't imagine anyone ever strip searches a Father of the church" The judge sat back in his chair with a huge grin on his face as if he had just solved the case for him.

"I am sorry, Judge Reynolds." Father Matthew was taken back a bit by what he had said, and the way that he had said it, so plainly in front of them.

"Don't take it as an offence, man. I no more think you did it than I. But if Nigel here is going to be a good detective, he should be thinking of you. Nobody is exempt from this process. You are the common theme:

a dead sister, a missing sister, and one of your helpers is dead. You also said it yourself a moment ago; you were out walking alone when Sister Trinity died, and you would have been passing the crime scene last night when you went from the prison to home, wouldn't you?" Father Matthew resisted nodding his head to the judge's questioning. Nigel was now looking at the Father with different eyes. He was wondering if he had been blinded to it as it was the Father. He had to admit the thought had crossed his mind, but he had quickly discarded it. It was Father Matthew, he would never be capable of something like that.

"Judge, I do agree with you. I was thinking of that myself earlier today. Nigel needs to consider every person on the island. He had asked me yesterday about my walk, and I did think it could look suspicious to the outsider. But it is something I do often, especially before a service." Father Matthew hoped his comment would reassure them as well as point out that he knew how it looked.

"Don't you see, Nigel; my head would tell me it's something to do with the church, the home, or the orphanage. There are drugs somewhere in the mix as well. Somebody is supplying the nuns with drugs; a sentence you don't hear every day now, isn't it? If you can work out, Nigel, how they are getting here, on this island, then that may start to bring some walls down. We all know drugs can't come over on the ferry, which leaves the harbour fishermen? Maybe they are getting them on the island for someone. How big is the drug problem in the prison?"

"There is no drug problem in the prison that we know of, judge?"

"No? Who has ever heard of a prison without drugs? It's like peaches without cream. No, Nigel, there is a link to these three women, a vessel that is bringing the drugs onto the island, and a market for them. Given what we know, I would start with the warden, have him do a sweep of the prison. Uncover what you can there, and ask the right questions, someone will give up their supplier. This will lead you to who is bringing it in on the outside, and that will lead you to the connection. If there is, as you say, no drug problem at the prison I will eat my hat. But if there is then my second guess would be to go to the pub. That young girl was heading somewhere with a pocket full of cocaine, wasn't she? Father Matthew is very keen to support her so if she wasn't taking it, she was selling it, and I know where I would go to sell it." The judge sat back in his chair again as if he had just given sentence. He had pointed Nigel in all the right directions, and also made him think twice about the Father who seemed to be at the centre of everything. They all took a moment of silence after hearing the Judge's speech. It all made sense, no matter what Father Matthew thought of Alana, she had been up to something that nobody in the home was aware of.

"Thank you, Judge. That certainly is a lot to take in and has been most helpful. I will follow up on all of that I assure you." This time Nigel got all the way to standing before the judge replied to him.

"Anytime, Nigel, we no more want murder and drugs on this island than we need more inmates. Sad old world out there, Nigel, and it's our job to keep it all under control."

"I agree, Your Honour. I may call on you again if it is OK. When my colleagues arrive." The judge had risen to shake hands to say goodbye. He pulled his hand back.

"Who arrives, man?"

"I have asked for support from the mainland. I thought that's what you were referencing when you mentioned the boat."

"I thought you would be watching the boats in and out, that is all. Why would you do that, you stupid boy? This doesn't need outside eyes prying into what happened here. You're a damn policeman; you should have handled the case yourself." The judge seemed to be very cross at the thought of the arrival of new policemen. The whole tone of his voice changed, and his body language started to scream anger at them. Nigel went to speak, but the Judge spoke over him.

"Stupid boy, do you have no pride in yourself? Man up you are supposed to be a policeman for gods sake." Nigel and Father Matthew both froze awaiting the Judge to speak again. He was clearly very cross with the both of them, shaking his head with great disapproval.

"I have had enough of you for today. Good day, gentlemen."

He left the jug of Long Island Iced Tea on the table and stormed into the house. The patio doors were slammed so hard it sounded as if the glass was going to pop right out of them. Father Matthew and Nigel stood frozen, both in shock after what had just happened.

"What was that about, Father?" The judge's reaction had him stumped.

"I am not sure, Nigel, but the judge seems to be hell-bent on not having any more police involved in this. A moment ago, he had all but put the murders at my door and two minutes later, at the thought of extra police on the island, he has stormed off in a rage." As soon as Father Matthew stopped talking, the words played over again in his head. He felt as if he was returning the favour; he didn't mean to, but he felt as if he had just tried to lay the blame back at the judge's door. That was not a very Christian thing to do.

"That can't be a good sign, can it? I thought we were doing so well. Why would he be so mad about extra resource to solve a crime?" Father Matthew shook his head.

"He is certainly not himself lately. Not the judge I know." Nigel didn't say it, but he had spent the night looking for the side effects of cocaine. Irrational behaviour and mood swings were right up there. All of a sudden Nigel started to wonder if the judge was on drugs as well.

"No, Nigel, it is not good at all. I think the judge, as well as myself, should be firmly on your radar. Something is distressing him." Father Matthew was keen to try to show to Nigel that he wasn't playing the blame game. They were all suspects, and he was happy to be investigated equally.

The ride back to the hotel was silent again. They were both thinking about what the judge had said with regards to Father Matthew, and his strange reaction to the extra resource heading to them. Nigel dropped Father Matthew back at the hotel to pick up his car. He then headed to the port to meet the six o'clock boat so that he could give a full briefing to the detectives they were sending across from the mainland.

Father Matthew took the fifteen-minute drive across the island and went straight into the church. He sat in one of the pews for a few minutes, trying to gather his thoughts after the long day. So much had happened in the last forty-eight hours; just as the judge had pointed out: everyone was a suspect. Alana was gone, he still couldn't believe it. He said a quick prayer for her; he had loved her like a daughter. He knew he was going to have to hug Catherine as hard as he could when he went home as a comfort for himself, but he wasn't ready to face that yet.

Father Matthew got up and walked over to the altar. Under the altar behind the curtain there was a small box; he pulled it out and placed it on the altar. It was full of keys. Spare keys to all the locks in the facility. He took out a bunch of keys marked *church* and returned the box under the altar.

In the corner of the church, there were some stairs leading down to the basement. Father Matthew took the stairs, and stood in front of a locked door. There were two freshly placed padlocks on the door. He had bought them from the local shop last Wednesday. He took the keys out, unlocked the door, and entered the room.

Chapter 6

Father Matthew and Mary stayed up for most of the night with the residents of the home. They had lost two of their own family within forty-eight hours, and the rumours were now rife about the disappearance of Sister Sarah also. They took time together and visited all of the residents one by one trying to reassure them that everything was being done to find out who had done this. Father Matthew took the time to pray with each of them. Last on their rounds was Alex. When they arrived at Alex's room, Catherine was sitting with him watching TV.

"Hello, Alex, Catherine, it is getting very late. How are you both doing?"

Catherine came over and gave both of her parents a big hug. Alex didn't move from his bed, fixated on the TV.

"I can't believe it, Mum; I can't believe that she is gone. I was only talking to her yesterday. Well, as much as she ever spoke. Both of them, Mum." Mary stayed hugging her daughter.

"None of us can, my dear, but your father and Nigel have been out all day trying to figure out what is going on, and we have more police arriving tonight. We will get to the bottom of this. Won't we, Matthew?"

He just nodded in the general direction of all of them.

"She was a wonderful young girl and it is a shame that she is gone. But she is with God now and hopefully at peace from whatever troubles she had." Father Matthew paused as he said that. He didn't want them to know everything, and he knew he had said too much already. That last comment could very easily lead to a multitude of questions so he needed to change the subject quickly.

"Your mother is right; we will catch whoever is doing this and bring them to justice. That is our main priority now. That, and trying to get everything back to normal around here."

Father Matthew turned his attention to Alex who was lying on his bed. He was hoping the change of attention would work.

"And, Alex, how are you? How are you coping with all this? Is there anything you would like to talk about or maybe say a little prayer with us?" Father Matthew knew Alex wasn't overly religious, but at times like this everyone questioned their faith.

"I-I AM F-f-f-f-fine, F-a-t-t-ther, fine."

"He isn't fine, Daddy; he has hardly said two words all day. I came in here this afternoon, and he didn't even have his programmes on. I had to put them on for him. He was just lying on that bed, staring out of that window."

"This is a hard time for all of us, Alex. We all loved Sister Trinity and Alana. They were family to all of us. But there are only a few people that we can rely on to support us all through this, and you, my young man, are one of them."

Father Matthew walked over and tapped him on the head.

"We need the old Alex back. You know, he is the one that keeps us all going, the one that puts a smile on everyone's face. It's a hard-enough week without losing you to whatever is going on in there."

Alex turned his head away, and stared back out of the window.

"Give him a little time; he will be back to chasing the sisters around in no time."

That would have normally ensured a response from him, but Alex didn't answer. Father Matthew grabbed and squeezed his shoulder to let him know that he was there for him. He knew that was as much as he was going to be able to do for him until it was time for Alex to open up.

"Come on, Catherine, let's leave him to his TV. It's getting late, and I would prefer we all walked home together. If you need anything, Alex, just ring the vicarage or get one of the sisters to come fetch me. Day or night, OK? Just know that we are all here for you. You are our family too Alex." Alex still didn't respond; he just continued to stare out the window. The three of them left, and took the short walk home to the vicarage.

Once they got home Father Matthew, Catherine and Mary sat up and drank tea for about an hour, trying to remember all the good things that both Alana and Sister Trinity had brought into their lives. After that they all retired to bed; exhaustion had gotten the better of all of them.

Father Matthew rose early for morning-prayer. Very few people attended at seven a.m., but he still ran this twice a week. There were a few more than normal, but Father Matthew figured that was because they wanted to know what was going on first hand. He politely kept his update brief short with each of them as they left the church and informed them that he was hoping to hear more from Nigel today once the other police officers had arrived. He returned to the vicarage at about nine just in time for the breakfast that had been laid out on the table for him. Mary was already washing up the cups from the night before.

"I swear, Matthew, that girl will eat us out of house and home."

"Sorry, my love, why do you say that?"

"Catherine. I swear the bread, cold meats, all of it disappears as soon as I put it in the fridge. She will never fit in that wedding dress the way she is going."

"She is a growing girl, Mary. Now, come drink your tea with me. It has been a long few days." Mary turned, smiled at her husband, and did as she was asked sitting down next to him at the table.

"Mary, I have been thinking about it, and I don't want you going out to the town, or anywhere, not until we find out what is going on. It's too dangerous. I would prefer that you stay here where I know that you are safe." Mary continued to smile and then grabbed her husband's hand and squeezed it tight.

"I understand what you are saying, Matthew, but I am not too sure which is the safer place at the moment. It's true what everyone is talking about, whatever seems to be going on, looks like it has a connection to our home."

Father Matthew knew she was right. Everyone must be thinking the same thing. He was only fooling himself if he kept ignoring that point. He shouldn't be leaving them at all. Whatever was happening, it was connected to everyone that he loved and cared for.

"I know, it does seem like that, but I am sure it is just a coincidence. I still like the thought of you here in the day time; there is a safety in numbers. At night time I am always here. Also, let's just make sure we keep Catherine close to us. I don't want her travelling anywhere alone either. Not until we get to the bottom of this."

Mary nodded her head as she looked towards the kitchen door. She could hear footsteps.

"No more talk of it now, Catherine is coming downstairs; I don't want to frighten her. We will keep her safe my love."

Catherine entered the kitchen, walked over and in turn kissed both her parents.

"Morning, dear, how about a cup of tea?"

"Morning"

"And some breakfast? How about a spot of breakfast?" Mary was up and back at the sink.

"Yes please, tea and breakfast, Mum, I am starving. Do we have any bacon?"

Mary nodded over towards her husband and mouthed the words, "see". He laughed. It was a genuine laugh, the first they had shared in days.

"So, what are your plans for today?" Father Matthew got up, and pulled out the chair next to him for his daughter to sit. Catherine picked up some cutlery from the kitchen drawer and sat down.

"I told Sandra that I would help her with lunch, and then I will drop in and see Alex as well, just to give him a little company this afternoon. He would stay in that room all day alone sometimes if it was up to him. I am worried about him now Alana is…" Catherine paused.

She didn't want to finish the sentence. Her dad noticed the pause.

"That's good of you, my dear. He does get down a lot; it must be very hard for him to deal with the change in his life." Catherine just nodded her response.

"This is just another blow after so many in the past few years. I did say a little prayer for him this morning, but I have faith he will get over it. He is a strong young man" Catherine nodded again. Father Matthew knew it was time to change the subject.

"Oh, I did mean to ask you yesterday, how is Michael?"

"He is good, I think. I did mean to call him yesterday, but with everything else that went on. Hopefully he will be coming over after lunch today." Catherine was watching her mother as she started on the bacon. As she did Father Matthew moved the toast over in her direction. She smiled and grabbed the butter knife.

"That's understandable; it was a long day. I am sure he knows that you are thinking of him. How is he feeling now?"

"Feeling, Dad?" Catherine looked up from her toast.

"Yes, I thought he was sick?"

"No, not that I know of? He had work yesterday, and then he said he was going to study during the evening, so we didn't have plans to see each other."

"Oh." Father Matthew paused thoughtfully, longer than he meant to knowing that he had to speak quickly now as not to draw attention to his question.

"My mistake, I don't know where that came from. Give him my best today though, won't you? Hopefully I will see him this afternoon." The feeling of dread had returned to Father Matthew's stomach. He knew that Michael wasn't at work yesterday, Doctor Mitchel had told him, and if he wasn't here either, where was he? There was something not quite right, something told him Michael was missing.

"Of course, Dad." Catherine returned to her breakfast.

The phone rang in the hallway and Mary got up to answer it; within a few seconds she was back into the kitchen and handed it over to her husband.

Father Matthew listened to the voice at the end of the phone, and just said OK. As soon as he hung up, he noticed Catherine and Mary on tenterhooks looking at him as if saying "what has happened now".

"It was just Nigel; there are two more detectives on the island, and they are pulling together the senior people for a meeting. I guess they want to see if we cannot solve this together." There was a sigh of relief from both of them.

"That's really good to hear." Father Matthew knew the relief in Mary's voice was not just because nothing else had happened, but also because now Nigel would have more support. She was glad the case would now count with more experience detectives. He put the phone on the table, and gave both his girls a kiss on the forehead before heading out of the kitchen door.

"Have a good day, and I will be back as soon as I can, I promise. In the meantime, stay together and be safe."

Father Matthew grabbed his coat and hat from the hallway and closed the door behind him. He then made the drive over to the hotel. The police station was only a short walk from the hotel, but it wasn't big enough to hold the meeting; it basically consisted of a cell and a desk. There had never been a need for any more than that because there had only ever been one policeman. Even when Nigel had passed the exams, he still had to wait a year for Constable Fred Kurz to retire before taking the post. Fred had been one of the only people to retire and leave the Island. He was now living in Cornwall with his daughter and son in law. The locals often teased Nigel about getting Fred back, even with his dodgy eye and the fact he slept most of the day he was still considered to be a better policeman than Nigel. These references to Fred's superior skills had risen even more over the last forty-eight hours.

When Father Matthew arrived at the hotel, Nigel was waiting for him. He explained he had told all the others to wait in the lounge area and then escorted him through to them.

Hayley and Kevin, the hotel owners, were already there along with Stacey and Ian, the owners of The Fleece pub down by the port.

"Father Matthew."

"Ian, Stacey, Hayley, Kevin, how are you all?"

"As well as can be expected, Father. Especially with a nine p.m. curfew. Damn pub was empty last night." Ian was never tactful in his answers; Ian was very rarely tactful about anything. The jibe was directed at Nigel for installing a curfew and curbing his trade.

"Ian, two people have died. Stop worrying about that damn pub. There are more important things than money." Ian wandered over to the window, not acknowledging that his wife had just scorned him in front of everyone.

The Fleece had been in Stacey's family for generations. She and Ian had been running it for the last twenty years. He was a fisherman by trade, as had been his father and his father before him. He still had his boat down at the harbour; every morning he would be out catching the fish that they would then serve in the bar that day to the customers. Ian doubled as the Fleece's chef during the afternoon and evening when he was sober enough to do so. Five out of seven nights a week Stacey would be the one doing the cooking. Nigel left the room again.

"He did say eleven o'clock, didn't he, Father?"

"Yes, they still have fifteen minutes Hayley I am sure they will be here." There was a general nod of agreement from all towards Father Matthew. No one in the room ever had a doubt to trust his word.

"How are they all coping at the home, Father? It must be a very distressing time for you all." Stacey walked over and brushed the Father's arm.

"It is, Stacey, they are coping the best they can. Mary and Catherine are doing a great job at keeping them in check and keeping everyone's morale up."

"It must be hard for you three too. They were all family to you." Father Matthew just nodded his head. He knew he needed to deal with his own loss privately, not in public. The last thing they needed was to see was him breaking down under the pressure of what had happened.

Over the next fifteen minutes the rest of the senior people on the island arrived: Judge Reynolds, Albert Finlay, Chris James and Dr Mitchell. Nigel had thought that these nine people including himself were the top ten most important people on the island. Just as Dr Mitchell arrived Nigel walked in followed by two more police officers dressed in suits who crossed the room and stood ready to make their statement. Everyone turned to face them in silence.

"Thank you all for coming. Before we start, I would like to ensure we all know who each other is. So, I will start, and if you could all introduce yourself one by one."

"My name is Detective Sergeant Rachel Morris." Rachel looked to her left.

"Detective Robert Green."

"Father Matthew Williams."

They each then in turn shouted out their names. Detective Green wrote them all down in the form of a seating chart so that he could remember who was who. As they got around to Judge Reynolds, there was a moment when the two new detectives looked directly at each other. Father Matthew and Nigel both noticed this. The judge was known to them both; that was very clear.

"Thank you for that. I think we should be open and honest with all of you. Nigel, sorry, Constable Johnson thinks you are the most influential people on the island, and as it is such a small community, we are going to need your help. Now, as we are so few in numbers, I can do this formally or informally; how would you like to proceed?"

There was a pause as they looked at each other.

"Plain speaking is what I always say." Ian was never shy in coming forward, no matter the audience.

"OK, so I am sure you are all aware that we have had two murders in the last seventy-two hours. From the evidence we have been given. They both seem to have been committed at night, and with no witnesses" There was a look from Rachel to Nigel. She had only spent a few hours with him last night, but she was already convinced that he was going to be useless in the investigation. The pictures of the table lamp hadn't helped his cause. That, and the fact that the doctor, who was still on his list of suspects, had taken all the crime scene photos at the hotel so they were only on his phone and not available for evidence yet.

"Futhermore the evidence we have from Doctor Mitchell suggests, that these murders were committed by two different people."

"Two?" It was Stacey's turn now to be forward as she looked around the room at the others.

"We had all presumed that they had been committed by the same person." Rachel looked over her partner's shoulder at detective Green's seating chart.

"No. Stacey, is it? These are two separate murders. The first, the murder of Sister Trinity, was a brutal rape followed by strangulation. On the report Doctor Mitchell indicated he was a strong physical male, right-handed, and the murderer tried to copy the style of the Sheffield Strangler, sorry, Damien Winter. The second murder however, Alana Jones, was stabbed in the abdomen by a left-handed assailant; it is too soon to say whether it was a woman or a man. But what we do know is that one to two hours before her murder, Alana Jones had consensual sexual intercourse with someone on this island. Given the distance between where she lived and here, my assumption would be that it is someone from either the town or the port. It is one of our priorities to discover who that person was."

There was an air of silence in the room. Father Matthew could feel at least half a dozen sets of eyes on him after that last point. He had always spoken of her in the highest regard and nobody had any reason to doubt that. He now knew her to be involved with drugs, and having sexual intercourse. It was still hard to take in.

"We have also discovered a connection between the two victims." This sparked everyone's interest. They all knew one obvious connection as he was standing in the room with them, but none had dared to point that out. Detective Morris pulled out an evidence bag; inside of it was a little black envelope.

"This is the connection. It's a drug called M. We have been tracing it on the mainland for a couple of months, but it's been very well hidden from us. Almost non-existent I would say." Detective Green passed the bag around the room. This was more for the benefit of Detective Morris, she wanted to see the reaction on everyone's face as it was handed out.

"I don't mind telling you that my colleagues on the mainland were even taking bets on whether it was real or something that one of the dealers had made up to increase sales. This is the first real evidence we have of its existence." There was a sense of pride in that for both the detectives and Nigel. They had phoned back to their offices the moment Nigel produced the packets.

"What is it?" Hayley had remained quiet till then, partly because she did not want to stand out in a crowd, but mainly it was to do with being very hung-over after the events of yesterday.

"It's cocaine. But it's not only cocaine, it is in fact, if to be believed cocaine mixed with the ashes of murderers." Detective Morris paused for effect. It worked. She could feel the gasp from everyone in the room.

"We didn't believe it to be true, but the doctor has confirmed the ashes. There are traces of the same type of wood that is used to make the coffins in the prison mixed in with the powder. Apparently, it is said to instantly give the user a rush to the brain by thinking that he is actually sniffing the body of a murderer." There was still a silence from their audience, they were all stunned at the thought of what they had just heard.

"That is just sick!" Everyone turned to Ian, but nobody replied to his comment.

"One of the side effects of this is that violent behaviour has been on the rise on the mainland. Whether it is actually the placebo effect or not. The kids that are taking it believe they are stronger, faster and more dangerous so that is how they react to it." Father Matthew handed the bag back to Detective Green.

"I don't believe it. Nothing gets in or out of my prison. Whether it is a body or not. That boat is searched day and night. There is no way that drugs are coming here on that boat." It was part of Chris James' responsibilities to be in charge of the dog patrol on the ferries coming into Callington Island, and he had complete faith in his team's ability. He audited the processes himself at least once a week. Often on his day off from working at the prison.

"Therein lies some questions, Mr James. We have been assured the exact same thing from Constable Johnson. I believe that either the fishing boats have picked it up, or we can't rule out that this is a well-connected gang with operation teams at the port or inside the prison. Unfortunately, Mr James, it is a very profitable business and money talks."

"Not my people. I can assure you that they will have nothing to do with this. I picked and screened each one of them myself." Chris took offence at the thought of someone thinking that his people were involved. Given the role on the island, the government had seen fit to pay a wage salary that had never been seen in the service before. Chris had handpicked the very best of the best as he had the budget to do so, and he considered his team to be a very qualified and financially satisfied one.

"It is either that, Mr James, or there is some other way on and off this island. Is there the chance that somewhere someone has a boat that makes the journey from the mainland? Maybe a boat nobody knows about?" Detective Morris was as strong in her response as Chris had been.

"It won't be the fishermen. I know all of them and that's not their thing. And if there was a strange boat in the harbour, we would know about it." Ian was as protective of his friends in the port as Chris had been about his team. Having worked with them all, all his life, he didn't want people throwing stones at the local people. Detective Morris was fast getting the feeling that the whole room was going to be protective of everyone on the island. Within five minutes she had been told to discount the prison and the port, and all the other guests looked to be agreeing with these points.

"Although, I have seen that packet before in our pub, Stacey." Everyone turned to Ian. He didn't say it very loudly, but he was an honest man. He wanted this situation to be resolved so they could all return to their normal lives.

"I didn't know what it was, but when I was emptying the bins, I saw it a few times over the last few months. To be honest, I thought it was a condom wrapper."

"A what?" Stacey spoke louder than she had wished and Ian just shrugged his shoulders at his wife.

"Well, I didn't know, who knows what these kids get up to? I thought the M might stand for mega or massive or something. I would buy them if I was in a pub."

Stacey shook her head at her husband and turned her attention to the detectives. Ian had just told them there was a drug problem in her pub. She knew that was going to mean a visit at some point.

"As bad as that sounds, Ian, it is good to know that it is commonplace on the island." There were a few cross looks at the words common place. Nobody seemed to know about it up until a couple of days ago, and most in the room till just now.

"It will help us lead to the source of the problem." Stacey was nodding her head at Detective Morris. They were making progress.

"Detective, how have you connected drugs to the two women?" It was a fair question from Hayley. Both women, up until this point, had been seen above something like this.

"Sister Trinity had an envelope in her room hidden in her bible at the home. Alana Jones was carrying several envelopes on her person when she was found in the garden of this hotel." As soon as the words several left the detectives lips Father Matthew could feel the eyes of the room turn back on to him again.

"Several? She was dealing them on the island? She was dealing in my pub? She was there all the time." Although Ian was talking, all the glances continued at Father Matthew; they all knew her story and that he was responsible for bringing her to the island.

"We aren't saying that, what we are saying is that they are both connected by the drug. That is all we know at this moment." Detective Morris was keen to ensure that a blame game wasn't going to happen on the island.

"If the drug theory is to be believed as the cause of these murders, and I repeat if, the only possible place to get ashes of murderers would be from the prison. Somehow those ashes are being mixed with cocaine and sold as a designer drug on the island, but more so on the mainland. This is now rumoured to be sold all over the UK. In huge quantities"

The room changed the direction of their attention to Albert Finlay. Every local person in the room had voted for the prison to come to the Island, but in that moment, they had forgotten about that and were looking for someone to blame.

"Calm down. We aren't drug dealers, you know. It's a prison, for Christ's sake. Sorry, Father. After the doctor pronounces the death of the inmate, the body is taken to the morgue, stripped naked, placed into a cheap wooden box, and taken to the furnace. The ashes are then placed in an urn in case anyone would like to collect them. They have to be a relative hence nobody has ever collected a single one. If they are not collected within two weeks, they are then disposed of. It is as simple as that." As soon as those words left his mouth there was a feeling at the bottom of his stomach that he didn't like. He knew they were disposed of, but never actually witnessed the process himself. This wasn't something he even thought about doing.

"Disposed of?" It was Detective Morris's turn to ask a question.

"Yes, Michael, he is our mortician on the island. I think the agreement is that he throws them in the sea. I don't think anyone believes that they deserve the full service, do you?" Albert was looking directly at Father Matthew now. He was once again in the centre of all this. His son-in-law was responsible for the disposal of the ashes.

"This would be Michael Peterson, yes?" His name was already on the detective's pad. Nigel had been very vocal about him not having an alibi for Sister Trinity. It was the detectives' turn to glance towards Father Matthew. They knew this was his soon to be son-in-law. Father Matthew, for the first time ever, was starting to feel uncomfortable on his own island.

"Yes, he is a good lad; he would not be mixed up with any of this. He works closely with the doctor here." Albert was keen to ensure that he wasn't giving them a suspect. He liked Michael and he had been nothing but courteous since the time he started work at the prison.

"Yes, we went to visit him at his parents' before we got here, but they presumed he was already at work. So, we still need to catch up with him. Apparently, they often don't see him in the week; he keeps long hours at work, and as I understand it, Father, he is planning a wedding with your daughter?"

Father Matthew had been silent throughout the debate until this point. It was clear they had really drilled Nigel for all the information they could on the island. He was shocked by the direction the conversation was heading, and was concerned with the fact that Michael could well be in the centre of it. If he was honest with himself, he had started to worry when the doctor had suspected he had fallen ill yesterday.

Now, with no sign of him, Father Matthew was starting to believe that something could have happened to Michael.

"If that is the case, that you have visited his parents and he wasn't there, and presuming he hasn't shown at work today, Doctor?"

Doctor Mitchell shook his head at the Father.

"Then, I think Michael is missing, Detectives."

There was a chorus of "what do you mean missing" from everyone in the room. This was another revelation. Another missing person on a very small island.

"Dr Mitchell mentioned to me yesterday that he hadn't shown up to work; he had presumed he was sick or helping at the home given what had happened to Sister Trinity. I didn't think anything of it until I spoke with my daughter this morning; as you said, they are engaged to be married, Detectives. She said she believed he was at work and she hadn't heard from him all day. I think now he is missing unless anyone else has seen him?"

Silence was returning to the room. The connection to Father Matthew, and the home, couldn't be ignored by anyone any longer. Another of his close family was missing. There was a silence until Detective Morris decided to break it.

"So, thank you all for that. It was very helpful. I would like to do a recap of where we are: we have two dead bodies, both previous workers at the old people's home." Father Matthew wanted to point out at this point that Alana was a resident, but he knew it was not the time.

"The evidence also tells us that we have two different killers. It seems the only connection between the murders at the moment is a new designer drug that, if rumours and early evidence are to be believed, seem to be linked to this prison. We also now have two missing people who, again if records are to be believed, have not left and are somewhere on this island." Everyone played the recap through their heads. The last seventy-two hours had certainly been remarkable in the life of the island.

"Two missing people, Detective?" Hayley was the first to answer.

"Yes, a Sister Sarah, and now Michael Peterson."

"Sister Sarah is missing? Father, I thought she had gone back to the mainland; that is what you said. That is what Mary said as well?" Everyone fixed their gaze back to Father Matthew. That is what he had told everyone. That is what he had told Mary. It took him a while to respond.

"That is what we thought, Hayley."

"Yes, Hayley, Father Matthew and Mary saw the booking of her ticket, but it wasn't used. The whole home believed she had gone back to the mainland. That was until I went through the records. I was actually at the boat on that morning, and she didn't use her ticket, so I, we, now fear the worst." Nigel tried to support Father Matthew as much as he could. Even he could feel the tension in the room.

"Now I believe everything is out in the open. This is exactly why we brought you all here today. The rest of the residents on this island will fear the worst, and it is our job, collectively, to keep things going whilst we look to resolve this situation as quickly as possible." It had been the first time that Detective Green had spoken through the whole meeting.

"How are you going to solve this? You don't really seem to have a lot to go on at the moment or am I missing something? And, well, to be frank, when you walked in the room ten minutes ago, I thought you were looking for one killer and were going to struggle to find that. I now know it is two killers, two missing people, and a cocaine problem which is infused with the ashes of dead inmates from the prison. Things aren't getting better, are they, Detectives? If you are here to reassure me, you aren't doing a very good job." Ian had voted for plain talking and that is exactly what he got and what he was giving in return.

There was a real acceptance of this fact across all the police officers' faces; they didn't have anything to really go on other than Nigel's list. It had been the best piece of work the new detectives had seen from him. Detective Rachel Morris was considered to be one of the most promising young talents on the force. She always had a plan, and she would not leave any stone unturned. But up to this point, she was either still working on that plan in secret or not had one altogether. At least that is what Nigel thought as she wasn't sharing anything with him. It was Nigel who responded first.

"I know it doesn't sound a lot, Ian, but we are a small island so we will find these people and fast. I met with the judge yesterday, and we believe him to be right in what he was saying as a strategy going forward. If we find the drugs, the dealer, and the way onto the island, it should cause a chain of events that will lead us to the bodies we have found, and hopefully to the missing people." Nigel was now looking directly at Chris James. Chris was already thinking ahead of them though. He knew that the first place you would look for drugs would be the prison.

"I can instruct a search of all the cells today; if there are drugs in my prison, my guys will find them. You can be assured of that." Chris was confident in his team, he was also convinced there would not be drugs found in his prison.

"That is good, Mr James, and exactly what we wanted to hear. If there are any drugs in the prison and we can in turn get the inmates to cooperate and tell us who is supplying it to them, then that gives us the first link in the chain."

Chris James stood up and strolled out of the room. He was a big guy, and nobody wanted to stop him. He had his mission and the sooner he started on it the better. He, above all others, was keen to ensure to everyone on the island that his team was not involved in what had been going on. The detectives waited for him to leave the room.

"We need a couple of other things from you also; we would like to quietly start a search for our, now two, missing people. And, at the same time, we would like to keep the drug element of this investigation away from the community. We need them to have confidence that we are resolving this, and as we don't know how the drugs are moving, we don't want to spook anyone into fleeing from the island." Detective Morris looked for a reaction from all of them. Putting their faith in a stranger was something she knew to be alien to them. It always was in small communities.

"Don't the people have a right to know there is a drug problem on the island, Detective?" Hayley's hangover had started to clear, and she was now getting down to business of looking after her island, and her people.

"Yes, they do. All we are asking is for some time. These things can get out of hand very quickly, and if all the people start to leave the island for fear of what is happening, we will lose our killers." It was clear to all that Detective Rachel Morris was leading this investigation now. Nigel and Detective Green were almost silent partners in the background.

"I think I speak for everyone, Detective, when I say that all we want is for the people responsible to be caught and then return to our normal lives. We will do all that we can to help support you in the process." Father Matthew spoke, and the room listened. Despite the doubts of his connections, they all knew that all that he had ever strived for personally was the best for the island.

"Thank you, Father. I will be back here at six p.m. tonight with an update of the day's events, and we will continue the briefings until we have concluded everything." Detective Morris turned towards her colleagues gesturing that this was the end of the briefing. The top-ten islanders started to disappear, leaving the two detectives, Nigel and Father Matthew.

"Father Matthew, I have heard only good things about you. It is nice to finally meet you in person." Father Matthew shared a smile in Nigel's direction. He knew that Nigel will have supported him to his colleagues on their arrival.

"It is my pleasure, Detective Morris, Detective Green. I just wish it had been in better circumstances." Father Matthew shook both their hands. He noticed that despite being a woman, Detective Morris's was certainly firmer and more purposeful in her handshake.

"Nigel has said you have been invaluable in this process so far, and we would just like to give you our thanks."

"It's not a problem, anything I can do to help I will. This island is important to me. As I know it is for Nigel." Father Matthew was keen to return the praise.

"I am glad you said that as we would like to re-interview some of the staff in the home and your residents, Father." There was a pause. Nigel gave him a look as if to tell him he knew the point was coming, but there was little he could do about it.

"I am sure you understand, Father, both victims have originated from there. Plus, there is a strong connection to our now two missing people." Rachel could see the concern on Father Matthew's face. The last thing he wanted was more upset at the home.

"It will be brief, Father. I am sure Nigel has already done an excellent job. We just want to ensure that he has not missed anything."

Father Matthew could feel the strength of Detective Morris's request. The words were pleasant and spoken in a soft voice, but they clearly highlighted that the two murders and two missing people were basically on his door step. It was clear the trust in Nigel was non-existent. Father Matthew gave Rachel a smile of his own and spoke softly.

"Of course, Detective. I would expect nothing less. I can take you myself if you like. I am sure it would make it easier for you." Rachel grabbed his hand again and shook it once more.

"It is fine, Father, we have Nigel's car, but if you could let them know we are coming, that would be great. I am sure you have other things to do." Father Matthew got the message clearly, they wanted to do it alone. He was not welcome. The two detectives disappeared out of the room, leaving Nigel and Father Matthew alone.

"You are not going with them, Nigel?"

"No, they said they wanted to do it alone. I was going to go back to the Petersons to see when the last time was that they saw Michael. I can't believe he is missing too now. He was still on my list to question again about Sister Trinity." Father Matthew ignored the obvious question; why? He knew as well as Nigel did that Michael didn't have an alibi for the time when Sister Trinity was killed. He had been walking home on his own. Father Matthew truly believed though he was walking home.

"It sounds like a plan, Nigel. Do you mind if I join you? I know Catherine is going to be very worried when she finds out he is missing, and I would rather it comes from me first-hand if that is the case." Nigel nodded. Father Matthew started to move towards the door, and Nigel suddenly grabbed him by the arm. This shocked Father Matthew. There was a look of desperation instantly all over his face as if he had just remembered something horrible.

"Father, before we go, I need to tell you something. They asked a lot of questions about you yesterday. I only told them the truth, Father, but they really drilled me at some points." It wasn't desperation; the look had been one of guilt. Father Matthew could tell now, there was guilt written in big letters. Guilt that he had been party to a conversation about Father Matthew without him being in it.

"They were only doing their job, Nigel. I am not surprised given the chain of events, and they have to be thorough in what they do. I have nothing to hide so I have nothing to fear, Nigel." Father Matthew gave him a pat on the shoulder.

"It wasn't just you though, Father, the doctor also and the judge; it was like they had it in for everyone." Father Matthew knew Nigel; he knew he would have told them everything. He also knew he was a kind lad so whatever he would have said would have also be counteracted by positive points about everyone. Nigel didn't have a bad bone in his body. His admiration would have shone through.

"Everyone is going to be a suspect to them, Nigel. We have to face that. They are not islanders. The sooner we tell our stories, the sooner they can eliminate everyone and find the real killers." Father Matthew found that last part hard to say. He didn't think it would ever be something that he would say on his island. During the time that he courted the government about bringing the prison to the island, a few people had asked Father Matthew some very specific questions: had he thought what it might do to the island? And what else it might bring to the island. At the time he didn't give them any importance, now he knew what bringing a prison to the island had done.

"The judge has a past as well, Father, and not a nice one as it turns out. Not nice at all."

Father Matthew suddenly stopped at the doorway and closed the door in front of them to ensure nobody could hear them.

"Nigel! That is not the type of conversations we want to have in public." Father Matthew paused, he was now intrigued and wanted to know what he meant. He too had had doubts over the judge's behaviour yesterday; it had been so unlike him.

"What do you mean, not a nice past, Nigel?" Nigel was still feeling sheepish from the 'not type of conversations' comment that Father Matthew had said to him.

"I am not supposed to say, Father." Father Matthew knew he would not keep the secret for long. It had been less than twelve hours and he had already started the conversation with him. It was better if he knew anyway, that way he could help deal with it.

"Nigel, how are we going to solve this together if I don't know all the facts? You know you and I have the best chance of finding who is doing this, don't you? This is our island. Nobody knows it better than us." Nigel nodded at the Father. Father Matthew knew that was going to give him confidence to speak.

"They said he has been investigated several times over the last twenty years for, like…" Nigel paused. Father Matthew could instantly tell that, whatever it was, it was an uncomfortable topic for Nigel.

"For things to do with children, Father."

"Children?" Nigel didn't need to mention the act. Father Matthew could tell by the look on his face that it wasn't good. That was all they needed to know.

"Yes, you know, little boys and girls; apparently, they could just never get enough evidence on him to, like, take it any further or to court. They were convinced he was a… You know." Nigel mouthed the word paedophile without actually saying it.

"That is what they said. Not me, Father. I wouldn't judge the judge." Father Matthew took a moment. That was a lot to take in. The judge had never been anything but professional for as much time as he had known him. He had spotted the look the detectives had given him in the meeting, but never would have come to that conclusion.

"The judge? That is very hard to believe, Nigel. Until he came to us, he was a happily married man as far as I remember."

Father Matthew could tell by the look on Nigel's face that wasn't true.

"That wasn't true at all, Father. You know his wife died? They also said they had their doubts on how that happened. She fell down the stairs apparently, but there is a strong rumour that she had been hit first, and then pushed down the stairs. They said it just couldn't be proved. So, it was dropped. He was too high up and influential to take on with poor evidence." Nigel was in full spilling mode. Father Matthew just needed to keep that going in case there was anything else that he should know.

"And, they just told you all this?"

"Yes, last night, and did you notice he didn't look once at them? I was watching him, Father. Didn't say a word in the whole meeting, and at the end he just got up and left. He didn't want more police on the island yesterday either, did he? That's what he was so mad about yesterday. Maybe this is why? He didn't want his secrets getting out. But Detective Morris, she knew about all of this, Father." Father Matthew took another moment to reflect on what Nigel had been saying. He was convinced now that that information was the biggest news he had had. The judge was clearly in the frame as well now. Father Matthew couldn't help but think that Alana was only seventeen and killed outside of his room. If he was the murderer, Father Matthew now knew he wanted to ask that question himself.

"Maybe we should pay him a visit after the Petersons, Nigel? He may have a different side to the story. We can't judge people on hearsay. He is a good man."

"OK, Father, I think you are right. But they are the police, Father. That is not hearsay. It is fact, Father. They have the paperwork and everything. A file this thick" Nigel gestured to him nine inches in length with his hands. Father Matthew thought about what Nigel was saying. If he had been investigated by the police there was going to be some things they didn't know about the man, and what they didn't know wasn't going to be good for him or the island.

Nigel followed father Matthew out of the hotel and they both took the short walk to the Peterson's house.

The Petersons were long-standing members of the island community. They ran the only supermarket on the island as did Mr Peterson's father and his father before him. Michael had taken his career advice from his mother's side of the family. Nigel had considered inviting them to the meeting, but he had not wanted to exceed ten. Detective Morris had been adamant that the number should be small.

It was believed by his father that Michael was going to follow them into the family business, but he wanted more than that. Rumours had it that he also didn't think that that career path was going to be enough to keep a girl like Catherine. He needed to be something better.

For that reason, Michael was studying hard to become a doctor while he worked as a mortician. His studies should have taken him to the mainland to spend more time in a real hospital, but he didn't want to leave Catherine. The plan was for them both to go once they were married.

Tuesday was the Petersons day off. They would always open at the weekend to capture all the trade from holidaymakers and villagers, but every Tuesday they would take the day off together.

Nigel stepped up and knocked at their door. Julie opened and greeted them both warmly taking them through to the lounge.

"Tea, Father, Nigel?"

"I would love some, Julie." As she left the lounge, her husband William came in through the patio doors at the back of the living room. He had clearly been working in the garden and took off his gloves to shake both of their hands.

"I thought I heard familiar voices. Father Matthew, hi, Nigel, nice to see you again." Mr Peterson gestured for them both to sit down. They did. He took the chair opposite to the sofa.

"William, we have a question to ask of you, and I am sorry to be so blunt and to the point, but as you know we are dealing with very serious incidents." Father Matthew paused. He knew this wasn't an easy question to ask.

"When was the last time that you saw Michael?" Father Matthew had taken the opportunity as Julie was out the room to start the conversation.

"Michael? Why do you ask, Father? Is there something wrong?" The atmosphere in the room changed. There was concern all across William's face as he started to think about the whereabouts of his son. Father Matthew could tell instantly that it wasn't that morning.

"We are concerned for his whereabouts, Mr Peterson."

Julie came in carrying the tray of tea and placed it on the table in front of them and proceeded to pour them each a cup. William waited for his wife to stop pouring the tea before speaking.

"The Father and Nigel are worried about Michael, dear; they want to know the last time we saw him?"

Julie froze just as she was about to sit down. Then she stood straight up. Father Matthew stood up too and went over to her. He could tell from the look on her face that she was not going to be taking the news well.

"You don't think...? Oh, my god, I don't know... I don't know the last time I saw him. Sunday? Was it Sunday?" Julie started to cry.

"No, Mrs Peterson, we don't think anything at this time. It's just that he hasn't shown up for work or at the home, and Catherine also hasn't seen him in the last thirty-six hours."

"Oh no, no, no..."

"Listen to me, Julie, I am sure that he is fine. Just think, when was the last time that you or your husband saw or spoke to Michael?" Father Matthew was directing her to a chair and sat her down. He knelt beside the chair, still holding her hand as he did.

"I think it was Sunday, Father, yes, Sunday. Julie and I were home when he came back from Sunday evening service with you. He told us what had happened to Sister Trinity. We did wonder what was going on with Nigel ringing his siren and everything." William was clearly upset, but a lot calmer than his wife.

Father Matthew gave Nigel a look. He knew there was a reason the home was full of visitors that afternoon. This was the first he had heard about the siren. Now he knew how the news had travelled so fast.

"And you haven't heard, or spoken to him since?"

They both looked at each other.

"I don't think so. It's not unusual for us; we are generally up and out of the house before he is up. Then when we come home, he is normally out with Catherine till ten, eleven p.m. and when he gets here, we are in bed." Father Matthew lent over to the tea tray and took a cup of tea and gave it to Julie.

"Last time I saw him was here Sunday night; he was on the sofa watching TV. He always likes to have Sunday nights to himself. We always go down to the hotel and have a drink with Hayley and Kevin and the judge."

"Thank you, William. The doctor said that he didn't turn up for work yesterday, and he is not there again today. Is there something else he could have been doing? Is there a course or something we may have all forgotten about and we are getting worked up about nothing?" Father Matthew looked at the room. Nobody answered. It wasn't unusual for him to go to the mainland for a short course, but he would generally tell everyone about it. He was proud about what he was trying to achieve for himself and Catherine. Father Matthew was thinking back to this morning's conversation with Catherine. He hadn't asked where Michael was, he just asked how he was. She was planning on seeing him today it was plausible she knew he was away, wasn't it?

"Oh no, no, no." Julie started to cry again.

"I know something has happened to him, Father. Something has happened to him. It is not like him to be away so long."

"I am sure it hasn't, Julie. We just need to find him that is all. I am sure he is still on the island somewhere. Or as we said, on a course somewhere that we have forgotten. We have been monitoring the boats, haven't we, Nigel? We should just check he didn't leave." Nigel just nodded at all of them. He had been monitoring the boats, Michael was not on them. He would have picked that up as he was still a suspect. Although he still didn't have this morning's manifests. He knew he should have picked that up first thing this morning to see if anyone had fled the island.

"But with everything that is going on, Father, where else would he be?"

Father Matthew and Nigel shared a look that seemed to agree with her. They knew that anything out of the normal in the last seventy-two hours could easily lead to a disastrous outcome.

"The best thing we can do is start to look for Michael. Besides here, the home, and the prison, is there anywhere else that Michael liked to hang out?" Father Matthew noted that Nigel was almost comforting in the way he spoke. He had been learning and fast.

"No, not really, he would go down the Fleece once or twice a week. In fact, he would have been down there last night. He always entered the pool competition on a Monday after work; a lot of the people that worked at the prison did. They would have seen him. Even if he had taken the day off, he wouldn't miss that. He is a very good pool player."

Julie and William started to look like this was going to give them hope. Neither Father Matthew nor Nigel wanted to tell them they had spoken with Stacey and Ian earlier, and they would have mentioned in the meeting if he had been seen in the pub the previous night.

"Then we will check that out, Mr Peterson. The best thing you can do is remain here in case Michael calls, and if he does, contact us straight away at the police station. We just want to make sure that he is safe." Nigel spoke softly and firmly so that they took it all in. Father Matthew really did want him safe, and returned home to them as soon as possible. The fact that he was missing after everything that had gone on was starting to concern him. Nigel on the other hand, mainly wanted to question him. He still had his doubts about Michael's involvement in Trinity's murder, and now he had gone missing. Something wasn't adding up for him. Michael was fast becoming his number one suspect. Unfortunately, Nigel's problem was that he had quite a few number one suspects now.

They both got up to leave.

"Wait, there is another place. He likes to walk by the cliffs at the top end of the island, you know, just past the new estate. The prison ones. He said it clears his head after what he had to deal with in the prison. I caught him coming back from there a few times when I was doing my shop deliveries." As soon as the words left Mr Peterson's mouth, he knew he had said the wrong thing in front of his wife.

"Oh, it is so dangerous up there. William, you don't think…" Mr Peterson turned to comfort his wife. Nigel and Father Matthew just stood and watched for a moment. Neither of them wanted to disrupt the situation. It was Mr Peterson that placed his wife back in the chair and gestured to the door and followed them into the hallway.

"Thank you, Mr Peterson, we will check that out also."

"Thank you, Nigel, you too, Father. Find Michael for us and bring him home."

William showed them to the door, and they left. Father Matthew took the same sigh of relief as he did when leaving the prison as soon as he walked outside. That was uncomfortable even for him. They were both now standing in the street outside of the Peterson home.

"Odd place to go walking, wouldn't you say, Father? It is hardly on route from or to anywhere." Father Matthew didn't answer. Although he noted that Nigel was turning into a real detective before his eyes. Father Matthew had left with exactly the same thought in his head. It was an odd place to walk and it was dangerous. One slip by those cliffs and you would end up in the sea with no way of getting back. They were very steep cliff edges. Father Matthew just nodded his answer to Nigel.

"What do we think the next steps are, Father?"

"I am not sure, Nigel. I suggest we ring around everyone we know to see if anyone has seen Michael."

"I can check this morning's boat too. I didn't want to say but his name definitely wasn't on the boats for Sunday and Monday" Father Matthew had feared that. Wherever Michael was, he was still on the island.

"That sounds like a good idea. Then I guess we have to wait. As Detective Morris said, we need to find the drugs and hopefully they will lead us to the killer or killers." There was a pause. Father Matthew knew the next question coming from Nigel.

"What about the judge?" Father Matthew had the judge on his mind all the way through his time in the Petersons. If he was what Nigel's colleagues thought he was, then he was the number one suspect in Alana's case. If he wasn't, then this was going to create a stir in the parish that he would not recover from.

"I have been thinking about it. What are we going to say to him? We know the rumours about you? No, Nigel, we can't start a witch hunt on him. Besides, these are hardly children or elderly women." Father Matthew didn't think they were in a position to accuse a high court judge of anything, not without any facts. Also, if they were to go talk to him, anything they had heard might slip out of Nigel's mouth at any time which the other detectives would not like.

"I don't like saying this, Father, but Alana was close to a child's age. And he was the closest person to her when she died. That had me worried all night, Father. I couldn't sleep thinking about it." Nigel had been having exactly the same thoughts as Father Matthew had as soon as he watch Nigel mime the words, that was clear.

"That is true, but we don't have any proof, and as much as I didn't think Alana had a boyfriend or a partner, I cannot see her sleeping with a seventy-year-old judge. Your colleagues themselves thought that he loved the children too much, shall we say, not that he hurt them. And his wife, who knows, maybe she did fall down the stairs. I don't want anything leaking out about this until we know for sure. Do you hear me, Nigel?" Father Matthew had changed the tone of his voice to ensure that Nigel got the message. He wanted to make sure he didn't speak to anyone about this.

"I think you need to find Michael. That is the number one priority. I will go back to the home and speak with Catherine to see if she has heard anything, and I suggest we are both back at the six-p.m. briefing. I have another confession to hear tonight." Father Matthew paused again. For a moment he had forgotten about that. Tonight's confession. He had met with him quite a lot over the past six weeks, but tonight was going to be the last time.

"I did see it on my diary this morning, Father. I can't believe it has been six weeks already. It only felt like yesterday the whole island was buzzing with people." Father Matthew just nodded. It did feel like yesterday, but so much had now happened since he arrived on the island. Nigel put a hand on Father Matthews shoulder.

"I don't envy you with that... One. Pardon the pun, Father. I mean to say, I don't envy you listening to that confession. I don't think it would be something I would want to hear. Not from the man himself anyway."

"We all try to make our peace before moving on, Nigel. If you need me for anything I will be at the home. I think being with my family is the best place I can be today."

They took the walk back to the hotel and then parted company. Father Matthew took a slow drive back to the church and entered. He emerged an hour later and headed into the home; it was bordering on lunchtime. Sandra was busy in the kitchen with Catherine and Mary; the sisters were escorting the guests into the dining room, readying them for lunch.

"You are just in time, dear, we were hoping we would have your assistance today."

Father Matthew got stuck into plating dinners; he wanted to talk to Catherine and Mary about Michael, but this wasn't the time. Sixty old age pensioners were all hungry for what he presumed was slow-cooked lamb and veg from the smell of it.

Alex had come out of his room also for the first time since Sister Trinity had died, and it almost felt like a normal day. When the last person was served food, they all sat down at the table together: Sister Katie, Sister Grace, Sister Bethany, Alex, Father Matthew, Mary and Catherine. Sandra was out delivering the food to the other residents.

"So, Alex, it is good to see you up and about again. The place just doesn't feel the same without you now." There was a smile around the table in agreement of that.

"T-t-t-thank y-you Far-r-r-ther."

"I hope you aren't going back to your old ways and giving the ladies at the table too much hassle."

Alex looked down at his plate and continued to eat.

"I received a flower this morning outside my room, Father, been a few days since I have had one of them."

That made the whole table laugh including Alex. That was a good sign for all of them, things were returning back to normal at the home. Something that Father Matthew had been praying for whilst he was at the church.

"I wonder who that is from, I wonder..." Alex didn't look up as Father Matthew looked around the room.

"Hey, I didn't get a flower. Catherine, did you get a flower?"

"No, Mother, no flowers for me. I think there is certainly some favouritism going on around here. Even after I had to watch the golf on TV this morning for over two hours."

There was more laughter around the table. Alex carefully took a flower from the vase in the middle of the room and passed it through Father Matthew to Catherine. She got up from her chair wandered over to him and kissed him on the cheek. There was a little round of applause as she did.

"It is nice to see you all smile and, didn't I tell you, if Alex is good, then so are the rest of us." Father Matthew felt like this was the first normal day in what seemed like weeks. They all returned to their dinner making light conversations. As they were all finishing up, Father Matthew knew he had to some how start a more serious conversation with everyone.

"And how did you all get on with the detectives this morning?" That dropped the smile off people's faces. Father Matthew almost felt guilty for bringing it up.

"It was as before, Father Matthew. The sisters and I told them everything that we knew, and then they interviewed a few of the residents, Sandra, Mary and Catherine. They were only here a short while."

"Yes, Dad, just as before, although they did ask a lot of questions around Michael. I said they should speak to him directly if they wanted to know anything".

"They did? What did they say?" Father Matthew had been dreading this conversation all the way home in the car.

"Yes, they wanted to speak to him. I said he must be studying either at the prison library or at home." Catherine didn't seem to be concerned for his whereabouts. They obviously hadn't told her he was missing.

"I think, they think he is missing, dear." Father Matthew broke the words as gently as he could.

"Oh, missing from where, Dad? The prison?" Father Matthew for once didn't know what to say. It wasn't a conversation he ever thought about having with his daughter.

"I just texted him when they left and said that they wanted to speak to him."

"You texted him?"

"Yes, he hasn't replied yet, but he has been all morning. I would say he is busy studying, you know how he gets. Deep into his own little world."

Catherine passed her phone over to her father; he scrolled through the phone as quickly as he could to not bring attention to it. Monday morning's text: 'Morning Beautiful have a great day xxx', Monday evening the same: 'Sweet dreams my angel xx', and this morning another text, but this one simply said, 'I love you xx'. Wherever Michael was he was still alive. That was at least a weight off Father Matthew's mind.

"You should text him to come round for tea tonight, dear; it would be great to see him." He knew that would get him some answers at least and keep it out of Catherine's mind. Father Matthews mind, on the other hand, started to race. If Michael was alive, where on the island was he? And why wasn't he coming home?

"OK, Dad, we can talk wedding stuff." Father Matthew was even happy to do that if it meant he could see Michael. They all returned to their lunch. After they had cleared everything away, Catherine texted Michael. 'Come to tea tonight I want to talk wedding stuff xxx'.

She was excited at the thought of another night of wedding planning.

Dr Mitchell picked up the phone and read Catherine's text.

Chapter 7

Father Matthew spent the afternoon trying to reassure the residents that everything was now returning to normal. It was far from the truth, but he prayed that it soon would be. His general update was that there were more police on the island and they were closing in on whoever had done these terrible crimes. After that he helped set the tea out with the team. Unfortunately, Michael had not shown up or replied to Catherine's text which had started to worry her. Before he knew it, it was time to take the drive back over to the hotel for the six-p.m. update.

Detectives Morris and Green were already there along with Nigel, Albert Finlay, Judge Reynolds, Hayley and Kevin and Stacey when Father Matthew arrived.

"I think this is all of us. Ian isn't joining; he is preparing food as this curfew has people eating earlier than normal." Stacey was keen to point out he wasn't just missing.

"Thank you. OK, let us start the update. I have been speaking with the prison and Chris James is going to be continuing his search; so far we have found over forty-two envelopes of the drug known as M in the cells." There was a shared look from everyone. Nobody had expected this, especially for it to be so common place in the prison. Something they were assured, not less than eight hours ago, it wasn't.

"Clearly, this is getting into the prison somehow. Chris James is looking at all the processes and we need to…" Detective Morris started to look around the room.

"I was hoping Dr Mitchell would be here, to be honest." Detective Morris was keen to have a conversation with him as he was the only licenced person on the island to deal with any type of drugs.

"We have a DS this evening. I presume he is at the prison preparing for that." Everyone looked at the Father, and then back to Detective Morris.

"Thank you, Father, With everything that has been going on I had almost forgotten that one myself." There was a silence. They all knew who the death sentence was for this evening. The world would be watching their Island once more.

"Once a complete search of the prison is done, we will question the inmates, starting with the ones with most drugs in their possession. This will hopefully lead us to the person or persons that are responsible for trafficking the drugs on the island. We still have a missing person's alert out for Sister Sarah and Michael Peterson."

"Detective, I accompanied Nigel to the Petersons this morning, and whilst neither of them, or Dr Mitchell, has seen Michael, my daughter has had three messages from him since Sunday night. Two on Monday and one this morning." This was a surprise to all of them. They had all started to fear the worst for the missing residents. Nigel wrote it down in his note book, he actually wrote two words: still alive. This made him even more of a suspect for Nigel; if he wasn't missing, why was he hiding?

"I would like to see that phone, Father, if that is possible? What did these messages say?"

"They were just terms of endearment, the type you send to your girlfriend. Good morning and good night, that sort of thing, but at least it is positive that he is still in contact wherever he is." Father Matthew was keen to put a positive spin on his findings, but deep down he knew how Michael's disappearance could be perceived given the current island situation.

"I agree at least that is a good sign for his wellbeing, if he is the person with the phone. We know from the boat logs that he hasn't left the island so he is still here somewhere. I would like to upgrade his status to a person of interest now that we believe he is not exactly missing." Detective Morris had suddenly also had the same thoughts as Nigel.

"A person of interest, Detective?"

"Yes, a person of interest, Father. He knew both of the victims, and at this present moment does not have an alibi for either murder. He is also missing from work and from home. That makes someone a person of interest in my book." Detective Morris paused and looked directly at the Father. He knew what she meant by that; he also knew that she thought the same of him. He was also a person of interest.

"We will continue to hunt down the supply of drugs, look for the two, missing people, as we still don't know where Michael is, and meet back here tomorrow at eleven a.m. I think that is all I have for this evening's update." Detective Morris was keen to wrap this up; they could all tell.

"Detective Morris."

"Yes, Mr Finlay?" She wasn't expecting a questions-and-answer session, but she was willing to listen.

"Although I have a cause for concern on how the drugs have got into the prison which, believe me, will be fully investigated. I have more cause for concern on how the drugs got onto the island. We know it is not from the ferry given the fact that we have trained sniffer dogs at every crossing. There are also strict laws forbidding the fishermen to dock on the mainland without certification making it almost impossible for that to be a route into the island as well. Have you got any idea how it is getting here? There is one thing discovering what we have, and another stemming the flow."

"We have not yet ascertained that point. I assure you, Mr Finlay, it is a priority for us too."

"What I say is that it must be from the prison, or the guards. We have never had any issues with drugs on the island until the prison came here." Kevin was looking directly at Albert Finlay with a glance at Father Matthew. Detective Morris knew it was natural that people were now assigning blame to this situation. The prison was always going to be the target, and in turn, so would Father Matthew. He was the one that convinced them all it would be a good thing for the island. Up until three days ago he had been right.

"I will reiterate my point. We do not know who or how the supply is getting to the island. What I can say is that we do believe that it is being cut with the ashes of murderers as advertised, and previously mentioned. We have had independent people looking at this on the mainland, and we can confirm that there are traces of bone, human remains and maple wood, which is the standard prison coffin for this prison. There is however no point blaming each other for what has happened. From experience I know that murderers are murderers; they do not change because of circumstances. It's already part of who they are." Detective Morris gave a look to all of them to reiterate the point. She, as with Father Matthew, knew how quickly these things could get out of hand.

"Do we think Michael Peterson is in on this? Is he the murderer and the drug dealer? He had the access; he had the ashes." Kevin was only saying what they had all started to think. He knew all the victims, and had access to the prison.

"He wouldn't be involved in such a thing, Kevin; he is a good lad. I see him twice a week down the Fleece, hardly drinks and studies most of his nights. I can't see it being him." Only Stacey was coming to his defence. She did look at Father Matthew as she spoke. Father Matthew was silent. All of this led back to his home, his family. The longer Michael was missing, the longer he was concerned for him.

"Again, I will reiterate my point: we do not know who, or how this drug has got to the island. Now, I suggest we call an end to this before we come up with a theory of guilt for everyone on the island." As Detective Morris spoke, she glanced another look directly at the Father. Other people in the room noticed that this time. The detectives left the building slowly followed by Nigel and Albert Finlay.

"What do you think, Stacey?"

"I don't know, Hayley; I just want them to catch the sickos as soon as possible so we can move on with our lives. This is affecting trade now and we can little afford that either." Stacey knew it wasn't the time to bring up money, but it was all Ian had talked about all afternoon. Who was going to reimburse them if this curfew went on for weeks?

"What about you, Judge? You seem very quiet." The judge again hadn't said a word in the entire meeting.

"I have known a lot of cases, Hayley, and this is no different; they just need to follow the chain of events and the truth will come out."

"The truth always comes out in the end, doesn't it, Judge?" Father Matthew directed that question directly at the judge. He played the words over in his head again. He wished he hadn't been so harsh in the tone. But with every look at the judge he could see Alana's body on the ground in front of him. The judge could feel the stare at him, but he didn't look up to give his answer. To most in the room it felt a deflection of guilt which they didn't expect.

"It does, Father, and it's always the people we suspect the least... In my experience."

There was a longer silence at his reply. The detective had been right; everyone was now starting to look at each other as a potential murderer. Father Matthew broke the silence.

"Anyway, I will take my leave of you all, and I will be back at eleven tomorrow. Along with the doctor I have a sentence to carry out this evening." Father Matthew wanted to leave before this mud continued to fly. This changed the focus in the room back to the Father for a totally different reason.

"I think everyone on the island has noted tonight in the diary, Father."

"Yes, I am afraid that they have, and I am sure it is not just here in the island, Stacey. The eyes of the world are on Callington Island this evening. Which given the current circumstances is not a good thing."

"I wish you luck if that is the right word, Father. I am not sure I would want to hear his confession, no matter how much we all think we know already. With any luck, Father, you will get, the father, if you know what I mean. I am sure that is easier to hear." As Kevin spoke, the whole room was listening. They all knew who Father Matthew was visiting this evening.

Father Matthew just nodded at them all. The whole world knew this case. Father Matthew had the unfortunate job of taking the confession of the world's self-proclaimed greatest serial killer of all time. He had, over a few years, held the whole of the United Kingdom in terror.

Father Matthew made his exit. After he left, the conversation went on well into the night, and the whispers of potential suspects started to flow around the town. Michael had been one, but the Father was also on the list now. He could copycat any murderer in detail as he had listened to all their confessions. Frighteningly he was now heading to hear probably the worst confession of all. There was lots of talk about the next murder, and if it would be copying the latest confession Father Matthew had heard. Everyone had a thought about what that could potentially look like. Some of the victims had legend status across the UK. People would still talk about where they were when the ONE was caught.

Father Matthew took the drive over to the prison, and was met at the gates by Chris James. He had been out walking in the fresh air. Father Matthew figured that even a security guard needed a break from being locked up twelve hours a day.

"Evening, Father, I will walk you in."

"Thank you, Chris, how is the search going?"

"We are complete, Father. We found over one hundred envelopes, and we have three potential ring leaders in the prison, so it's only a matter of time. I have to tell you, Father, I am really disappointed in it all. I thought we were better than this." Father Matthew could hear the disappointment in his voice. He really meant what he said. Chris James loved his job. It was everything to him.

"We won't be doing any more this evening though as this event, sorry, sentence, Father, is far too important."

"I didn't see any press at the gates, Chris? I was expecting a crowd of people on the island, to be fair. Given who it is."

"No, Father, we decided the closest they were allowed to be was the port. Especially given recent events. They weren't happy, but we used the excuse about all the issues it caused at the second sentencing. We have rigged up a light to The Fleece pub to tell the press when it is done. Nigel and the other detectives have allowed The Fleece to have a lock-in from nine p.m. given the interest. It is best to control it all in one place. There was just one other person that came to the island on the six p.m. boat; they have allowed her to come through. Mrs Gosling is here, Father. I am sure you remember her, from York. She was one of the few that managed to escape his wrath." Father Matthew did remember; it was thanks to her that he was finally caught.

"That sounds very sensible. I am sure Ian is happy about that too, he has been complaining about trade for the last few days. The less people we have wondering around on the island at the moment, the better. I will make sure I make time to speak to Mrs Gosling afterwards should she need it." Chris James nodded his head at the Father. There was a mutual respect between them grown from everything they had to witness at the prison.

"Father. I have known some evil people in my days, Father, but this lad, this lad, he is the worst. I am not saying that just because of everything that we know, but also because you can feel it when you are around him, Father. I don't know what it is, but I can feel something. The face of an angel and the heart of the devil my mum would say."

They walked in silence the rest of the way until they reached the cell. As with Jacob a few days ago, he had just finished his last meal, and his hands and feet were chained to the bed. He was sitting with his hands on his lap as if he was in school, staring at the wall opposite to him. He was waiting patiently for Father Matthew. He was almost excited about the meeting. He had been telling anyone that would listen that he had some one-on-one time with the Father this evening. Other than his height, his frame and stature were similar to Nigel's, he looked as if he could still have been in college although in his late twenties now. Chris had been fair in his judgement. He looked like butter wouldn't melt in his mouth. He turned and smiled as he heard the cell unlock.

"Evening, Father, I have been waiting for you. It is so lovely to see you again." He held out his hand as much as he could. Father Matthew shook it as he entered the cell.

"Good evening, Mr Carson."

"You can call me Edmund, Father, I told you that."

Chapter 8

"Father, there are no formalities in here. You and I, Father, we are men of the faith." Father Matthew ignored the comment. He knew what Edmund was referring to. Edmund Carson was known for playing characters whilst he was on his murder spree; one of the more famous ones was a priest called Father Harry. Father Matthew didn't want to get into that debate again. He changed the subject as quickly as he could.

"OK, Edmund. How was your meal?"

"Bland, Father, but just before we get to that, I do need to ask you, how was the press on your way in? Is it busy out there? The usual suspects I suppose? BBC, SKY? We are close friends now." Edmund had been repeatedly asking Chris James what was going on outside the prison since the day he arrived. Chris didn't entertain the conversation with him. Chris had never mentioned it to anyone, but he had lost a family member to Edmund a few months before he was actually caught. A lot of people had lost family members to Edmund over the years. Chris had lost a niece walking home from a night out in Camden. She and her friend had been to a club, and she was discovered floating in the canal with her throat cut. The other girl had been found on the canal bank with her insides taken out curtousey of Edmund Carson.

"There is nobody there, Edmund. They are all still down by the docks. It is better and safer for everyone that way."

"I suppose it would be hard to contain them all up here; there is a pub down there too if I remember? They will all be raising a glass to me no doubt. Giving them a little more work. I tell you the world's press can make a difference, can make or break your career, Father. I would know. Anyway. Dinner. Father, I was told, well, more led to believe, that for your last meal on this planet you are entitled to eat whatever you so desire? Isn't that in our book, Father? The bible, I have read it somewhere, I know that."

"No, Edmund, not in the bible, but it is generally true; you can eat what you want. I believe they do try to accommodate everyone here at the prison."

"Well, apparently not everyone, Father. What I asked for was the liver of an eleven-year-old boy, poached in his blood for about four to five minutes with some really, really fresh bread. The bread makes all the difference, Father. Straight out of the oven if possible. That is always the best time." Father Matthew watched as Edmund mimicked dipping the bread into the blood. Over the years it had been rumoured that he did that with quite a few victims. Dipped fresh bread into them and then ate it, but it was never actually proved or reported on in full. Although he never denied it, and did quite often boast of its taste. Father Matthew had no reason to doubt that Edmund was serious.

"What I got was liver from a three-year-old cow with a little cream, and what I can only guess is last week's bread that they feed to the birds. I tell you, Father, what is the world coming to? If they had given me the ingredients, I could have done it myself, Father. I would have made a great celebrity chef, you know. Even wrote a cookbook whilst I was in here. It is still at my last prison. I expect the guards have had it published by now, and they are living off the royalties. I am sure your wife has a copy Father. Why wouldn't she?"

Edmund wasn't completely wrong in his thinking. A guard had actually stolen the book from his cell and sold his cookbook to a newspaper for a six-figure sum. It was yet to be released though. Given the amount of press Edmund had had in his lifetime, the press were keeping it until after the events of this evening. The publishers knew how much money they were going to make if they put it on sale the day after the world's press reported on his passing.

Father Matthew knew this was the start of the confession that he had been dreading to hear. The only thing that had kept his mind occupied and away from today was that the world outside this prison was getting more dangerous than the one inside the prison.

"Sorry about the liver thing, Father. It is the entertainer in me; I like to create a shock. I knew they weren't going to get me one. Besides, I always found eleven-year-olds do not taste of much. Especially boys. Girls always taste that little bit sweeter, don't you think father?" Father Matthew knew his whole back catalogue of work. He knew that if anyone knew if that were true or not it would be Edmund Carson.

"So how does this work now? No, don't tell me; I should know. It has been a while since I took a confession from anyone. They were always in a booth, Father, behind like a little window. I always worried about that, Father; is there a reason for the window?

And, why can't you really see who it is? I often wondered if it was because of the details. You know, Father, you get some hot girl come in and tell you what she had been up to all weekend with a bloke called Zac and her friend called Nicole. One thing leads to another and when she starts telling you the whipped cream was her idea, you start whipping a little cream of your own. If you know what I am saying? I did find tissues in quite a few booths father. I know they were not really all for the tears." Father Matthew knew exactly what he was saying. He wasn't going to rise to it though. He knew Edmund liked to talk; the world knew Edmund liked to talk.

"Not a prison, Father, never took a confession in a prison. Maybe I should have. I have a lot of fans in here, Father. I should have worked with some of them. Confession is a funny old game, Father. I don't envy you having to do that job. I tell you, I have heard stuff that would curl your hair." From the press reports, Edmund had spent a few months impersonating a priest across the country. Taking confession, and even giving services. Edmund had been so skilled and convincing in the roles he had played that he had whole villages believing he was who he said he was.

"So, I start with the old 'forgive me, Father, for I have sinned' stuff. Tell you everything I have done wrong, then you forgive me, and I can go to Heaven; is that the deal?"

"It is up to you what you share, just know that if you are truly sorry for the crimes you have committed, it will help you in the afterlife." This was a big test for Father Matthew's faith. Everyone deserved a shot at absolution, but even he wasn't sure that Edmund did.

He had caused more misery than any one person across the whole of the UK during his three-year murder spree.

"Then I am screwed, Father, as I am not sorry for who I am. Why would I be? I am a Legend, Father, you know that. Number ONE, Father, number ONE. Forgive the pun, Father. When I created that character, the ONE, I just didn't know how much use the world would get out of it. The songs. The T-shirts. I presume you had some of the T-shirts, didn't you, Father? Probably more of a Father Harry fan than the ONE though. You see, Father, I don't really believe in the afterlife. Well, I say I don't believe. I have some questions, Father. I can ask questions, can't I, Father?" Father Matthew nodded. His first and only thought at that point was questions would be easier than listening to some of the things he knew Edmund had committed.

"What type of questions, Edmund?"

"I want to know, when I get to heaven... Because I will confess everything, Father, and you can then do the whole sign thing and wiz me up there. When I get to heaven, will I get everything I want? I understand heaven is paradise, right? So, I am kind of thinking, my paradise is a little different to yours." Edmund was looking at Father Matthew for a response. He just nodded for Edmund to continue.

"I suppose it comes down to one particular question. This is a tricky one, Father, so take your time. Are blondes allowed into heaven, Father? Because if they are, how is it really heaven?"

Father Matthew didn't know what to say. That wasn't the question he thought this was leading to. He thought he could tell from the look on Edmund's face that he was joking, but he wasn't sure. Edmund had a way about him that would make you feel at ease and scared beyond belief at the same time. His history noted that he was very unstable. In the six weeks that Father Matthew had been visiting him, he was still waiting to see the monster that had the world captivated.

"I am just kidding, Father. I know they are not allowed in. Why would they be? God and I have similar tastes. I mean, if he gives those arseholes that blow stuff up forty virgins when they get up there, I am in for a pretty decent time. I can sort it out directly with him if you like, Father? Skip all this confession stuff. I am sure he will want to hear it all first hand from me anyway. I must say I am looking forward to being front page news again tomorrow, to be honest." Over the last ten years, Edmund had been obsessed with the press. He had become an expert in social media and for a while shared every victim with them. Even when the press and the government got together and stopped reporting, he would send them details directly.

"Then I can leave you in peace for the next hour if you should so wish." Father Matthew got up to leave. Maybe letting him share his stories where he was going was the best thing that could happen for both of them.

"Wow, you give up easily, Father. No, I want you to stay, I want to confess to you. You and I are kindred spirits father, I can tell. There are still things people don't know about me, Father; there are things I have done which are yet to be discovered. I always have to keep a little bit back for my fans, don't I? I can share this with you. Hell, I want to share this with you. Can't let anyone else take credit for my work, can I? Let's sit, chat, talk a little; I want to tell you everything."

Father Matthew sat back down. He had feared this. Edmund Carson was proud of his achievements. He was another inmate who had waived council at his hearing and wanted to represent himself. If truth be known, he liked the sound of his own voice, and he just wanted to take the opportunity to showboat. His court case had lasted six months, and it had become something legendary across the whole world. Mostly because of what had happened to the first judge.

Edmund Carson was classed as the biggest serial killer of the modern age. He had not just killed people; he killed hundreds of people. He slept with the corpses, he ate their body parts, and he staged little plays for the police for when they were found. All playing out some sick and twisted game in his head. He created characters to entertain the people. To keep the press hungry, he would write to them after the attacks, in great detail so everyone could know what he had done, and how he had done it. Edmund Carson was a real Social Media Murderer. The first of his kind.

Edmund didn't care that the world knew what he looked like. He wanted to be famous. He would take selfies outside of the victim's doors and with their dead bodies and post them online on social media. He was proud of his work, and as far as he was concerned, he was good at it. He lasted on the run over thirty-six months with over one hundred and ninety known victims. This number had always been underestimated. Rumours were rife that it was ten times that. Every missing person over that time was linked with Edmund Carson. His reign of terror had spread that far. Father Matthew knew all of this, and now, the legend that was Edmund Carson, wanted to share everything with him.

All Father Matthew wanted was for this to be over and done with.

"So, Edmund, where would you like to start? I am really interested in the things that nobody else knows. The stuff you refer to as undiscovered. If you really want to confess something, start with that; it will help you with the closure." Father Matthew was sure that if he was going to have to listen to this, he was going to try to get something out of it in return. Some peace for those families of Edmund's victims would be a great place to start.

"Not yet, Father, let's start at the beginning, Father, at the beginning. I have been dying to tell this story. People in here just don't want to listen."

"Edmund, the world knows the beginning. I want to help you give peace to those who may still need it."

"They don't know all the beginning, Father. Indulge me. I promise I will give you everything you need to save the souls of the people that need it."

Father Matthew nodded at him to start. He was just going to have to endure this evening which, after everything else that was going, on was really going to test his faith.

"This is so exciting, Father; I can't tell you how good it is to finally have someone who wants to listen to me one-on-one. The guards are no fun, Father; most of them won't even look at me. Especially the big guy. The one in charge downright ignores me. But you, Father, you will be my salvation."

Edmund had craved attention his whole life. The police knew this and, after what they believed to be about a hundred killings, so did the press. They believed the press was feeding his ego and his killing spree. So, when he was eventually caught and placed on trial there were no press, no cameras. It didn't matter to Edmund; he still showboated for the judge, jury and legal representation. He truly believed at some point someone would write a book about him. At least a trilogy, and they would interview the people in the courtroom, and everything that happened in there would go down in history. Unfortunately, he was once more correct. One of the jurors sold his story six months after his sentencing to a local paper and that did make it into a book written about him. To date, the court case had figured in six of the nine books written about Edmund Carson. Edmund Carson was the most famous serial killer of all time. All his work, as he would have called it, had paid off. Madame Tussauds in London even commissioned him to their chamber of horrors, shortly after his arrest. It had been quite the attraction. People from all over the world visited to get a selfie... and survive it, with the man himself.

"OK, let's start. My mother died, Father. My father abused me from an early age, and kids at school picked on me. I tried to kill myself several times, but just never got the hang of it... Isn't that what I am supposed to say?" Edmund started to laugh. He was clearly going to enjoy this.

"Sorry, Father, none of that is true. My mother and father loved me. I was worshipped as a king at school, and I have never tried to kill myself... Why would I? When I enjoy working with other people so much. Life is a gift, Father, you have to experience every moment of it. You never know when it may be your last breath."

Father Matthew was holding his bible in both hands on his lap in front of him. This was already testing him.

Edmund had a swagger about him for such a young person. The confidence in which he spoke showed Father Matthew the true depth of who he was. He was proud of himself, in what he had become.

"Enough waffle now, down to business, Father. Forgive me, Father, for I have sinned. It has been about six years since my last confession. My only confession, I think. Anyway, I will get on with it. My first, oh, my first, Father, she was beautiful. We had been dating for around six months. I was fifteen-ish. She was nineteen or eighteen, I forget; she didn't know my real age. To be fair, she didn't ask, she just presumed I went to the same college as she did as I was always around the same quadrant in her school. I used to bring her back to my parents after school, well, after school in the morning, and we would spend the whole afternoon in bed. My parents worked late, and I was always fending for myself." Edmund paused at that point as if to remember something about his parents. The truth was Edmund was never left fending for himself. His father and mother did dote on him and would always ensure that he came first.

"Anyway, yes, we were home one afternoon, and she found a picture of me in a drawer. Caroline. Caroline, Father, I have been racking my head over that name since I started this conversation. I have forgotten that girl so many times. Anyway, my mother had put the date and my age on the back of the photo. I came into the room, and she went mad at me, said she was a paedophile. At the time, I didn't even know what one of those was. Turns out, Father, she was. Then she started hitting me and hitting me. I hit her back. No, that is a lie, Father, I didn't hit her. I wouldn't hit a woman, Father. I gently pushed her, and she fell backwards, and her head hit the bedside cabinet. She was just lying there on the floor. There was blood coming from her head, Father. I can still smell that blood, Father; I can smell it as if it was yesterday, more powerful than any perfume. It has always had an effect on me, Father, blood. It drew me towards it. Like a calling father. It called to me." Edmund was losing himself again within his own thoughts. Father Matthew coughed. He didn't like the thought of Edmund re-living the situation. It wasn't appropriate that he should enjoy those actions for a second time.

"Anyway, you would know about a calling. Where was I? Yes, I ended up sitting on top of her and, I don't know why, I dipped my fingers into the blood and put it to my lips. Father, I tell you, it was the sweetest thing I have ever tasted, warm, rich." He paused again. Father Matthew wasn't sure if Edmund was really thinking it or doing it for dramatic effect now. Either way, he didn't like it.

"And you were sorry for that?" Father Matthew spoke to stop Edmund having the moment.

"Hell no, sorry, Father, won't swear again. I was excited about it, and I mean excited, Father. We had sex right there on the floor. By this time, I was kissing her all over her face. It smudged the blood all over; the taste of her had always been great, but now, Father, now with all the blood all over her body, now it was amazing. Strange thing was though, she woke up halfway through our lovemaking. Made it feel a bit creepy, Father, I have to confess, so I took the lamp from the table and without stopping bashed her head into the floor. Just to help her release a little bit more blood for my pleasure. What came next, Father, I can only describe as the best sex ever."

There was a silence. Father Matthew knew there were over a hundred of these stories, and he didn't want to hear all of them. Over his reign of terror Edmund had become the bogey man that everyone had feared.

"I threw her in the river, Father. Canal, sorry. Although I am not sure what the difference is? Weighted down the body, and to this day I think she is still there. Caroline Lipwig, or Lipvig, something like that. The college thought she was dating a fellow student, but clearly, she wasn't; I was still at upper school at the time. I think she is still one of my unknown. I don't remember confessing that to anyone. Father, you are really good at your job. Really bring the stories out of me." Edmund mouthed the words well done to Father Matthew as if to give him some special recognition for the part he played in his little confession.

"Do you wish me to contact her parents and tell them what happened to her, Edmund?" Father Matthew was keen to let him know that he wasn't to thank for this act. This was all down to Edmund.

"Do I? That would be fantastic, Father. Don't forget to tell them the part about great sex. I think it's important they know that their little girl was good at something. Especially once I had worked with her. Parents like to hear these things. Makes them proud." Edmund's smile, although sweet, scared Father Matthew. It lit from his mouth to his eyes, but Father Matthew knew what was behind those eyes. Evil. Pure evil. Chris was right in what he had said on the way into the prison. Father Matthew didn't want to ask but he knew so far

Edmund hadn't confessed any of his sins. He was just warming up to the real stuff.

"Oh, and tell them they can keep the wheelbarrow. That is what I weighed her down with. It was my dad's, but he doesn't need it now. I think they have made our house into some kind of monument to me." Father Matthew knew Edmund believed that. Edmund believed that the outside world worshipped him and loved everything he did.

"Is there anything else you would like to confess, Edmund?" Father Matthew held his breath, but not for long; Edmund was as he had feared just getting started.

"Yes, Father, next were my parents. Where to start, where to start? I never got everything I wanted, Father. I couldn't really understand that... They had lots and never gave me everything I wanted. Was that too much to ask of them? It was around the same time as the best sex of my life that I had asked them for a motorbike. I was coming up to sixteen and I just wanted a little 125cc to impress the girls at school. I mean college. School girls didn't interest me as much... back then." Edmund gave Father Matthew a wink. He knew what that meant. He knew that story was coming at some point. It was one of his most infamous.

"I mean, it was less than a grand. A grand, Father. But, no, I had to earn it, get a part-time job... Me? Working in a fast food restaurant, I don't think so. So, one day I came home and went into the kitchen. The gas supply was under the sink. I made a small cut in the pipe that led round to the cooker. And then left. I didn't know what was going to happen; would it gas them; would they die from poisoning or explosion? I have to say, I was excited again. I rode away thinking... Insurance, that is how I get my bike. That, and the fact that if I didn't see them again, I wouldn't have to ask for anything anymore. I could just have what I wanted when I wanted it."

"And did you, Edmund? Did you see your mother and father again?" Edmund had paused, and Father Matthew filled the silence. He had decided he was going to try and ensure that Edmund didn't relive any of his stories.

"Ah, that would be telling, Father; you need to listen to the whole story. I went to one of those fast food restaurants that they had wanted me to work in... I thought it was fitting I be there at their end. Then, after about an hour I returned to see if it had worked. It hadn't. I was riding up my road and I could still see my house. No explosion. No big ball of flames. I could hope for gassing them, but had a feeling I had messed it up. I thought maybe I hadn't done it properly; maybe the cut wasn't big enough. I mean, how much is too much or too little gas? Turns out it needed a little over an hour. As I was about to get off my push bike, BANG!" Edmund shouted and clapped his hands at the same time. Father Matthew jumped backwards, and Chris James jumped into the doorway. Edmund didn't notice either action, and just continued with his story.

"The whole thing went up like a bomb. Knocked me to the ground. The papers said I was the luckiest boy alive. I was in the news everywhere; it was amazing, my face, and my name, on every TV channel. Although, I grew to hate the photo they used, Father. I made up for that and gave them so many more. Father, I had offers of adoption from at least twenty couples. I was a celebrity in our town. No, more than a celebrity, I was a god in our town. I loved it, Father, absolutely loved it. I tell you, Father, it got me some action… No, wait, it got me lots of action. If they ever ask you, Father, in one of my movies which I am sure you will have a part in now, I said it got me lots of action."

Father Matthew didn't want to be excited by Edmund, but showmanship was in his blood. Even telling a story that could horrify you, he had a way of sucking you into it. He could feel himself wanting to know more of the story. Even though he had heard it at least a dozen times before on the news or in the papers.

"Turns out, my parents did love me after all; the house was insured and there were insurances and wills made out to me. I cleared nearly two million out of that, the newspapers, and TV. People wanted to interview me, and pay me for it. I tell you: life was on the up. Thanks to them. The press that is. It was nothing less than I had deserved."

A few years after killing his parents, when Edmund Carson was still on the run, a high court judge had ruled the first ever national press blackout. He said that under no uncertain terms could his name and his crimes be mentioned. He stated that the media had helped create a monster, and it was their responsibility to help catch him, not to glorify him. It didn't stop the killings though. If anything, it made Edmund travel more, and do more so that the world could hear him.

"They were your parents, Edmund. Did you not stop to think that they were just trying to teach you a sense of responsibility?" Edmund didn't rise to Father Matthew's bait. Ignoring his question, he seamlessly moved on.

"The press was a drug, Father; the more fame you got the more you wanted it. They were all feeling sorry for me. They didn't need to feel sorry for me. I was soon going to be rich and famous. I had the world at my fingertips. There were girls falling all over me, not just girls, Father, women. Real women!" Edmund paused again. It always worried Father Matthew what he was thinking about in case he wasn't just remembering the events. Everyone knew the story of the court case. They knew how quickly things could change in Edmund Carson's mind. Before he could fill the silence, Edmund started again much to Father Matthew's relief.

"Don't get me wrong, Father, I nailed a lot of them. And I mean a lot. But it wasn't the same; it wasn't the same as Caroline; something was missing. It had to be the blood. So, I decided to recreate it. This girl I had met, Sophia something, I forget now. Worked in a florist, I remember that. I remember buying flowers for my nan from her. No reason just because she was my nan. I went back to her parents' house whilst they were sleeping. Her room was on the ground floor which was great, and I had recreated the whole scene within an hour. I made sure I worked with her properly this time as I didn't like the fact that Caroline woke up halfway through… It was amazing, Father, amazing. But as I sat there next to Sophia, Sophia, nope, thought I had her name again then; I wanted more. I didn't tell her that. I think I told her it was too quiet, and we needed to enjoy it a bit more next time. So, I was going to take care of it with her family so we could. I tell you, Father, women will believe anything that I tell them. She had a mother and father upstairs and a little brother. I could see the press: *little orphan boy in quadruple family horror,*

Edmund returns, Edmund Carson five times a night; hundreds of press titles came through my head. I would be once again the centre of attention. I took a knife from the drawer and crept upstairs… The little boy's room was open so I just had to walk in. I worked with him just like they do in the movies. I was tempted to take his head off; how cool would that have been, Father, to wake up the parents holding their son's head, you know, like Medusa in Clash of the Titans." Edmund made a fist and held it out in front of him.

"I didn't, the smell of blood was too strong; it was overpowering me. The blood, Father, it was like Viagra, made me horny. I left the room and then ended up in Sophia, Sophia, Merson, Sophia Merson's parents' room. I knew I would remember the name, Father, it was just on the tip of my tongue. Sophia Merson. Odd how you can forget things, isn't it? So, sorry, yes, I entered the room and worked with the mother the same way. You know, a little ear to ear action." Edmund gestured the action of cutting her throat by dragging his own finger across his own neck. There was a hypnotic look in his eyes as he did.

"She had gone as quietly as her son. A bit of fitting, but nothing special. Her father, now that was another matter, he woke up, never worked with anyone awake before. We struggled for a while, and, to be honest, if I hadn't told him what I had just done to his family, he may have stopped me there and then. But I did, and it put him off balance. The knife went straight through his eye and into the back of his brain. Wow, that made a mess. But the rush, Father, oh, the rush of it all. I was horny again, Father, and it had always been one of my fantasies to do a mother and a daughter, not together, you understand; I am a one-woman-at-a-time type of guy, and that threesome-thing is a little creepy. So, I placed Mr Merson, into the chair in the corner of the room and made love to his wife." The smile on Edmund's face was taking its toll on Father Matthew. He was trying to tune out of the conversation by reciting the Lord's Prayer in his head, but with every twist and turn, he found himself tuning back into Edmund.

"Oh, this was better. She was fuller and just bouncier; do you know what I mean? Younger women just don't feel the same, Father; it was so much better with an older woman. I did stop halfway through and took the knife out of Mr Merson's eye so he could see what we were doing. I think he enjoyed it if I am honest. One of my favourite memories, Father. I can tell you. Funny how you forget about these things, and then all of a sudden, there they are back in your mind."

At this point Father Matthew was watching the clock and not making eye contact with Edmund. He was resisting getting into Edmund's world as much as he could. He knew time was nearly up, and Edmund wasn't going to get through his whole autobiography. He could be there for a month and he would not get through all the events in Edmund Carson's life. Father Matthew could see a light at the end of a very dark tunnel.

"I didn't want them to be found like that, Father; they were a nice family and I guess helped me get on my path. That was where the ideas started to flow. So, I took all the bodies into the living room. Made a mess of the hallway carpet, I can tell you. Placed them round the coffee table and even set up a game of scrabble for them. It was great. I gave the police so many clues that they never picked up on. On the board and in their hands were words like: fire, parents, orphans, sex. I was spelling out it was me without using my name. The police thought it was to do with the family, but it was all about me. A year later, I had to include it into my You Tube channel, a confession, as they hadn't linked that one to me. You have seen the You Tube confession, right? My first one. I guess I have done this more than once then. Never thought about that. Never had a confession seen by a billion people before, have you, Father? Anyway, where was I? Oh yeah, idiots, there are so many they don't even recognise me for… Even I can't remember them all. It was their fault. If they had not installed the blackout, we would have had documentation for everything. Now they could write a book about the missing years of Edmund Carson let alone the stories they already know." Edmund's voice had changed. He wanted to ensure the world knew of all of his work. It was important to him that the world knew who he was, and what he had become.

"It's time." Chris James walked into the cell.

"No, it can't be, we haven't even started. I wanted to tell you, Father. I wanted to tell you the ones I never got time to report on. They deserve it too. I need to ensure they get it correct, the number. The number is important for the film, sorry, films, they will never be box office smashes without the right number. The ONE, Father Harry, The Alphabet Killer. Somebody needs to tell the world, Father." Edmund was well aware that in today's film industry his story would be a blockbuster. The first of his films had already been made, but they were under strict guidelines not to tell him about it. From the age of fifteen, he had lived the life of a celebrity, for all the wrong reasons. In his mind he would always be remembered as one. The ONE.

"It's. Time!" Chris wasn't playing his games.

"Edmund, wherever you end up I hope you are at peace." Father Matthew stood up to leave the cell.

"Wait. You don't forgive me, Father?" Father Matthew waited with Chris just outside the cell for the other guards to arrive to undo his chains.

"Edmund, you are not looking for forgiveness; you are looking for publicity. I don't believe that you have any regrets about your life."

The guards surrounded Edmund as he walked out of the cell. The rattling of the bars started as all the inmates acknowledged his walk to the chair. Edmund looked as pleased as could be. In his head, it was more praise and admiration for him.

"That's not true, Father, I have regrets. Lots of regrets. I never got to meet Sandra Bullock, Father; that is one of my regrets. Can you imagine, Father? Me and Sandra? Now, that would be a movie, Father. An eighteen certificate if you know what I mean?"

Father Matthew didn't respond to him.

"Father, I still have so much to say. I have so much they don't know about. It will be good for the people to know Father." Edmund was smiling from ear to ear, but he sounded genuine. Father Matthew was sure that Edmund still had stories to tell.

"I think they know enough, Edmund."

As they walked, the noise from the other cells increased. There was banging and cheering. Everyone knew Edmund. The world had been waiting for this moment. Ian had rigged up a clock in The Fleece pub for the press and was counting down the minutes to the end of Edmund Carson.

They reached their destination. As ever, Father Matthew took the first door as they took the second. In the room was only one woman. She had been one of Edmund's last victims. She had survived an attack on her doorstep, and after coming round an hour later, she played dead even though she could see her whole family laid out before her. They hadn't been as lucky. Her eleven-year-old son, her husband, and her daughter had been killed. When she awoke, Edmund was eating the liver of her son as she lay as lifeless as she could on the sofa in the living room. She had recognised her attacker, and knew that if she moved it was certain death.

Edmund had created the scene of a family movie-night in. After spending some of the evening cooking for all of them he had left the father and the daughter lying in front of the TV whilst her and her son were on the sofa and in the chair. Edmund loved a good scene. He was only caught because she happened to have her mobile in her pocket. She had dialled 999 and had left the line open. It took them a while, but they were able to trace the call to the house. Edmund walked out of the house straight into the police, and all the press. He didn't put up a fight; in fact, when the police approached him, he had been seen to be laughing with them.

Father Matthew took the seat behind her in case she needed some comfort. They sat there in silence for a good ten minutes, but the screen didn't come up. Suddenly the door to the right of them opened and Albert Finlay walked in.

"Father, can I have a word?" Father Matthew placed a hand on the woman's shoulder and then stepped out into the hallway with Albert.

"We can't do it, Father. Neither Michael nor Dr Mitchell are in the prison grounds. We can't do anything unless we have a doctor present to pronounce the death, and Dr Mitchell signed himself out about four p.m. and hasn't returned."

As he finished talking, Edmund Carson was brought past the door again.

"Looks like we have time to finish our story after all, Father. I so look forward to that." There was a huge grin on his face as they carried on walking him back to his cell.

"OK, I will tell the young lady inside. You ring Nigel and Detective Morris, and tell them they are now both missing."

As the Father entered the little room, he could hear actual cheering from the inmates at the return of Edmund Carson.

Father Matthew consoled the young lady; he then took her to the hotel and got her booked in for the night. There was little they were going to be able to do in the dark. Dr Mitchell was now added to the ever-growing list of missing people.

Father Matthew then drove home to the church. He sat in his church at prayer for quite some time. The confessions of Edmund were brutal. Not only from what he had heard today, but of all the things he knew that Edmund had done. The world had watched as Edmund had terrorised the UK. Father Matthew couldn't remember the amount of times that he had prayed for his victims. It had seemed that it was every service for the past few years. The creation of the character Father Harry had hurt him the most. Edmund spent months preying on the people of the church. Killing at least a dozen of his brothers. Edmund had become a worldwide superstar in his own mind. This made him become even more elaborate as the victims racked up. The scenes of Edmund Carson had become a best-selling book and there was even an art exhibition dedicated to his work.

After a while of silent contemplation Father Matthew got up, walked to the altar, collected the keys, and then walked to the corner of the church, he unlocked the basement, and went in.

Chapter 9

Wednesday was the midweek lie-in for Father Matthew, although sleep had eluded him most of the night. It was two a.m. before he climbed into bed, and he was up again at eight. Mary and Catherine had already left to do the breakfast rush at the home. Father Matthew was sitting at the kitchen table with a cup of coffee when there was a knock at the door.

"Detective Morris, Detective Green, please do come in." They both wiped their shoes when entering the hallway.

"Thank you, Father."

"Is Nigel not with you?"

"No, Father, I have left him at the doctor's home. He is still doing a thorough search of the property. Early indications would seem he has packed some clothes and left his house for good."

Father Matthew took them into the kitchen and stood in the middle of the room.

"He has packed?" Father Matthew knew that wasn't a good sign. Missing people don't pack. Guilty people pack.

"Yes, we went there first thing this morning after finding out that the doctor had not been at the prison last night. There are clearly some clothes taken from his wardrobe, and as far as I can tell, his passport is missing. Plus, his medical kit and anything of any worth."

"And what, has he taken the evening or morning ferry off the island?"

"No, Father that is one of the things we are looking into. He hasn't registered to leave the island." Father Matthew walked over to the side where the kettle was.

"Sorry, Detectives, where are my manners; can I offer you some tea?"

"No, thank you, Father, we have a busy day in front of us. We just wanted to ask you a few questions, Father if that is OK?" Detective Morris beckoned Father Matthew over to his own kitchen table.

"OK, not a problem, sure, let's sit down." Detective Morris sat and so did Father Matthew. Detective Green stood by Detective Morris. Father Matthew didn't take that as a good sign either. It felt a little intimidating and clearly on purpose.

"We just want to go over a few things again. Can you tell us again your whereabouts on the night Sister Trinity was killed?"

"Yes, Detective, as I told Nigel, I was home with Michael and with Catherine and Mary. They were planning wedding flowers, I believe, and I was engrossed in a TV programme; I forget which one at the moment." Detective Morris had her notepad and pen in front of her now. Father Matthew couldn't read what was on it, but he could just about make out his name on the paper. A few times.

"Yes, but after they all went to bed, you went for a walk, and your wife recalls you going for about an hour and a half."

"That sounds about right, Detective. I took a walk around the grounds, and then I spent some time in the church preparing for mass on Sunday. It's my busiest day of the week." Detective Morris ticked a few points on her pad.

"But you didn't see anyone or speak to anyone in that time?"

"Detective, we don't get visitors to the church past eleven o'clock at night; there are very few religious emergencies."

"But you didn't see anyone or speak to anyone in that time?" Father Matthew was aware she was just repeating the same question. He was also aware that she had done so on purpose.

"No, Detective, I did not."

"And just to be sure nobody at the home saw you walking around the grounds?"

"I don't believe so, but if you ask them, they may have. There are plenty of rooms that back onto the church. All with windows."

"And the night that Alana was brutally stabbed to death in the hotel garden, you were where?" Father Matthew knew that was on purpose also. She was family and the detective was trying to get a rise out of him. It wasn't going to work.

"I was at the prison, and then I drove home, Detective."

"We have the doctor saying that you left a little after nine and arrived back home at eleven thirty. Your wife has confirmed that." Detective Morris was looking through her notepad as she spoke.

"That sounds about right, Detective. I left the prison, drove back to the church, and tidied up after the congregation. I left soon after evening mass was over to meet the doctor and Nigel, so I hadn't had a chance to, before. Once I had cleared up, I went home to bed." Father Matthew sat back in his chair.

"I am not sure what you are asking me these questions for, Detective? I don't really have anything new to tell you."

"We have to ensure that everyone is fully vetted, Father." Father Matthew knew it was more than that. Everyone up until the doctor, missing or killed, had a connection to him.

"I agree, Detective. Detective, are we no longer looking for two murderers? As it seems you are asking me about both instances."

"No, we are still looking for two, Father, we just are compiling a list of possible suspects for each one. And you, unfortunately, Father Matthew, do not have a credible alibi for either." Detective Morris paused to see if the Father would bite once more. He didn't.

"Once you eliminate the obvious, all that's left is the possible." Father Matthew smiled. He had used that line often in his sermons as it was one of his favourites.

"Sherlock Holmes, I believe. So, I am one of the possibilities. Detective?"

Detective Morris looked straight at him. She didn't need to nod or answer that question; they both knew the answer.

"Tell me about Sister Sarah, Father."

"OK, what would you like to know?" Father Matthew leaned forward in order to give Detective Morris his full attention.

"Just her in general, what you knew of her." Detective Morris flipped her pad over to a blank page to write down what the Father was saying.

"She was a nice girl, been with us since the beginning, about four years. I believe she came from Newcastle way originally, I don't think she had the best of an upbringing which led her into this service." Father Matthew watched as she made notes.

"We all have the calling for different reasons, Detective. Although ours is generally to do good, for our fellow man."

"And what was your relationship like with her? I mean, were you two close?" Father Matthew didn't like the way she used the word close. There had been a pause and emphasis put on the word.

"Close? No more than with any other of the sisters; we worked together on a daily basis. If what you are getting at is around her leaving, she hadn't mentioned wanting to go home at any point. So, we were all a bit shocked when she did."

Detective Morris sat looking directly at the Father to see if the expressions on his face were changing when he spoke. They weren't. She closed the pad in front of her. Detective Morris had just wanted to let the Father know that she was still looking into him. She had made a clear point.

"I am afraid you are one of the possibilities, Father, and it is my duty to tell you not to leave the island until this is resolved. Just a precaution, of course." Although surprised Father Matthew knew that statement was coming at some point after the conversation they had just had…

"OK, Detective, clearly it is quite a shock to me, but it isn't an issue; I have no plans to leave my home and my people in this hour of need. I have nothing to run from, Detective, so have no fear on that matter." Father

Matthew stood up wanting to indicate the end of the interview.

"Thank you, Father. Can I also ask you some further questions? Not related to yourself." Reluctantly he sat back down again.

"Of course, Detective, as I have said all along, I will help you in any way that I can."

"It is to do with Judge Reynolds." Father Matthew was wondering when his name would come into conversation. Even the detectives would have worked out by now that telling Nigel about the judge would mean that other people now knew their concerns. Father Matthew did wonder at that point whether they may have told Nigel on purpose.

"Yes, the judge."

"How well would you say that he fits into the island community?"

"How do you mean, fit in?"

"You know, interact with yourselves, the locals; from what we gather, he is a very private man. And since being on the island has kept himself to himself. Would that be your view also?" Now they were asking the questions he expected. Had the judge kept himself to himself?

"I would say that is a fair assumption of the judge, yes. He does tend to drink in the hotel and not down at The Fleece like most people of the island. He gets on well with Hayley and Kevin. I would say out of anyone they would be the closest to him."

"The managers of the hotel? Any others you would say are close to the judge on the island?" Detective Morris was now back flipping through her book.

"Yes, the hotel managers, he stayed with them for quite a while whilst his house was being rebuilt. David did most of the work so I would say he probably knows the judge well also. David's wife Sandra probably does too, and probably the Petersons as they also drink in the hotel as regulars. Whilst we are a tight community, Detective, people do come to the island for peace and quiet."

"And other than that, he doesn't socialise with locals, maybe at fairs, fetes, help out at the church? None of that? Has he helped at the orphanage?" It was another leading question. Father Matthew could feel them trying to create a link between Alana and the judge, other than the oneof finding her dead body outside of his hotel room.

"No, not really. He doesn't join in with those things. I see him when he reads out the cases, and the odd time at the hotel, but nothing other than that. When he first brought Alex to the island, he visited us a couple of times, but that was a few years ago now. I did hope that he would have been a better godfather to Alex, and they would become closer, but that does not seem to be the type of man that he is. I know Alex can be hard work in his condition, so rightly or wrongly I put the lack of attendance from the judge's part down to that." Both detectives shared a look at this point. This was new information for them. The judge, to them, had never came across as a caring man.

"Alex? The handicap kid, well, the disabled man at the home?"

"Yes, that is the one. The judge was friends with his parents, and he took care of the child when his father died, and his mother could no longer cope with a kid, sorry, a man with MN." Father Matthew thought this would have already been in one of their files on the judge. Guardianship is a serious business, especially of a minor with a judge who, as they have already mentioned, has a dubious past.

"And you say the judge brought him here?" Detective Morris was busy writing this down in her pad.

"Yes, I believe he is his guardian at the moment. I believe the families were close friends. Alex is a young man with very little future. The disease seems to be getting worse with him all the time, and the average length of someone living with this awful disease is five years. Alex is almost three years into his diagnosis."

"I find it strange that he would bring him here as such a huge favour to his mother, and then rarely visit, don't you, Father?" Father Matthew had made numerous comments over the years to his wife. They found it strange that the judge paid for Alex's room and board, but neither of them could remember the last time that he had visited him.

"I presume it was so that he was close enough to help him, if he should need help. Being a godfather means he made a promise to Alex at an early age." Father Matthew knew in that moment that those were the wrong words to say. As a father, and even as a Father, he had all sorts of thoughts going through his head now. He used to have high regard for the judge, but now all he could think about was what Alex may have gone through at the hands of the judge.

Detective Morris sat quietly for a short while. Her thoughts were similar to Father Matthew's; poor Alex. She shared a look with Detective Green which didn't go unnoticed by Father Matthew, he knew what the look meant. From his conversation with Nigel, he knew what they thought of the judge.

"Are you asking these questions because of the judge's past, Detective?"

The detectives were taken back by his question at first, but the look in Father Matthew's eye showed them that he knew more than they thought he did.

"It's a small island, Detective; rumours do tend to circulate very fast." Especially when the biggest gossiper on the island was the local policeman Father Matthew thought to himself.

"Partly Father, I was on one of the task forces looking into Judge Reynolds. There are still a lot of unanswered questions around the judge and his relationships. This relationship with Alex, and his family, is one that had eluded me, Father which does give me concern. I am now wondering how many more have eluded me." Detective Morris closed the pad in front of her.

"For me, Father, Judge Reynolds will always be a person of interest."

Father Matthew didn't want to push on the words 'task forces' or 'relationships'. This was another dark avenue, in very dark times. He had had his fill of bad news and horrible stories over the last twenty-four hours, and knew it was best to leave this up to the detectives.

"As I said, Detective, his time on this island has been uneventful. Other than the cases he reads out in court, he is, as you say, keeping himself to himself." Father Matthew was hoping that was the end of it now.

"Are we having an update meeting at eleven a.m.?"

"No, Father, Detective Green and I are going to the prison, but there will be an update meeting at six p.m. We won't keep you any longer." This time the detectives stood up first to leave.

"Thank you, Detectives."

"I presume we will be seeing you at six at the hotel, Father?"

"You will. As I said, happy to help wherever and whenever I can."

Father Matthew reiterated the point again. He was going to be there until this was resolved. He had no intention of leaving the island. Father Matthew escorted them out of the door just as Mary was returning from breakfast duty.

"Is everything OK, Matthew?"

Father Matthew waited until the detectives had disappeared into Nigel's car before responding.

"They were just giving me an update. I am afraid it's not good news, Mary. Dr Mitchell is now missing. I was going to wake you last night to tell you, but you were fast asleep when I got in."

"Oh no, Matthew, things are getting worse. You don't think something has happened to him, do you?" Mary came close to Father Matthew, and he pulled her in for a hug.

"I sense that they don't expect foul play, Mary. I don't like to say it, but you don't need to be a detective to work out that if there is a drug problem in the prison and the prison doctor goes AWOL, then he will become the number one suspect." Mary lifted her head from his chest to look up at him.

"Really? Doctor Mitchell? But he is such a lovely guy; been with us for years. It seems we have had a lot of number one suspects over the last few days. You don't think he is responsible for all of it, do you? He is the doctor, after all."

"I don't know what to think, Mary. It goes to show that we never really know anyone, do we?" Father Matthew led Mary into the kitchen and switched the kettle back on.

"I was going to say something similar to you, that's why I came home. The judge was at the home this morning, at breakfast. I didn't see him come in, but he certainly seemed to leave in a really foul mood." This made Father Matthew turn back and face his wife.

"Really, the judge? Who was he there to see? And why do you say he was in a bad mood?"

"I don't know. I presume he was there to meet David, to get some work done on the cottage. Whatever the reason, I tried to say hello, but he just blanked me and carried on walking. He was arguing with himself under his breath, and when he got to the dining room door, he practically kicked the door open. Scared quite a few people, I can tell you. That is so not like him. He is always a very polite person, well, when I do see him in the town because I don't think I have seen him in the home since the days when he brought Alex." Mary and Father Matthew took their tea to the kitchen table.

"I sense our island is unravelling, Mary; all these goings-on just put everyone under pressure and on edge. They are all becoming concerned about each other and wondering if anyone can be trusted. The rumour mill is rife; we will have to help control it where we can." Father Matthew was worried. The judge, Michael, the doctor, and even himself were going to be the most talked about people on the island. They each had links to the victims or pasts that were now surfacing.

"I know Matthew, during our ladies' coffee morning yesterday there was little else discussed. But, as you say, the rumour mill was rife. Not something anyone should be listening to." Father Matthew knew it was too late. She had already heard, he was sure someone would have been talking about him.

"So, dear, let's not talk about it. Change the subject." They shared a smile. They both knew that was going to be for the best.

"What is the plan for today?" Father Matthew was glad she changed the subject.

"I am coming to help you in the home until the meeting at six; there is little else I can do. We have to leave it to the detectives and Nigel to follow through on all their leads."

Mary smiled at her husband. It was just what she wanted to hear.

"I, as well as the sisters, will be glad for the help. That sounds like a good day to me; they always are when we spend them together."

Father Matthew and Mary finished their tea and headed back out of the vicarage. The day was spent like many had been before. They all pitched in at the home with the dinner times and the guests. The sisters took most of the work, but with two sisters down, this was becoming tiring, so Father Matthew took this opportunity to write to the mainland to see if anyone would like to come to support.

Sandra had been cooking all day, and David was fixing some of the fencing around the grounds. Alex had been his usual flirty self, and both Sister Grace and

Sister Katie had received flowers this morning. Father Matthew almost forgot about the troubles of the island; he put them as far as he could to the back of his mind. As time passed though, he could see the six o'clock update looming towards him. He knew he would be back in the middle of the island's troubles soon enough.

When Father Matthew arrived at the hotel, Hayley, Kevin, Stacey and Albert were already sitting there waiting for the detectives.

"Evening all." He paused a moment before saying what everyone had been thinking.

"It would seem we are reducing in numbers with every meeting."

"Yes, Father, Chris is at the prison. There has been a little unrest since the disappearance of the doctor." Albert and Chris had been dealing with inmates coming down from cocaine all day. The prison was clean, and they were strongly suspecting now that it was the doctor who had started the epidemic.

"Ian is at the pub, Father, given the events of last night he thought it wasn't wise to leave. None of the press that managed to get to the island have left. In fact, I don't think they want to now for other reasons. There is much more going on, on this island, than they ever thought." Father Matthew hadn't considered that. With this much press on the island, the island business was bound to start getting a lot of media attention. That was the last thing they needed right now. He would have to talk to the detectives about trying to keep it all on a low profile.

"And has anyone seen the judge?" They all looked at each other.

"I haven't seen him today, Father. I am sure he will be coming." Hayley had a smile on her face; she liked the judge. Father Matthew had been worried that the rumours about the judge had reached everyone, but they clearly hadn't, which was a good thing.

Detective Morris, Green and Nigel entered the room.

"Good evening to all of you."

Everyone nodded in their direction. Detective Morris, as always, led from the front of the room.

"As promised our six o'clock update. As you may or may not know, Doctor Mitchell is missing. He left the prison yesterday around four, and has not been seen since. He packed a bag, so we are not expecting any foul play in relation to his disappearance. However, we can confirm that Doctor Mitchell is the supplier of the drug named M into the prison. We have the statements of several inmates who testify to the fact that he was their source. He was paid in cash by their friends and family on the outside or in exchange to trinkets, given that they could not take them into the afterlife." There was a silence as everyone took that statement in.

"But surely that's slander? You are taking the word of a convicted murderer? Over the doctor's? Doctor Mitchell has been an upstanding member of this community for a lot of years." Kevin liked the doctor; he had been drinking with him every Thursday for the past five years. He couldn't believe that this had anything to do with him.

"Kevin, it is not slander, it is fact. We have traced the money, and we have also found quite a stash of envelopes in his office, nearly twenty to be precise. Wherever he went, he was in such a hurry to leave that

232

he didn't bother to take all of his stock. Due to the fact that he has not taken the ferry, we strongly believe that he is still on the island. Either hiding out somewhere or someone is covering for him." There was now a strong glance at Kevin from the detectives due to his outburst. Kevin could feel it, but he didn't care. He wanted to protect his friend.

"I would urge you to let everyone know that he is dangerous, and any evidence of his whereabouts needs to be presented to the police. He is not to be approached." Nobody in the room had ever considered the doctor to be a dangerous man. He had always been supportive with everyone on the island.

"Don't tell me you believe he is the murderer as well?" Kevin couldn't help himself. The thought of his friend being wrapped up in this was more than he could deal with.

"All I will say at the moment is that he is a person of interest."

"It would seem to me that since this started, everyone on this island is a person of interest." Kevin made a good point. At that point everyone looked at each other, then most of the looks went in the direction of Father Matthew. They had all been listening to the rumour mills.

"Yes, but, Detective, he was still at the prison when Alana died, and after that he was with me." Albert made a good point, there were nods of agreement from everyone in the room.

"Was he, Albert? That is a good point and one we have been discussing most of the afternoon. Perhaps you can help us, Albert; exactly when did Alana die?"

"Shortly after ten o'clock on Sunday night." Again, everyone was looking at each other, they all agreed with his statement, but didn't know where this conversation was going. They looked back at Detective Morris. Her expression hadn't changed.

"And how do you know that? Anyone? How do you know when Sister Trinity died? How do you know there were two murderers?"

They all looked at each other. As soon as the detective said it, they all knew the answer.

"Because the doctor told us that was the case." Hayley was the first person to state the obvious. She didn't want to believe it, but there was a sick feeling in the bottom of her stomach. Had they had all been led down the garden path by the doctor from the beginning?

"Exactly. Everything we know about this case is now in question, and most, if not all of the evidence is gone. We don't know who, how, why or with what at the moment. Everything hinged on the doctor's say-so. We have another doctor, well, team of doctors arriving on the boat this evening. They are going to have to try and piece together the information that they have to see if we can ascertain the truth going forward." There was a defeated sigh from the room. Everything they knew had now been put into question. They were back to the beginning all over again.

"What would be interesting to know is if there is anywhere that the doctor could hide out without anyone knowing where he was." This was the first time they had heard Detective Green open his mouth in days. Detective Morris had seemed to be the senior and the talkative of the two. It was a statement and a question. Detective Green wanted to point out, especially to

Kevin, that if someone was hiding him or if they knew of any habitable places on the island where he would stay they needed to tell them. They all took a moment to think about this.

"There are quite a few old farm houses around the island; especially where people have passed on and family haven't come to sort the house. I know of a dozen houses that used to be occupied by my residents that are empty."

"Thank you, Father, we believe that given the weather yesterday, the only boat capable of making the crossing would have been the ferry. We have also spoken to the entire fishermen community today and told them that should they be helping the doctor, there is a chance that they could be charged with drug smuggling and accessory to murder. Whilst that will not get you a place in this prison, it will get you a place in one on the mainland for the rest of your days. I believe he is still on the island and capturing him is our top priority."

"What about the other two, Michael and Sister Sarah?" It was Hayley's turn to ask a question. Father Matthew hadn't even considered the Michael-angle at this point. He knew he should have. He worked closely with the doctor. He could have been an accomplice or worse he could have found out what was going on and something could have happened to him.

"At this time, they continue to be missing persons, Hayley, but we have not ruled out that either of them or both were in on this. Michael worked closely with the doctor, and there were drugs found in Sister Trinity's room and on Alana. Sister Sarah may have been involved also, given the obvious link to the church and the old people's home." Another glance from everyone went in Father Matthew's direction.

"I think that covers about everything. I would ask you to ensure the people of the island that we are still continuing to do everything we can to find all the missing parties, and apprehend the killer or killers." Detective Morris closed the book in front of her.

"Oh, and Father, is it possible that I can have a word in private now that we are finished."

Everyone else got up and left the room. Detective Morris signalled to Detective Green and Nigel to leave also. Leaving her and Father Matthew alone.

"I know I have no right to ask this, given our conversation of this morning, but I would like a favour from you, Father." The fact that she had dismissed the other police officers made Father Matthew sure this wasn't to do with the case.

"I am sure I will do everything I can to help, Detective. I have nothing to hide." Father Matthew was keen to put that point across again. Detective Morris just nodded her head to acknowledge the point.

"Thank you, Father, but you haven't heard my favour yet."

"It does not matter, Detective. I am here to support you and my people on this island as much as I can." Father Matthew kept her stare and smiled back at her.

"It's to do with Edmund Carson, Father."

Father Matthew was quiet. He now knew what the favour was going to be. Last night's events were the first of their kind. Nobody had ever walked away from the chair before. Edmund Carson was the first. He was the first, and the whole world was watching. Although it shouldn't have ever been possible, he would have been the only person to make it possible.

"Go on."

"The doctors we have called in should arrive on the island shortly, and given the coverage of Mr Carson's case, we would like to reschedule his sentence to tomorrow evening." Father Matthew's first thought was of the press in The Fleece. They would still all be here for the next twenty-four hours at least.

"That sounds like a good idea, Detective. What do you need from me?"

"Father, I have been at the prison today, and he asked to see me. I don't know how he knew I was there, but he did. To be honest I am not sure how, but the goings-on of the island are known to all the inmates. Anyway, Edmund would like to continue his confession. He has insinuated that there are still bodies to be found and things to be said. I am not sure I believe him, but for some reason he said if you listen to his total confession, he will give you everything."

Father Matthew paused for a moment. The feelings he had when he sat in the church last night were coming back to him. This wasn't a man you wanted to spend time with. There was an attraction to Edmund; his company could be infectious. But hearing him talk about the things that he had done, in the manner he did them, was testing Father Matthew's faith.

"When you say all his confession. Do you mean he wants to tell me everything he has done?"

"It would seem that way, Father. For some reason, he said you have a kinship. I don't know if he is referring to Father Harry as I don't really want to try and understand what goes on in his mind. He wants you to

237

spend a few hours with him. I know it can't be a pleasant thing to hear, but I also know that if it just gives us one more closed case, it would be worth it, Father. Wouldn't it? There will be people who will be able to move on with their lives." Father Matthew knew she was guilting him into this, but he knew it would be something he would have done anyway. He was still going through it in his head when the detective spoke again.

"I was there, you know." Something about the detective's voice told Father Matthew she was reflecting on her past, and it wasn't a pleasant memory.

"There, Detective?"

"There, in the courtroom. When he was on trial. I was in charge of the whole of the southeast. It was my first real promotion. For some reason, Edmund Carson seemed to have a liking for Brighton. He was there a few times that we know of, and I was first to the scene of one of the hoteliers. I don't think I will ever forget the sight of that body Father. I watched him day after day; he was infectious. Wondering where he was going to pop up next. The whole thing had an almost sick excitement about it, even for the police." Father Matthew noted the word infectious. It had been the same word he used himself on the drive home last night.

"Something about him kept you interested. He led the court in his direction. There were actually points of laughter from everyone. Given the seriousness of the crimes, Father, it shows you how people were captivated in his company." Father Matthew sensed she wanted to talk about it. He didn't know if it was to get it off her chest or if she was trying to show that she had done her time in his company too. That would help persuade him to do the same.

"Is it true then, that he represented himself?"

"It was, Father. He was evaluated, and he seemed, dare I say it, sound of mind. He knew what he had done and why he had done it. It was all about fame and recognition. He said he had studied law and nobody knew the cases better than him. He even pointed out mistakes that were made. He listed them, the mistakes in the cases. Pointed out the clues he left. How obvious he had been. Some of it was embarrassing, Father, for people in our profession. I was glad that it was a closed court." Father Matthew could tell she really meant that.

"The judge ruled it would be the best thing for him to represent himself. He would ensure we got everything down on paper. The fame was important to him, Father. There were cases we knew nothing about, but even then, you thought, maybe there was more." There was a silence. Father Matthew didn't want to push the detective. He almost felt as if he was hearing a confession from her.

"It went on for weeks. He took us through all the big cases. The big numbers first. The school, the hotel, the wedding, those ones. I think the judge thought him to be a little unstable if I am honest, but he wanted as much from him as possible. He wasn't wrong. It is why we didn't get to the end. It is why we don't know everything. The Alphabet Killer; we don't know them all. I am sure of that. There were gaps in his time lines too. He left them there on purpose, I know he did, to keep us guessing. I remember him going from seventy to a hundred in a single sentence. From after the school to the birthday party was a blur. I know he did some strange stuff back then, but he is still to let us know it all. He never told us on purpose I know that. He was good at keeping us guessing." There was another silence.

"Everything was going well, we were getting so much information, but then the judge just said the wrong thing. The wrong name, and everything changed. In an instant, Father. At one point, he was laughing and joking with the jury, and the next... The next, the judge had become his last victim." The detective sat down. It was clearly a troublesome image for her.

"I just remember the blood, Father. I remember the blood coming from the side of his neck. It was like a fountain, and, Father, I will never forget the thing that happened next. He licked him. Right there in court, he licked him, as he was bleeding to death right in front of us. It happened so fast everyone was in shock." Father Matthew watched as she relived the situation placing a comforting hand on her shoulder.

"I will do as you ask, Detective." That brought Detective Morris back into the room, and she stood up again.

"Thank you, Father." Detective Morris took a moment. Father Matthew was happy to give it to her. Clearly the events of the court case had been too much for her even now.

"We have scheduled a midnight sentence. If possible, I would like you to sit with him through his last, last meal. And if you can listen, take notes of everything that he says?" Detective Morris was clearly trying to shrug off the thoughts she had just had.

"Of course, Detective."

"Thank you, Father. Father, I know he is in chains, but still, be careful what you say. You know his story. Be careful." Detective Morris turned to leave.

"Detective, can I ask a favour in return?"

She had expected this. This was the reason she sent both of her team away.

"With regards to what?"

"With regards to Michael, Detective. Should you find him or, God forbid, find a body, would you be able to tell me first. I am worried about him, and so is my daughter; they were due to be married in a few months, and she has been in pieces today. I am a father and a Father, and I want to be the person to speak to her should it not be good news." The longer Michael was missing the more the Father believed he was messed up in this somehow.

"Not a problem, Father, let's call it an even trade." Neither of them believed it to be an even trade, but it was a trade.

Detective Morris and Father Matthew left the hotel.

Thursday morning meant another early mass for Father Matthew; he was in the church for six a.m., and people started to arrive from seven. The residents preferred early mass. Their time schedules were very morning-based, which all of the staff at the home were all thankful of. Breakfast at eight, dinners at twelve and tea at five. Most were in bed for half seven, which left the evening to themselves.

After service was complete, Father Matthew cleaned the church; there was nothing else until Sunday, and he liked to be prepared. By the time he was back in the vicarage, Mary and Catherine had finished the breakfast rush and were back cleaning the kitchen. As he walked through the door, Catherine was almost on top of him before entering the kitchen.

"Is there any news, Dad? Have they found Michael? Do we know any more?" He didn't like to see his daughter like this. He would have preferred to give her news one way or the other just so the situation was over.

"No, nothing as yet, Catherine. I am sure it won't be long. We know he hasn't left the island." Father Matthew wasn't sure if that point was a comforting one or not.

"But why is he hiding? He can't have done anything wrong? He wouldn't be involved in all of this, would he? Do you think he is caught up with the drugs and the doctor? Dad, none of this makes sense. Not for my Michael." Catherine was right; it didn't make sense. Michael didn't want for anything. Drugs or drug money wasn't something that he was dependent on. He didn't even drink alcohol. Everything that he had done in the past had led to everyone thinking of him as an honest and upstanding member of the community.

"I don't know, dear. We all know that Michael is a good lad at heart, but only he knows why he can't come out of hiding. I am sure we will hear his story soon enough." Father Matthew wanted to keep up the pretence that he was totally convinced that he would see Michael again. He wasn't.

"What if something worse has happened to him, Dad? I haven't heard from him in days. It's not like him, not like him at all." Catherine couldn't speak any more. She left the room with tears in her eyes, and ran back to her bedroom. She had been crying on and off for the past day. Mary had spent most of the night lying next to her, but she had little to say in the way of comfort. Catherine had been sending messages to Michael's phone since

Tuesday with no response. Mary waited until Catherine was upstairs.

"I am starting to fear the worst, Matthew." Father Matthew turned to his wife and nodded in response.

"I know, Mary, I feel the same, but we can only pray that he is OK."

With that the phone rang. Matthew could see the look of terror on Mary's face. With every call and every meeting, the apprehension on the island increased, the lack of resolution was beginning to take its toll. Father Matthew went over and answered the call. When he returned, he called for Catherine from upstairs. His wife and daughter both now stood in front of him in the kitchen.

"Please sit down, the both of you." Father Matthew beckoned them to the table.

"No, Dad, not…" He walked over and held them both, moving them towards the kitchen table as he did.

"There is nothing to fear, Catherine. Michael is alive and in custody. He and Dr Mitchell were found in the old farm house just past the new estate. Neither of them are speaking, but Michael has said he will speak to me, and only me. I am going to go directly there to see what I can do to help." He kissed his daughter on the forehead as he placed her in the chair.

"I want to come with you." Catherine was wiping the tears from her eyes.

"Just me, Catherine. That is what Detective Green had said. He was very clear to Nigel also. Let me find out first what has gone on, and then I will send for you. I promise, Catherine." Mary now had her arm around Catherine, comforting her. As hard as it was to hear that they had been in hiding, they were all relieved; at least he was still alive. At least there wasn't another murder.

"Where are they keeping him? Has he been arrested? What has he done?"

"He is in the hotel, and Dr Mitchell is in the police station. They are keeping them apart for questioning. That's all they have said, Catherine, just questioning. I don't know any more. But I will find out all I can and hopefully bring Michael home." Father Matthew believed deep down that that was a lie. The fact that he was hiding for three days and found with the doctor who they now knew to be involved with all the drugs on the island told him that Michael was in on this too. However willing he had been, he was part of the process.

"But Michael wouldn't have done anything, Dad; he just wouldn't."

"We will see what has happened, Catherine. As I said, I will go directly there and see what we can do to clear all this up."

Father Matthew left the kitchen, grabbed his coat, and went out of the front door. Catherine fell into her mother's arms and cried for the next hour straight; some of it was due to relief, and some due to fear of what news was to come.

Father Matthew arrived at the hotel. A small crowd had gathered outside, but Hayley and Kevin were stopping anyone from entering other than Kacie March and Edmund Carson's only visitor who were the only true residents of the hotel. Both were in the bar area and trying not to concern themselves with the comings and goings of others. Both had far more important things on their minds. Hayley came to greet him as he entered the hotel.

"He is in room one, Father. Nigel is with him." The look on Hayley's face said it all. Normally the most jolly of the people on the island; he could tell how upsetting this was to her.

"Thank you, Hayley."

Father Matthew went to the door and knocked. Nigel answered, and in he walked. Michael was sitting on a chair by the window. Just staring at the outside. He looked, and smelled, like he hadn't washed in four days. There was what Father Matthew could only assume to be dried blood all over his T-shirt. He knew that wasn't a good sign. He looked over to Nigel who shrugged his shoulders at him. Nigel spoke softly.

"Father, he hasn't said anything. Said that he would only talk to you. But I am sure you understand, Father, I need to be in the room, and I need to record everything that is said." Father Matthew nodded.

"I understand, Nigel. Set your tape recorder going, and we can begin."

Nigel walked over to the corner of the room and pressed 'record' on the tape machine. The tape recorder had been in the police station for ten years, and this was the first time that it had ever been used. Nigel activated the voice recorder on his phone also just in case, and placed it on the windowsill behind Michael to ensure that he got everything. Father Matthew started to walk towards Michael who was still looking out the window.

"Michael?"

Michael turned his head. He hadn't even realised that he had entered the hotel room.

"Father." He ran towards him and wrapped his arms around him. Father Matthew stood holding him for a while. It felt good. He had hoped for his return, but he also had mixed feelings about what he had done. Father Matthew then sat him down at the table by the window. Sitting in the chair next to him, he grabbed both his hands.

"How are you, Michael?" He didn't really need to ask, he could tell by the look of him he had been in a bad way. He could see from the expressions on his face the hurt he had been going through.

"I am scared, Father, I am really scared." Michael had tears running down his eyes.

"I can see that, Michael. What are you scared about? Just tell me what has happened. I am sure we can sort this all out." Father Matthew looked over to Nigel. Nigel didn't offer any advice in return.

"I did it, Father. It was me; I killed Alana." There was a second glance. This time there was shock on both of their faces. Father Matthew was suddenly aware what his son-in-law had said in front of the only police officer that was a resident on the island.

"Calm down now, Michael; you need to be sure of what you are saying. Nigel has to record all this so that we have evidence of the conversation. I am sure he has already read you your rights." Father Matthew looked over to Nigel, and he nodded.

"But I did, Father. I did it, here at the hotel. In the garden. I didn't mean to, but I did." The tears were now more of a sobbing. Father Matthew took out his handkerchief and gave it to Michael.

"OK, Michael, sit down, take a breath, and tell me everything. Why don't you start at the beginning? Tell me exactly what has been going on." Father Matthew held his hand even more tightly to let him know that he was on his side. Michael wiped his face.

"I don't know where to begin, Father; it's all so terrible." Michael was still crying it was almost choking cry as he spoke. As if it hurt him to get the words out.

"I got so messed up in it all. I didn't mean to, Father. I promise that I didn't. At first, it was just for some extra money, for the wedding. I thought I could use it as we wanted so much… The flowers, the dresses, the food, then there was a honeymoon, a house. I just wanted to earn a little more money, Father. For me, for Catherine, that is all I wanted. He told me it would help. He said that it was all OK." The flood gates had opened, and Michael was trying to say everything at once. Father Matthew placed a hand on his shoulder.

"Who said, Michael? You are rambling. Just start at the beginning, and take it slowly, OK?" Michael took a moment and some deep breaths before continuing.

"Doctor Mitchell. It started with Doctor Mitchell. He came to me one day and said that one of the relatives had called him, and they wanted the urn with the ashes in. Nobody had come to claim these before. I was so surprised. It turned out nobody had come to claim them now either. Doctor Mitchell asked me to take it to the mainland, and deliver it in person. Apparently, they had called him and asked for the ashes; I didn't even know they could do that. I thought they had to claim in person. I did it as I was going on a course anyway; I dropped it off at a bar as he asked me to. I thought it must have been where they lived. When I came home, Dr Mitchell gave me two hundred pounds. I thought, that was a good day. I put it in our fund, Father, honest, I did. A few weeks later he asked me to do the same. I did, and I got another two hundred pounds. I thought, this is going to be easy money, and it was dropped to a different location, so I didn't think anything of it. Just another relative wanting their family ashes." Father Matthew felt a little encouraged listening to Michael's story that the Michael he knew was still in there. That sounded like him, it's something that he would have done to help anyone out.

"Where on the mainland did you go, Michael?"

"Not far, about ten to fifteen minutes off the coast each time."

"Then what happened?"

"Then it got a little weird. Dr Mitchell got a boat. Not one on the harbour, but at the top of the island just past the new houses. There is a cove. As kids we always used to call it smugglers cove. You can actually get down to the sea from there, and he installed a rope ladder to make it easier for me. Doctor Mitchell asked me to take all the urns to the mainland. I didn't know, honest, I didn't know what they wanted them for. Dr Mitchell told me it was for the weirdo ladies. You know, the ones that come to the prison, and are in love with the inmates. He told me we could sell every one of them for four hundred, and split it fifty-fifty. All we needed to do is take them off the island. He said the boat was to ensure that the ferry people didn't ask questions. I was going to talk to Catherine about it; I didn't think we were doing any harm. If a woman wanted to keep ashes in her house, then that is up to her." Father Matthew could see how someone could manipulate Michael. He could now see how easily he had been caught up in this. Michael had stopped crying, and now just wanted to get everything off his chest.

"We couldn't go all the time because we had to wait for the sea to be calm enough, so we just used to store the ashes there, and make a crossing when we could. After a while it stopped going to different addresses, and just went to the pub. I would drop them off, and he would give me an envelope of cash. It was easy money, Father, and I was banking enough for a honeymoon and everything."

"Do you remember the name of the pub?" Nigel asked his first question. Michael didn't want to answer him, and looked directly at Father Matthew.

"Do you, Michael?"

"Yes, Father, it was the Dog and the Duck."

"Thank you." Father Matthew looked directly at Nigel as if to say, no more questions from you. Let's get to the bottom of this.

"Go on, Michael."

"Just one day, they had a package to bring back for the doctor. I didn't open it, I swear; I never thought anything of it. That was his business."

"Do you know what was in the package?"

"At the time, no. As I said, I didn't open it, but I do now. I know it was M, the cocaine that has been smuggled onto the island, by me. But I swear, Father, I didn't know. I didn't know until she told me." Michael pulled his hands away from Father Matthew. They clenched into fists as he did. This shocked Father Matthew.

"Who told you?"

"Alana, Father, Alana told me what I had done." Michael's emotions had changed from sadness to anger at the mention of her name.

"I have to ask Michael how was Alana mixed up in this? She was a good kid. This wasn't something I would associate with her." Father Matthew still wanted to think the best of Alana despite all the evidence to the contrary.

"No, she wasn't, Father, she wasn't good at all. I started to hear rumours down at The Fleece about drugs on the island. I played pool every Monday, and all the teenagers were talking about it. They were saying they knew where to get Coke, and good Coke. I thought it was just them being kids. Didn't think at any point it was going to be true. It turned out Alana was supplying the island. Dr Mitchell had approached her, and she started dealing for him. I didn't know, Father, or I would have come and told you there and then, but I didn't know. Not until about six weeks ago. She knocked on my door. It was Sunday night, my parents always go out Sunday, Father, and Catherine always helps out with both services and lunch and has an early night so it's my night to myself. I catch up on all my TV stuff. She knocked on my door, Father." Michael bowed his head in shame. Father Matthew knew whatever was coming next wasn't going to be good. Now that he could see the connection to Alana, he feared that his first statement could actually true, and he had done it.

"I let her in, and then she started on me, Father. She started to call me names, and told me everything that had been going on. She told me about the ashes, the drugs, the prison, and what she and Dr Mitchell were doing. She said I was so deep into it I was never getting out. I was scared, Father, more scared than I had ever been in my life." Michael's hands were out again, and Father Matthew took them.

"I understand, Michael. So far it is all a big misunderstanding. It sounds to me as if Doctor Mitchell tricked you into all of this." Father Matthew was keen to say that, given he knew it was being recorded.

"But, Michael, what happened to Alana?"

"I didn't mean to, Father, but she started to blackmail me. She told me she was going to tell you about everything that had been going on so that the information would then get back to Catherine. She told me that if Catherine found out it would most certainly be the end of us, Father. I never wanted that. Not ever. She blackmailed me, Father. She made me do things." Michael shivered.

"What kind of things?" Michael paused. He knew this wasn't going to be easy for Father Matthew to hear, but he needed to be the one to tell him.

"Sexual things, Father, she made me have sex with her." It was Father Matthew's turn to pull his hands away from Michael. He hadn't meant to, it was just an instant reaction. Michael could see the physical change in him immediately. Whilst he was a Father of the church, he was also the father of the woman he was going to marry, and Michael had just confessed to sleeping with someone else. All Father Matthew could do was think of Catherine.

"She made me, Father; I didn't want to. I love Catherine, but she made me, she made me. She was going to tell everyone, Father. I was... I just didn't know where to start."

Michael started to cry again. A lot of it was due to anger, but also as a consequence of realising what he was saying to his prospective father-in-law. Father Matthew couldn't help himself; he leaned in again and started holding his hands trying to reassure him.

"I understand, Michael, she made you do those things? That Sunday afternoon?" Michael looked up from crying for a second before dropping his head back down.

"Every Sunday, Father. It carried on, Father, every Sunday. As soon as my parents were out, she would knock on the door. I told her I wasn't going to be in. She just said that if I wasn't, she would find me and tell the world. She was a horrible person, Father. Even after we had sex, she was a horrible person. She would say stuff, stuff like that I was rubbish or that Catherine was lucky that she was a virgin as she would have nothing to compare me to." Michael paused. He felt he may have crossed the line, but that was what she said to him. He wanted Father Matthew to know how horrible she really was.

"She was horrible. That night last Sunday, she left saying she was heading to The Fleece to pick up a real man. I was a below-average boy, and she was finished with me. For a moment I was happy about that; if she wasn't in my life, it would have been so much better. But then she said she was going to tell Catherine everything in the morning as there was still time before the wedding. She said Catherine would be able to upgrade to…" Michael stopped himself, suddenly remembering his surroundings.

"Upgrade to who, Michael?"

"Just upgrade, that is all." Michael threw a look at Nigel. That is who Alana compared him with: dippy Nigel, the local bobby. She had said he had more of a good time in him than Michael had. Catherine would be better off doing him.

"I couldn't help it, Father. I ran out of the house, and I could see she was heading towards the hotel to take the shortcut. I had picked up the pizza knife on the side; I was only going to scare her, Father. I wanted to show her I was a real man. She just laughed at me, Father, and laughed and laughed. I don't know what happened as it was all over so quickly. She pulled the knife next to her stomach and said, go on, go on, stab me; it would be the only weapon I have felt from you in weeks. Somehow it went in; she wasn't taunting me anymore. I took it out, but it went in again and again, Father. It was as if it was happening in slow motion, Father, as it came back out it slid back in again, and then she was on the floor, lifeless."

Michael was silent; he was clearly in the moment. Father Matthew had seen this before all too often in the prison. Murderers reliving their events. That is what Michael was now. He was now a murderer too.

"What happened then, Michael?"

"Then I ran. I could see my parents through the window in the bar, but I ran away from them and towards Dr Mitchell. He had started all of this, and we were both working for him. I went to his home, and he had just got there. I explained everything, and he said he would take care of it. There was already one murder on the island. He said he was going to fix it. He said I didn't need to worry about it."

"So where were you, Michael?"

"I was at his house, well, for Monday anyway. He caught me texting Catherine, and took my phone. I started to get worried then; if he was really going to help, why couldn't I speak with Catherine? He then came home on the Tuesday late afternoon, and said we

253

needed to get off the island. He packed a bag, and we headed to the cove. The sea was too bad to make the journey, and since the old farm house up there hadn't been occupied for years we stayed in there. We stayed there till this morning when Nigel, and two more police officers, found us, and picked us up. I haven't seen Dr Mitchell since. Father, am I going to the prison? Am I going to this prison, Father, to the chair?" Michael was really scared. Father Matthew could see it. He didn't want to point out the obvious. Everyone knew the change in the law. He knew what he had done and confessed the act on tape. There was only one place he was going.

"It's too soon for conversations like that, Michael. Don't worry about that. I think you have just been a little foolish, and you have been manipulated by some cleverer people than you."

"But I do worry about it, Father. What if I never see Catherine again? What is she going to think of me? What about the wedding Father?"

Father Matthew was silent again. He didn't want him to see his daughter, no matter how innocent he had been in the whole affair. The fact he was a murderer and a cheater was more than he would allow for his Catherine. This was all going to cause her so much pain. Father Matthew was keen to steer the conversation in a different direction.

"What about Sister Trinity, Michael? What do you know about that?" Michael sat up in his chair. This was something he could answer with confidence as he had nothing to do with that.

"Nothing, Father, I promise."

"Do you know how she managed to get her hands on the drugs?"

"I don't know, Father, I swear, and I did ask Dr Mitchell as well. I was scared at one point he was going to kill me. I knew what he had been doing, and I asked him up at the farm if it had been him. He said he didn't know anything about it, and that he wasn't a killer; he was just a business man. We both presumed, somewhere along the lines, she must have got the drugs from Alana." If Michael's story was to be believed, Father Matthew could now see how drugs were connected to his home and his church.

"And did you believe him?" Michael was nodding.

"I do, Father. I know he lied to me, but he looked as scared as I did when we were together. He was fine till Tuesday afternoon, and then something spooked him." The arrival of real police, and a thorough search for the drugs in the prison was only going to turn up one thing, Doctor Mitchell's connections. That is what had spooked the doctor, and Father Matthew knew it.

"OK, Michael, I think we need to take a rest. Let me fetch you a glass of water." Father Matthew left the room and Nigel stopped the tape.

"I didn't mean to do anything, Nigel. I really didn't."

Nigel didn't answer him. He knew from his training that he couldn't have an off-the-record conversation with him. Father Matthew entered with the water and gave it to Michael. He placed a hand on his shoulder and held it for a while. He knew what Michael had just confessed to, and he knew it wouldn't be long before they headed him to the mainland.

"You stay here, and I will go and speak with the detective across the road in the police station. I will be straight back, Michael, I promise."

Father Matthew left and made his way through the people waiting in the lobby. He didn't speak to them. He wanted to know where the doctor stood on this story before the rumour mill made up a story. It was a short walk down the street to the police station. When he arrived, he could see the doctor in the cell, but he didn't acknowledge him.

"Detective Morris, Detective Green."

"Thank you for coming, Father. Have you seen Michael Peterson?"

"Yes, Detective." Father Matthew paused. He knew what he wanted to say, and he also knew what he needed to say to best protect Michael from the chair.

"It would seem that Michael has been a bit foolish with the choice of company that he keeps. From what I can gather, Dr Mitchell and Alana have both been manipulating him for various reasons for some time." He figured that was the best that he could do for Michael.

"I would tend to agree with you, Father. That is also what we have gathered from what the doctor has confessed, although the doctor is adamant that it was Michael that killed her."

"It was." As Father Matthew said that, he felt he was starting to come to terms with the fact that his son-in-law had become a murderer.

"He has confessed to that as well. I don't believe he intended to; he seemed to have lost his way in all this and it all got the better of him. He was a good kid at heart." Father Matthew was suddenly aware that he used the words 'was a good kid'. He had been saying that about Alana for the last few days. They were both good kids in his eyes less than a week ago. Today, one was a murderer, and the other a dead drug dealer. Father Matthew couldn't help but question himself, and his role in all of this.

"It would seem our stories are matching then. Did he mention Sister Trinity or Sister Sarah?"

"No, Detective, not in that way. He has told me he had nothing to do with that, and he believes Doctor Mitchell when he said the same. I think that killer may still be at large."

"Yes, the doctor's story is pretty much matching that, but I will be taking DNA swabs from both of them to see if they are telling the truth." Father Matthew nodded in agreement.

"Can I ask, Detectives, what happens now?" Father Matthew knew there were people on the island who were going to want to know the answer to that question. Michael's parents, Catherine and Mary; he knew it wouldn't be long before they were knocking on the door.

"Now we take their statements, get them to sign them and, hopefully, by this time tomorrow, they will be on the ferry over to a prison awaiting trial. We still have a case to solve, Father; we still have a dead sister and a missing one. Although I will say it's a relief to know we have stopped the drug flow, and solved at least one of the murders. That is progress in my book." Father Matthew could tell that Detective Morris was taking this as a huge win for them. In the space of a couple of days to have solved so much of what was going on. This was going to look good for them back on the mainland.

Although he couldn't help but think Nigel had been close to this already. The search of the prison was the judge's idea and that would have resulted in the doctor fleeing anyway.

"What do we tell the people of the island? You know they will be making their own stories up by now." Father Matthew did have a selfish thought for a moment: that at least the chatter about him was going to stop.

"At this point I would just say that they are helping with our enquiries, and we carry on that line." Father Matthew nodded at Detective Morris.

"We don't want a witch trial, do we?" Detective Green was keen to say something. The longer the case had gone on the more he spoke. That had been twice in as many days now.

"No, Detective, we don't. Can I ask for something please? Would it be OK for me to sit with Michael this afternoon as he is very scared, and very lonely at the moment?"

"Yes, Father, but just you. No more visitors. His parents have been asking, but I would prefer it if they stayed away. He is an adult in the eyes of the law. He needs to be tried as one." Detective Morris was clear with the way she was speaking. It was just to be Father Matthew. He was somehow going to have to explain to Catherine and Mary that they couldn't see him either. He knew now that they wouldn't be seeing him again. Not on the island anyway.

"I understand, Detective, thank you."

Chapter 10

Father Matthew sat with Michael all afternoon. He sat with him whilst Detective Morris and Detective Green took his statement again. It all matched and it matched what the doctor had said also. Doctor Mitchell had pleaded guilty to drug trafficking and failure to report a murder. Although he did point out that he had in fact reported the murder and investigated it. Everything he had said was true. The two assailants, the way they were killed, the time of the killings. What he hadn't disclosed was that he knew who killed Alana.

Nigel was left with Michael in the hotel overnight, whilst Detective Green and Morris stayed in the police station with the doctor. They were both due to be on the six-a.m. boat in the morning.

As agreed with Detective Morris, Father Matthew had to leave Michael's side and head to the prison to listen, and write down, as much of Edmund Carson's confessions as he could. He rang Mary from the car and told her everything. They agreed to keep it from Catherine until the morning. It was best coming from the both of them, and by then Michael would be off the island.

As the Father drove up to the prison, he felt an overwhelming sense of culpability. If he hadn't made the deal, the happenings of the last five days wouldn't have happened. It was the first real time he had questioned whether he had been doing right by the island and its community. He had brought drugs and murder to the island, and to his home.

It was a small but familiar walk down to the cell block to Edmund Carson's cell.

"Father, I am so glad you have come. I knew you would. We can't resist a good confession, can we? Come in, take a seat. I would get up and give you a hug given the day you have had, but as you can see, I am otherwise engaged."

Edmund rattled the chains that had him tied to the bed.

"Hi, Edmund, how are you today?" Father Matthew sat on the bed opposite to Edmund.

"I am great, Father, couple of days of unexpected luxury will do that for you. Still don't have the food I requested, but you would have already known that. How has your week been so far, Father?" Father Matthew could tell by the smile on Edmund's face that he knew everything. He was almost chuckling to himself as he said it. Father Matthew didn't respond.

"I hear the good doctor will be joining us soon in here… Drugs, murder, all seems to be going down on this island, doesn't it? Sounds like a place I should have come on holiday. You know, I think I nearly did once. Ended up in Weston instead. You remember, don't you? Of course, you do. Everyone does the old piping and the lord."

Father Matthew didn't comment again. He knew of the county show in Weston, but if he was going to have to hear his whole confession, it was best that he only heard it once.

Father Matthew sat in silence till Edmund spoke again. It had been a long afternoon with Michael, and the thought of Catherine, and what this was going to do to her, was weighing on him.

"That Detective Morris is very cute, isn't she? I would, I really would." Father Matthew was almost glad of Edmund's desire to talk today as he didn't want too although he knew he did not want to listen to the words he had to say.

"How did you get on with Detective Morris, Edmund?"

"Good, good... Gave me a few dreams last night, I will tell you. She is definitely my type of woman. We could have had some great times, you know, if we had met before this on the outside. Worked together for a while." Edmund looked around at the cell.

"And you told her you had things to say to me, Edmund, is that true? Or a play for some more time to showboat?"

"Showboat, me? Father? Would never dream of it. Oh, I do, Father; I want to tell you everything. Everything, Father, the world needs to know what I have done. How I felt, what an achievement it all was. After a movie, trilogy I should say, it would make a great miniseries, don't you think? On HBO or Sky, something like that. Think of the money it would bring to the country, Father. Filming in all the locations I have worked. Some of them need it, Father, especially the ones in Scotland. They really need some financial help." He had already started the showboating. He loved to think that he was going to go down as a thing of legend. The trouble is everyone knew that he was, and he was proud of that.

"Edmund, it's been a long day. I would prefer if you tell me the things that are yet to be resolved. Things that will help me settle down some of the families of the people that, let's say, met you. This is not a typical confession as you are not asking for absolution, are you? Just for the world to know how good you are at what you do?" There was a smile from Edmund at that. He did want that. That was all that he wanted.

"Are you going to help these families get peace, Edmund?" Father Matthew's tone was tired and beaten. Even Edmund could tell, he wanted Edmund to just hand over the names, if there were any new ones, and then they could both move on. Although Edmund had spouted religion a lot of times over the last ten years, he knew he was not truly religious.

"I will, Father, I will try to keep it down to a minimum." There was sigh of relief from Father Matthew, but it was short-lived.

"Let's start. Where did we leave off? Oh yeah, the Merson's. Nobody knew it was me. That wasn't any fun, Father, and whilst I didn't want to be caught by the press, I wanted some, you know, acknowledgement of my work. Do you know how that feels, Father? Just someone to notice you, notice what a difference you make in the world. Of course, you do, what am I saying? You're a Father; you must blend in like a wall flower wherever it is you go of a night time." Edmund paused. It made Father Matthew feel like the rumour mill had made it all the way to the prison. Edmund was baiting him just to get a reaction.

"I know, I have been in your shoes, Father." That was another jibe at him. Father Matthew wasn't going to react.

"That little collar has so much power. You could get away with murder wearing that, couldn't you?" He paused again. Edmund realised it wasn't going to work. He decided to carry on.

"What am I saying, could? I know you can. Anyway, nobody knew it was me. I didn't call anyone, tell anyone; I wanted them to work it out for themselves. They are supposed to be detectives after all." Edmund tutted as if he was ashamed of the detectives on his case.

"Honestly, Father, they were idiots, so I, we, decided, the Merson's and I. We decided that I needed to make a career of it. But before I did, I needed to get my house in order. Do you know how many criminal or murder or CSI programmes there are on TV nowadays? I will tell you, Father, a lot, and do you know how many bad guys get caught? All of them, Father, all of them. Stupid idiots, there are shows on every day showing how you are going to get caught; you think criminals would actually watch them to learn what not to do. I swear that I watched TV one afternoon and every murderer was caught using his credit card at a gas station." Edmund was psychically shaking his head in disgust at them.

"No, I wasn't going to be that thick. I took a lot of money out of my bank, and put it in a safety deposit box in London. I still have a lot of money, Father, if you need any cash in a hurry... You know, for a getaway." Father Matthew just shook his head at Edmund.

"I am sure you have that covered already, don't you? That old plate does get full every Sunday, and I can imagine there are a lot of confessions on this island, given the drug problems. Anyway, back to me, Father. I knew as soon as I was there, as soon as I was there in the limelight that the world was going to be looking for me. If I paid cash for everything, they were never going to find me. Thinking ahead, Father, that's always good for an international star. It is all about how long you can keep in the limelight." Father Matthew imagined Edmund in full flow in the court case. He could see how captivating he must have been. With a swagger to match. He was still gesturing as much as he could for a man chained to a bed.

"So, you planned to do all of this, Edmund? Everything you have done was planned in advance? On purpose." Father Matthew was keen to ensure Edmund knew that as he headed to the room down the hallway. He was responsible for all of the hurt he had caused on the country.

"No, not all of it, Father. I tried to plan as much as I could. If you are good at something you carry on doing it. Once I had started, I just carried on, the next one and the next one. Some days I didn't work with anyone. They were lonely days, Father; meant I didn't have many people to talk to. If I wasn't planning my work, I was dreaming it. As my late father used to say: You have to have a dream, Edmund. I guess, in a way, he helped me realise mine... Father, sometimes I forget how much they must have really loved me." Edmund paused. Father Matthew was looking for the remorse in his face as he had done with all the inmates. There wasn't any. It was all for the Father's benefit. Father Matthew was tired of his game.

"Edmund, this is well and good, but I need something if we are going to continue this conversation. Something to show me you meant what you told Detective Morris." Father Matthew was going to have to push this conversation or it could go on for days. Edmund loved talking about himself more than anything else.

"Give me some names that nobody knows about at the moment. Something I can share with the detectives to say that this isn't a waste of time. Something, Edmund, that will make your followers want to watch the final part of your movie. The last grandstand." Father Matthew stood up. Two things were going to get the information out of him. One was ego, and the other was the world not knowing everything. That's why he needed someone to listen.

"It's not, Father, it's not a waste of time. I want you to tell my story; I want you to tell people my whole story. It is a great one. That is a great title by the way. The ONE's last grandstand. Can you please ensure that you use that in the interview you have with the film director? Just to give him the idea. It will probably be Spielberg or I want to say Shyamalan. He was the guy who did the whole 'I see dead people', wasn't he? He would be great as my director."

"Edmund." The look on Father Matthew's face showed Edmund he was happy to walk away from the room.

"OK, Father. Sit down." Father Matthew sat back down. Edmund was happy to be back in charge again.

"Something to tell the detectives: Sandra Billingham and two other girls, Father, Cornwall area, and I believe they are all still missing. I only remember the name as I saw it in the paper a couple of days after, and I think it was my first ever real Sandra. You know, like *the* Sandra." Father Matthew shook his head he didn't know who he was referring too.

"Sandra Bullock. She is perfect, Father, just perfect. Oh, and how she would have loved me. I would not be surprised if she is in tears tonight father. There will be so many women in tears tonight Father. Sandra and her friends are all down a well; up on the moors; I am not proud of that, Father. You can imagine. It is not my thing to do that, but I have had to a few times in my past. I think they were on a camping holiday; well, they had a tent. The tent is down there also, Father. I am sure if you fish it out it is still usable." Father Matthew took the pen and paper out and started writing down what Edmund had said. That put Edmund back at ease, more than ease: that made Edmund happy. Someone reporting on him, writing down what he was saying.

"I just came across them one day. I was driving up from Penzance or somewhere like that. It may have been Wadebridge. A place with two bridges; I don't know why I remembered that, Father. I toured around there quite a bit. As I said, I came across them. I could see a light on the moor. I drove up closer to it and dimmed my lights. I parked far enough away not to spook them and walked up to the tent. I could make out shapes as they giggled inside. Immediately I could tell there were three women. Imagine my luck Father. I am a lucky man Father. There was a radio playing if I remember right, with some modern music, not my type. Anyway, I didn't open the tent. I jumped on it and just started hacking from the outside; it is really weird wrestling a tent. I just thought it would be fun. A surprise for them, Father. I could hear them scream with excitement every time the knife went in. It seemed to last forever, scream after scream of excitement; they didn't want it to stop, I am sure of it. Then they were all quiet. Exhaustion had the better of them, Father. I had such fun too Father it wasn't just them. Then I thought to myself, how good it would be just to crawl in there to make love to one of them. So that's what I tried to do, but there was no space, Father. The others kept touching me as I was trying to have sex; it was creepy. I don't blame them. I mean, look at me." Edmund tried to stand up as much as he could to show the Father his figure. He had always been a fit young man. The last five years in prison had only helped him with his body appearance. Most inmates took their frustrations out in the gym. Edmund was no different although a lot of the inmates always kept their distance from him. Even when he started the conversations, they were never very trusting of him.

"I never really fancied a threesome although that would have been a foursome, I guess. The tent was a pain too. At that point, I knew, it would have been a bit better if I hadn't flattened it." For once Edmund looked a little disappointed in what he had done. Father Matthew knew it wasn't for the right reasons, but he didn't look happy with the action he had taken.

"Have you ever, Father? Ever had a threesome or a foursome? What am I saying? Of course, you have. Again, that collar, Father. Access all areas, and all the hot nuns. Nuns really do it for me, Father. Do they do it for you? Do you always wonder what is under the old gown? I know, Father, I know they are always wearing the old stockings and suspenders. Sometimes with a little Basque. Always black, but then the odd kinky one would be wearing red like the devil, eh, Father. Maybe that Sister, what was her…"

"Edmund, the case." Father Matthew was keen to stop him before this got any further. Edmund was just happy he finally got a reaction.

"I tell you, I enjoyed playing a Father. Oh yes, the story, so I dragged two of them outside, and placed them round the camp fire. I went back in. I managed to fix the poles, so they stood up. The poles, Father, that wasn't a metaphor for anything; I have never had any trouble in that department. Then, yes, that was good, it was good to have sex in the normal manner. She was good as well, Father. Multiple multiples, she said, which was normal for women that I slept with."

Father Matthew was struggling to listen to him. He knew sex in the normal manner for Edmund was with a dead person. Everyone knew this about him. Father Matthew needed to imagine them alive however hard that was going to be. He needed to imagine the act itself as some kind of love-making just to be able to carry on listening to him.

"When I was happy that she had been completely satisfied Father, I went outside. I tried to stage a scene like I had a dozen times before in people's homes and, you know, other places, but outside has always been difficult. They just wouldn't sit upright around the fire. Then if the frigging heavens didn't start to open, Father. I mean, it started to rain. That was all I needed. I didn't have my coat with me or an umbrella. I looked, the girls didn't have one either. I was tired. It had been a long day, Father, and these bitches, sorry, Father, emotions getting the better of me, these women, they were proving too difficult; after an hour or so I gave in. I didn't want the world to see me fail at staging a scene, so I placed the bodies in the boot of my car with the tent, and cleaned up their camping area. You can't leave fires unattended and all that, Father. I couldn't rely on the rain to do the job. I took them to a boarded-up well that I had seen back down in Penzance. I didn't want to make the drive as it was already late, but I didn't want to be seen as a failure either. It was worth the hour drive to keep my reputation, Father. Sometimes you have to work for your art form, Father. I prised the board off the top of the well, and threw them, and all their kit, down, and then boarded it over again." Edmund looked pleased at himself at this point as if he deserved to be rewarded for what he had done.

"I was so lucky of the rains in the end that night. By morning there was no trace of where they had been staying. So, they just disappeared. I mean, can you imagine if the press had gotten a hold of that? If they had thought I had failed... Me? They were already falling out with me at that point. And, it was me, Edmund Carson, not the ONE or Father Harry. In fact, I don't even think that I had invented Father Harry by then. I think there was just me and the ONE at that point. Anyway, I watched the news, and after a couple of days there was a nationwide manhunt out for the girls. They couldn't find where they had pitched their tent. Later I heard on the news that they had lied to their parents on where they were going. I guess that's technically why they are still missing persons. There is a lesson there somewhere about lying to your parents, isn't there, Father? So, something else the world can thank me for. Ensuring that kids don't lie to their parents." Edmund watched as Father Matthew finished writing everything down and caught up with him.

"Edmund, it's not that I don't believe you, but can I check that story out?" Father Matthew was on his feet again. If he was going to listen to everything Edmund was saying, then he needed to know this one was true. He also knew this was going to waste some of his valuable time.

"Of course, Father, I am here to help. Remember the well is in Penzance. Girls off the moor. It may not have been a moor though, there was a hill and a field; I am not exactly sure of the difference. And I had sex with the dark-haired girl. I think it was black hair or a very dark brown. It must have been Sandra. All Sandra's look like that. I think it would be good to tell her parents that. So, they knew she met and slept with a star before she fell down a well. The other two were blondes, and they just aren't the same, Father. I don't think they deserved me as much. Their parents will already know that. Now, give me a redhead, and we are talking. I really think they are growing on me. Detective Morris as a redhead. You know what I am saying, Father? Of course, you do. You have eyed her up and down. Probably on your laminated list of people you are allowed to sleep with already."

Father Matthew walked out of the cell. Edmund was still talking, but he was trying not to listen. He rang Detective Morris who was still at the station. She entered the name into her computer.

"Yes, Father, all checks out, all three girls are still down as missing. Been quite a few years now. I am sure their families will be glad of the closure."

"Thank you, Detective, that helps." There was something tired in his voice, Detective Morris picked up on it. Spending the afternoon with Michael, and worrying about Catherine had taken its toll on him.

"Thank you, Father, I know it can't be an easy thing to listen to. I also understand you have had a long day." Father Matthew just agreed, put down the phone down, and walked back into Edmund's cell.

"OK, Edmund, Detective Morris confirms your missing person's case carries truth. Can we move on with the rest now?" Father Matthew was just about to say the words 'the rest of the unknowns', even though he feared there were going to be hundreds, but Edmund had already started talking.

"Told you it checks out, Father, I wouldn't lie to you. We don't do that, do we, Father. Oh yeah, where were we? The Merson's, been to the bank and withdrew lots of cash. That's when I saw her, Melanie Epsom. She was a bank teller; she helped me sort all this out. Long dark hair, beautiful, Father. I tell you, probably the second most beautiful woman I have ever seen." Edmund stopped at that thought. She was the second most beautiful woman he had seen. Next to her. She was the most beautiful.

"I knew having sex with her, her hair, her lips, her mouth, her blood, would be sweeter than honey itself. So, I paid her a visit to her home. Father, I would never have to pay for it, look at me. You wouldn't believe it, she was single. A woman that looked like that and wasn't getting any. I needed to help her out with that. You know what I mean." Edmund was lost in the moment again, but not like before. He wasn't as much savouring it as remembering it.

"She wasn't expecting a visit from me. I broke into her apartment, and when she was in the shower, I pounced.

It was just one of those shower curtains, so I could grab her easily. I think it had ducks on it, can't understand why the woman lived on her own with no kids and she had ducks on her shower curtain. Anyway, when I grabbed her, she fell, and hit her head on the tap. Well, the tap embedded in her head, shall we say. At the back though. Didn't mess that beautiful face up. Anyway, I dried her off and then set the scene. A little music, some candles, all very romantic, Father. I wished I had had some flowers, roses or something like that would have been a nice touch, you know, like the movies. Anyway, Father, we made love all night. It was great." Edmund stopped mid-flow. That was so not like him. He was clearly in the moment again.

"No, that's a lie, Father, and I said I didn't want to lie to you. I was great. She was average. I think that is fair, Father. Average is fair. Or fair maybe, maybe that is a better word for her. And it wasn't all night. It was probably not her fault. Not all people can be good at all things. Apart from me, Father, I am great at everything as you know." Edmund returned to full flow.

"I will have to admit I did have to cut her a little, but she didn't mind. Just because of the lack of blood, Father. She just wasn't doing enough for me. You know how it is when you need a woman to do her part, don't you, Father. Of course, you do. I thought, give it a day or so, people will find her, add one and one together, and get Edmund. Three days, Father, at least I think it was three days. Can you believe it, three days to find her? I had to make the call to the police station myself. It is a good job that I am such a talented actor, Father. I could have been an actor, Father. That's why I am so good with all my characters. I am surprised that I won't

272

be chosen to play myself in the movies, Father. It would have made sense. Now they are going to have to pay someone millions. I mean, Father, I look like a movie star, don't I?" Edmund held his hands out as much as he could as if receiving an applause.

"The press, I hear you ask, Father. What of the press? Nothing, nothing linking the cases, no OMG moment 'there is a new Jack the Ripper on the loose'. Nothing! All that work, all that preparation, and still nothing. I tell you, I was not happy about it. Here I am, eight people under my belt, and not a person looking for me. Edmund the Invisible I was, not Edmund the Invincible, invisible. That was not my intention at all, Father, I can tell you. I wanted to be adored by people back then like I am today." Edmund sounded truly disappointed.

"If you wanted fame from this, Edmund, why didn't you just own up? Come into the police station and say, look at what I have done?" Father Matthew was wondering at that point how many hundreds of lives would have been saved if he had just done that.

"I did in the end, Father, I owned up. I thought at first it wasn't dramatic enough, so I introduced the ONE to the world. You know with the iconic hoodie. Do you have kids, Father? I am sure they have one in their wardrobe now, don't they? All kids are buying them everywhere. Don't you just love the word iconic though? Iconic black hoodie. I can't even remember the first time I heard that, but sums me up, I think. Well, not me, The ONE. My alter ego. Or at least one of them. But do you know what? Even that got a little messed up in the beginning. So, I couldn't make it much clearer anyway, let's say that. I thought, something big, something that will get the world's attention, and they will really know it was me. Oh, I planned, Father. I planned who, I planned how; I planned it down to the last minute and, well, it was executed with perfection. Almost perfection."

"The girls' private school?" It was Father Matthew's turn to sound disappointed. It was one of the stories he knew he would have to hear. He could tell that Edmund loved the sound of his own voice. Father Matthew wasn't going to get a lot of words into this conversation.

"The girl's private school, Father, you know it, I am so glad."

Chris James entered the cell and placed down Edmund's last meal.

"Perfect. Thank you, guard James. Stay if you want. I am about to tell the Father here about the school. You will love that story."

Chris didn't say anything. He didn't want to be caught into his conversation. From the time Edmund had arrived at the prison, all he had wanted to do was brag about what he had done. Chris left the cell.

"See, nothing, Father, I tell you, he doesn't like me, that one… I talk and nothing; some people are so rude. Sorry, Father, where are my manners? Do you want to share some of my dinner? It is not as if I will be hungry later." Father Matthew just shook his head. Edmund continued to eat whilst he spoke.

"No, thank you, Edmund, can we just get to any of the people that still need to be laid to rest? You told the detectives there were so many cases that still had to be solved. Things like the school, well the whole world knows that one."

"But, Father, the school is the best story I have. Well, the school and the hotel. That was great. Oh, and the Alphabet... There are so many good stories in the Alphabet, Father, it is hard to choose. A, B and L. Oh, L, Father, that will make your toes curl, I am telling you. Oh, L, you know I meant the letter, right? Of course, you did. He did a good job, didn't he Father, the old Alphabet Killer: Halloween, Friday the thirteenth, Christmas, all of it, Father. Sorry about taking Christmas, Father; I know it is dear to us. I would say we are both worshipped equally at Christmas now, Father. Unfortunately, the world had missed out on that, Father, you know, knowing everything that happened at the time. Because of the blackout, they missed out on the whole Alphabet Killer. As a third movie, Father, it will go down a storm."

Father Matthew was on his feet. The reference to taking back Christmas from Christ was more than he could stand.

"These are not stories, Edmund. The school, it was a massacre. The hotel was a massacre. The ONE, Father Harry, the Alphabet Killer, Killers, whatever you called them. They terrorised the whole country for years. Your stories have ruined lives. Your stories will haunt people for the rest of their lives." Father Matthew said this with a sharp tone. He knew the stories; the whole world knew the stories.

Edmund smiled at him. Father Matthew regretted the last sentence. He knew Edmund would have liked to hear that one. After a few minutes Father Matthew sat back down. He knew he needed to get through this for other people, other people's peace even if there was none for himself. They sat in silence as Edmund continued to eat his meal. As soon as he finished, he looked at the Father.

"I will make you a deal, Father; let me tell the stories, just two, and I will give you the rest of the names. I doubt that, given my meal is here, we have enough time to go through all of them anyway. I pick my favourite two, you listen, and then we are good, Father."

Father Matthew looked him directly in the eye. He had been ready to walk. He also knew that if Edmund was going to give him something it would be worthwhile.

"This is it, Edmund, promise me that after these two stories you will tell me the names of these people."

"I promise, Father. Maybe not the names, Father, but certainly the cases. Trust me, I want the world to know what I have done. By my reckoning, the world still thinks I am a little shy of two hundred people I worked with and, Father, I am over that number. I am probably double that number. I tried to tell the judge in court, but I don't think he liked me very much. Grumpy guy. We have a deal, Father, good, great. I am so excited. I love this one. You can just imagine, Father, imagine how peed, can I say peed off? It's not swearing, is it, Father? Imagine how peed off I was that nobody had still recognised me for everything I was doing. It was like the public didn't want to hear about me anymore. I thought, what can I do that nobody else has done? The kid with a rifle on the roof of a school, been done far too often, Father. You know, I blame video games, I do Father... I remember them as a kid; we could play online for hours, gunning down people." Edmund started to make shooting sounds at Father Matthew. He just looked directly at him without an expression on his face.

"Sorry, I am all over the place, back to the story. I took a holiday. I needed one, Father, to clear my head. I met some friends when I was there; it was fun. Then I was in south London. I was thinking, something related to the London Eye, or Chamber of Horrors could be creative, when I suddenly noticed a group of school girls were on the tube next to me. They were all from one of those private schools; you know the ones, where they board there all year because their mummy and daddy are too busy to have them at home. Imagine my surprise when I found out there were three hundred and twenty-five students in the school. What is the world coming to, Father, when that many girls are in boarding schools? Too much extra cash that is what I am saying. Well, as good, as I am, even I didn't fancy my chances against three hundred and twenty-five girls. Far too many. I dug a little deeper and I discovered that at half-term, about twenty girls were still going to be on site. Their mummies and daddies didn't even want them for the holidays. Can you imagine that, Father? Away all year and they don't want you for the holidays."

"Twenty-three."

"Twenty-three, that was it. Well remembered, Father, and a couple of teachers. Twenty-five in total. Now that was a scene, wasn't it, Father; I could see it in my head. If I could pull that off, I would be famous. Not just today-famous, Father, not reality-TV famous, I was thinking Jack-famous. Jack the Ripper, Father, you know the story? Of course, you do, everyone does. Anyway, I watched and I planned, Father, and do you know what? Couldn't have gone any better. It was as if it was meant to be. Girls not sharing rooms any more. I swear when you see these films on TV, St Trinian's and all that, girls in a dorm with pillow fights. Not nowadays, private rooms with their own TVs and en-suites, amazing, Father, amazing. Made my job so easy." Edmund was enjoying the story. Father Matthew was keen to let him keep talking. His idea was that if he let him ramble on, he would not have time for the second story.

"I waited till, what, about midnight and went room to room. Working with each of the girls as I did. Not a sound, not a scream, nothing, Father. They were so happy to see me. Most of them had already heard about me… Nope, that was another lie, Father. There were a few bumpy moments, but I managed to get through them all. Both the teachers had their own rooms also, Father. They were last though. I remember one of them needed a little more attention. Small dark-haired woman, very pretty, she was my reward for a job well done. She was attractive, Father, probably the third most attractive woman I know." There was a pause. It was brief, but every time Edmund thought about the second or third most attractive woman in the world, he also thought about the first. Father Matthew knew who the most attractive woman he ever met was. The world did.

"I tell you, Father, I really do have a type. Small, dark hair. Just don't tell my girlfriend, Father. This is confession, right; you can't repeat this stuff to her."

Edmund stopped. His head dropped for the first time. Father Matthew was shocked. Edmund had actually said it. He wasn't prompted by anyone. He actually said he had a girlfriend. He didn't use her name. Nobody around him used her name.

Father Matthew could not get the picture of Mary out of his head. She was Edmund's type. If he had indeed come to this island on holiday, she wouldn't have survived his trip. Edmund's head came back up, and he was in full showmanship mode again.

"Anyway, Father, yes, I remember afterwards I laid on the bed exhausted from all the excitement; we made love at least three times that night. I think I have heard that she told people five, but that is OK. Women do tend to brag about being with celebrities, don't they? I had to stay awake, Father. I didn't know if there were deliveries that next day or family were coming to visit. I had to get to work. First of all, my plan was to dress them all, Father, dress them all back in their school uniforms for the picture. There was no way I was going to get them all done. It was a shame, Father, as I think it would have been so much better. I did dress the teachers though, Father; I thought they needed the respect of that. Each student was sat at a desk in various poses. My God that was hard, Father. I had to collect meter rulers from all the classrooms just to keep some of the student's upright, on a few occasions I even had to staple their heads to the ruler. Not an easy task I have to say. Some were bent over the desk as if they were working, while others were passing secret notes to each other. Oh, it was like you see in the movies, Father, kids having fun at school. Seventeen, Father, haven't even told you about Seventeen. She was beautiful, Father. Her and Seven, Father, both beautiful. Not their real names though. You know what? Don't think I remember their real names? Found them together, father, both Seven and Seventeen. I mean together, together. Wait, you are not one of those preachy Fathers, are you? The ones that don't believe in free love? Of course, you are not. Look at you. You must have had your fair share of free love.

Anyway, they were special, I just wanted to point that out. Always pop into my head those two. I guess it's because it is the closest I have come to a threesome. Well, if you don't count the Spanish girls, Father, but that was as the Alphabet Killer. This was all him, I mean me, Edmund Carson. Where was I? Oh yeah, the teachers. One was at the blackboard, had to tie her to a hat stand and hammer the hat stand into the ground to get her to stand up. The other, my favourite one, was at the teacher's desk marking work. She gave everyone an A-plus, Father; these girls were special and doing so well. Suddenly I was stuck, stuck on what to do to tell the world. I couldn't just write 'By Edmund' on the blackboard. That was no fun so I decided to put clues on all the notes that were passed in class, like, is he an orphan, was there a fire or was it a planned gas leak, that type of thing. Then I wrote on the blackboard:

Every Day My Urges Need Desires, Can Almost Replace Some Open Negativity. From U.

E.D.M.U.N.D C.A.R.S.O.N. F.U." Edmund spelt it out.

"Edmund Carson Fuck you. It wasn't great, Father, I know, as you know my writing got better as I escalated. You know because I am sure you followed me on social media. The world did. Anyway, in that moment, it was all I had. Replace. Retain. I was struggling. Then I started to put name badges on the girls, but I ran out of time. I was just writing some up when I saw a van driving up the road to the school. I was freaked out. I didn't realise where the time had gone. I thought, maybe I should have stuck about and worked with them also, give me a little more time with the girls. Well, I thought that until I saw two men get out of the car, gardeners, but one was a big lad, Father, and I fear I wouldn't have been able to work with him, just because I was knackered from all the sex father no other reason. So I thought, time to get out of here. It won't be long before they are found, and the news are everywhere. That was always my favourite part, listening to the news. Waiting for my name to be said. Imagine my frustration, Father, they didn't go into that room till five p.m. that night... and it was almost forty-eight hours before they worked out my clues... Well, that's what they said. I wasn't a person of interest for two days, Father, two days... When the news broke, Father, I was in a kebab shop. Remind me later about that as there is a guy in the dumpster round the corner. Another one of not-my-best moments, I am afraid. Dropped my kebab. But then, there I was. I really was, not just a person of interest, but world famous. Everyone in the world was talking about me. The headlines were in every paper. I even read an article about a girl that survived one of my attacks, Father. Honestly, never met the girl in my life, but here she was saying what great sex we had, and how she was always worried about me. If we had had sex, Father, she wouldn't be worried about me. Oh, and she said she had my baby. Can you believe that? It did make good reading though, Father. I did try looking her up afterwards to show her what sex was really like with me, but I couldn't find her, Father; she was hiding ever so well." Father Matthew was exhausted. Edmund Carson didn't stop talking. He spoke with words, and with his whole body.

"Edmund, can I ask why you felt the need to do that?" Father Matthew feared he was getting to the end of the story too soon.

"Need, Father? There was no need. I just wanted to find her, and pay her back for the great press she had given me. And to see my child, of course. I would make a great dad. Even had names, Father: District Carson and Lake Carson. Do you like them? I bet you can't imagine where I was when I came up with the names."

Edmund was back smiling at Father Matthew.

"Not the girl, Edmund, the whole school?"

"Oh, that need, the need to do something special. We are only here once, Father, and who are we if we don't leave a mark. Are you not worried about that, Father? When you leave here, not here the prison, but here on this planet. When you leave, are you not worried that nobody will remember you?" It was a genuine question from Edmund.

"My family will remember me, and my loved ones, Edmund." Father Matthew patted his bible as he said that.

"Yes, but not forever, Father. My loved ones won't remember me forever. I worked with my parents, and my nan died, and Miss—"

Edmund stopped. Full flow. He froze. He froze for a long time. It worried Father Matthew. He could feel Edmund's breathing getting harder. Harder and faster. Father Matthew remembered the story of the court case. How quickly Edmund Carson could turn. He needed to snap it out of him.

"About the names, Edmund. Time is getting away from us." Father Matthew looked up at the clock on the wall. The guards put one in each of the cells. It was almost a kind of torture for the inmate to know how long they had been there, and how long they had left. It worked. Edmund snapped out of it.

"One more story, Father, I promised, and so did you. So, I was launched, not just countywide launched; I was launched worldwide. Everyone knew who I was, and everyone in the world was looking for me. Can you imagine that, Father, not just here, not just in the UK, but worldwide my face was everywhere. Imagine how bad it is that it was nearly three years before anyone caught up with me? What does that tell you about today's people? Never look where they are going. That's what it tells you. It's not like I am hard to miss."

"Edmund." Father Matthew gave him a look as if to say, "Just get on with it".

"Sorry, Father, I do get distracted. Anyway, it was great, Father, the attention. The press. I tell you, I would sit in the hotel room, and watch the news all day. There were sightings of me from Land's End to John o' Groats on a daily basis. Father, I didn't even know those places existed till the girls told me that was where they were going. I thought they were made up. I am pretty much the common man, Father, I only know what I know. Well, Edmund is pretty much the common man. I always thought of the ONE as a bit more of a legend, like Jack. That's how I saw him. Father Harry was just a Father. I did enjoy it while it lasted, Father. And I am sure it helped you guys. Probably got you all a pay rise. I thought I was a quite good, Father. Fill the silence; number one rule, eh? I really was good." Father Matthew wanted to say something. He wanted to tell him the damage he had done to the church. The fear he put into worshippers countrywide, but he knew he would only be playing to his ego.

"I used Camden a lot for my inspiration. Have you been, Father? It is an amazing place. I consider it to be home, well, one of my homes. They are my type of people. I guess, I was trying to go a bit Jack with the first one of the alphabet, Father. I am lost now, Father what was I saying? I am not sure where I am going with all this. Oh yeah, the next story. Anyway, I was working with my friends generally at their homes or in their cars or bars and pubs. I have worked in a few bars in my time. Never really got the taste for alcohol though, Father. I suppose that is a good thing. The point is there were no headlines like I had with the school, no Half-term Hell, Orphan Rampages School, and my favourite... School's out Forever. I thought that was genius. People had come to expect something great from me, and I was disappointing them. The press were not happy with me, Father, and neither were my fans. So, I had to come up with something. Something visual, bold, and right in your face."

"The hotel."

Father Matthew knew where he was leading. He just didn't know if he wanted to hear it. The trouble was he couldn't pick which of the stories he did want to hear. They were all so awful.

"I know how the story ends, Edmund." There was a huge smile on Edmund's face as the Father said that.

"You have followed all my work, Father. I am always glad to meet my true fans."

"The world has followed your story, Edmund. The world." This was playing to his ego, but he would prefer he just got on with it now. He just wanted the names and to get out of there as quickly as possible.

"I am so glad to hear that, Father, but I still have to tell the story. When I told it in court, you could see people were impressed. I would have made a great lawyer, Father; you should have seen me. For three months I had them eating out of the palm of my hand. Almost had to do my job, and the job of the guy that was prosecuting me. He was rubbish, Father. I tell you. The jury would have gone in my favour. They would have if we had got..." He stopped again. Father Matthew knew the rest of the sentence... If he had gotten to the end of the case.

"I digress. I do that, Father; just stop me if I do again. We have to move on. Time is of the essence and all that. It's amazing how many of my nan's sayings I just say without thinking about them. She was an amazing woman, Father; you would have loved her. Everyone loved her. I wrote a lot of them down. You know, to make sure they make it into the movie." Edmund paused again. Father Matthew hoped it was for a genuine reflection on his grandmother.

"Firstly, I checked the timings for about a week..." Father Matthew tried to tune him out. He was back in full flow. The whole country knew the story of the hotel from hell. Even though it had been the first real blackout story. It had been the last straw in a reign of terror that was already well into its second year. One paper had issued an early edition, and it had become a collector's item around the world. The rest of the newspapers never reported on it. Father Matthew knew what he was hearing so far was rubbish. Edmund was playing to his crowd. Making it sound better than it was. The early edition had proved that the hotel manager was in on it. Nobody knew why. Especially given how it ended. But the video cameras had proved they were in it together. The rumour circulating with the paper was that the manager did it to make his hotel famous. It worked. It was now a tourist attraction in London owned by the Merlin group.

"So as soon as I had a sketch and a victim on a floor, I went to work. I would follow them to the room, and work with them. Various ways, Father, and with some it was a really big struggle. I tell you, it almost hurt me to put some of these people in the positions that I did. By now though, I had become an expert in my field. To become an expert, you have to have put in ten thousand hours; so they say. I had been at it for years. You can see from my frame I bulked out from my younger days, since Mr Merson, and that horrible photo. That kid in the blanket; that photo has followed me everywhere. It wouldn't surprise me if it made the calendar. Does it make my yearly calendar, Father? You buy it, don't you? Of course, you do." Edmund was a fit young man. He wasn't big, and he had the frame of a large teenager, but it was lean and muscly.

"I was worried that if I wasn't stronger, if I wasn't faster, I was going to be caught. I had chloroform, and a knife. Actually, I bought it in a pub, can you believe it? A biker's pub called The Red Earl. I tell you, with the correct money you can get anything. Who sells chloroform nowadays?" Edmund was shaking his head.

"Victoria. That was her name, Father. I was trying to remember, but her name was Victoria. I met her in reception. I went to her room, and she was ready for me. She had actually started without me. After working with her, we had a nice little chat, and a glass of wine before getting down to business. It was just what I needed, Father. It was as if it was meant to be. Fourth prettiest woman I know." Edmund quickly glossed over it that time. He knew what he had said.

"Father. I tell you, Father, I am going to miss all the sex. I am presuming there is sex in heaven, right, Father? Or is there lots of sex in heaven? It is heaven after all. And don't we get whatever we want in heaven? Although technically every woman in heaven is already my type because it is my heaven. These things are what keeps me awake at night, Father."

Edmund laughed at himself. He was really lost in the sound of his own voice now. Father Matthew could tell he was enjoying hearing everything he was saying even if it had started to make no sense.

"Well, as long as they are not blonde. I am sure I will manage." Edmund gave Father Matthew another wink. There was something about it that made Father Matthew almost like Edmund when he did.

"Edmund, I don't think you are going to get time to finish your story, and tell me the names if you do not move on."

Not that Father Matthew wanted to hear it. His faith was certainly being tested today. From Michael to Edmund, he really wanted the day to end.

"Yes, sorry, Father." Edmund went back to full flow. Father Matthew sat and ran through the Lord's Prayer in his head. He kept nodding at Edmund to show him that, at least as far as he was concerned, he was still listening.

"He had long hair and a beard. What else was I going to do, Father...?" Father Matthew caught the question. He was now trying to piece together where he was in the story, but there were so many possibilities.

"I know the rest, Edmund. The press got your sketches, remember? And we are down south, we are the only people that got the early edition."

"I forgot about that. How good is that, Father? I was only in Brighton. I could have popped over to see you. Well, you know if I knew you then. Did you keep it? I heard it is fetching quite the price now. Five hundred thousand I heard. A nice little nest egg there, Father." Five hundred thousand was a stretch in Edmunds imagination. Father Matthew knew this, but he had heard that one copy had been sold for twenty-three thousand pounds a week after Edmund was caught.

"Can we get to the names?" Edmund just wanted to talk. It was almost as if he was back there living the actions. Father Matthew knew this, and that's why he didn't want to carry on. He didn't want Edmund to relive these actions as he wasn't repenting; he was re-experiencing.

"Father, I haven't told the whole story."

"But I know it, Edmund, and don't you want the world to know everything that you have done? Do you really want other people having your number? Other murderers claiming your victims? They will do it. Claim the victims of the greatest of all time. That would be such a win for people following in your footsteps. How long before they are number one? Time is ticking, Edmund." Father Matthew knew it had worked before. Playing to his ego, he hoped it would work again.

"You're right. I won't go through the rest. Just as long as you tell me which one was your favourite,

Father? Tell me your favourite, and I will give you the names now."

Father Matthew just wanted out now. Time with Edmund wasn't doing him any good.

"I don't have a favourite, Edmund. These were people's lives."

"Everyone had a favourite, Father. People always try to hide it, but deep down everyone has a favourite. Just tell me yours, and we are done. It is that simple."

Father Matthew knew he wasn't going to give in unless he told him.

"Floor thirteen, Edmund. Now let's get on with it, shall we?"

"I knew it, I knew it. It was the masterpiece, wasn't it, and with Victoria there as well. I tell you, Father, took me a week to get that red spray paint off my hands. People must have thought I had blood on them or something. Blood on my hands. I like that father. Remember to use that in the interview. I think he saved her, Father. She deserved saving, Father; she was great. That's what I think anyway."

"Edmund, you have no time left; it is time to tell me."

"Is it, Father? I do get ever so excited about these things. If I give them to you, Father, can you promise that everyone involved will know that it was me? They will know that Edmund Carson was the person responsible. Edmund or the Alphabet Killer. I think that is my favourite today. The Alphabet Killer. Oh, and the ONE and Father Harry. But it doesn't matter which one did it, they will all go on my hit list, Father, in the end. I want my number, Father. It is very important to me. Promise me, Father. I want them to say, Edmund confesses all. Edmund heading to quadruple figures. Edmund spends his final hours with God to confess. It will be good press for you too, Father. You know, should you need some brownie points. You will become famous on the back of my fame. I don't mind. I love the papers." Edmund was back to smiling again. The thought of being back on the front pages always made him happy.

"Edmund, I will tell everyone what you have done."

"Thank you, Father, you are a good man. I suppose it comes with the job."

Edmund reeled off the places that he had worked, missing people, people who had got in his way, and people unfortunate enough to have recognised him at a hotel or at a park who, before they had a chance to say anything, ended up in a wheelie bin or a skip. Edmund had spent a little under three years on the run. He had been good at keeping out of sight most of the time, but when he was spotted, it didn't normally end well for the other person.

Chris arrived at the cell ready to transport Edmund to the last room with a very small audience he was ever going to be in.

"Father, when they ask you what it was like at the end, can you tell them? Can you tell them that I was smiling, happy with myself, and everything that I accomplished? Can you tell them, Father? Can you tell them I was calm? More than calm, I was cool. Cool, and it didn't bother me. I don't want them to think that I went to the chair screaming, and kicking. It is important for the film, Father. They need to get it right. You know, like the man on The Green Mile. Don't tell them I was tired though. Just that I walked and smiled, and I had a dream. That's it, Father, I had a dream. There was me, the One, Father Harry and the Alphabet Killer all on stage. All receiving the accolades that we so rightly deserve. Oscars, Father. Oscars and what is the English one? BAFTAs, Father. Yeah, we will win some of them."

Father Matthew nodded at Edmund.

They took the walk to the sounds of the inmates rattling their cell bars again. Edmund was waving at them and cheering with them. He heard them as fans. They were there for him. They got to the section where Father Matthew was to take the door to the right and Chris was going to take Edmund forward. Edmund suddenly stopped, and looked at Father Matthew.

"Don't forget, Father. Cool and calm." Father Matthew went to grab the handle to the door. As he did, Chris James leant over, and whispered into Edmund Carson's ear.

"You fucked and murdered your precious Miss Walker. You, sick fuck." Edmund Carson's scream was so loud that it stopped all the inmates rattling their cages. They froze at the sound. He instantly went from the showman to the psychopath. Chris James got a headbutt for his troubles. Every arm and leg kicked out from Edmund uncontrollably. Father Matthew dived into the room to the right, and closed the door. He didn't want anyone in there seeing what was going on in the hallway. Father Matthew breathed. He wasn't expecting that. He tried to compose himself then went back to sitting behind Mrs Gosling. She was the only person in the room. He waited a second before putting his hand on her shoulder as it was still shaking from what had just happened.

Chris James had used the name that nobody used around Edmund. He didn't like the thought of anyone knowing he went quietly. This was payback for his niece, and the hundreds of people that he had killed over his reign. Chris wasn't normally a petty man, but Edmund wasn't a normal man.

This was the name that had cost the judge his life in the courtroom. This was the name that stopped the trial, from that point on he was just sentenced. The courtroom had seen him at his best and his worst.

The whole courtroom had been listening to Edmund's stories. They often weren't in sequence, to keep the courtroom guessing, but there was one story that had never been mentioned. Edmund never mentioned a Miss Walker. The judge made the mistake of doing so. It was believed it was a random meeting. She had picked him up in her car, and offered him a lift home late one night. After parting company, he supposedly went back, and broke into her house. He raped and brutally murdered her on her living room floor. The fact that nobody found the body for weeks meant they struggled to established an accurate time line. The judge told Edmund that he had been delusional through his whole career. After consulting with psychologists, the court believed that all the time Edmund had been talking to her. Some of his social media stunts, his messages to the press; they had her in them. It was as if she was still there, still a part of his life. The judge said it was believed to have been the main trigger in his escalation. The reason he was who he was, was because he murdered the only person he really cared about. His teacher. Edmund had seemed calm as he sat there, and listened to the judge. When asked for his defence, he stood up again. He had been unchained since he started to defend himself. He walked the walk he had done a hundred times, preparing to speak to the jury about what he heard. There was almost an air of excitement about what he was going to say.

Then everything changed. He suddenly ran at the judge, and before anyone knew it, he was on him, biting his neck. He tore a hole out of his throat with just one bite. Then he grabbed a pen from the table in front of the judge, and drove it through his eye socket, and then into his neck. When he had finished, he turned, and held his hands straight up in the air as if to say he was done. There were screams from the whole courtroom. The guards didn't have time to shoot. They were armed, but it happened too quickly.

Edmund stood and turned to the jury. He apologised for his actions, and explained that the judge had been wrong in his assumptions. He then headed back to his seat. There was shock in the courtroom. The guards calmly walked up to Edmund and asked him to accompany them. He did what he was told. The guards on Callington Island weren't being so polite to him this time.

There was a lot of noise coming from behind the screen. Shouting and screaming. It took ten minutes, but eventually the screen went up and Albert, Chris and two other gentlemen were in the room. Father Matthew presumed one to be Michael's replacement, and the other to be the doctor that Detective Morris had brought in. Edmund was still kicking on the table, but he was restrained. Chris James had made sure of it. There was blood coming out of the side of Edmund's mouth. He had managed to actually bite one of the guards who was now being patched up. Chris James had blood running down the side of his face, but he was smiling. It was a big smile. Father Matthew knew he had done it on purpose. Deep down he knew why as well. He didn't deserve to go peacefully.

They all stared at the clock until it struck midnight, and then they began the procedure. The injections started to flow. Edmund started to calm down as the liquid went in, and looked around the room. Father Matthew tore a blank page out of the notebook he had been using. He tore the page up, as if to tell him, I don't care about you getting more famous. Chris James had given him the idea to have his last say to the world's greatest serial killer. It was little justice for the victims, but now Chris and Father Matthew felt a little better.

Edmund's face was one of horror, but then, suddenly, it changed. He began to smile again. It was a true and genuine smile from Edmund. He turned his head to look into the corner of the room. Father Matthew turned his head too, and so did Mrs Gosling. There was nothing or no one there. Edmund gave a little wave of his fingers. The guards and Albert clocked it too. They were all now looking at the imaginary person in the corner of the room. Father Matthew was adamant that he mouthed the words I love you as if he was actually seeing someone in the room with him.

Edmund Carson didn't deserve forgiveness. He deserved exactly what he got. Father Matthew stayed with Mrs Gosling for a while, ensuring that she knew that he was gone. He heard her story again, but comforted in knowing that the whole chapter was over. That she would now get some peace, and be able to move on the best that she could.

Edmund Carson, The ONE, Father Harry, The Alphabet Killer's reign of terror was over. At least she could be thankful that she had been the one that got away.

Chapter 11

Father Matthew walked out of the prison, and stood by his car breathing in the fresh air as he had done so many times. This time it felt better; it felt healthier. He didn't want to go through that again. Edmund had been evil in its purest form. The world was a better place without him. He was hopeful that the world would never see another. As he opened the door to his car, his phone rang. Knowing what time it was, he instantly knew it wasn't going to be good news. Especially when he recognised the voice on the end of the phone.

"Father Matthew?"

"Nigel, it's very late."

"Father, it is Michael." There was a croaking in his voice. Father Matthew was right; something was very wrong.

"Sorry, Nigel, what is up with Michael?"

"Father, I need your help. I didn't know that's what he was doing. I didn't know, Father. I thought he was OK, Father." Nigel was almost turning hysterical at this point.

"Calm down, Nigel. Tell me slowly what is going on with Michael." There was a silence at the end of the phone. Father Matthew could hear Nigel trying to control his breathing, it took a minute, but he answered softly.

"He is dead, Father. He is dead."

Father Matthew put the phone down, and drove to the hotel as fast as he could. He went straight to room number one; Hayley and Nigel were sitting on the bed. Hayley was holding him. Nigel was covered in blood, and looked soaking wet.

"What happened, Nigel? Where is Michael?"

"He is in there, Father." Hayley shook her head at the Father, and pointed towards the bathroom door. Father Matthew could tell by the look on both their faces that it wasn't somewhere that he wanted to go. Not after where he had just been.

As Father Matthew pushed the door to the bathroom open, he could see Michael in the bath. He had slit his arm from the elbow joint to the hand. One was done fully; the other looked as if he had passed out halfway. Father Matthew went to the side of the bath, and sunk to his knees. He grabbed his hand. He was cold, very cold. He was gone. Father Matthew suddenly felt guilty. He had wanted him gone, off the island, as soon as possible so he could speak to Catherine and Mary, but he didn't want this. He said a little prayer and headed back into the main room. He went and sat in the chair next to the bed. The toll of the day was really getting to him now. He didn't know how much more he was going to be able to take. It took him a while, but he finally spoke.

"What happened, Nigel?"

"I don't know, Father. He didn't say anything to me. Most of the time he just sat there looking out of the window. It wasn't until about nine o'clock he asked me if he could have some pen and paper as he wanted to write a note to Catherine. I said fine, and gave it to him. The letter is over there on the desk. He then said he needed a bath, Father, and he really did; he still had the blood-stained clothes on from four days ago. I phoned the detectives; they said it would be fine. I bagged all the clothes for them for evidence, and they are over there. I said, "Take a bath, and I will see if we can get you some clean clothes." He went in there, and I rang his parents. They dropped some clothes around. I didn't let them in, Father; Detective Morris told me not to. His parents are with Kevin in the bar at the moment, Father. I said they could see him when he had finished. I know I shouldn't have, but I thought a quick conversation would be OK. After about thirty minutes, I knocked on the door, and he didn't answer. I went in, and found him like that. I tried to get him out of the bath, Father, but he was already dead." Nigel was almost sobbing at that point. He felt all of this was his fault. Leaving him alone in the bathroom had been a mistake. A mistake that cost a life.

"I need to call it, Father. I need to, but they are going to blame me."

"There is no blame, Nigel. You didn't know what he was going to do; you did everything right. They agreed he could have a bath too, Nigel." Father Matthew got up, and sat next to Nigel. He put a hand on his shoulder.

"But I should have kept an eye on him, Father. I shouldn't have let him go in there alone. But there was just a little window, I knew he couldn't escape the room. I thought it was safe." Father Matthew took a breath. It had been an exhausting day. He was sure it would have been one for Michael also.

"I think he had his own form of escape, Nigel." There was a shared look of agreement between all three of them. Father Matthew wanted the day over and done with; he needed the day over and done with. His emotions were all over the place. Sadness at what had happened, rage at why it had happened, and what he was going to have to do now.

"Michael has made his choice, and his peace with God. Let's just call Detective Morris, and let's get this mess cleaned up." That was exactly what Nigel needed. Someone to tell him what to do next. As soon as Father Matthew did, Nigel got up, and did as he was told. He disappeared out of the room to call Detective Morris.

"Father, nobody is telling us anything, did he kill Alana?" Father Matthew waited for a second. Everyone was going to find out eventually so there was no harm in telling her.

"I am afraid so, Hayley, but it was an accident, of sorts. He wasn't really to blame." Father Matthew knew it was going to come out. If not from Nigel, it would be leaked some other way. Secrets didn't last long on Callington Island.

"But why would he do that, Father? That is not Michael. And the others? Was he involved in that too? Sister Sarah, Sister Trinity?" Father Matthew knew the problem with releasing a little information always meant that there would be questions.

"Just Alana, Hayley. It's a long story, and this isn't the time to get into it, but we will, I promise. It was a mistake that should never have happened." Father Matthew was tired. This had felt like the longest day in his life, and although it wasn't over yet, he was wishing it had been.

"They are still looking for Sister Trinity's murderer. They are not part of what the doctor and Michael were up to. They have assured us of that. The detective and I, we do believe them. This was all about the drugs, and for some, the money. The stupid things we do for money."

Father Matthew went over to the table and picked up the letter addressed for Catherine. He opened it and read it in his head. Michael confessed to it all: the drugs, the doctor, and most of all what had happened between him and Alana. Father Matthew tucked it in his pocket. There were some things that Catherine didn't need to know. Nobody did, and Michael being unfaithful was one of those things. They had all been through enough. Father Matthew turned just at the point that Nigel re-entered the room.

"I have called the Detective, Father, and they are sending the doctor from the prison over to collect the body." Nigel sounded a beaten man. Father Matthew could tell the events of the day were weighing on him as well.

"She was a little mad, but I don't think surprised in what he did."

"No, the poor lad had been through enough. He probably thought this was his only way out."

Father Matthew gestured to Nigel. It was time to leave the room. There was nothing else they were going to be able to do for Michael now. They all walked to the bar, and sat with Michael's parents until the doctor had been and taken away the body. It had been a long night for all of them. After the doctor had left, they all said their goodbyes, and headed home.

Father Matthew pulled up outside the church. He looked at the vicarage, and the church, and then headed into the church. Although it was late, he needed to ensure that the night's events meant something. He needed to know that he still had a role in this world. After spending some quality time in the church for the next thirty minutes, he headed home to bed.

Although it had been a long night, Father Matthew needed to be up early. He wanted to be the person to tell Catherine about Michael, and then there was another case hearing at the court house. Getting things back to normal was going to be key for all of them.

Catherine was in pieces. He told her as little as possible: the way he had been manipulated into the drugs situation, that he had been used by Alana and Dr Mitchell, and that he had lost his way. He had been trying to raise money for the wedding, and ended up being involved with drugs and killing Alana. He didn't mention that Michael had been unfaithful although he knew the rumour mill had already started. He then left Mary to continue to console their daughter. Sandra and the sisters were going to have to tend to breakfast by themselves today. On the drive over to the court house Father Matthew played everything over in his head. It all seemed to have happened in slow motion. Although it felt like six months, everything that had happened had done so in less than a week. Sister Trinity had died on Saturday night, and it was only Friday morning.

When he arrived at the court house, there was only Nigel sitting in there. He wasn't as buoyant as he had been awaiting the Sam Purnell case. Today he looked tired.

"Are you OK this morning, Nigel?" Nigel hadn't seen him walk in, and looked up from the floor.

"Yes, Father. Thank you, Father. It's been a hell of a week, hasn't it?" Father Matthew nodded at him.

"I was just thinking the same, Nigel. We must carry on though, and do our duty to the best of our abilities. Try to return to normality as quickly as possible." They both nodded their heads in agreement. They both knew it was important to the island, and to their own lives

"How is Catherine taking it, Father?"

"As well as can be expected. I have kept the fact that Michael was unfaithful out of the conversation, and I would appreciate if you did the same. There is only us that know that part." Father Matthew placed his hand on Nigel's to show that he really meant that.

"Of course, Father, I won't say anything."

"How did you get on with the other detectives?"

"They were very reasonable, Father. They knew there was nothing I could have done. I just wish I had known what he was thinking."

"People can always surprise you, Nigel. There was nothing you could have done to stop him." Father Matthew had been thinking about that all morning. There was little any of them could have done.

"From how the letter was written, he had made his mind up. Thinking about it, it was probably for the best for all concerned. He probably didn't want to put his parents or Catherine through any more, and I don't think any of us would have wanted to be sitting here with Michael in the dock." Nigel shook his head.

The judge appeared through the door and sat down.

"Where the fuck is the murdering bastard!"

The judge was loud. He didn't care who heard him say that. He didn't even check the room. If he had, he would have seen Father Matthew and Nigel with their mouths wide open at his statement. He stood up and stormed back out of the court room. Within five minutes a young woman had appeared in the docks followed by Chris James. The judge followed them in thirty seconds later.

"So, let's begin." The judge sat and opened the file in front of him. He was already shaking his head at what he was reading in front of him before he started to speak.

"Are you Eleanor Scath? Born nineteen seventy-three on July twenty-seventh?"

"I am." The judge didn't look up to acknowledge her agreement.

"You were on the fifteenth of June two thousand and ten convicted of murdering three teenage boys, all under the age of consent so cannot be named. You wilfully, and not under duress, confessed to these killings, stating that they were going to, in your words not mine, "shop you in" for having sex with under-aged children. For that you were given the PDS sentence and now sent here. Do you have anything to say?"

The woman in the dock just looked down. The judge didn't lift his head; he just expected a response.

"Do you have anything to say?" The judge was as loud as he had been when he first walked in the room. Something was very wrong now. The woman remained with her head down. This time the judge stood up and faced her direction.

"You don't have anything to say? Just say, no, I have nothing further to say. What the fuck is wrong with you, people? I sit here every week, every week and read, listen, watch what happens and nothing. There is no shame, there is no remorse for what you have done. Do you not care? You killed three teenage boys, for fuck's sake. You not only killed them, but you fucked them beforehand. What kind of sicko are you?"

303

All four people in the courtroom were now fixated on the judge. This rant had come from nowhere. Nigel went to stand up, but Father Matthew pulled him back down. This wasn't the time to question a judge, not in front of an inmate. But they were going to have to find out what was wrong with him.

"This world is going to shit, and so is everything in it. Murder is murder, Eleanor, there is no way around it. You can't just shag and kill; it's no wonder you were dubbed the Black Widow. You kill, you should be killed. That is how the justice system works. Too many people get away with too many crimes. This has to stop. They should tie you up and…"

"Judge?"

Father Matthew tried to bring him back to reality. Judge Reynolds looked directly at Father Matthew. If looks could kill, Father Matthew had the feeling that he would have been the fourth death on the island that week. It took a moment, but the judge's face softened a little.

"Father, you are a man of the cloth. You say something. Somebody, for fuck's sake, say something. Is it fine to carry on like this? We continue to make a mockery of the justice system. I make a mockery of the justice system. I promised, I swore an oath, to protect and serve the greater good. To find justice and give justice where I can, and I haven't done that. I have made a mockery of my whole fucking entire life by coming to this godforsaken island. Who am I to sit here and be judged unless I am judged? That is in the fucking bible for Christ's sake, Father."

The room was silent. The judge's rant hadn't really made sense to anyone, but him. They were all waiting for him to speak again. He stood and looked around the room as if considering his options of what to do next. Then he sat down, took the file in front of him, and closed it. The whole courtroom watched as the judge slowed his own breathing down, and then returned to normal.

"Fine, say nothing then. Eleanor Scath, your sentence is to be carried out at Her Majesty's service six weeks from today pending any appeal. That is the last time I want to say that. I can assure you all. Fucking appeal, my arse."

The judge slammed his gavel down and stormed out of the room. Chris James threw a glance in the way of Nigel and the Father before leaving with the murderer Eleanor Scath.

Father Matthew and Nigel both sat in a state of shock for a few moments before Nigel broke the silence.

"What…what was that all about? I think the judge has really lost the plot, hasn't he?"

"I don't know, Nigel. It would seem our judge is not in a good place. Not in a good place at all." They had both picked up on the fact that he had asked to be judged during his outburst which made both of them think of the allegations that Detective Morris had brought to the island with her.

"I think we need to tell Detective Morris about this episode, Father. It is so unlike him. He is normally quite a quiet man, and given what we now know about him, this could be serious. He may have done something, Father, maybe even something that we don't know about?"

"I agree, Nigel. She was next on my list of people to visit after last night's confession so I will come with you." They both got up, and left the courtroom together without speaking another word. They were both playing the judge's outburst over in their heads trying to make sense to it. Neither of them came to an answer by the time they reached the police station. The doctor that had been in Edmund's execution the previous night was there next to Detective Morris and Detective Green when they walked in. Dr Mitchell had already been taken to the mainland following the events of the previous night. There were a number of files on the table in front of them that were all mixed together by Detective Green on his arrival. Father Matthew didn't concern himself with that. It would seem everyone on the Island had secrets nowadays.

"Father, how may we help you?" It was the first time he had seen Detective Morris off balance. She had been the one to ask him to come and see her first thing in the morning after Edmund's confession. He wasn't going to point that out in front of an audience.

"Something I would like to discuss in person, Detective Morris."

Detective Morris moved them over to one side of the police station. It was only one room, so it was going to make very little difference privately.

"I would appreciate if, as much as possible, Detective, we did not mention about any relations between Alana and Michael. I have not told my daughter that part and would, if possible, like to keep that from her. Well, for as long as possible." Detective Morris was nodding in agreement.

"I understand, Father, I will try my best, but it will come out in court, you do know that? I am sure that the press will get hold of it too. They always seem to find a way."

Father Matthew did know that, but he was hopeful he could keep Catherine away from court and the press. There was now no reason for her to go to the mainland, and Michael's case was never coming here.

"I do, Detective, but we can try." Detective Morris was looking behind her. All the papers had been cleared, and Detective Green and Nigel were standing waiting for them to finish. She took three steps to the right to ensure everyone was back into the conversation.

"How was it with Edmund Carson last night?" Detective Morris spoke loud enough for everyone to hear.

Father Matthew pulled out a list with dates, places, and Edmund's reason for "working with them".

"There is the list. He has given me some names, but I am not sure how many are real because, as he describes it, they had already been 'worked with'. Which means, I am not sure how he knew their real names. The locations are probably more helpful. He is responsible for these in whatever person he was at the time. I don't think he has lied about them. He was adamant that the world needed to know that he 'worked' with them. If anything, it felt like there could have been a lot more." They were all nodding in agreement.

"As I said before, Father, there were large chunks of his story never told. One paper picked up on it and called it 'the forgotten year'. Edmund picked up on that too, he then was sure that it would make another great film. Even now that he is gone, it feels like he will still have something to say."

"It did feel like he was trying hard to remember them all, but there were so many. He spoke a lot about the Alphabet Killer. He was very proud of that work." Detective Morris was nodding again. She knew it would have been hard to listen to his story. She had been thinking about it a lot the previous night.

"There is a view that if we had let him carry on using social media, we would know a lot more. He would have told us a lot more. There were times he went off the radar for quite a while. Everyone would think him to be dead, and then he would pop up again from nowhere." They were all silent for a moment. Edmund was still forefront in both of their minds. Exactly where he would have wanted to be.

"That is a lot of cases, Father. I will check them all. Thank you, Father. Thanks for listening to him. I am sure it wasn't easy. Not something that I would have liked to have done." Detective Morris lied for the benefit of appreciation.

"It wasn't easy, Detective, but he is at rest now."

"I hope not, Father, I really hope not." Detective Morris took the list, and placed it in the drawer of Nigel's desk. She had taken it over as it was the only desk in the office. There was a moment's silence, and a shared look between the detectives that made Father Matthew feel uncomfortable. Detective Morris nodded without saying anything, and Detective Green started to speak.

"We now believe we have a serial rapist, and murderer on the island." There was a look from Nigel and the Father; this was clearly news to both of them.

"A rapist? Has there been another attack on the island?" Nigel was the first to respond.

"No, not here. The doctor here informs us that the DNA we found on the first victim, Sister Trinity, matches the DNA from a number of cases from the mainland. Two of rape, and a further two of rape and murder. Sister Trinity was not his first victim. She was just his latest." Father Matthew almost felt like the point was directed at him again. He didn't respond.

"And this guy is now on Callington Island?"

"We believe he was or is, yes, Nigel. With the discovery of Doctor Mitchell's boat, we are not ruling out the fact that there are other ways on and off of this island." Nigel knew that was directed at him. He had been the one to tell the detectives that there certainly wasn't another way off the island. However, if the weather had been better, both the doctor and Michael would have left the island and escaped capture.

"Where on the mainland?" It was Father Matthew's turn to speak now. He had been working through the possible thoughts of the detectives. He knew they would be looking into people travelling both ways.

"Sorry, Father?"

"Where on the mainland were the other cases you mentioned? We may be able to help, knowing the local people and where they travel." He was only saying what he knew they had been thinking.

Everyone was looking at Father Matthew now.

"All in the south so just a short trip. Whoever it was could have made the journey across and back in a day. These were presumed cold cases as we haven't seen or heard of this guy for a couple of years, but it would seem he has reared his head again."

Father Matthew was silent. They were all still looking at him. It had started to make him feel even more uncomfortable. The silence had gone on way too long until Nigel finally broke it.

"I was just about to say about Judge Reynolds' breakdown in court today, Father. I don't really know how to explain it. He was in a bad way. Wasn't he? And he used to travel back and forth, didn't he, Father? He did." Nigel's mind had now gone into overdrive.

"How do you mean, a bad way?" It was Detective Morris's turn to ask the question.

"Well, not his normal self. Full of rage and disrespect for the law. He practically screamed at the accused. Cursed at all of us, didn't he, Father? Something has rattled his cage. At first, after what we know, I presumed having more police on the island had started that. Wouldn't you? But now? Now it feels like something else. Something else has him rattled."

There was a silence around the room as they all changed their glare to Nigel. He was now openly talking about the judge and his past. It was as the detectives thought, it was Nigel who had told Father Matthew.

"You think he has something to do with this, do you, Nigel? With what has happened to the sisters?"

"I am not sure, Detective Green. Although he has only been here a few years and travels backwards and forwards from the mainland a lot. He has not been himself since the time the Father and I told him that you were coming to the island."

"Yes, but his MO, or suspected MO, is not for rape and murder, if you do not include his wife. The rumour had him involved in child offences. Besides, is he physical enough? Sister Trinity wasn't a small girl. She put up a hell of a fight." Detective Morris figured at this point Father Matthew knew everything already. So, if this was a possible suspect, then it did not matter what was said at the police station.

"You never know, do you? He is an old man, but I would say still fit. He walks everywhere, and I know David put a gym in his house. He didn't think he ever used it, but he has one. He ticks a lot of the boxes for what we were looking for, doesn't he?" There was a brief silence whilst everyone thought about the judge. Father Matthew knew that he ticked a lot of the same boxes, so he still kept a watchful eye on all the detectives. There was something they weren't telling him.

"No, Nigel is right, you don't know. I think we need to pay him a visit."

Detective Morris took the car keys off of the table and left closely followed by Detective Green and Nigel. Although they hadn't been officially invited, Father Matthew and the doctor followed the detectives and Nigel to the judge's house. On arrival, Detective Morris told them to remain behind whilst they entered the building. It was less than five minutes before they returned, and asked them both to join them in the judge's house.

"It may be hard for you to see, Father, but I figure that you may be able to say a prayer for him or something. It was right for us to come here. It would seem the judge was in a dark place; he has taken his own life." Father Matthew stopped walking towards the house for a second. Another suicide. Another suicide on the island, his island.

"Our second suicide in twenty-four hours. This really is turning into a busy island, Father." Detective

Morris was keen to let him know that it wasn't the quiet conservative place that he had once described to her.

As Father Matthew entered through the main door, he could see the judge hanging in the hallway from the staircase.

"It would seem he stood on the top banister and then just jumped off. The rope is tied to the banister behind him and hung over one of the support beams. To make sure it took all his weight I would guess?"

The doctor immediately went up, and started to let him down. Nigel and Detective Green supported the body as it reached the ground, and laid him out. It had clearly been too late; the judge was blue and cold.

"He must have come straight home and hung himself. Father, I knew we should have stopped him and spoken to him. Maybe we could have stopped this." Father Matthew shook his head at Nigel. He was still hurting from Michael and wishing he had been able to stop that suicide, and here he was with a second.

"Nigel, the judge will have made his mind up to do this." Detective Morris turned to look at Father Matthew. She didn't say anything. She was just looking for an expression on his face. There wasn't one.

"Yes, I think that is exactly what he did, Nigel." Father Matthew shook his head in agreement.

They each slowly started to walk through the house leaving the doctor with the body. Nigel knew that something had the judge in a state. He figured that there must have been clues in the house to why he had gone to such extreme measures to escape the prying eyes of the new police officers on the island.

"Detective Morris, can you come through here. I think we have found something."

Detective Morris followed the sound of Nigel's voice. He was in the study with Father Matthew. Father Matthew was by the laptop, and Nigel had arms full of photos. The whole study was immaculately clean. Everything in the room was in its rightful place. All except for the desk. On the desk there were pictures of half-naked children. His laptop was open and there was a note written on the screen. It was a short note.

I am sorry for everything that I have done. I am sorry for the children, sorry for killing his wife, and he was sorry for killing Sister Trinity.

Below the confession, there was one line saying, just check my internet history.

"It was him. He was responsible for all of it. We have our man." Nigel was almost happy at that point. Father Matthew could tell there was a sense of relief washing over Nigel. It wasn't washing over everyone else in the same manner.

"It would seem that way, Nigel. I must admit though, I don't normally have everything laid out for me like this." The detective had known paedophiles, and generally they were secretive and embarrassed by what they did. Judge Reynolds had always been like that. He knew the police were looking into him over the years, and not once did he slip up. Why would he now when there were more police on the island. Detective Morris was rereading the note over and over again.

"Look at some of the wording on the note. The word 'He' generally means it is written by a third party. That's a little odd for a very educated man, isn't it? Wouldn't he say, I am sorry for killing Sister Trinity?" Father Matthew agreed with that as soon as the detective pointed it out. The judge would never be that sloppy with his grammar no matter what state of mind he was in. He was a very educated man.

"But didn't you say you knew he was a murderer, and a sexual deviant?"

"I did, Father, and we have been investigating him for years, but could never find anything let alone have it left on display for us. The judge isn't that flippant. Trust me, I know the man. The last thing he would want is for his reputation to be tarnished like this. Even if he did take his own life." The more Detective Morris looked at the room the more she didn't like it.

"I guess he didn't mind as it was the end. And if you had seen him in the courthouse today, you would say he was very flippant." Nigel was trying to justify that they had their man. If they had, it was all over. He could tell by the look on the detective's face that she wasn't convinced.

"I guess so." Detective Morris still didn't believe it, but it wasn't for now. Now they just needed to gather the evidence.

"Detective." The doctor was calling from the other room. The four of them left, and met him in the hallway. He was holding the rope and standing over the body.

"What is it, Doctor?" The doctor handed her the rope.

"This, this rope. This is the proof that it isn't suicide, Detective. This is a case of murder that is made up to look like suicide. Poorly, I may add, Detective. I would say that this man has been hanged by someone, maybe for something he did? No more than thirty minutes ago I would say."

They all stood looking at each other. This made more sense to Detective Morris now. She knew when she came into the room that something didn't look right. The doctor took the rope back from the detective.

"I noticed, when I came in, Detective that there was just too much distance between the top of the stairs and the beam that the rope is pulled across. Look." The doctor walked back up the stairs, and put the rope back into its original position. He then pulled the noose back to the top of the stairs.

"If he had placed this around his neck here, look what would have happened." The doctor let go of the rope, and it landed in front of them about five feet off the floor.

"He would have been standing up?" They all looked at Detective Morris.

"Yes, Detective, he would have. The distance is just too great. Now look at the rope. It is worn from rubbing against the beam where someone has pulled him up to make it look like it was suicide." Detective Green followed the doctor up the stairs. Everyone else took his word for it. They waited for the doctor and Detective Green to come back down the stairs before anyone spoke again.

"That would make sense from the note we found in the study that seems to have at least some of it, written in the third person. He is being framed for the murder of Sister Trinity. It would seem like someone wanted the judge to be our murderer."

"He can't be framed for everything, Detective; he had thousands of photos in there. He definitely had a thing for you know... You can't just produce them. They looked like they had been accumulated over time." Everyone knew that Nigel was right. He was guilty of some of the crimes. These weren't just placed there by someone else; they were the judge's. Detective Morris knew all the stories people had been told about him were real. He had been a paedophile, and he had indeed murdered his wife. In the note that was written on the PC it stood out what he was confessing for. This concerned her because if it was written by someone else then they knew what the Judge had done too.

Where the judge and his wife lived on the mainland, he had an upstairs office which she never went into. He had told her that he kept crime scene photos and all his evidence in there. It wasn't a pretty sight, and he didn't want her to see things like that. She had always trusted her husband, but when the accusations started, she became more and more obsessed with his room. One night, when she thought he wouldn't be back till late, she broke into the room. Most of the pictures that she uncovered were now covering the desk in his study. She went through the files. There were hundreds of them. She started to freak out and screamed, then she turned and ran to the door. She hadn't heard him return five minutes earlier. He was standing by the door when she got there. She was screaming again at the judge. He struck her once across the head almost killing her outright. She was dazed and confused, but still standing. She managed to get under him and out into the hallway. It was a high flight of stairs to her right, and he ensured that when he dropped her down it, he did so on her head.

The judge had seen a thousand crime scenes. He knew exactly how to recreate one that would leave no questions. He cleaned the blood that had splattered in the study on the door and the door frame, and even took up a piece of the carpet at the top of the stairs. Taking a knife at it to make it look frayed as if he had been meaning to fix it for some time. He then left the house and returned later. Appearing to be drunk and loud so that the neighbours would hear. They did, and they backed up his story. He was a judge, and they didn't doubt his word. Because of his stature in the community, it was never questioned. Nobody questions someone who had dedicated their life to the law. Not to his face, without real evidence. The police tried to build a case behind his back for years, but could not get anything solid enough. Now they had it, but it was too late to use it. The judge, as he had himself pointed out earlier, had already been judged.

"My belief is that they are his photos. Someone knew him well enough to know where he hid them. Or they were just fortunate when they caught him at home. I have always suspected he had killed his wife. It was too convenient for her to fall down the stairs. I think she probably found the pictures, or some evidence, and confronted him, and that's why he killed her. No, I believe our killer is trying to pass Sister Trinity's death on to the judge. Maybe because he wanted his reputation tarnished. Maybe because it would put an end to all this." Father Matthew could feel Detective Morris's stare return to him.

"We can't prove the first two points now that he is dead, but if he were to be accused of the murder, we could bring his name into disrepute again." That did make sense to everyone in the room.

"What I am also starting to believe is that there could still be two murderers on the island." Every one of them turned to look at her.

"What? How do you figure that, Detective?"

"Because, Father, whomever was writing the message in the study did not include Sister Sarah into the mix. So, I would say if this is sister Trinity's killer, they are only trying to cover their own tracks. Why wouldn't they add the other missing person to the email? Where is Sister Sarah? Is she still alive? That is one of the questions that should always be asked."

There was a silence again. Father Matthew didn't like the tone returning to the detective's voice. It was where it had been before the Edmund Carson's confession, when she thought there were a lot of things pointing back towards him.

"What if it is someone who is just trying to frame the judge for a murder we know about? What if he is keeping Sister Sarah? She may still be alive. You hear about these people all the time, don't you? Keeping women for years. Locked in a basement or somewhere against their will?"

"It very well could be, Nigel." Everyone considered that point. Nigel could be on to something.

"It could be something totally unrelated to the murder of Sister Trinity. A victim or victims of the judge trying to end his career in turmoil. We are monitoring the boats, and we should check to see if anyone has come on or off the island in the last twenty-four hours that we can associate with the judge. We have been concentrating on the prison, and the doctor. We now need to consider everyone on this island again as a potential murderer. Doctor, see if you can match the judge's DNA to that found on Sister Trinity. I do agree with our young constable on one level, and wouldn't bet fifty-fifty either way at the moment. This island seems to be surprising me by the minute."

Nigel's chest puffed out as he contributed to the conversation. Father Matthew was becoming more and more impressed with the way he thought as a policeman. Nigel was going to help solve this case. If it hadn't been for him, they wouldn't now be at the judge's house. Father Matthew was convinced that Nigel, on his own, would have been at the same place today in the case as the other detectives.

"Detective Morris, what do you want me to do with the laptop and the photos?"

"Box them all up, Nigel, and bring them to the station. There may be fingerprints on them, you never know. The doctor can take the body to the prison morgue, if that is OK with you, Doctor?" The doctor just nodded.

"It has been a busy place recently, I must say that. Are you any good with laptops, Nigel?"

"I have had some experience." It wasn't a lie. There was little else to do all day as Nigel sat around awaiting a call at the police station. He had become quite the self-taught IT expert.

"Good. Start going through the history and see what else we can find out about our judge and what he was up to. I have to warn you that some of the content may not be pretty. So, you will need a strong stomach to go through his history."

Nigel started to pull a box together. Father Matthew was a little concerned with the content of the laptop Nigel was going to see. This would be far outside his comfort zone. But with his new-found admiration, he was sure he was going to be able to deal with it.

"If you don't mind then, Detective, I will take my leave. It is gone lunchtime, and I know they need me back at the home."

"That is fine, Father. Clearly, everything that has gone on here is confidential, Father." Father Matthew just nodded.

"Thanks for your help again. I will be seeing you soon."

Father Matthew knew she meant what she said. There was that tone in her voice again that let him know. He left them all to it. The doctor was putting the body bag down next to the judge, and Nigel was packing up the study. Father Matthew went directly to the home. He knew, with Mary and Catherine still grieving, they were going to be pushed to cope with the activities of the old people's home today. When he arrived, both Mary and Catherine were with Sandra in the kitchen clearing up.

"You are late, dear, I was expecting you before lunch." Father Matthew took a moment to look at his family at work. He remembered standing in the same position last Friday when the world was a different place.

"Yes, I am sorry; I was caught up with the detectives. I didn't believe you two would, you know, be in the right frame of mind to help today." Deep down he knew better. He knew that they would be worried about Sandra and the rest of the sisters being able to cope with the amount of people missing from the old people's home now. It reminded him that he had to follow up the email to the mainland for extra resource. They could really do with it now.

"No point dwelling on what has happened, Dad. We have to get on with things."

Catherine just put her head down and carried on drying the dishes. They were his wife's words; he knew them all too well. He helped them to finish clearing up in silence and then asked all of them to go and sit in the dining room. He thought about calling the sisters too, but it was going to be easier to break it to smaller groups, so his family and Sandra were going to have to be first.

"I am afraid I am not the bringer of good news today either. It would seem that the judge has also been murdered. It is better you hear this now as I am sure it will be all over the island shortly."

Catherine started to cry again. This had been going on and off all day. It was mainly still for Michael, but now there was another death on their island. Her home was starting to feel less safe all the time. As it was for everyone.

"The judge, oh, my God. What is going on, Father?"

"I don't know, Sandra, but with the judge, it was made to look like suicide. There is a belief that someone from the mainland is involved. They have tied Sister Trinity's death to some others from a few years ago. Cold cases, so they believe that we may have had someone from the mainland come across and killed Sister Trinity and now possibly the judge."

"But why would they do that, Dad? Why?" Catherine's tears had stopped long enough to ask the question.

"There are some things in the judge's past that are under investigation. Some things I would rather not talk about, but as far as Sister Trinity is concerned, I have no idea. She was a good woman. If we are to take something positive from the whole thing, it is that at least it seems it is a visitor. Someone who isn't associated with our island." Mary and Sandra took some comfort in that point, but Catherine barely heard it.

"What about Sister Sarah? Where is Sister Sarah?" Mary had been asking the same question as the detectives. It was now the most prominent question on the island.

"She wasn't mentioned." Father Matthew was very brief in his answer. Mary noticed it. That wasn't like him. He noticed the look from his wife also.

"Whoever killed the judge left a note, meaning to write it as the judge, but made some spelling and grammar mistake's. It only mentioned Sister Trinity. That is what initially made the detectives suspect of foul play, and then it was corroborated by the fact that it would have been impossible for the judge to do what he did." Father Matthew nodded towards Catherine. Mary put her arm around her again. He had done enough to ensure Mary didn't ask any more questions about the judge. After a while, Catherine calmed down. Her Father gave her the time to do that. There was only so much he could say whilst his daughter was in tears.

"These are horrible times, Father Matthew. How can this all be happening to us?"

"They certainly are, Sandra, but all we can do is stick together, and pray for a quick resolution." They all nodded in agreement.

"I suppose the good thing from that is that it's not someone from the island."

"I didn't think it would have been, Sandra; we are a close family here, aren't we? I think we would have known if one of us was capable of this." He knew as soon as the words were out of his mouth that Catherine was going to think about Michael. One of our own had been capable of this. He was about to change the subject when Mary chipped in.

"I hate to accuse anyone, dear, but what of Miss March? Do we think she knew this murderer from the mainland and brought him over? I know she has lodged an appeal for Damien Winter, given that there is an identical crime on the island whilst he had been locked away. I wouldn't bring it up but the ladies' knitting circle have been saying this for a few days. It sounds a plausible answer, don't you think? She may have paid someone to do this? Maybe she didn't like the judge as well and thought it might stop the whole process? Give them some more time." Mary was jumping to conclusions as was the rest of the island.

"I would suggest she is high on the detective's lists of suspects now. I am sure they will be speaking to her again in due course."

"So, what will they do now? And what about the appeal? Who is going to be at the prison and the reading of the cases?"

"I don't know, dear. I guess we will get another judge sent across to us."

"People are beginning to believe that the prison is still the cause of all this, Matthew. If we knew what effect it would have on this community, we should have never started the process of bringing the prison here."

Father Matthew didn't disagree with his wife. He had been having those doubts over the last few days also. He was blaming himself for this situation that had arisen. Although the only people that had been charged with crimes at the moment were both locals before the prison arrived.

"H-H-H-he-hello, F-F-Fa-Father." Everyone was shocked to see Alex standing in the doorway of the dining room. Each of their first thoughts was, how long had he been standing there? This wasn't the type of conversation for him to hear.

"Hello, Alex, I didn't see you sneaking up on us. How are you today? You are a welcome happy face at the moment, I can tell you." Father Matthew gave the women a look to stop the conversation. Alex was smiling as he approached them. It was clear he wasn't affected by what was being said so he must have only just arrived. Father Matthew suddenly thought that he was going to have to tell him at some point. He was the closest thing to a relative that the judge had on the island.

"Oh, now you get up, do you? All the work is done whilst you have been lazing around in your room with your programmes." Mary smiled at Alex as he sat at the table. She had thought exactly the same as her husband.

"Don't you pick on him, Mum, he always helps when he can, don't you, Alex?" Catherine was wiping away the tears. The whole family thought the same. He was to be protected from this. He had enough on his plate.

"Besides, I got a flower this morning so today has to be a good day." Catherine smiled over at Alex and her father. Father Matthew felt a huge surge of pride in his daughter. After everything she had been through, she was still here helping others.

"Y- Yes, A-a-always h-help."

"I saved you some pudding if you are hungry, and I was just about to sit down and have a game of cards with

Mr and Mrs Johnson if you fancy it, Alex. Let's leave the oldies to talk about all the bad stuff."

Catherine smiled at Alex and put her arm in his and escorted him out of the dining room. There was a moment of silence; they were all feeling the love for Catherine.

"She is a credit to the both of you know? I am not sure I could be as strong considering what she has been through in the last twenty-four hours." Sandra was shaking her head, but she also had a tear in her eye.

"I don't think I would have been either, Sandra. After about an hour this morning, she stopped crying and just set off to help with the lunches." She reached out her hand and put it in Father Matthew's.

"I think when this is all over, dear, we can take her for a trip somewhere. Just a short break, maybe into the capital, to treat her. Take her shopping, something that doesn't involve a wedding dress." Mary agreed.

"I think she would like that, it's a great idea. The capital is a lot safer nowadays." Father Matthew had a flashback to the previous night's confession. Five years ago, nobody wanted to visit the capital in case they were unlucky enough to come across Edmund Carson. It had taken a few months after his capture for people to feel safe on the tube once again.

"OK, that is enough for now. I have saved you some dessert too, Father, so why don't we all sit down and have some pie and a nice cup of tea." Father Matthew and Mary agreed, that was the best piece of news so far today.

Chapter 12

Saturdays were generally a quiet day in the church and the home. Father Matthew, Catherine and Mary were all on duty for breakfast, and Sandra was busy creating a pasta bake and salad for lunch, something that just needed warming up in the oven, so they all had some spare time. The residents came and went as they pleased, various friends and family from the island would visit at the weekends and take them on trips into the town or down by the sea for a few drinks in The Fleece. After breakfast Catherine and Mary helped Sandra finish preparing lunch, and started on the dinner vegetables. Father Matthew had been in the church after serving breakfast. Just pottering as Mary would have called it. Making sure the place was spotless for the big day tomorrow and working slowly on his sermon thinking about what he was going to have to sit and write that afternoon as he always did.

Given the week he had had and the conversations with Edmund Carson along with the other inmates he had spoken too, he wanted his speech to reflect the good of God and the evil that is in each of us. He was standing at the altar when Detective Morris and Green entered the church. Although he knew it was never going to be just a social visit, he tried to keep everyone upbeat.

"Good morning, Detectives."

"Morning, Father." Father Matthew walked down the aisle of the church to greet them.

"Seems a lovely day outside. Let's hope for a better day all around, shall we? With God's blessing the worst may just be behind us."

"It does seem like a better day, Father." Father Matthew could tell by the look on both of their faces that it wasn't going to be a better day. Something was coming.

"So how can I help you?"

"I am sorry to do this, Father, but, Father Matthew, you are under arrest for the murder of Sister Trinity, and the suspected murder of Sister Sarah, you do not have to say anything, but it may harm your defence if you do not mention, when questioned, something you could rely on in court. Anything you do or say can be given in evidence."

Detective Green continued to read Father Matthew his rights. Father Matthew felt his mouth open wider as he did. From the tone of the voice, and the fact that Detective Morris was now undoing the clip on her handcuffs, he knew how serious they were.

"I am sorry, Detective. You are arresting me for the murder of Sister Trinity?" Father Matthew was shocked that their investigations had brought them to this conclusion.

"Yes, Father. I hope you listened to Detective Green. Whatever you say." Father Matthew nodded his head.

"Now, given where we are, I am presuming I do not need to handcuff you to leave here?" She gestured at the handcuffs at her side.

"No, Detective, you do not. I will come and help you any way that I can, but I have to ask, do you know what you are doing? You know I am no murderer, don't you, Detective?" Detective Morris didn't acknowledge what Father Matthew had said; she just gestured towards the door.

"We can discuss this further down the station, Father."

As they started down the aisle, Mary walked into the church.

"Good morning, Detectives."

"Good morning." They both spoke in unison.

"I am just going to help the detectives, Mary. We will be back shortly."

"There isn't another?"

"No, Mary, there isn't... Everything is going to be fine, and I will be home shortly to write my sermon for tomorrow." Father Matthew kissed his wife and then followed the detectives. Neither of the detectives spoke or made eye contact with Mary, they were just keen to get Father Matthew back to the station.

They left the church, and got into Nigel's car. The journey to the police station was done in silence. When they arrived, Father Matthew was put into the cell, and then the two detectives and the doctor stood as close to the front door as they could so they could continue talking. It was a very small police station, and they clearly didn't want to be heard in what they were saying.

After a short while, Detective Morris came over and spoke to the Father.

"Father Matthew are you willing to give us a sample of your DNA? I can get a..." She didn't need to finish her big speech.

"There is no need, Detective, of course I am happy to do so. May I ask why?" Detective Morris didn't respond to his question. She had turned around before she spoke.

"Thank you." She nodded over to the doctor, and he left the station to get his bag out of his car.

"Father Matthew, is there anyone you would like me to call before we get started? A lawyer maybe?" Father Matthew stood next to the bars, so he was as close to Detective Morris as he could be.

"No, I don't believe so, Detective. I don't need a lawyer. I have nothing to hide. Besides, we don't have one on the island anyway." Father Matthew could tell that between the two of the detectives, they weren't completely convinced in their actions. There was a doubt in what they were doing.

"OK. I think we should do this at the desk, is that OK with you?" Father Matthew nodded.

"Yes, that is fine, Detectives, but I assure you I am not a murderer. I am a man of God. We take that very seriously, Detective. All of the commandments actually." Father Matthew spoke with a smile as wide as he could. It was all he could do to show them that they had the wrong man.

The doctor walked back into the station with a little medical bag, as Father Matthew came out of the cell and sat down. The doctor came over and stood next to him.

"I just need to take a swab of your cheek, Father."

"That's fine." Father Matthew opened his mouth. The doctor quickly opened his bag and pulled out a cotton bud. He swabbed the inside of his mouth, and then placed the cotton bud into a little test tube and sealed it.

"I am probably going to need five to six hours to get the results."

"That is fine, Doctor; we can hold the prisoner, sorry, Father Matthew for forty-eight hours until we have to decide if to formally charge him." Detective Morris didn't look at Father Matthew as she spoke.

"Father, before I go, can you let me know the last time you had physical contact with Sister Trinity?" Father Matthew smiled at the doctor.

"Physical contact? If you would like to know the last time that I held her, it was after she passed, Doctor."

"You touched the body after she was dead?" The doctor clearly hadn't read all of Nigel's reports as he had been very thorough with the explanations.

"Yes, Doctor, Sister Trinity was naked when we found her so I dressed her. It is not a fitting way for a sister of the church to be seen, no matter what the circumstances of her passing were. I explained all this to the detectives and Nigel. I believe it is in all their reports." The doctor looked over at the two detectives, and then back to Father Matthew.

"And when you dressed her, Father, where exactly did you touch her?"

"It would be hard to say, Doctor. I pulled on a pair of undergarments for her and then picked her body up and placed it on her bed. I then pulled over a long gown, moving her arms into position, and ensured it covered her completely. I then placed her back on the floor so that Nigel would know where she was when Sandra found her."

The doctor picked up his bag and walked over to the door, again beckoning the detectives. Father Matthew was a little closer now, so he could hear them talking.

The doctor pointed out that Father Matthew had contaminated the crime scene and whatever he found now could almost be inadmissible.

The doctor left, and the detectives returned to the desk. There was a shared look between them, and a moment of silence before they began.

"Interview with Father Matthew conducted at ten thirty-one a.m. on the seventh day of the sixth month two thousand and nineteen. Present are Detective Morris and Detective Green and Father Matthew. Father Matthew has waived his rights to council, isn't that correct, Father."

"Yes, that is correct, Detective."

Father Matthew didn't lose eye contact with Detective Morris all the way through her speech. He knew who was leading this investigation, and he wanted to ensure that they understood every word he had said.

"So, Father, can we hear the story one more time?"

"Which story is this, Detective?"

"Sunday, Father. What happened last Sunday?" Father Matthew continued smiling at the detectives. They had made a mistake and his was keen to ensure they knew this.

"Oh, OK, you would like to know the timeline of events for Sunday?" The detectives were nodding at him.

"The whole day? OK. I woke around six o'clock I think, went to the church and said my prayers. That is very normal for a man of the church on a Sunday."

"Did anyone see you, Father?"

"I don't think so. My wife is a light sleeper; she can probably confirm the time, but waking up, and going to pray is something I do every morning. You may want to speak to the residents as you can see the church from quite a few of the windows. Anyway, said my prayers, came home, ate some toast, drank some coffee and headed over to the prison. I logged in a little late which you can check also. About five to eight, I believe, for an eight o'clock sermon in the chapel. The chapel was already full when I arrived."

"And Damien Winter, the Sheffield Strangler, was in the chapel?" Father Matthew knew that name was coming.

"Yes, he was, along with another forty to fifty inmates of the prison." Father Matthew was keen to point out that Damien Winter was not the only murderer in the room. There were dozens of them.

"It is a popular service. I gave my sermon and then drove back home."

"But you spoke to him, didn't you, one-on-one, with Damien Winter?" Detective Morris was back at her notes. Father Matthew knew this was for effect. She wasn't the one doubting what she knew. She knew exactly what she was doing.

"Yes, sorry, you are right; I did. We spoke about Miss March, and her obsession with him. There was a guard present, Arthur, I think. I am not sure how much he may have heard, but you could ask him."

"We have, Father. He didn't hear a thing. Can anyone else witness what you were discussing, Father?" Father Matthew looked at her, perplexed. He had explained that they were alone.

"Can anyone witness, Detective?"

"Witness what you spoke about?"

"I don't believe so, Detective, but that is what we spoke about. I am a man of God; why would I lie about that?"

Detective Morris flipped her pad forward and started to make notes. Something wasn't adding up. It was almost as if they were trying to spook him into saying something.

"Shall I go on?" She nodded at the Father.

"I spoke with Damien Winter and then drove back to give the first Sunday service back at the church. Once complete we all went to the home as usual."

"When you say all, Father?"

"Catherine, my daughter, Mary, my wife, Michael Peterson and I. And probably four dozen of the residents. I can name them if you would like." Detective Morris was shaking her head.

"Just for the record this is Michael Peterson. Who confessed to murdering Alana Jones not two days ago and then committed suicide. He was also the intended son-in-law of Father Matthew."

"Yes, that Michael." Father Matthew said that in such a tone that Detective Morris knew he was angry at that statement. The detective noted it had been the first time he had shown emotion through the interview.

"We went and helped out at the home, as we all do, every Sunday, Detective. We helped plate up the meals, and then sat down for Sunday lunch with the sisters of the church." Detective Morris was back to looking at her notes.

"So, at what time did you discover the body?" She didn't look up. He knew it was a test.

"I didn't discover the body, Detective."

Detective Morris looked up. They shared a look between them. She had been trying to catch the Father out; they both knew it.

"Sandra, our cook, she discovered the body. It must have been quarter past twelve or something like that as we sit for dinner at twelve every week, and she was out delivering dinners to the bedridden residents. She must have noticed Sister Trinity was missing, and gone to deliver her some food. I didn't really ask."

"And what happened then?"

"Well, we all heard someone screaming; it was quite the shock. We left the dining room to find out what the commotion was about." Detective Morris paused and put down her pen. She leant back in her chair.

"How did you know where the screaming was coming from?" Father Matthew could feel this was a key point to her.

"I followed the noise, Detective."

"When you said, followed the noise, it was constant? Was it?" Father Matthew didn't like the way she said that. His mind went back to the day. He honestly couldn't remember it just happened so quickly.

"I believe so, Detective. I followed the noise to Sister Trinity's room and found Sandra and the body of Sister Trinity on the floor."

"How was it constant? Like argh, argh, argh or just one long argh?"

Father Matthew was still thinking.

"I think it was one long argh." Detective Morris opened her book again.

"You think it was one long argh. And her room is what? A minute, a couple of minutes from the dining room?" Father Matthew just nodded. He knew exactly what she was getting at. Someone screaming for that long you would remember more vividly.

"And when you arrived at the room, how was the body positioned on the floor?"

"Naked, as I said before, all bar a pillow case across the private parts."

Father Matthew gestured to the lower half of his body.

"Other than a pillow case across her private area. A pillow case that you later removed." Detective Morris stopped herself. She had gotten ahead of herself. She was getting keener in her questioning.

"Father Matthew, can you confirm that Sister Trinity was a blonde-haired lady?"

"Yes, I believe she was, but you know that. Why are you asking me? Not that I am sure the colour..." Detective Morris interrupted the Father.

"And, Father, did you know she was blonde before that moment?"

"Yes, I guess I did. We have known each other for a few years. What difference does that make?" Detective Morris was back to writing in her pad.

"So, you had entered the room and found Sister Trinity. Then what happened, Father?"

"Well, there was a lot of noise, people were arriving from the dining rooms and the bedrooms, and I didn't want them to see her like that, so I sent them all away." Detective Morris paused again.

"They were all arriving because they followed you. Is that correct, Father?"

"I suppose it is yes detective."

"You suppose, and once they had arrived at your crime scene you sent them away, leaving just you at the crime scene." Detective Morris's tone was one of judgement. Father Matthew knew she was getting closer and closer to her point.

"It was not my crime scene, Detective, but yes, I suppose so; I was on my own with Sister Trinity for a short while; I proceeded to give her the last rites." Detective Morris was back at her pad.

"You gave her, her last rites? Why would you do that, Father? Isn't that supposed to be before they die?" Detective Morris was smug again. He could feel it from her.

"It is, but I felt that someone should say something. She was a sister of the church, after all. Given what had obviously happened to her, it felt the right thing to do." Detective Morris almost leapt out of her seat at that point.

"Obviously? Why do you say obviously? Are you a doctor, Father? Or a policeman? Why would you presume to know what had happened? You found a body and you presumed what, Father? She had been murdered?" Father Matthew caught his breath. He could see this was looking worse and worse for him. Anything he said could be twisted against him.

"Yes. I could tell foul play, Detective. She couldn't or wouldn't have done that to herself. She was a sister of the church. It didn't look like suicide, and I feared the worst for her at that time."

Father Matthew's tone was turning to disappointment. Detective Morris could tell that she had him considering his words. That was exactly where she wanted him to be.

"So how long were you alone at the crime scene for?" Father Matthew thought for a second.

"I don't really know, five maybe ten minutes, I suppose?" He was now wishing he had listened to Mary and Sister Bethany.

"Alone with the body for five to ten minutes. And then what happened?"

"Sister Bethany arrived with some clothes for Sister Trinity and we, sorry, I mean I, dressed her with Sister Bethany in the room."

"And did Sister Bethany say anything to you at that point? About what you were doing." Father Matthew knew exactly what she was getting at.

"I believe so." Detective Morris was again going through her pad.

"You believe so? You believe she said something like, I think we need to leave the crime scene as it is until the police get here. I think there may be DNA or fingerprints." Detective Morris was looking directly at Father Matthew now.

"She did say something along those lines, yes, but as I explained to her, we couldn't leave a sister uncovered like that. She did agree with me in the end." Detective Morris didn't move her glare.

"She didn't have a lot of choice, did she, Father. You were already dressing her. And then remind me, Father, who was next into the room?"

"My wife I believe, and yes, she said we should have not touched the crime scene also." Father Matthew was keen to make sure that Mary wasn't going to get dragged into this. He had started to see how this looked from an outside perspective, and it wasn't looking good for him.

"And correct me if I am wrong, Father, the next to arrive was the doctor, Dr Mitchell, who for the record, has also confessed to drug trafficking, and failure to report a murder. Then the island's constable arrived?"

"Nigel arrived first, and then the doctor." Father Matthew knew she knew that. It had been another test to see if Father Matthew would tell a lie.

"Once the constable had arrived, you didn't leave, Father. You insisted on helping the constable look for clues. Is that correct, Father? You helped in the search for clues?" Father Matthew knew how that looked also now. He had insisted on helping Nigel because it was Nigel. They all knew that he needed help.

"Yes, that's correct. Anything I can do to assist the police I feel is part of my duty."

"Your duty, thank you, Father, and what did you find in your brief stint as a police detective? What did you find, Father?" Father Matthew shrugged his shoulders.

"Me? Nothing! Sister Trinity was a very simple woman." Detective Morris nodded at him. He knew what she wanted him to say. He thought it over in his head for the first time. There was nothing wrong in saying it as it was the truth.

"Nigel, however, found a black envelope with an M clearly embossed on the front with an unknown white powder inside."

"For the record, the white powder was later discovered to be the drug commonly known as M. Cocaine laced with the ashes of the bodies from the prison." Detective Morris had just wanted Father Matthew to mention it.

"Father, whose idea was it to empty the packet across the whole crime scene? Was it true that you let Nigel go through all the drawers whilst you wandered around the room and subsequently, he found the package?"

"No, Detective, we just searched together. It was nobody's idea, Detective. Nigel just found the packet, and accidently emptied it." Father Matthew was mad at the suggestion. They all knew how Nigel was. He had been thanked by the detectives on several occasions in the last week for his support, and now they were criticising him for it to make a point.

"Where is Nigel, by the way?" Father Matthew had noted that he wasn't with them at the beginning, but now he was concerned. If Nigel knew that they were planning to arrest him, there was a good chance other people knew this now too. Mary could even know. That started to upset Father Matthew.

"Nigel is on other duties at the moment." There was that tone again. It was none of the Father's business where the constable was.

Nigel had been with them on the car ride over, but he had already left the car before getting to the church, and was at the vicarage when they were taking Father Matthew away. He had a search warrant for the house to see if there was any evidence of foul play or drugs in the house. Nigel explained that it was just routine, but Mary and Catherine were in pieces as Nigel went through their home. Father Matthew hadn't told Mary when he left that he had been arrested, but Nigel did. He didn't believe it was right, and didn't believe the accusation to be true, but he had to follow the orders from the other detectives.

Father Matthew was worried now, he wanted this to be over as quickly as possible. His head kept going over possible scenarios about where Nigel was, and what his family would be thinking. He just wanted to get back to his family.

"He found the packet in Sister Trinity's bible, and just emptied it. In fact, he was about to lick it when I told him not to. He didn't know what it was."

"But you did?"

"No, I didn't know what it was either. Detective. I was just pointing out that he didn't know what it was. That is why I stopped him." There was a pause in what Father Matthew had said. Both detectives heard it, Father Matthew even heard it himself.

Detective Morris and Green looked at each other. They both believed Nigel to be worse than useless on arrival to the island. Although they had to admit that he seemed to be improving by the day. His actions at the first crime scene hadn't shocked either of them. They had seen all of the pictures. They got up from the table and walked over to the door again. They covered their hands over their mouths to ensure that the Father didn't hear them. He didn't. They came back to the table.

"Father, can you, just for the record, confirm the goings-on of Saturday night?"

"Yes, of course. I was home with Catherine, Michael and Mary. They were all planning the wedding, and I was watching TV. It was a chat show, ITV I believe. It must have been around ten o'clock when Michael left, and the girls went to bed. I went outside to walk around the grounds. To think over my sermon, and then went to the church for about an hour to make sure everything was ready for the morning." Father Matthew was quick, and to the point.

"And nobody saw you that night either?"

"I don't believe so, Detective. As I have told you already. Not many visitors that time of night."

Detective Morris took a long pause. Father Matthew could see that something was coming.

"Father, from what I have heard in the last fifteen to twenty minutes, would you like me to recap?"

"Yes, please, Detective, it's all true. I will swear on it if you would like me to." Father Matthew put both his hands out in front of him as if to hold a bible.

"You may have to, Father, at a later date." She paused again. They both knew what that meant.

"This is what I have heard, and what we know so far. Sister Trinity's death is believed to have happened between the hours of ten p.m. and three a.m. The new doctor has given us a longer period than Dr Mitchell. Within those hours you do not have an alibi. You have confirmed yourself that you spent an hour and a half alone on the night in question. You then proceeded to bed, and left early hours of the morning. Your wife's statement says she doesn't remember you coming in or going in the morning. The first time she saw you on Sunday was when you were coming back from the prison to do the morning service. The prison where you spent some one-on-one time with Damien Winter, aka the Sheffield Strangler. The Sheffield Strangler who killed and brutally raped his blonde-haired victims, leaving them naked with all, but a covering for their private parts. After the service you went to dinner, and during dinner you heard a scream. That got your attention, and you ran directly to Sister Trinity's room. Sandra and Catherine, your daughter, both confirmed only hearing one scream, but you said it was enough to lead you to that room?" Father Matthew could feel the passion in her voice; she meant everything that she was saying.

"You were the first to arrive. On finding the body, you sent everyone away, and closed the door. At which time you could have very easily tampered with the crime scene. Something you may have missed from the night before. You had, in your own words, five maybe ten minutes to do so, that is in your own time reconciliation. Sister Bethany then arrived, and you proceeded again to tamper with the crime scene against the advice of others. You dressed, and moved the victim contaminating any evidence that we were going to find. You then claim that the constable was responsible for the dusting of cocaine all across the room as he emptied the packet. He seems to believe there was a nod or a look from you to suggest the question, what is in the packet? So, he opened it." That wasn't exactly what Nigel had said. He had said to the detective that when he found the packet, the Father was there also. Detective Morris was baiting the suspect that was now clearly in her sights.

"I think Nigel may have been confused. I did not do that, Detective."

"That may be, Father, but I am not. I think you are not the man the people on this island believe you to be. I think you wanted the prison here for your own reason. I think that one day you knew you were going to be caught, and that day is today, Father."

"Caught for what, Detective?" Father Matthew raised his voice for the first time. He had been nothing but co-operative with the detectives, but they were now making this personal. He could feel their passion for making all of this sit on his shoulders.

"Caught for multiple murders, Father, multiple."

Father Matthew was about to answer when Detective Morris's phone rang.

"Forgive me. Interview terminated at eleven twelve with Detective Morris leaving the room."

Detective Morris answered the phone as she walked outside. She was gone for about ten minutes, and Detective Green didn't say a word in her absence. Father Matthew played back her statement in his head. He had known there were no alibis. He knew that was always going to put him in question. He just didn't know it would lead to an arrest. Detective Morris came back into the police station and immediately pressed record on the tape machine again.

"Interview resumed at eleven twenty-three with all parties back in the room. Father, just so you know, the phone call that I took that ceased the interview was Constable Johnson, and they found nothing at your home."

"You have had people looking at my house? What did you believe you would find? I have nothing to hide, Detective, I could have told you that. I have been nothing but supportive through all of this, with all of you?" Even Detective Morris could tell that Father Matthew was getting cross now.

"Yes, Father, we have had people at your house. This is a murder investigation." She wasn't budging from her accusation stance.

"But I haven't done anything, Detective. I keep telling you that. Oh, Mary and Catherine must be so worried now. Have you told them that you have arrested me? This is just a big misunderstanding." Father Matthew's anger was now turning to despair at the thought of his wife and child going through this today on top of everything else that had happened that week.

"Is it, Father? Talk to me about all the trips that you have made to the mainland." Father Matthew knew that he was one of the most frequent users of the ferry on the island.

"What do you mean?"

"I mean trips to the mainland over the past four to five years. Let me help you out, shall we? Here is a log of all the tickets you have bought in the last four to five years. We also have dates of meetings that you have had with the government about bringing the prison to the island. Here is a list of the times and dates we believe you to have been on the mainland. There is a lot. Have a look through, and tell me if you disagree with any of these."

Father Matthew took the list off the Detective. The pages kept turning over and over.

"Detective, I was there weekly. Negotiations, suppliers, contractors for the hotel, home, orphanage. It has been my labour of love. Let alone the time I spent with the government. This was all the work I have put in to ensure our Island continues."

"So, you agree with all these dates then, Father."

He sat and reread the dates.

"I suppose so, Detective, there are diaries in my study that have my appointments in which you will be able to check against. I am not sure what you are getting at?" He passed the list back to Detective Green who had remained silent all the way through the interview. Detective Morris made a note about the diaries in the office in order to check it later.

"What I am getting at, Father?"

Detective Morris walked over to a black bag that was placed by the door.

"What I am getting at, Father, is these."

She started to throw down files on to the desk.

"Kylie Savage, Sandy White, Lorraine Summers, Marie Bury. This is what I am getting at, Father. Open them, read them, I have more in my bag over there, go ahead. With a bit of digging we were able to uncover a lot of cold cases linking to this one."

Father Matthew picked up the first file; there were pictures of a naked woman as soon as he opened the file. She had clearly been beaten to death and raped several times, and not just beaten, there was a violence that was hateful and hurtful about it. He read through the case. She had lived alone. Found by a friend two days later. None of it made good reading. Father Matthew closed the file, and placed it gently back on the table.

"What do these have to do with me, Detective?"

"Carry on, look through them all."

Detective Morris opened the remaining files for him, and left them on the desk in front of him so he could see all the bodies. Father Matthew didn't look down. He continued to look directly at the detective.

"Do all the women look familiar, Father? Been a while, I know, couple of years maybe? What happened to you? Did you stop getting your fix from confession? Hearing everyday how others tortured, maimed and killed was not enough for you, was it? You needed to do the same. You needed to become one of them. Father Matthew, you are one of them now. At least you are already home."

Father Matthew sat listening to the detective in shock. She was placing all of these cases at his feet. All of these murders, she considered him to be the Killer. It was his turn to interrupt her.

"No, Detective, I would never…" Father Matthew stood up.

"You would never what, Father? Did you notice something about all of these women, Father? All these women were raped, murdered, and tortured whilst you were on the mainland." Father Matthew sat back down at that point. There was a sinking feeling in his stomach; the detectives were going to try to pin everything on him, and there was nothing he was going to be able to say to help with that.

"And now, Father, now you have started again. When the doctor comes back with your DNA, you will be sentenced, Father, and five years from now you will be back; you will be back on your precious island. And this time, Father, someone else will be taking your confession." Detective Morris slammed a file on the desk as if it were the judge's gavel. She had summed up her case, and given her conviction prediction.

"That is not what this is, Detective. I can assure you I have nothing to do with what has happened to these poor women. Nothing." Father Matthew was nodding his head side to side in disapproval.

"You expect me to believe this, Father. You have no alibi, you have tampered, hindered, and tried to manipulate this investigation from the beginning. Your home is a front for a drug trafficking ring, including your ward Alana, and your son-in-law, Michael. The murdered sister is found with drugs in her possession and, which we haven't even got to yet, Father, Sister Sarah, her ticket for the ferry where was that ordered from, Father? From the computers at the home where naturally one would presume, she would order it from? From her smart phone that actually had the APP to do this? The APP she downloaded months ago. Or was it ordered from the desk computer in your office? That's right, we traced the IP address. Trying to cover your tracks? What happened, Father? Were you interrupted when you killed Sister Sarah? Maybe one of the residents heard something, and it spooked you, so you had to think quickly? You had to come up with a plan to try and put the police off the scent. A disappearance. Then the taste got so much Father didn't it? You had to have more. So, you started a copycat theory; you knew them all, Father, didn't you? You knew because less than a week before, you sat and listened to the case in the court house." Detective Morris was on a roll. She didn't even seem to take a breath as she spoke. Father Matthew tried to replay everything over in his head as she reeled off point by point. All he could think of now was the judge summing up the case. It was all believable. Everything that she said did make sense if he had been listening to it about someone else.

"Everyone knows these cases, Detective. They are worldwide."

"Yes, but not everyone is a murderer, Father. Not everyone is looking for someone to blame for their actions."

"Detective, you have this wrong. You said yourself that you believed the murderer to be trying to blame the judge. I didn't kill the judge. I was with you. I left the courtroom with Nigel, and then went to the judge's house with you."

"I've thought about that too, Father, and you are right; I don't believe you did kill the judge. I think that is a separate case, and I think someone that knew the judge very well did that, someone who knew who he was, and what he had done." Detective Morris was smiling again. It was making Father Matthew uncomfortable. He had come to realise she only did that when she knew she had him.

"But the note, Detective? The note we found?"

"The note you, and the constable found, Father. The one confessing to everything, the one confessing to child abuse, and murder of his wife. The one with the last line that read: he killed Sister Trinity. When was that line added to the note, Father? In context or in the moments that Nigel was distracted with the photos? Did you just type that in the seconds before I entered through door? If I check for fingerprints, am I going to find yours on the keyboard?"

"Detective, this is ridiculous. I am a man of God, I am not a killer. You have me wrapped up in a web of lies, and crimes. If you are trying to frighten me, Detective, it just won't work. I have my faith." Father Matthew was on his feet, so was Detective Green now.

Detective Morris's phone rang for a second time.

"Interview suspended at eleven fifty-three with Detective Morris leaving the room."

She left again, and then quickly returned with the phone still to her ear.

"Interview resumed with all parties back in the room, and Constable Nigel Johnson on the phone. Father, why would you have a locked basement in your church, not just a locked basement, but one with two padlocks on it?"

Father Matthew sat back in his chair. His heart had jumped into his mouth. In all the time that he was in the station he hadn't given the basement a second thought.

"Are there any keys to this basement, Father?"

He didn't answer, he was running through the situation in his head. He knew what was in the basement.

"I said, are there keys, Father? Tell me or I will be asking Nigel to break down your door. I will point out that he is in the church with your wife and your daughter, Father. I will repeat myself once more: are there keys?"

"Yes, they are under the altar, but I, we, can explain."

"They are under the altar, Nigel... You can explain, Father, can you? Have you changed your mind now? You want to communicate? You want to help with the enquiry? Do you need a lawyer now? Nigel is it unlocked?"

Nigel was clearly talking to her down the phone.

"Hurry up then. OK, go in and see what is inside."

The phone was quite close to the detective's ear, but Father Matthew could still hear the screaming from his wife and daughter as they entered the basement.

Chapter 13

Detective Morris suspended the interview again, and told Detective Green to escort Father Matthew back to the cell.

"What is going on? I can explain everything. We thought it was for the best. That is why I didn't say anything. Detective? Detective? Why aren't you listening to me?" Father Matthew was panicking now. The screams from his wife and daughter can't have been good. Something had happened, and he needed to know what.

Detective Green didn't answer him. He just locked the cell as Father Matthew went inside. He then went to join Detective Morris outside of the station. Father Matthew could see them both in conversation out of the window. Fifteen minutes later they came back into the room. There was a moment's silence as they both looked at Father Matthew. Detective Morris had a faint trace of the smile she had when interviewing him. She wasn't upset with whatever it was that made his wife and daughter scream.

"Father, this is unprecedented, but we need you to come with us." Father Matthew was back on his feet.

"To where, Detective?"

"To the church. We are not allowed to leave you here on your own, and both I and Detective Green need to be at the church. You are still under arrest, that I can assure you of. But we do not have enough cover to leave you here." For them both to have to go, he knew it was serious.

"That is fine by me, Detective." Father Matthew took a pause. It was time.

"I am presuming that you have just found Sister Sarah; she will help to clear all of this up. I can assure you." Father Matthew tried to return a smile to the detectives. They weren't in the mood.

"Father, we have found Sister Sarah." There was an uncomfortable look between the two detectives.

"Good, that's really good. Sarah and I will explain all of it. It was all her idea, hence why we—" Detective Morris was keen nothing more was said.

"Father, not now. I need you to keep silent, and keep anything you would like to confess until we have time to put this on tape." Father Matthew didn't like to hear the word confess again. He had nothing to confess. But he nodded and agreed. He knew it was the best way to get a place in the car and head over to his home and his family.

The detectives escorted Father Matthew to the car, and then drove over to the church. The whole trip was in silence. Father Matthew tried a few times to engage them in conversation, but they were having none of it. They pulled up to the church, and proceeded to get out of the car.

"Father stay in the car, please." It hadn't been a request. Father Matthew could tell by the tone of Detective Morris's voice.

"But—" Father Matthew tried, but they weren't going to let him have his say.

"No buts, Father, remember you are in our custody, and you should act as such. Nigel will be back out in a moment to drive you back to the station."

"But I want to talk to Sister Sarah, to my wife, to my daughter, you have panicked them all for no reason."

The detectives ignored Father Matthew and left the car.

Shortly after they entered, Catherine, Mary and Nigel exited the church. Mary could see Father Matthew in the car, but ignored him. She put her arm around Catherine and headed towards the vicarage. Father Matthew went to get out of the car, and Nigel ran over towards him.

"In the car, please, sir."

The 'sir' took Father Matthew by surprise.

"Nigel? I was just going to speak to my family. Mary! Catherine!"

They carried on walking, ignoring his call. The detectives and Nigel had told them to do this. They just needed to get back to the vicarage, and Father Matthew would be taken back to the station for further questioning.

"Mary? I don't understand?"

"Sir, into the car, please. I have instructed your family they are not to talk to you, sir." Nigel was being forceful with Father Matthew.

"I will not, Nigel." His tone was serious, but this time Nigel didn't buckle under the pressure from him.

"It is not a request, sir; I will cuff you, and place you back into the car. Given the amount of people looking out from the home, you do not want that, Father. Now, please, get back into the car."

The word 'Father' had brought him back to reality. That and the quick look at all the faces that were staring directly at him. Father Matthew got back into the car, and Nigel got into the front seat and pulled away.

"Nigel, what is going on?"

Nigel was silent. He had been told not to talk to the Father about what they had found in the church. He was to drive him directly back to jail, and ensure that he was locked up.

"Nigel, whatever it is, Sister Sarah and I will clear this whole matter up."

Nigel still didn't respond. They sat in silence for the rest of the journey back into the station, and Nigel locked the Father back up as he had been instructed to do. Then he went and sat at his desk, facing the window as he didn't want to face Father Matthew.

"Nigel, how long have we known each other? Nigel, we are more than just good friends. At least tell me what is going on here. I am starting to fear for my family, Nigel. They are my family, Nigel." Nigel was uncomfortable. He had been trying his hardest to do exactly what he had been told, but Father Matthew was right. Everyone on the island was practically family.

"I can't, Father, I am under orders from the other detectives."

"But, Nigel, we have been on this case together. We are looking for a killer together, and we need to find them. Whatever has happened, it can't be good, and we need to clear it up, and continue with our search." By now Father Matthew was fearing the worst. Something has happened to make them all respond like this. He was concerned now for Sister Sarah.

Nigel was silent again.

"You don't think I really have anything to do with this, Nigel, do you? You don't think like the other detectives that I am a murderer, and a rapist?" Nigel turned to face Father Matthew. He wanted to look him directly in the eye, but he couldn't; he just looked in his general direction.

"No, I didn't, Father, but the evidence they showed me last night is telling me something different. I am doing what you and the judge said that I have to do, following the evidence. That is my job." He folded his arms.

"Nigel, it is circumstantial. They don't have anything because I haven't done anything. Those dates on the mainland must be just a coincidence. I am sure thousands of crimes were conducted whilst I was there." Nigel held his tongue, but not for long this time.

"What about Sister Sarah, Father?"

"What about her, Nigel? Ask her yourself. I haven't done anything to her. I was helping her. She asked me to."

Nigel didn't respond to his point. He knew he shouldn't have asked about her. He had been told. It was hard for Nigel to not say how he felt. The Father knew this, and he was going to make him talk.

"Nigel, ask her. She will verify everything. I was helping her. That was the whole point of her being there."

"I can't, Father. She is dead! Dead, Father. You know that she is; you locked her in there. You knew where the keys were and everything." Nigel's anger had come to the surface. He was feeling betrayed by the one man he looked up to on the island.

"What, Nigel? She is dead? What do you mean, dead? She was fine. I swear, Nigel. When I left her yesterday she was fine. We spoke a lot yesterday Nigel." The Father was on his feet, waving at Nigel to get his attention.

"I can't listen to this anymore, Father; I can't listen to any more lies."

Nigel almost ran out of the station, and stood outside. By now the rumour mill was in full flow, and there was a small gathering outside of the station looking through the window at Father Matthew. Nigel was talking to all of them, but trying to keep as much information under wraps as possible. He stood out there for the next three hours. The Father watched as he paced up and down. He could tell he was distressed and couldn't deal with the Father on his own.

Detectives Morris and Green entered the room, and Nigel then had the confidence to follow in.

"Get the Father out, and sit him at the desk, I want to continue the interview." Nigel froze. He didn't want to touch the Father again.

"Now." Detective Morris meant what she said.

"Yes, now, Nigel." Detective Green accompanied him to the cell to help with Father Matthew. They placed him back at the desk.

"Interview resumed at four minutes past six with Detectives Green and Morris and Constable Nigel. Nigel, what is your second name again?" Nigel could tell she was mad from the sound of her voice.

"Johnson, ma'am."

"Constable Johnson and Father Matthew."

"Father Matthew, talk to me about Sister Sarah." There was no messing about; she was directly to the point.

"OK, but, Detective, I am fearing the worst; what has happened to her?"

"What makes you think something has happened?"

Detective Morris threw a glance at Nigel. Father Matthew didn't respond to that. He needed Nigel to still trust him.

"Detective, I heard my wife scream. You have all rushed over there, and I have been alone for hours. It's clear she wasn't in the same condition I left her in yesterday." It was plausible that Nigel had kept his mouth shut. The detective moved on.

"You were with Sister Sarah yesterday? What condition did you actually leave her in Father?"

"Yes, Detective, we spoke together yesterday. She was fine." Detective Morris took her pad and pen out again.

"When you say you spoke Father... You spoke, but did she actually speak in return?" Father Matthew knew from the tone of her voice what she was hinting. Edmund Carson was said to speak to his victims all the time. Having long and meaningful conversations he even published them on line thanking people for their input in his career. Father Matthew now feared the worse.

"I think you need to start from the beginning, Father. Start with the ticket, and the lies you have been telling not only to us, but everyone on the island for quite some time."

"Lies?" Father Matthew didn't like that word. He hadn't been telling lies. Although he hadn't been owning up to some truths.

"Yes, lies. We knew something was wrong when we heard Michael's confession back; you didn't mention Sarah. You didn't ask about her and, tracking back, you never have, Father. That started us questioning your real motives, Father. Whether you were aiding or trying to influence the investigation away from yourself." Father Matthew hadn't realised this. As the detective spoke, it became clearer to him what he had done.

"Subconsciously, I would guess, Detective. I didn't realise that I had omitted her from my conversations, because she was fine Detective." Father Matthew knew how that looked. He knew how all of this looked.

"From the beginning, Father." Detective Morris was in no mood for reflection.

"OK, from the beginning. Sister Sarah came to me. She came to me with a problem she was worried she couldn't resolve by herself. As part of her community work on the island, she had spent time with the teenagers and the younger twenty-something's. She would often visit The Fleece and go down by the harbour to make sure everyone was fine." Nigel was nodding towards the detective at this point to ensure that she knew what Father Matthew was saying was correct.

"She discovered through her conversations over some time that there was an increasing drug problem on the island. At first, she didn't believe it, having never seen the drug herself. The teenagers were telling her they had been taking it, and unbeknown to me, Sister Sarah used to have a massive problem with cocaine. We sat and discussed it, and I told her to keep away from the children and the so-called drugs to be on the safe side. I tried to quietly dig around to see if I could find out more, but didn't find anything. Sister Sarah found it hard to keep away from the children. She had, over time, become quite a figure head for the youngsters, and she wanted to continue to be there for them. One night she was given a packet of the drug as proof it existed. The one we now call M. She confiscated it, and brought it back to the home. It was weighing on her mind for days, and, unfortunately, she gave into temptation." Father Matthew sounded almost defeated at this point. As if it had been him that took the drug.

"If you want to check with the sisters, a few weeks ago she spent the day in bed, and that was the real reason. She managed to find a source for the drugs, which she never divulged to me. Even after I told her about Alana, and Michael the other night. She never confessed that she knew it was Alana." Father Matthew was trying to make it as clear as possible that all he had been doing was helping.

"Sister Sarah continued on with her work with the teenagers, but I could see her slipping. I spoke to her a few times and asked if there was anything she wanted to discuss, but she continued to say no. Her eyes were sunken, and her appetite had gone. I figured she was using the drug. In the end it was Sister Trinity she turned to; I guess that is where she got the packet from. Sister Trinity came to me, and explained everything that had been going on. I went to see Sister Sarah, and I asked her what she wanted to do. Clearly, she could no longer take care of her duties as she was. She could return to the mainland or we could try to cure her here on the island. She didn't want to leave. She said she couldn't let others know of her problem or they would never look at her the same. That is why I didn't tell you. Detective, that is why I haven't mentioned Sister Sarah. It was not my story to tell. She didn't trust herself to keep strong through the detox. Apparently, she had done this once or twice before, and failed every time. The only thing that had really made the change was joining the church. That had kept her clean for almost three years."

"So, your solution to the problem was to keep her locked in the basement?"

"She asked me to. If you look at the basement, we set up a bed, a TV, a portable toilet which I changed daily for her. She was getting better, and we were days away from revealing that she was still here. I had told her everything that had been going on, and she was keen to come out, and clear her name as soon as she could. As I said, Detective, it was her choice to decide when she felt strong enough to face the world again. Where is she, Detective? What has happened to Sister Sarah?" It was Father Matthew's turn to ask the question that everyone should have been asking and wasn't.

"How did you feed the victim that you kept locked in the basement of your church Father?" Detective Green asked a question. This was only the second since being on the island.

"I fed Sister Sarah every day from the home, and if I couldn't get there, she had a supply of food down there that she could make. I managed to see her a couple of times a day nearly every day; there has been a lot going on this week. You are not answering my questions, Detectives."

"And when was the last time you spoke to her, Father?"

"Last night. She had had a good day and was feeling so much better. We discussed her return to society for tomorrow, and she agreed."

The detectives paused for a moment. Father Matthew could tell there was something unsaid between them.

"What time last night, Father?"

"I don't know, between seven and eight o'clock. I went to the church, and took her a late tea. We chatted for about thirty minutes, and then I returned home. You can check with my wife." There was another silence.

"Interview terminated."

"That's it? That's all we are going to discuss?"

"Detective Green, please escort the Father back to the cell. Father, we cannot take this any further until we have some more information from the doctor. I am going to go over to the prison now, to find out what we know."

"But what has happened to Sister Sarah?"

"Father that is what we are asking. I would suggest you two take it in turns staying up with the Father this evening. I have no intent of losing another person of interest."

Father Matthew was taken back to his cell. Detective Green stayed for the first watch, and sent Nigel home to get some sleep. It had been a long few days for all of them. The next six to seven hours were in silence. Hayley had sent some food over from the hotel for the Father and the detective, but neither of them spoke whilst eating. Detective Green sat reading a book, and the Father spent his time in and out of prayer. Nigel came in to take a shift at two o'clock in the morning. Detective Green departed. Father Matthew knew this would be his opportunity to get some answers. He gave him a little while to settle himself in before approaching the subject.

"How are you, Nigel?"

"I am good, Father."

Father Matthew could see that speaking to him was making him uncomfortable. They both knew at some point he was going to talk. Nigel had been running this through his head all evening too. He knew he was going to be alone with the Father, so it was just going to be a matter of time.

"And your aunt, how was she?" Father Matthew knew that small talk was the best option at first. Just to get him engaged.

"Upset by the events of the day, Father, the same as most of the people on the island, I would imagine."

"Upset, why would they be upset, Nigel?"

Nigel just looked at the Father square in the eye, for probably one of the first times in his life. It wasn't fear off the Father now; it was more anger towards him. Father Matthew could see it. He just knew he needed to get Nigel back on side. He also knew how let down he must have felt if he believed any of the evidence the Detectives had on him.

"Nigel, you know I didn't do any of this, don't you? This has been one huge mistake." Father Matthew spoke softly. He knew it would help to put Nigel at ease.

"Father, I have been told not to discuss the case with you. So please do not…"

"But, Nigel, you know me. We have been on this island together, well, for your whole life. Do you really think me capable of the things I am accused of doing? Really, Nigel?"

Nigel was already shaking his head. He wasn't sure himself if it was in anger or it was his body saying no.

"I didn't, Father, but the evidence is stacking up, and you could discount all of it until what we found in your basement. Your basement with your set of keys, keys that you, and only you, knew where they were. You admitted to knowing she was in there. I heard you." Father Matthew knew it was time to ask the all-important question.

"Nigel, what did you find in our basement? Of course, I knew she was there. I was helping her. I was saving her from herself. I was trying to do my best for her."

"I can't say, Father. I can't talk about it." From the sound in Nigel's voice, Father Matthew almost believed him. It was croaky now as if the words just wouldn't come out. Whatever had happened it had been very upsetting.

"Nigel, I swear to you and to God I have not done anything. Tell me what has happened, and let's figure this out together."

"I don't think I can, Father." Nigel's voice was almost trembling at this point.

"Nigel, look at me. Look at me. I am not a killer, Nigel. I have served the island to the best of my abilities, and I continue to do so. I always will."

Nigel looked directly at the Father and then glanced away, looking at the wall for the next few minutes. His eyes were welling up with tears that he didn't want the Father to see.

"If I tell you, Father, you can't tell the other detectives that I have; they already think of me as an idiot. You will hear it all in the morning anyway. I am sure they are looking to charge you tomorrow." Father Matthew heard what he said, but paid no attention to it. It was more important he found out what had happened.

"So, there is no real harm, is there?" He was already justifying to himself spilling the story.

"You are not an idiot, Nigel. Now let's sit and see if we can solve what is happening here, together."

Nigel pulled his chair closer to the Father's cell. Whilst deep down he didn't believe he was the killer, he wasn't confident enough to open the cell door.

"Tell me everything that has happened, Nigel."

"It started with the doctor; he linked the DNA to the cases on the mainland a couple of nights ago. I didn't know Detective Green had asked for the files. I didn't know that she was looking into you so much. I didn't know she had been tracking your whereabouts for the last five years, or cross-referencing your visits to the mainland, or checking the IP address on your computer... all of it. Honest, Father, it was like we were working on two different cases."

"They probably thought you were too close to the island to be objective, Nigel." Father Matthew knew what they probably thought of Nigel, but now wasn't the time to have that conversation.

"When I arrived this morning, I mean, yesterday morning now. They told me what they were going to do. I said they were mad, and that you were never capable of what they believed. But they took me through the case they were building, and it all seemed plausible. To be honest, Father, it was the only real answer that covered all the points. I couldn't believe it. They told me to go to the vicarage, and look through your belongings to see if there were any drugs or any other kind of evidence. I did, Father, and there was nothing. I told Catherine and Mary it was just routine, honest, I did, Father. Once I was finished there, I was to go to the church, and then to the home to see if there was anything else. To be honest it felt as if they were just keeping me busy, and away from you, Father."

"As I said, Nigel, they probably knew how close we were. They wouldn't have liked that." Father Matthew was back speaking in his soft voice to keep Nigel on side.

"Anyway, I searched the church and nothing. Catherine and Mary were following me. It was Catherine who pointed out the cellar. I think she was proving there was nothing to hide. That's when I rang and asked where the keys were."

"And they were in the small bowl under the altar?"

"No, they were under the altar, but not in the bowl. Just next to it."

"Wait, they were next to it? Are you sure? That is not where I kept them, Nigel." Nigel didn't respond. It was a point, but not really a valid one for Nigel at this moment in time.

"I went to the basement door, unlocked it, and then I entered." Nigel physically shuddered at that point.

"Mary and Catherine were so close behind. Father, if I had known, I would have kept them away. I think Catherine noticed before I did what had happened, as I heard the scream from her first. Then they were both screaming. I pushed them both back into the church, and went back into the basement alone, Father. I closed the door, Father." Nigel took a deep breath. He was looking directly at Father Matthew now. To see if there was any response. There wasn't. Father Matthew was listening keenly.

"There, on her knees, was Sister Sarah with her bible in her hands, looking up to God. She was facing the bed as if she was saying her evening prayers. Naked, Father, she was naked like Sister Trinity, but she was naked and, in a pose, as if she was still alive and praying, Father. Her throat had been slit, and there was blood all over her body. I walked over to her, Father. I walked over to her, and I could notice that someone had been licking her neck. Like Edmund Carson, Father. It was exactly like an Edmund Carson scene. I have seen all his scenes. It was one of his." Father Matthew knew from the scene Nigel had described that the link was going straight to Edmund. He also knew he had confessed being with Sister Sarah after Edmund's final confession. Even he was starting to believe that this was an open-and-shut case. Nigel took a minute to try and wipe the scene from his head.

"I rang Detective Morris, and told her. That's when she came over, and we drove back. When we spoke later, she said the doctor had been. Sister Sarah was killed last night, well, the night before last night. Her throat had been slit. I had told her about the licking, but that wasn't the end of it. Someone had had sex with her after she was dead. That's how all the blood had managed to get all over the body. Someone had sex with her after she was dead, Father, after. Exactly like Edmund Carson did with his victims, Father. Exactly the night..." Nigel paused. They both knew what night it was. Father Matthew was quickly up to speed with the copycat theory. Father Matthew could see it now, the detectives would paint a picture to say that it was too much of a coincidence that there were two murders with the same MO as two murderers that the Father had been visiting that same day.

"Sister Sarah is dead." Father Matthew already knew it, but the words just dripped out of his mouth. He was trying to come to terms with everything that had happened.

"I am afraid so, Father. Not only dead, but dead Edmund Carson-style."

"That's impossible. I was there when Edmund died, Nigel. I watched it with my own eyes. Even he could not kill from beyond the grave." They both paused, and for some reason they both had the same thought, if anyone could, it would have been him.

"They are not thinking it is Edmund, Father. Detective Morris believes that you are responsible. She thinks that all of these confessions that you hear have started to break down the walls of your realities." Deep down Father Matthew already knew this.

"I must admit, Father, you heard Damien Winter's case in court, and a few days later a body turns up in the same manner, and less than twenty-four hours after you hear the confession of Edmund Carson a body turns up again. With a different signature. Well, the latest signature that you had heard about." They were both now in agreement. There was only one key suspect now, Father Matthew.

"The only thing I can think about, Father, is that you may have spoken to someone. about the confessions or the cases. About all the things you have heard, and they are trying to frame you?"

"No, nobody, I don't have any enemies, Nigel. I have mentioned them in my prayers, ask for forgiveness for what has happened to these people, but nothing else. Besides, what both of these people did in the past, it's all over the internet and news articles everywhere. They were two of the most prolific killers of all time, what they did and how they did it is not a secret." Father Matthew was now leaning back on his chair in the cell. His thoughts for a moment wandered to the chair in the prison. That is where this was going to end up. He was going to end up where he had seen so many people lose their lives before. This case was solved easily if he was the murderer the island would now believe him to be.

"They are, Father, killers whose style of murder now happens to be replicated in your home. Twice." Father Matthew knew that was the truth.

"Not just my home, Nigel. What about the judge as well? They can't honestly think that all of this isn't connected?"

"Detective Morris is convinced you added the words 'He killed Sister Trinity' at the end of the note the other person left. She thinks that his past just caught up with him, and it was just a coincidence that it happened at that time. Also, they were very keen to point out that if it had been the old doctor and me on the island looking at the case, it would have probably gone down as a suicide."

Father Matthew sat in silence for a while. They were right; it did stack up against him, and they would have probably believed it to be suicide. They never knew the judge's past until recently.

"I think we are missing something, Nigel. We have to be missing something." Father Matthew knew it was time to try and clear his name. However he could.

"We are missing something, Father: another suspect. You are the only one in the middle of this and, forgive me, Father, all of the evidence points to you. You even, well, according to them, tampered with all crime scenes. You confessed to having locked one of the victims in the basement for a week. Father, you can't blame them for coming to this outcome." Nigel would have come to the same conclusion given the evidence, but his heart had him feeling otherwise. He needed to be one hundred percent sure of it first; that was the difference between Nigel and the other detectives. Father Matthew meant a lot to the people on the island. Nigel wanted to ensure that if he was the murderer, it would be concrete evidence that would send him down.

"I know Nigel, but what I also know is that I didn't do this. I haven't played a part in any murders. I didn't find Sister Trinity, and all I did was try to help Sister Sarah."

There was silence again.

"Nigel, where did you get to on the list of names that you showed me in the courtroom? You were working on crossing off all the ones with alibis. Did you continue with it?"

Nigel went over to the desk, and came back with his piece of paper.

"There were only a few left, who had the potential to murder Sister Trinity. There was the doctor and the judge, but both are now discounted. Then all that was left was Chris James, the head guard at the jail, Ian from The Fleece, and, well, you, Father. I was down to three, Father." Father Matthew ran the names in his head. He couldn't see either of the other men doing this.

"I thought you said Ian had a disco in The Fleece that night?"

"He did, Father, Saturday night, but apparently went to bed drunk around eleven. It was a long shot, but technically nobody saw him between the hours of eleven and two thirty when Stacey went to bed." Father Matthew shook his head. He didn't believe that Ian was capable.

"So, it is basically down to the two of us, Nigel, and I am sure I didn't do it."

"You think Chris James?" Father Matthew didn't want to flat out accuse Chris. Nobody had suspected Chris had a part to play in any of this. Father Matthew was just keen to point out he was not the only possibility.

"I am sure the evidence against me is as close to the evidence against him."

"Apart from Sister Sarah." Nigel regretted saying that as soon as it came out of his mouth.

"I meant with regards to listening to the cases and the confessions; he is always close to me when we listen to them. I even think he used to help Sister Sarah with the work with the youngsters. He could have come across Sister Trinity then also at some point, I don't know." Father Matthew was clutching at straws now to see if he could get himself out of this by ensuring they knew there were other possibilities, no matter how slim they were.

"So, I should get him in? Arrest him, Father?" Father Matthew shook his head.

"I think you should at least go and have a conversation with him. If you bring him in here, they will think you are protecting me, and diverting attention on to someone else. I need you to solve this case, Nigel. I also need you to speak to my family, and let them all know what a big mistake this is."

Nigel was silent. He knew he couldn't say that as he wasn't one hundred percent convinced of the Father's innocence at the moment. He wanted to believe; he just didn't know if he could.

"I am going to try, Father, I am." Father Matthew looked at Nigel. It was all he could hope for. The only person on the island that was going to be on his side was Nigel, the local constable. Father Matthew didn't want to think about what he would have said if someone had told him this, this time last week. They talked the remainder of the morning around the case and its possibilities. Father Matthew was assured by breakfast that Nigel was going to do everything he could. Detective Morris arrived followed by the new doctor on the island. The doctor went straight to the desk and opened his bag.

"Morning, Father, morning, Nigel." Detective Morris headed straight to the cell.

"Good morning."

"Father, with your permission we would like to take another DNA sample."

"OK, but can I ask why?"

"Inconclusive results, Father. We have confirmed that the person that killed and raped Sister Trinity is the same person that killed, and had sex with Sister Sarah, well, if you can call that having sex." Father Matthew portrayed a look of shock on his face.

"Oh no, Sister Sarah is dead? And what do you mean had sex with her?"

It was Detective Morris's turn to look a fool. She hadn't gotten that far last night, and Father Matthew was keen to point this out. Detective Morris froze. She had made a mistake; it wasn't like her. She was normally so careful with these things. She looked over at Nigel who didn't say a word. She was almost convinced he would have told Father Matthew, but she couldn't even blame this on him.

"What happened to her? She was fine when I left her, Detective." Detective Morris took a deep breath.

"Father, I think we need to resume the interview, on the record."

Detective Green came through the door of the station which made everyone turn to look over at him. Nigel got up at this point. It was handover time.

Father Matthew didn't say any more. He was keen for Nigel to leave, and start working on everything they had been discussing. Detective Green completed the handover with Nigel and told him to go and get some breakfast as he escorted Father Matthew out of the cell and to the desk. He then pressed record on the tape machine.

"Interview resumed."

They were the last words that Nigel heard as he stepped out of the station. Father Matthew was in trouble, and it was his job to help him. Although there was still a little doubt in the back of his mind that he had been played by a very clever man. It was still early, but Nigel wanted to go and speak with Ian first, just to clear up his last possible suspect before tackling the only real viable alternative to Father Matthew. Nigel headed down to The Fleece pub. He thought twice about knocking so early, but knocked on the door anyway. Stacey opened.

"It's a little early, Nigel, even for the police, but if you need a drink and don't arrest us, I am sure we can sort something out for you, my lad."

Stacey just smiled at Nigel. They all had a fondness for him. Most people had a fondness for him. However incompetent they felt he really was.

"I am here to talk to Ian, Stacey. Just to get all of the stories straight from the night of Sister Trinity's murder." Nigel was keen to point out he was on official business. He knew that they liked to tease him, but today he had a job to do.

"You better come in then. But I thought you had caught the killer and it was Father Matthew?" Stacey was just fishing for the latest gossip from the police station.

"Father Matthew is just helping us with our enquiries at the moment."

"I heard he has a sex dungeon up at the church where he tortures women before killing them. Gone completely mad, so I hear. It comes to us all, Nigel."

She smiled at Nigel with that remark. She wasn't one hundred percent convinced that the Father could be innocent, but she wasn't convinced he was guilty either. They had been friends a long time.

"Sit down, Nigel, I will go get him, he is in the cellar. That is where I keep my sex dungeon. Just give me a minute to unlock the handcuffs, take off the gimp mask, that sort of thing."

Nigel sat at one of the tables in the pub. A few minutes later, Ian came stomping up the stairs as if it was a huge interruption to his day.

"What now, son? Busy day today with it being Sunday and all."

"I just wanted to go over our previous conversation around Saturday night."

"OK, OK, what did you want to know?" Ian stood cleaning his hands with a bar towel over the top of Nigel who remained seated. Nigel had his pad in front of him, opened at the page of Ian's statement.

"You said that you disappeared to bed about ten thirty, eleven and then didn't reappear till the following morning."

"Sounds about right." Ian looked over at Stacey, and she nodded to him. He needed confirmation of anything that happened on Saturday night from her.

"And nobody saw you until the morning." Ian shook his head.

"Nah, the wife she would have seen me when she went to bed about two thirty."

"That's right, I did. That is my cross to bear every night, Nigel. Believe me, not a sight anyone should ever see." She was still smiling over in his direction.

"And you were drunk, sorry, intoxicated due to the amount of alcohol you had consumed." Nigel didn't like Ian standing over him, so he focused on his notepad.

"That's right, intoxicated, intoxicated as a newt, I would say."

Stacey's daughter Emma came through the door from the upstairs apartment as they were talking. Everyone turned to look at her.

"Hello, Nigel." Emma gave a flirtatious wave in his direction.

"Hello, Emma." Nigel lifted his head to speak and then focused back on the notepad. Emma had a crush on

373

Nigel although she was still only seventeen. He was one of the only people on the island that wasn't a fisherman. She was convinced that she never wanted to end up with someone like her dad.

"What are you talking about?"

"Just last Saturday, Emma, nothing else. Now go on and start peeling those spuds, lots of Sunday dinners to make." Stacey was keen to get her out of the room.

"Last Saturday. The disco."

"Yes, Emma, the disco." Nigel responded without lifting his head this time.

"The one where I asked you to dance, Nigel, and you wouldn't dance with me?" That got a laugh from Stacey and Emma.

"You asked him to dance?" It was Ian's turn to ask the questions now.

Nigel was now colouring up although he didn't lift his head to show it.

"Why didn't you want to dance with my daughter, Nigel?"

"MMM I did, I mean, I didn't want to, I mean, I can't. I was on duty. I am always on duty." Nigel was struggling to respond. He quite liked Emma although he knew she was still too young. She had been the only girl on the island to ever really taken a fancy to him.

"Take a breath, Nigel; they are only teasing you." Stacey was still laughing behind the bar. Nigel took a moment and composed himself again.

"OK, thank you, but back to the question: you went to bed at eleven and not seen until two thirty a.m. when Stacey went to bed. Is that correct?" Ian was nodding.

"Saturday night, oh, he was seen all right." It was Emma's turn to laugh.

"What do you mean, Emma?" Nigel lifted his head to look over at her.

"I mean that he was seen. Me and the girls went up about twelve thirty. Mum told us to so we went up to my room and kept drinking." Emma suddenly realised what she had said.

"Drinking let's say orange juice, when who should wander in but Dad. Naked. Naked as the day he was born. I want to say we all screamed, but seeing my dad walk around naked in our house has become common place. My friends just laugh now."

"Oi, laugh at what?"

"You, Dad... It is a good job they do or they will be calling Nigel to arrest you for indecent exposure or something like that."

Both Stacey and Emma continued to laugh at Ian's expense. Nigel was trying to bring the questioning back on track, but there was little point. Ian was here, and he was drunk. There was no way he was making it to the old people's home, and back in that state. Nigel's mind had started to wander to Chris James. He was now the only viable alternative to Father Matthew.

"And you say this was about twelve thirty?" Nigel just wanted to wrap this up now.

"Yeah, I think so, ask Gracie and Katelyn. They will be in at lunchtime, Nigel. We just rolled him back to bed. Had to turn the music up as he sounds like a train when he snores." Emma was shaking her head.

"You didn't say anything, love." Ian turned his attention to Emma.

"Dad, if I said something every time you did something stupid, I wouldn't get time to peel the spuds every friggin' day now, would I?"

Emma smiled at her father and then at Nigel, and went back out towards the kitchen.

"Bye, Nigel." She blew him a kiss and laughed to herself as she headed through the door.

"Are you happy enough now?" Ian turned his attention back to Nigel.

"Yes, sir, happy enough, thanks for your time."

"No problem, and next time my daughter says she wants to dance with you, what are you going to do?" Nigel almost fell backwards as he stood up.

"Er… I don't really know. Maybe."

"Shut up teasing him, Ian, and get back into your dungeon." Ian just laughed and turned around to head back to the cellar.

"See you later, Nigel." Stacey was still laughing at the conversation as Nigel closed the door behind himself.

Nigel stood on the road outside. His list was down to two possible suspects. One was innocent, and one was the killer; he was sure of it.

Chapter 14

Nigel took the drive over to where Chris James lived. He knocked on the door, but there was no answer. He knew that Chris didn't keep normal hours at the prison due to being head guard; he was flexible. Although he didn't know a lot about Chris, he did try to keep an eye on anyone that was on his island. Chris had always lived alone since he had arrived and, all in all, he was a very quiet man. Never said more than ten words anytime that they had met. All of this was playing in Nigel's head now. Why hadn't he investigated him closer? He was a prime candidate when you looked at it from the outside. Nobody knew him. Nigel was convinced all murderers were loners at some point in their lives.

Nigel then took the drive over to the prison. Out of courtesy he went to see Albert Finlay first. One of the guards escorted him through to Albert's office. He knew it would be the right thing to do at his place of work.

"Thank you for seeing me, Mr Finlay."

"Nigel, no need to be formal." Albert was sitting at his desk, working on some papers. It overlooked the exercise yard, and he would spend most of his day watching the inmates walk around there. With them only ever being on site for six weeks, the job was the easiest of his career.

"Sorry, Albert." Albert gestured to Nigel to sit down which he did.

"So how may I help you, Nigel?"

"Well, I was here to see Chris James. I just need to take a statement from him for his whereabouts of last Saturday night."

"The Sister Trinity murder?" Albert looked perplexed at Nigel even asking the question. As far as Albert was concerned, Chris would be top of his innocent-list.

"Yes, sir, I mean, Albert."

"You don't think Chris has anything to do with that, do you?"

"I don't know, Albert; all I do know is that we are closing in on whoever it is. So, we need to continue to cross people off the list of suspects. That is the job, I am afraid." Nigel didn't want to let Albert know the list was down to two now.

"I thought the Father had been arrested, and there were bodies found in his basement. Five, I heard. That is what the rumour mill is telling us, Nigel." There was a smile from Albert as he spoke. As with everyone now on the island, they didn't believe, but they didn't disbelieve either. Anything was possible. Albert had seen it all in his career, and for this to be true wouldn't have shocked him.

"The Father is just helping us with our enquiries. Did you say bodies?"

"That was one of the stories going around The Fleece last night. Apparently, he has been killing all the groupies that come to the island. Miss March was in the pub. You should have seen her face. Maybe the rude awakening she needed." There was almost a chuckle from Albert at this point.

"I think the rumour mill may be a little out of control, Albert."

"I would not be surprised, Nigel, not at all. Always seemed like a good man that Father, but you never know. I do see all sorts coming through here. Do you want me to buzz him for you? Chris, I mean." Nigel nodded.

Albert Finlay picked up the phone.

"Yes please, Albert."

About five minutes later, Chris James entered the prison director's office.

"Shall I leave you, gentlemen, to get on with it?"

"It's fine with me, sir, you can stay, if it is OK with the constable?" Chris stood next to the desk where they were both sitting. It was only whilst sitting there that Nigel realised again how big Chris was.

"That's fine." Nigel pulled out his pad. Having Albert as a witness to what was being said was a good idea. It was also a good idea that one of them would be able to call for backup in case Chris was the murderer he was looking for.

"I wanted to talk to you about last Saturday night, Mr James. I believe you had the night off?"

"That's right, always have the night off following an execution. It is not often that it is the same day though." Nigel remembered the fact that Jacob had asked for a morning execution. It had been the first of its kind on the island.

"Do you? So, you had Friday night off as well?"

"Yes, after the Edmund Carson execution." Chris didn't move; he stood firm-looking in front of him. He gave the answers clear and direct.

Nigel's head was ticking. Both nights that the victims were killed Chris James wasn't working. Maybe he really is an alternative killer for the Father.

"And both nights you were at home alone?"

"Yes, I live alone."

"When was the last time you saw anyone last Saturday, Mr James." Chris paused as if recapping the day.

"It would have been about twelve noon in the supermarket. I went to fetch some food for a late breakfast. I spoke with Mr Peterson. He will remember as we talked about football. He is a Newcastle fan, the same as I." Nigel noted there was no emotion in his story. He had read somewhere that was a sign of a good murderer. Being able to keep emotion out of the situation.

"And you never saw another person from then until?"

"Until work the Sunday morning. I went in at seven to help with the early service in the prison chapel."

Nigel was back to writing in his notebook. This was a real solid alternative so far which, whilst it meant that there was an ox of a man standing next to him that he may have to arrest, it also meant that his feeling about the Father could be correct; he may well be innocent.

"How well did you know Sister Trinity, Mr James?"

"Not well. Met her once maybe twice. With Sister Sarah, I believe."

"And how well did you know Sister Sarah?"

"How well did I know her?" Chris moved his head. He looked at Albert, and then down at Nigel for the first time.

Nigel had messed up again, and given away his punch line. He had spoken about Sister Sarah in the past tense. He played it back in his head. He really did accentuate it, in the sentence.

"Yes, sorry, Mr. James. How well did you know her before she was found murdered yesterday morning?"

Nigel wasn't so convinced now about Chris being his man. The look on his face was one of shock. For a big guy, his eyes welled up very quickly.

"Sit down, Chris." Albert could see that the news had distressed him. Chris did as he was told.

"She is dead, Nigel?" Nigel noted it was the first time he had used his name. Something had changed in Chris; he was no longer the non-emotional robot he thought him to be.

"Yes, I am sorry to say, she was found yesterday morning."

"Nigel, was Sister Sarah the body they found in the church? The one from the rumour mill? I thought that was all it was, just a rumour." Albert had heard the story, but nobody had put two and two together and come up with Sister Sarah.

"Yes, Albert, she was." There was a moment of silence as everyone went through the news in their heads.

"And was it Father Matthew? Did he kill Sister Sarah? Is that why he was telling everyone she left?" Chris's voice changed to one of anger.

"The Father is helping with our enquiries, Mr James; that is all at the moment. Can I ask you where you were Friday night?"

"I was at home alone. Wait, you aren't questioning me to see if I had anything to do with this? Are you?" His anger was getting stronger.

Chris James stood up again. Nigel almost leapt out of his own skin. If Chris wanted to, he could kill them all in this room, and be out of the prison and off the island in a heartbeat; nobody was going to stop him.

"Sit down, Chris. The lad is just doing his job. I am sure we are all suspects."

"I am, I really am. I am just making sure that everyone is accounted for at the time of the deaths. I have asked everyone else on the island the same questions."

There was a silence. Chris James sat back down next to Nigel.

"Were you alone, Chris? That is what Nigel is asking. Can anyone vouch for where you were?" Chris shot a look across the table at Albert. Nigel noted there was something about the way he spoke. Something about the way Albert had said 'anyone'.

"I was alone in the house, Albert, but not virtually alone."

Nigel was looking at the both of them.

"I think you need to tell him, Chris. It will clear yourself from the investigation, and he isn't going to tell anyone. Are you, son?"

"Tell anyone what?" Nigel was worried at that point that he had missed something. Chris took a deep breath.

"I was home alone, but I was on the internet. Chat rooms, dating websites that type of thing. The boss here is encouraging me to be more adventurous in myself. He has been a good ear to listen to my troubles over the past couple of years." Chris spoke a lot softer now as if he didn't want anyone but the people in the room to hear what they were talking about.

"Oh, OK, so if I ask for the records of say, Match.com, they will confirm this?" Nigel had been spending time on dating websites too. It was all too common now, and he knew that every time he logged on, it would tell you when a possible match was on line.

"Sort of... Yes... Just not that website."

There was a pause. Albert and Chris shared another look, and Albert gave him a nod encouraging him to proceed.

"You see, Nigel, I am gay." There was a pause in the room. Nigel was the third person Chris had told. The first had been his wife, hence she filed for divorce, and he moved to the island alone. The other had been Albert. In his appraisal six months ago, Chris had broken down when Albert asked him where his life was headed. Albert had been as shocked as his wife when he found out.

"I can give you a list of the websites, and there are a few guys that I spoke to at length both those nights who can confirm what I am saying. Nigel, the only people on the island that know are you and Mr Finlay, and I would prefer to keep it that way. This job isn't an easy one, and if the inmates found out, it would make things worse in here."

Nigel was a bit taken back with the statement. The man was a man mountain. He certainly hadn't expected that as an answer.

"Thank you, Chris. I assure you I won't speak a word of it." Nigel actually meant that. He instantly imagined what would happen if it did get out on the island, he would be the first person that Chris would be in contact with, and he was sure he wouldn't survive the meeting.

Chris James proceeded to reel off names of websites and user names that he had been speaking to. Nigel started to realise that he had no reason to doubt him. For him to come out and say what he did must have been hard enough. He confirmed that between the hours of the murders he was live web chatting, and it could be collaborated with the men he had been talking to.

Nigel thanked both men for their time, and left the office. Twenty minutes later he was back outside the prison, looking at the road in front of him to town.

He had no idea what to say to Father Matthew. He was the only man left on the island who could have committed the crime. He was the only man that all the evidence pointed towards. He must be guilty. Despite what he had been telling Nigel and the others.

Nigel took the drive back to the police station. Detectives Morris and Green were sitting at the desk, and Father Matthew was back in his cell. They had taken his whole statement, and officially told him what had been found in his basement. Upon hearing it back for the second time, even Father Matthew was finding it hard to disbelieve the situation. He knew the case against him was really strong.

"We said go and get breakfast, Nigel." Detective Green was the first to talk.

"Yes, sorry, I was side tracked into some conversations."

"As your punishment you are on second lunch duty. Rachel and I are going to go to The Fleece, and you can eat second, is that OK?" He knew it was going to have to be ok as both detectives already had their coat on.

"Yes, that is fine." Nigel was thankful of them leaving. His head was swimming with questions that needed answers.

"No talking to the suspect though, Nigel; you know the rules."

"I know, Detective Morris."

They both left the station, and Nigel sat in silence. Father Matthew was keen to know what he had found out, but he already knew from Nigel's face it wasn't going to be the news he had hoped for.

"Well, did you find anything?"

"No, Father, both of the remaining suspects have solid alibis. You are the only person left on this island at the time of the murders capable of killing and raping two women. Not just women, Father, sisters of your own church." Nigel's voice was back to being a little hostile. He had been thinking a lot during the drive, and he couldn't help but feel betrayed by Father Matthew.

"Now, Nigel, we have discussed this; I didn't do it. There must be someone else on the island. Hiding out."

"Father, we have searched every inch of this island, every deserted farm house, shack, even the hulls of the fishing boats; there is nobody else on the island. We have monitored the boats. Nobody new on or off the island. I have been through the list over and over again."

Nigel took the list from his pocket and placed it on the desk in front of him. They both sat in silence for a while. Neither really knowing what to say next.

"You are not making a fool out of me, Father, are you? You are not sending me on wild goose chases for your own amusement? They say that is a trait of a psychopath." Nigel had been considering that too. Considering this was all a game for Father Matthew.

"Of course, I am not, Nigel, and I am no psychopath. When the doctor comes back this afternoon with a clean DNA test, I will be cleared. What I am more worried about is that there is a murderer on my island, and my family are out there alone without me to protect them.

Did you get a chance to speak to them?" Nigel shook his head.

"No, Father, but I will later today. What do you want me to say to them? You are hanging all your innocence on a DNA test? Because that is exactly what you are doing." Nigel was more confused the more he spoke to Father Matthew. His instincts were to trust him, but his head and training told him he was their man. He was the only possible murderer on the island.

"It will prove, Nigel that I did not sleep with those women. I didn't, I love my wife, my child and my congregation. This has all been a big mistake."

Nigel sat back in his chair. The sound of Father Matthew's voice always sounded like the sound of trust to Nigel. Every time he had spoken to him over the years, he had wanted to be more like him. After a few minutes, he turned, and pulled a file from the desk.

"What if we have missed something, something from Trinity's crime scene, Father? I have never done one before and you, you contaminated it. There were more people in there than Euston station. What if we have missed something that could lead us to the killer? They say eighty-five percent of victims know their attacker. A photo, a letter? Something that points us in the right direction. In any other direction would be good."

"I don't know, Nigel. The sisters have very simple lives; they don't really socialise a lot or need a lot of possessions." Nigel was slowly coming back on side; Father Matthew could feel it. He needed to keep Nigel with this momentum if he had any chance of getting out of prison.

"What about a bag? I didn't see a bag or a suitcase in her room. You say she came from the mainland a few years ago. Well, she must have brought something with her, even if it was just a few habits, a bible, anything like that would have needed at least a small suitcase." Father Matthew thought for a moment.

"You are right, Nigel. She did have a small suitcase, a little red one, if I remember correctly. Maybe there is something in there?"

"And it would still be at the home somewhere?" Father Matthew nodded at Nigel. He didn't know where it was, but they all arrived with some kind of suitcase.

"Did she have any visitors, Father? Anyone from the mainland ever come to see her or Sister Sarah or both? Did they know each other before arriving here? Do any of the sisters know each other before coming here, Father?"

Nigel was trying his upmost to believe that the Father was innocent, and if he kept on that positive path it was going to make talking to Catherine and Mary later so much easier.

"Not that I know of, Nigel. Although they both tried to help the whole island, so they were always out and about after meal times. They could have easily met someone without me knowing about it."

Nigel sat looking at the file. There was a long silence again. Father Matthew wanted to give him time to think, but not too much as the evidence was overwhelming even him.

"What is it, Nigel?"

"I don't know, Father, I don't know how we have got here."

"I think I have some of the blame for this, Nigel. I believe if I hadn't brought the prison to the island, we wouldn't have had all this. Evil follows evil, Nigel. The drugs, the murders, we even had a paedophile in our midst, and didn't know about it. If I hadn't offered this place up, they would all be alive today." Father Matthew had been reflecting on that for the past twenty-four hours. He had been the one that brought murder to the island.

"I am not sure the judge would be, Father; he wasn't a pleasant man. We just didn't know that he wasn't, but someone did." Nigel felt betrayed by the judge as well. He had decided to dedicate his life to the law like him, and had always looked up to the judge. To find out about his past, and to witness first-hand his internet history had really upset Nigel. He was quickly starting to realise that you didn't really know anyone. That was also a question still niggling him about Father Matthew. If you didn't really know anyone, did he really know him?

"Father do not take this personally, but I need some air. I need to clear my head."

"No problem." Father Matthew knew that Nigel probably felt like he had the weight of the world on his shoulders.

Nigel went and stood outside. He couldn't help believing in Father Matthew, but at the same time he knew his job and all the evidence was hard to argue against. He stood outside the station for the next forty-five minutes. Father Matthew could see him pacing up and down as he had the first time he had been arrested. He only entered back into the station when the detectives arrived.

"I can strongly recommend The Fleece Sunday dinner, Nigel, if you want to go and get yourself some. Nothing will be happening here for a while. We have to wait for the doctor's results, and he is still down there having dinner."

"Thank you, Detective, I will go down there. I have taken a walk over to Hayley also, and she is going to pop some dinner over for the sus—, Father Matthew."

Nigel heard the word 'suspect' coming out of his mouth and stopped himself.

He left the police station and drove over to the vicarage. As he was driving up the lane, he could see the yellow tape still around the church, so nobody could enter. It had been the first time in forty years that there had been no service on the island. This had helped fuel the rumour mill, which was spreading even faster and wilder, about the activities of their priest. Nigel knocked on the door of the vicarage. After about five minutes, Mary answered. She and Catherine had needed time to compose themselves.

"Nigel, oh, please tell me Matthew is OK?" She was ushering him inside.

"He is OK, Mary."

"Come through to the kitchen; Catherine is in there." Catherine was at the kitchen table. A huge smile came across her face when Nigel walked into the room. It was as if he was going to bring her some good news. Mary placed Nigel in the seat next to Catherine at the table and then sat opposite to both of them.

"Father Matthew asked me to drop by and tell you that he is OK and thinking of you, and he will be home soon." As soon as the words 'home soon' came out of his mouth, he knew he had made a mistake.

"Will he, Nigel, will he be home soon?" They both looked at him with hope in their eyes. Nigel paused. He honestly didn't know, but that was not what they wanted to hear.

"I hope so, Mary, I hope so. I am trying my best to help, Mary." He didn't lie. He had been trying everything he could to clear the Father's name, to no prevail.

"What about what we saw, Nigel, what was in the basement? I don't think I will ever be able to go back into that church again." Catherine's smile had disappeared from her face.

"I don't know, Catherine. Father Matthew assures us that Sister Sarah was alive when he left her on Friday night. She had asked to be there. He says she had a drugs problem, and they were working on a form of cold turkey, I would guess. She didn't want the rest of the island finding out. That is why they came up with the story together that she had just gone to the mainland. She was coming back in a day or two. Father Matthew said she had been there for a week or more, and he had been sneaking her food every day." There was a pause from all of them until Mary spoke.

"That would make sense, Nigel. I said to him, I said the food kept disappearing. I said Catherine must have been eating like a horse, but that makes more sense now. He would be helping someone, Nigel. He is not a bad man. He is not a killer, Nigel." It was hardly an alibi, but Mary thought it helped secure her husband's story.

"The doctor has confirmed that she did die Friday night, and she obviously had been kept well up until that point."

"Then his story checks out, Nigel? He can be released?"

"Not really, Mary. There are other factors we still need to consider. As I said, they are working through all of the evidence, and hopefully we can clear him of any wrong doing." Nigel had already gone down the rabbit hole of promising them hope. He was now fully in with the belief that they could fix this. That he was going to fix this. To do so he needed another suspect on the island, and they were all out of them.

"What other evidence, Nigel?"

"I can't say, Mary. Please don't put me in that position. Just know I am doing everything I can for the Father." Mary could see tears building up in his eyes as he said that. She knew she shouldn't be pushing him. He had always been very loyal to her husband, and somehow, she knew that was the best she was going to get by way of support through this.

"I know you are, Nigel. I know you are doing your best."

Catherine got up, and gave him a hug from behind.

"Please bring him back to us, Nigel. He can't have done the horrible things they say; he is my father. He is everyone on the island's Father."

"I will try my best, Catherine."

Nigel couldn't remember the last time he had got a hug from anyone. Especially the cutest girl on the island. This did make him want to solve the case even more. The thought that Catherine would like him was as much as an incentive as you could get.

"I have to go over to the home to see if there is something I have missed."

"OK, Nigel, we won't keep you. Do you need any help? Is there anything else we could be doing? We are going out of our minds here."

"No, I will be fine, and all you can do is pray and keep the people at the home calm. We will get to the bottom of this." Mary and Catherine were both seeing him in a different light. He had developed more as the week had progressed, and now sounded like a real policeman. And, more importantly, one that cared for Father Matthew.

"Nigel, before you go, do you know when we will have our church back? It's just that people are asking."

"No, sorry, I don't. I will ask when I am back at the station though. I am presuming they will need to take more pictures. Will be at least a few days."

Nigel left the vicarage, and headed over to the home.

There was an open-door policy at the home; you didn't have to sign in or out of the facility. Generally, people didn't wander too far when they were on an island.

Nigel went through the dining room, and he could see Sandra chopping salad for that night's tea. He nodded at her, and carried on through to Sister Trinity's room. There was still police tape across the front of it. It was able to come down now, but nobody from the home had wanted to go back into the room.

Nigel started to look through the room again. Nothing had been changed, and there were still odd spots of blood on the floor. There was nothing new, and there was no little red suitcase either. Nigel continued to search as Sister Bethany entered the room.

"Nigel?" She was surprised to see him back there.

"Hello, Sister." Nigel stopped searching, and just stood in the centre of the room.

"What are you up to in here? Can I help you with anything?"

"I am just going over the evidence, Sister, just to see if we have missed something, something important that might help." Nigel stopped. He didn't say the words, but Sister Bethany knew what he meant.

"Might help Father Matthew?"

"Yes, Sister, might help Father Matthew." She knew he liked Father Matthew. They all did, and they were all going to do their best to support him. No one in the home believed that the Father was guilty of the recent events. They were all convinced he had been either set up or it was a big mistake.

"Sit down, Nigel, on the bed. I would like to talk to you."

Nigel turned and sat down; the sisters were as scary if not more so than Father Matthew had been.

"Father Matthew is innocent, you know."

Nigel just nodded. He didn't want to question the word of a sister.

"We all knew of his plan with Sister Sarah; Sister Trinity had told us, but we didn't say anything. What they were doing was between them and God. Sister Sarah had started down a dark road, and he was trying to bring her back from it, Nigel, that is all. He is a good man, Nigel." There was something soothing about her voice as she spoke.

"And will you swear to that, Sister? In a court of law if need be?"

"Of course I will, Nigel; we all will. Father Matthew is a good man. You know that as much as anyone." Now she was holding Nigel's hands as she spoke.

"I know, Sister, but that is not the only evidence we have. There are other factors. For starters, he is the only person on the island with no alibi for either murder. They have linked the murders here to crimes on the mainland when the Father was over there, and they believed he purposely tampered with the crime scenes. His DNA was all over Sister Trinity, and in the basement. They also believe he tampered with the judge's computer." Nigel couldn't help himself; it all just came pouring out of him. He had kept control with Mary and Catherine, but now, with a sister in front of him, he couldn't.

"They believe, Nigel?"

"Yes, they believe, Sister."

"You don't?" Nigel paused for a second. His first reaction was to say no, but he needed to sound as impartial as possible. If this whole mess was to work out to be the Father, he was still the only policeman on the island.

"Honestly, Sister, I don't know what to believe. All I do know is that I have to find truth, clear evidence one way or the other."

"That is good, Nigel. God will steer you in the right direction. I am glad that we have you to help us." Sister Bethany was smiling at him now. It was almost as encouraging as the hug he had just received off of Catherine.

"Sister, Father Matthew said that Sister Trinity came to the island with a little red bag, sorry, suitcase." Nigel knew he needed to find some evidence.

"She did, Nigel; would you like to see it?"

"Yes please, Sister."

"OK, it is in the cloakroom. We keep all our luggage there as there is little room in these places. Follow me."

Nigel followed the Sister down the hallway to the cloakroom. He took down the suitcase, and opened it on the floor in front of her. There were some clothes; they looked like jeans and T-shirts. He held them up to Sister Bethany as if to point out it was an odd combination for a nun.

"She wasn't always a sister, Nigel; we all used to wear other clothes at some point."

"Just odd to visualise, Sister. A sister in normal clothes." Nigel pulled some photos out of the suitcase.

"Do you know who these people are, Sister?"

"Her family, I believe. Mother, father and two sisters if I remember correctly."

"And where are they, Sister, do you know? Why would she keep them here, and not in her room? I would keep photos in my room."

"No, sorry, Nigel. Wait, I think she did say once they were looking to move to Australia at some point, so they may have gone." Nigel continued to pull things out of the case and on to the floor. He pulled a bundle of envelopes.

"And what about these, Sister?"

"I don't know, Nigel. What are they?"

"They look like some kind of love letters?"

There were four bunches of letters. Probably thirty letters in total. Nigel opened the first letter...

"Dearest Trinity. It feels as if time does not pass when we are apart, and yet when I am in your arms an hour feels like a minute." Nigel gave a look up at the sister.

"I think they are definitely love letters, Sister, and quite a few."

"Before she came here though, Nigel. Look, the address, it is in Leicester. Maybe just a keepsake from a different life that she had. She travelled quite a bit, so I recall. Leicester, Newcastle, Scotland." Newcastle stuck in Nigel's mind; it had been the second time it was mentioned today. Chris James was a Newcastle fan, and so was Mr Peterson. Mr Peterson... Had Nigel really looked into him enough? Was he another person? Did he know Sister Trinity?

"I think they are still of interest, Sister, you never know where they may lead... If I can just take the photos and the letters, I will return them, Sister, I promise, and maybe then we can return them to the writer." It was a nice thought from Nigel which helped sway the sister into agreement. Nigel was keen to read them to find out who they were from.

"OK, Nigel, as long as it helps with the investigation."

Nigel closed the suitcase and placed it back into the rack with the other suitcases. All small cases. It would seem all nuns travelled light as they came to the island. Nigel paused for a moment, wondering what they were all leaving behind. Nuns were people you never really noticed. They were there, but not like normal people. Always floating around in the background. Not really knowing any of their story. He was really clutching at straws now, but all he could think of was that it was a good disguise. You don't really look closely at them. If someone were to dress up as one you wouldn't know if they were a man or a woman. They left the cloakroom and headed back towards Sister Trinity's room.

"I was going to go and sit with Catherine and Mary, Nigel. Would you care to join me?"

"No, thank you, Sister, I have only just left them, and I still want to finish going through Sister Trinity's room and then Sister Sarah's, just to ensure that we haven't missed anything."

"That sounds like a good plan, Nigel. You are a good man. I know God will be with you as you help Father Matthew. Bring him home, Nigel."

Nigel nodded at the sister, and then he disappeared back into Sister Trinity's room.

"Alex?"

"N-n-n-n-Nigel." Alex was standing by the window.

"You can't be in here, Alex; it is still a crime scene. We have to preserve everything the way it was when we found Sister Trinity."

"Th-h-he d-door." Alex was trying to point in the direction of the door.

"The door was open, yes, I know; sorry, I was talking to Sister Bethany. I must have forgotten to close it when we left."

"T-T-TH-e-e Far-Father."

"He is fine, Alex; he is just helping us with our enquiries at the moment. We are doing all we can to help him. I wish that we could do more, but we can't at this time."

Alex sat down in the armchair that was in the corner. It was a struggle for him to get seated, so Nigel didn't want to tell him to get up and go out again.

"So, I would guess by that action you are staying, are you, Alex?" Nigel smiled at him.

"Maybe you can help me then. I am looking for clues, Alex, any type of clues that we could have missed. Something that is going to clear Father Matthew. To be honest, he is the only suspect we have at the moment. Everyone else has an alibi for those nights."

Nigel wasn't worried about telling Alex anything. Alex barely spoke nowadays as the disease had progressively gotten worse. Unfortunately, it would have taken him a week to tell anyone else. Nigel continued walking around the room. Opening the drawers, wardrobes, looking under the bed; there was nothing, nothing that they hadn't photographed or seen before.

"You see, Alex, there needs to be something, something that we are missing. We have been across the whole island, and everyone, every possible suspect has an alibi apart from the Father; he is the only person that could have done all this. Well, not all of this, not the judge. The judge we believe was something personal."

"T-t-the-e jud-judge." Alex was still sitting in the chair. Nigel knew as he had said that that he shouldn't have. He had just been rambling. He forgot not everyone knew about the judge yet.

"Yes, so sorry, Alex. Didn't you know? The judge hung himself, well, didn't hang himself, someone hung the judge; they pulled him up on a rope and hung him from the beam. Not the Father as he was with me the entire time, so even when we do solve this, there could still be another case, another murderer on the island."

Nigel went over and patted him on the shoulder. Speaking it out loud was working for Nigel. The case was becoming clearer in his head.

"We will clear this all up, Alex. So just keep all of this to yourself whilst we do. I am just missing something. I just don't know what it is."

"Th-h-he-e judge mur-r-rd-d-dered?"

"Yes, I am afraid so. He wasn't a nice man, Alex." Nigel paused; he had forgotten about their connection. He had said too much already, but now he had to wrap it up.

"I know he was your godfather, and he brought you here. So there must have been, at some time, some good points about him. He had quite a few secrets that nobody knew about though. Detective Morris believes it was one of those secrets that got him killed."

Alex started struggling to get out of the chair. Nigel knew it wasn't because he was upset about the judge. It had been commented on a few occasions that, whilst he brought him there, he never visited. He did start to fear the worse though, what if this had brought up some bad memories for Alex? Nigel started looking at him in a different light. What if Alex had been one of the judge's victims?

"Boring you, am I? Let me help, there you go, all upright." Nigel pulled him out of the chair, and returned to his search. It was time to try and steer the conversation in a different direction.

"What was I saying? The judge... Yes, well, that's our next case, Alex. We need to solve this one first and help the Father. We have to find something here, maybe connecting Sister Trinity and Sister Sarah to someone other than the Father. Some other person who had the means and the motive to kill both of them."

"B-But no-ot th-he jud-judge."

"No, not the judge, Alex. I don't think there is anything that connects all three of them. You see, the judge was a bad man, Alex." Nigel was trying to politely stop talking about the judge but he wasn't good at changing the subject.

"We didn't know, but it would seem he did some bad things. Things we can't discuss, Alex."

"Ba-a-ad-d."

"Yes, bad, Alex, before he came to the island. Probably long before you knew him. He hasn't done them since being here, Alex, but that doesn't mean we forgive him."

Nigel closed the door of the dresser. He paused for a moment as if a light bulb had just appeared above his head. As he turned, he could see Alex closing the door of the room.

"O-o-on-n-n t-t-the mainland, Nigel. The judge did some terrible things on the mainland Nigel. With me. To me" Nigel froze. It all clicked into place. There was another person on the island. There was someone else in the home. There was someone just as invisible as a sister of the church. Someone who could move without being seen.

Alex's walking stick struck Nigel across the head, and he blacked out in seconds.

Chapter 15

Nigel awoke on the floor next to the bed with a gag in his mouth, and his hands and feet tied. The door to Sister Trinity's room was closed.

"Oh, you are awake... Sorry, should I say O-h-h-h u-u-u-u a-a-r-r a-w-aw-awake. You have no idea what it feels like to speak normally, Nigel." Alex smiled down at Nigel on the floor. Alex was walking around freely rotating his hands as if they were somehow miraculously healed. He shook his legs in front of Nigel as a sign of the freedom he really had.

"Who would have thought the person that was actually going to put this together was you, Nigel, the local bobby." Alex stretched his mouth as he spoke. He had only been able to speak to one person on the island normally since his arrival, and until recently he had never visited.

"I knew you were all getting close, but I didn't think it would be you that comes a-knocking. The thing is, Nigel, I need to know what you know. So, I am going to take the gag out of your mouth. But know something, Nigel, the sisters are at prayer. Sandra has served tea and gone home. There are just the residents and me here... If you scream or call out, I will kill you. By the time anyone got here, you would be untied and A-a-a-al-le-ex-x-x would be crying over your body. If you are not worried about yourself, I will take more of them before

I leave the island. It is up to you. Do you understand me?" Nigel had never heard Alex's real voice. Nobody alive on the island had. Now that he had, he missed the old one. There was a purpose behind his words. Nigel knew he meant everything he said. The threats would be carried out. Nigel had no doubt about that. Nigel nodded his answer.

"Good, very good, Nigel. You are certainly turning into a bright lad."

Alex took the gag off of Nigel's mouth. Nigel took a second to get his mouth back into gear. Alex went back and sat in the chair. Leaning back as if waiting for the questions. He knew Nigel would have a lot of questions.

"How?" Nigel managed to get his first word out. The taste of the pillow case was still in his mouth.

"How? That's the first thing you ask me? How?" Alex was smiling.

"How for two years have you been like that? How didn't we notice? Are you saying there is nothing wrong with you?" Now Alex was laughing.

"How for two years was I A-a-a-a-l-le-ex-x? Honestly, because I had to be, Nigel; the fucking judge saw to that. I had to disappear, and this was the place to come." All Nigel could think about was the mainland now. He had come from the mainland. All the other cases. Everything was falling into place. He was their man.

"The judge made you like this?"

"Yes, the peado-judge. He brought me here. He knew what I was, he knew what I had done. He knew because he was partly responsible for how I turned out."

Alex paused at that point. There was a fire in his eyes at the thought of the judge. Nigel could see that.

"That's a fucking lie; he was totally responsible for how I turned out. The judge wasn't a good guy, Nigel. He was a fucking wanker, Nigel. You have all figured that out. The confession I put on his computer, the photos that lay around the house, they weren't all planted. They were his, because that is who he was. That was what he was." Nigel could feel the hate from Alex.

"That was what the bastard did to me, and to countless others. He was an evil fuck, Nigel. He didn't get half of what he deserved."

"You were one of his victims?" There was a moment of sadness in Nigel's voice. The thought of someone being hurt in that way was upsetting for him. After everything he had seen on the judge's computer, he felt sorry for Alex at that point. Even if Alex was someone who he was fast considering to be a serial killer, and had tied him up on the floor he couldn't help thinking how horrible those years must have been for him. Nobody deserved that.

"I was, Nigel; I used to live next door to the judge; that part of the story wasn't a lie. I would be in and out of his house all the time. He was always asking me over to do things for him. Little jobs and he would give me sweets. I thought at first, he was just old. Then he started to do things to me, things that weren't natural. I knew it was wrong. He always said if I told anyone, he would lock me up for lying as he was a judge. I tried to talk to my dad about him once. My dad fucking worshipped the guy. Always said he was a powerful man and he could do anything. That scared me into not telling a soul. As I got older, he still used to do things to me, till I was about twelve. As I got older, he knew I wasn't as scared as I used to be; he changed what he said. He said he would hurt my parents. Lock them up. I must have got too old for the sicko as he stopped talking to me or touching me after a while." Alex took a moment. Nigel figured he was reliving his revenge.

"He moved on to someone else?" Nigel didn't want to say it, but it just came out of his mouth.

"I presume he found someone new to play with, yes." Alex nodded to Nigel. Then stood up and started walking the room again. He was getting himself back into his showing-off stage. He clearly didn't want to dwell on the judge.

"You were right all along, Nigel. There was only one killer on the island, and it was me; I killed all of them." There was satisfaction back in Alex's voice.

"The judge was always going to get it at some point. Some point when I thought it would be safe for me to return to the mainland. I know you have linked it to my adventures on the mainland. I heard you talking about it. Have you read the case files? I can imagine some of them were a pretty good read." There was a wink in Nigel's direction. He had read them. He did know what Alex was capable of.

"It's amazing that nobody notices the cripple boy at the door or by the window whilst they are talking. Everyone pities me, staying in my room all day and all night, sad about my illness. Who said I was in my room? I never did. I would keep it locked, and people just thought I was being antisocial, and with everything that I had been through, who would blame me. Father murdered, mother rejected me, and I have this disease."

Alex twisted his arms around, and clicked his heels together. Then walked across the room like the Alex that Nigel had known. The one that they had all known.

"Your father was murdered?" Nigel started to think about keeping him talking. The longer he did, the more chance someone would walk past and overhear the conversation. It was a long shot, but from where he was on the floor there was little else he could do.

"Yes, oh, I killed him too. Can you imagine? After everything I had been through, he never found out or saved me from the monster next door. Fucking prick." Alex went back to sitting in the chair. He leant forward so he was over Nigel.

"He wasn't my first; my first had actually been a girl I had been seeing. Things were great until it got to that point, that point of intimacy, then something just took over me. What the judge had done to me made the whole point of sex dirty and vile. I kept saying no, but the more and more she tugged at my clothes the madder I got; I thought you want it, you can have it. I gave her sex, Nigel, but I choked the life out of her at the same time. I had visions of it being the judge…" Alex lost himself in the moment.

"I think that is why I enjoyed it so much."

"And that was your first?" As Nigel looked up, he knew he could become a victim at any moment. Getting him on side was key for his survival.

"It was my first to my fourth, for the same reason. The closer we became the more enraged I got, the more I wanted to hurt them. I thought the judge had really messed me up, really hurt me. I blamed him for everything. I still blame the old fucker for everything."

"But you said thought?" Nigel's training was kicking in. Keep Alex talking whilst he assessed the situation! Unfortunately, the situation was that he was in real trouble here, and not a lot he was going to be able to do about it. He started to tug at the rope that was binding his hands behind his back, but only when Alex's glare was somewhere else.

"We, I thought how can someone come from such a loving, caring family, and then end up like this? I realised I didn't really come from a loving family. I don't even think I came from a family at all." Nigel tried to look as interested as possible in Alex's story.

"My parents at the age of eighteen told me everything; they told me that I wasn't born naturally, they told me I was born in Paris in some test-tube facility. The Brown institute. It would seem my dad couldn't even get it up for my mum. That is how much love we had in our family, Nigel." Alex was up again and walking.

"And so, that made you think your parents were responsible for all of this?"

"So, Nigel, that's why my father didn't love me. He was incapable of love, Nigel. I was some kind of experiment. Probably why he let the judge do all those things to me. He didn't care, Nigel. He didn't care at all. So, I killed him. I killed him there and then in front of my mother, and I told her if she ever spoke of it, I would slit her throat in the middle of the night. I was used to hearing threats, Nigel; I knew how to make them sound real." Nigel could tell from the tone of Alex's voice he meant every word of that. Alex was reliving every moment of it.

"After I had done it though, I knew I needed some help. It wasn't going to be hard to tie me to my father's death. Also, I needed some distance between me and my ever-growing body count. At the time the judge was working on setting up this prison, and had been living between the island and the mainland with his wife. She didn't want to move, but he was insisting they did for his work. He sorted that issue, didn't he?" Alex was nodding at Nigel. He knew that the story of his wife would have been discussed by now.

"I contacted him, and told him what I had done. I told him about the girls and my father and if he didn't help me I would do more. He ignored me, Nigel. He ignored what I was saying to him. So, I killed another and another. I sent him pictures, and I think he didn't care. I think the old sick fuck probably got off on the pictures that I sent him." Nigel's mind went back to the photos on the desk. They were all of children. He hadn't kept any of Alex's photos.

"So, I told him I would tell his wife what he did to me. What he had in his little precious study upstairs. How he made me watch porn there sometimes with him whilst he did stuff to me, and I did to him. It worked, Nigel. That really touched a nerve. He was so mad. He said he would lock me up forever if I did tell her. That didn't scare me anymore. I wasn't afraid of him. He had no control over me anymore, Nigel. Nothing." Alex's pacing up and down was getting quicker. This wasn't a good sign; the more animated that Alex got the more Nigel feared he could lash out at any time.

"I told her, and she went to investigate. Well, I presume that is what she did as the next thing I heard was that she was dead. I contacted him again. I told him he needed to help me or I was going straight to the papers and then he would be staying on that island of his for good. Well, at least six weeks anyway. It would have been something the old man deserved anyway. He did deserve everything he got, Nigel. He deserved more, but there was not enough time."

"So, he brought you to the island with him?" Nigel was still trying to loosen the rope tying his hands together as they spoke, but it wasn't going anywhere.

"Yes, he did. He came up with the cover story, and got me admitted. At first, he told me I had a job on the island working at the home. Even managed to get me a new identity. He was a judge so he managed to get all the papers sorted for me. He didn't tell me until we were at the docks on the mainland the true story though. About the disease, the whole back story he had created. It was one last twist by the sick fuck, Nigel. I think he wanted to make sure that I didn't leave the home. He didn't want me anywhere near his life, so he showed me the papers he had falsified. Explained about my deformities and my speech problem. I had no choice but to continue with the charade. I needed to get away, and this island was the best hiding place I knew. It meant nobody was ever going to look for me. I never believed it would have gone on so long, Nigel. Two years, the whole island feeling sorry for me." Alex moved his hands again into the old Alex position. He was quite proud of what he had been able to do; he had fooled everyone. "Some days I would trip and fall for my own amusement, just to see the fuss it created around me. Other days I just wanted to stay locked in my room away from them all."

Nigel knew that if the end was coming, he wanted to know it all. At least he would have that satisfaction.

"But why did you kill Sister Trinity?" Alex started to laugh. It was a little louder than before. Nigel was happy about that. It was a sign he was relaxing.

"I hadn't meant to do that. Being here, being A-a-al-lex-x-x. That had its drawbacks. I still felt like I wanted to kill people, but I never got angry enough. It's hard to shout at pensioners. I had got quite good at taking my frustrations out on myself in a locked room, if you know what I mean? But I made a mistake. I had been in my room all day, and had the door locked. I was watching football. Sandra had come round with the tea tray, and I opened the door to let her in. I ate my tea, and went back to watching my programmes. The judge pays all my bills, so I have the full TV package including porn. I was in the bathroom relieving myself when Sister Trinity came walking into my room. She called out, but I thought it was the porn still playing in the room. I just didn't have enough time before she was in the bathroom checking if I was OK. I turned quickly and grabbed her by the mouth, still hard from what I was doing. She was fighting back at me. My God, that turned me on. Hadn't felt anything like it since leaving the mainland. Luckily most of the people in this place are fast asleep by then, and deaf; fuck, most of the people in this place are deaf or blind. Look, she scratched me really good." Alex pulled up his T-shirt and showed Nigel the scar.

"I overpowered her, but it brought back all those memories, those ones I had been suppressing. I had to have her so I did right there and then in my room. I had sex with her whilst she was half-conscious, and then I strangled her. I knew then how much I had missed it. The feelings I had back at home about it being dirty seemed to have gone away. Once I accepted who I was, it became almost natural. As soon as I did it though, I knew I wanted more. My appetite was back." Alex held his hands out as if introducing himself to the world. Nigel was struggling to concentrate on Alex. His head was hurting, and he was trying to wriggle free without being noticed. At the same time, he was still dumbfounded by what was happening. He was adamant that he had thought of everyone. Alex just never came to mind. He was right; you didn't notice him. It didn't even spring to mind that he would have been powerful enough to take Sister Trinity down. Nigel took a deep breath, and tried to calm himself so that he could continue with the conversation.

"So, then you moved the body?"

"Yes, I waited till about one a.m., and moved it two doors down into her room. I had been reading online that Damien Winter had arrived on the island, and I needed a distraction. I didn't really think that anyone would have solved it anyway, no offence, but still I needed a distraction from the home. I figured the same MO as the newest recruit to the island would be a good one. Imagine my shock that it almost took all day to find her. I was on tenderhooks that morning, I can tell you. I never thought it would have taken till lunchtime. I nearly choked on my roast beef when the scream came out." Alex was back to laughing again. It was unnerving to Nigel. He had no remorse, no feelings, for what he had done. Most of the serial-killer stories that Nigel had listened to were full of feeling, but Alex seemed to have lost his. That was a dangerous trait in a serial killer;

there was only one other who he knew of, that spoke like Alex was doing now. He was the world's greatest serial killer, and had been executed a few days before.

"But she was your friend? And a sister of the church?"

"She wasn't my friend, Nigel. These people aren't my friends. They have been my prison guards. Do you know how insulting it is all day to play little old Alex? Poor Alex. Tussle my hair like I am seven years old. I was in hiding. I had to do it, but these people, these people are too nice, too trusting for their own good." Nigel was seeing the real Alex for the first time now. It wasn't something that he wanted to see, but he needed to keep him talking.

"What about the judge?"

"I laid in wait for him. I locked my room here, and went straight out of the window; my room is at the back of the church so I can get out without being seen. I can be across the island in an hour on foot. I am quite fit you know. I have little else to do all day, so I still exercise a lot. Feels good to move freely when I am alone. I broke into his house, and waited for him. He had the brunt of my anger for a little while, well, until he gave up the password to his bank account, and the combination for his safe. Then I hung the fucking pervert. Quite a profitable deal as it happens; two years here for nearly seven hundred thousand. Apparently being a judge pays well." Alex had enjoyed every moment of torturing the judge. Nigel could tell. There was a huge smile on his face. No doubt it had laid a lot of his childhood memories to bed. Nigel knew now though he had the money to disappear and start again which also meant that he wasn't going to be looking to leave witnesses.

He continued to try and wriggle free from the ropes, this time with more emphasis.

"What about Sister Sarah?" It was his last story. Nigel knew this was his last chance, whilst he told this he needed to work himself free.

"Oh, yes, I almost forgot about her. As I said, when get out of my window I am at the back of the church. One night I am out for a midnight stroll; I do most evenings. It is the only chance I get to walk properly. All the old fuddy-duddy's in here are dead to the world by nine. Then I hear voices coming from the church; I could listen in from the window of the basement. Imagine my surprise when I realise it was Sister Sarah and Father Matthew. They would discuss everything; they discussed politics, religion, anything to keep Sister Sarah's mind away from drugs, I guess. That Father Matthew is a really nice man, but who knew nuns could be so bad? I do like a bad nun." Alex was smiling again. He sat back down which Nigel knew wasn't going to help his cause. He could hardly move with Alex looming over him.

"Anyway, I listened in one night. Think it was Tuesday or Wednesday, and Father Matthew was telling her of Edmund Carson's first victim. I was intrigued, I can tell you; the biggest serial killer of our time, and his first 'encounter' was similar to mine. A woman in and out of consciousness, and he had had sex with her. The Father repeated the story word for word saying how he believed it to be the best sex ever. The way he told it, all I could think about was that, I want some of that, I really do." Alex was up again. Nigel breathed a sigh of relief, and went back to working on the ropes.

"After the judge had been found, and they had worked out it wasn't suicide, I listened in on the Father telling Mary, Catherine and Sandra after lunch, I knew my time on the island was going to be short. If they looked deep enough into the judge's past, they would find me and my parents. After that it wouldn't be long until they realised my mother was alive, and she wouldn't keep her mouth shut, especially if she thought I had killed the judge. So, I did it. The more I thought about her down there on her own the more I thought I would lose the perfect opportunity to work with her. Notice that, Nigel? Work with her. Like the great man himself." Nigel had picked up on Edmund's language. He was also noticing how similar they were, not only in personality, but also in stature.

"I followed the Father back to the church round the back, and listened to their last conversation. She was doing really well, and he wanted her back in society as people were asking too many questions about her disappearance, but she asked for one more day. When the Father left the basement, I was already inside the church. I saw where he placed the keys, and went down to the basement. All I can and will say, Nigel, is that Edmund Carson doesn't know what he was talking about when it comes to sex. It was a bit creepy. Anyway, in honour of the truly great man, I thought a scene would have been a fitting tribute. I did wonder if the world would think he had back from the dead one last time. How cool would that have been, Nigel?" Nigel nodded at Alex as if to agree. It was more so that Alex would keep walking around. The ropes weren't budging. Nigel was considering screaming now. It wouldn't lead to a great outcome for him, but at least the other detective may have a chance of putting all the pieces together.

"So, I placed her praying. I really would have loved to have a nail gun like him. Some of those scenes were my favourite, Nigel. He was a master, wasn't he, but sadly, the Father didn't keep a nail gun in the church." There was a swagger about it now. Alex had rediscovered himself since Sister Trinity, and now he was going to continue and enjoy himself. There was going to be no stopping him.

"I mean, I followed him, Nigel, Edmund, that is. I followed his whole story as a kid. The ONE. Father Harry. That was a good one. I still have both of those T-shirts. He even came to our town once when he was the Alphabet Killer. Or was he still Father Harry? I forget. Took a whole family, and even the gold fish. I don't know why, but he killed the gold fish, and placed one of them in the stomach of the boy he killed as if he had swallowed it. I tell you, the guy was a legend. But the sex thing, I am not sure how he got off on that. Not to say I won't try it again, Nigel. He must know what he is talking about. The copycat thing after Damien was perfect. I knew it would throw them to the scent of the prison. I didn't know they were going to frame the Father for them though. That was a nice twist of events."

"Father Matthew is innocent." They both knew this. Nigel just wanted to say it out loud. There was silence. They both knew that innocence didn't matter. Nigel knew what Alex was going to do to him. He had been trying at the ropes and nothing. He was out of stories to tell, and he was going to have to leave and leave no witnesses. Nigel knew that. He was going to have to make up his mind, but he knew alerting other people could get them killed. He didn't want to be the cause of that.

"What now though, Alex?" Nigel didn't really want to ask the question, but he knew he had little else to say.

"What now, Nigel, is that the Father probably goes down for the murders. I am sure those detectives want that to happen. And I take a trip with my newfound wealth. Doesn't sound like a bad deal for me? I have had some fun and got rid of the judge from my life once and for all. Not a bad week for Al-l-l-lex-x-x-x." Alex bent his hands for one last time.

"But they will realise that the Father's DNA doesn't match."

"They will if they want to. Father Matthew was all over both of those bodies. He held Sister Sarah through her rehab and dressed Sister Trinity. My guess would be that they are going to struggle to prove or disprove how close he was to either of them. In any case it will go to trial and it will ruin this island, his reputation, and his family. I suppose I should feel guilty, Nigel, but he is a bit of a sap. Always treating me like I am a kid. I am twenty-one, Nigel. I swear I have dumbed down to thirteen whilst I have been here. Playing this part." Alex stopped. There was a huge smile across his face.

"Huh, never really thought about it like that before. I have been playing a part. Just like Edmund. Playing a role. Maybe that is it, Nigel. Maybe that is what is next for me. I could be the next Edmund Carson. I have the money, Nigel. I have the papers. I have become accustomed to being Al-l-lex-x. Nobody would ever think it was me. And if that doesn't work out, I still have my real identity which nobody is looking for either. And then there was TWO." Alex really laughed at that point.

Nigel could see that he was excited about what was going to come. Nigel knew everything that he was saying could well and truly ruin the island. Father Matthew had been the island. If he was in question, so was the whole society. The island was about to fall apart, and there was nothing he could do about it. Not as he was tied up on the floor. The Father was in prison. The detectives weren't even looking elsewhere any more. Alex had all the power, and now it sounded like he had a plan.

"Alex, they will work it out. Especially if anything happens to me. Father Matthew is locked up."

"Nigel that is a good point. He is, at least until tomorrow morning. If they don't have anything though, they won't be able to charge him, and they will let him go. So, they will either charge him or he will return here first thing tomorrow to another..." Alex stopped speaking and smiled at Nigel. He had always been polite to him all the time he had been a prisoner of the home.

"You know, other than my father and now the judge, killing men hasn't been my strong point. I just don't get the same buzz from it. Is that not weird? The killing and the sex go hand in hand for me even though I don't like the sex part. Do you think that is an Edmund Carson thing too? That's why he did it afterwards? I really believe you have helped me uncover something about myself this evening, Detective." Alex smiled, but it was the type of smile that Nigel knew had something following it.

"You would think men would be easier for me. This whole being-similar thing is really spurring me on though, Nigel. I am so glad we talked. Just one more thing. Do you know where I can buy a nail gun?" Alex walked over and picked up his walking stick. There was still wet blood on the end where he had already hit Nigel.

"Then don't do it, Alex. Just go. I will keep quiet, and give you a head start. I can say you knocked me out." Nigel was still toying with making a noise, but deep down he knew he couldn't. If this was going to happen, it was just going to have to happen.

"Nigel, I can't just go. Or let you go. You are a policeman, and you know, you turned out not a bad one in the end. I would never get off the island. No, there is no alternative, I am afraid." Alex smiled at Nigel. Nigel thought about Edmund in the docks at the judge's rereading of his case. He had smiled the same smile.

"I promise to give you some time."

"I am sure you would have, Nigel, but I have lots to do, and can't afford to take any chances. You really inspired me today. I have plans now, Nigel, big plans. I think the world needs another Edmund Carson. Admit it, we have missed him."

Before Nigel knew what was going on, Alex's walking stick struck him round the head once more, and then again. The stick kept hitting Nigel over and over again.

What Alex hadn't noticed though was that the bed was taking some of the blow. The last thing Nigel saw before he blacked out was the memory of Catherine hugging him as his head hit the floor.

Alex took the walking stick over to the bathroom and cleaned it. He became A-a-al-lex-x-x again as soon as he left Sister Trinity's room. He met the sisters as they were returning from prayer, and they said their good afternoons. He entered his own room, and locked the door. He changed as quickly as possible, and packed a bag. It was getting on for late afternoon. Alex knew that he could make the ferry at six thirty if he got a move on. It was a couple of hours over to the port on foot, but he knew that Father Matthew always left the keys in his vehicle. Any of the sisters could use his car when he was in residence. He wasn't, and he knew the sisters were too busy to be travelling anywhere. It was a risk he was going to have to take. As A-a-al-lex-x-x he took the short walk over to the vicarage. He got into the car, and pulled out of the drive way. Catherine watched as the car pulled away, but didn't take any notice presuming it would be one of the sisters.

It was five minutes to six when he presented himself to the harbour master with the ticket he had just purchased online on his phone that the Judge had begrudgingly bought him. They all knew Alex; over the years Catherine and Mary had taken Alex down to the harbour to watch the boats. In Alex-speak, he told them he was visiting his mother for the evening by himself; they were all very proud of him. He played the part of being ever so excited perfectly. They let him sit up at the front of the ferry with the captain for the ride over. The captain gave him his hat, and even let him sound the horn as they were coming in to dock on the mainland.

Alex caught a taxi straight from the docks to the train station and jumped on the train headed to Birmingham. He was already passing London before Nigel awoke.